THE KILLER'S
CO-OP

~ A Robert Schwimer Mystery ~

By RICHARD HOWES

The Killer's Co-op
All rights reserved
Copyright © 2011 by Richard Howes

ISBN-13:   978-1463501518

ISBN-10:   146350151X

About the Author:

Richard Howes is an avid mystery buff, a thirty-year computer programmer (he started quite young, possibly in-utero), and avid horseman and adventurer. He's ridden horses for nearly twenty years, started in hunter-jumper and flat classes, moved into team penning, and cattle sorting, and ended up earning a World Champion buckle in the sport known as Cowboy Mounted Shooting - yes, that's right - he shoots guns from the back of a horse. (Well enough to have trained Mounted Police units in the same activity - and he is eternally grateful for the opportunity.) He's known as a wild horse trainer and all around horseman.

He likes most any comedy, including those ever under-appreciated classics such as The Three Amigos, anything with John Cleese and the other Pythons, Keeping Up Appearances, Are You being Served, Rowan Atkinson, Roberto Benigni, etc, etc, etc. He is also extremely funny... just ask him. (Copyrights held by their respective holders.)

He started writing his first novel about a young wizard before JK wrote her first novel about a young wizard. He expanded it into three books, and is currently expanding it into seven or twelve books... Don't look for that soon. Instead look for mysteries, westerns, fantasy, sci-fi (maybe) and comedies... What's that? Oh, okay... His muse says no comedies. and um... she wants him to write a romantic drama.

This book is dedicated to Kristie,
the love of my life and my inspiration,
and to Casey and Lane Ashton
for their support.

Many thanks to
Createspace.com
and their employees.

Chapter 1

Terrance Silverman saw lots of strange things during his years sleeping in public parks and cemeteries, but nothing stranger than a dog dragging a detached human arm down the railroad tracks. The full moon glinted in the dog's eyes as it stopped to growl at him. It was then Terrance realized the dog was actually a coyote, not unlike the wild dogs he listened to all summer as they howled into the eastern Massachusetts nights.

The coyote dropped the arm, let out three quick yips, and proceeded to drag the arm by the shirtsleeve. The arm was heavy and the coyote looked at Terrance once more, snipped twice, and ran off into the woods leaving his prize behind. Terrance skirted around the arm, trying as hard as he could to avert his eyes. The watch on the wrist glared at him like a solitary eye filled with accusation. He hurried down the railroad tracks, wondering if he had drank too much. Then he saw the rest of the body parts.

He stopped to stare in awe as memories of violence and carnage flooded his mind. He tried to think, but his mind was on old army buddies and death. He knew he needed to act but his feet stood frozen. He slowly realized where he was. He knew there was a road nearby, under the railroad bridge. He knew there was a path that led down to the road, through a church yard where he sometimes ate breakfast.

Wrapping his rain coat closer around himself, Terrance willed his body to move forward. Step by step he made his way along the tracks. As he left the body behind he thought to cross the railroad bridge and go to the park where he had planned to sleep. There was a sheltered corner by a Civil War memorial that he found warm and protected from rain. But there was a body, and like before, he knew he would be blamed. He could run but his feet stopped moving. He could forget he found the body. He could walk all night and be twenty miles away by morning, except the bartender would know when he had left the tavern, and there were the people he worked for at the school and the church. They would know he had been living nearby.

The last time he reported a body he had been illegally detained for months, but he had no lawyer. With winter coming soon jail would provide food and shelter. He tried to convince himself it would be like in the army. Everything he needed would be supplied. Everything he might want was unnecessary. Memories of the army brought him back to the body. He would not want his bones gnawed on by a coyote. He did not want the same for anyone.

His feet moved again, past the fence, towards the road. It was early... very early and traffic would be non-existent, but he would stop a car and ask for help. Ask them to call 911.

Chapter 2

The false dawn glowed in the eastern Massachusetts sky as Plymouth County Acting-Sheriff Robert Schwimer pulled his black Taurus Interceptor onto the crumbling asphalt sidewalk behind an Abington Police Department Crown Victoria. The lights of the Massachusetts coroner van flashed a fiery orange across the granite Central Street railroad bridge retaining walls. To the north the Mount Vernon church and parochial school stood on the hillside quietly overlooking the scene. It was still too early for Sunday Services to start. Farther up the road, a sedan flashed its hazard lights. An Abington Police patrol car was parked on the south side of the narrow underpass. A yellow-vested police officer directed the few cars trying to reach Route 58.

A short man dressed in a heavy canvas raincoat and grimy blue jeans sat sullenly on the wall. A dirty knit cap was pulled far down over his brow. His hands were handcuffed behind his back with a flexible nylon double-cuff. A small backpack lay on the grass beside him.

On the grassy hill above the road, Bob saw the tall athletic Deputy Peter Jackson arguing with the taller heavy-handed coroner, Frank Wysup, who smoked a cigarette angrily. The red embers glowered in the dark and reflected off his silvery hair and gray skin. Ashes fell onto Frank's tan overcoat and he brushed them off. Another Abington policeman stood beside Peter with a look of amusement on his face.

Bob retrieved a flashlight from his glove box. He got out of the car and wrapped his heavy wool coat around his middle-aged build. He pushed his black cowboy hat down further on his dark haired head as he trotted up the stairs and across the wet grass. The morning dew soaked his shoes.

In the dark, he could pass as young as late twenties, only because his thirty-five years had been good to him. A few gray hairs gave him away.

'Distinguished,' his wife, Mary, said when she first noticed.

'Earned,' he'd replied.

He was cursed with being average. Average meant he worked harder to be better, and he figured its advantages were found in fitting in, blending in, and going unnoticed. Being underestimated was often a plus in police work. He prayed he would never be as annoying as Columbo, but still the man got the job done.

"Good morning Peter. Frank." Bob nodded to the coroner.

"Hello Robert," Frank Wysup said with a tinge of contempt in his voice. Frank lit another cigarette.

"Good morning Detective," Peter said, "I told Doctor Wysup that you wanted to see the body first. Not disturb any evidence." Peter was tall, young, dark haired, and built like a football player.

"Thank you, Peter. Doctor Wysup. I've been meaning to talk to you."

"He wouldn't let me go up there." Frank Wysup indicated the railroad tracks above the road.

"Yes. I know."

"I'm the state coroner and a licensed doctor for Christ's sake. I know how to handle evidence. I used to work for Boston PD Forensics. I used to be the Plymouth County Medical Examiner." Frank tapped another cigarette from a pack of unfiltered Camels, forgetting he had just lit a new one.

"I told him to secure the scene until I arrived."

"But I've got jurisdiction…"

"Not until the Staties' say so."

Frank continued his protest, which Bob ignored. He put his hand out to welcome the local police officer.

"Good morning. I'm Detective Schwimer, County Sheriff's Office."

The officer looked at the hand suspiciously for a moment before shaking it, "Jerry Morrissy. Abington. Thanks for coming out."

"Yes. My job. You know…"

"Our lieutenant is on his way… Here he is now." Officer

Morrissy pointed to a cruiser pulling up.

"Excellent. Who's in the other car?" Bob gestured to the sedan with the hazard lights on.

Peter flipped open a small notebook and read, "Civvies. Tom Rivers, Carol Rivers. They called 911 when this guy flagged them down. They've been waiting for hours, even after they were told they could leave. Officer Morrissy was first on scene and had Abington dispatch call us in. They also called in to the Kingston-Plymouth Railroad. They've held up the commuter trains until we can clear the tracks."

"Who is he?" Bob pointed a thumb at the man in the raincoat and handcuffs who still sat on the wall, head bowed.

"Terrance Silverman, according to an expired Michigan gaming card. He doesn't have any other ID. He said he used to work in a Motor City casino. Says he's been homeless for several years. He claims," Peter read from his notebook, "*He doesn't want any accusations like Raynham*, whatever that means. He said that is why he flagged down a car to report the body. The only thing I found on him was a bottle of Jack Daniels, mostly empty."

"Flagged down a car?"

"It must of taken hours…"

"The Abington Police department is less than a quarter mile down the road."

Peter shrugged. "He must not have known that."

"We can assume… He didn't give any more about Raynham?"

"No idea what he was talking about."

"Where's the body?"

"Right up here. I didn't let anyone go over, like you said. It's a mess."

The local lieutenant came up the stairs.

"Who are you?" he asked as he looked up at Bob.

Bob smiled down at the local lieutenant. "Detective Schwimer, County."

"What do we have here?"

"Your name, for starters."

"Singer. Lieutenant." The officer's eyes became steely. "This is a local crime. We can handle it."

"Your dispatch called in the B.C.I."

"Yeah?"

Bob sighed, "Yes. Do you have a state-of-the-art forensics lab?"

"No."

"Then do you mind if we use ours?"

Singer dropped his eyes. "That sounds okay."

"Thanks."

"The death will be reported to the State Police."

Bob smiled.

Singer's face flattened. "That was not a question. I'll do it."

"Please do. Thank you."

"What does that mean?"

Bob pointed to the suspect. "What do you know about this Terrance Silverman guy?"

Singer looked over at Silverman still sitting on the wall. "He looks homeless."

"Ever seen him before? Pick him up for begging? Vagrancy?" Bob looked from Singer to Morrissy.

"No. I've never seen him," said Morrissy.

"I'll run his name through the database," Singer replied.

"Terrance Silverman. If he hasn't been pan-handling maybe he has some cash stashed away. He can wait. Let's see what we have up here." Bob turned to Peter and motioned toward the railroad tracks. They passed Frank, who fell in beside Singer as they crossed the grass in front of the church rectory.

Frank turned to the Lieutenant and asked, "What's that about?"

"Let's find out," Singer replied.

The four men slipped through a cut in the tall chain link fence that bordered the railroad tracks. Inside the fence, they pushed through overgrown weeds until reaching the gravel railroad bed. As they walked Bob saw small gray and red spots and splotches scattered in the brush. His flashlight flickered upon the torso of a human beside the tracks.

"The train did its job," Peter said.

"This is a massacre. Don't go any further." Bob motioned to them to stop. He unlocked his cell phone and dialed a number.

"Terri? I need your help," Bob said into the phone as a priest came out of the church rectory and stood on the porch watching them. Bob pointed to Peter and then to the priest. Peter nodded and moved off to interview the man.

"This is James." A man's voice came over the phone.

'*Crap*,' Bob thought. "James. How are you? It's early," he said.

"It's okay. How's Mary?"

"Good. You?"

"That's not why you called at quarter-to-five in the morning. Here's Terri."

"Thank you."

"Bob? Where and what's going on?" Terri asked.

"Central Street in Abington. Got a corpse... parts of a corpse."

"Parts?"

"And... pieces."

"Cool." Her bright young voice rose, as it always did when things got gory.

"If you say so. Pretty sickening from where I'm standing." Bob never did understand Terri's fascination with the dead, but he figured it made her good at her job. "How soon can you get here with the van and a crew?"

"Half an hour, plus or minus. Make that minus."

"Get on it."

"Wait. Why didn't you call me earlier?"

"Because you work too much as it is. No sense if this turned out to be nothing."

"What would nothing be?" Terri asked.

"A dog, raccoon."

"It's not."

"No. It isn't. Come down here. A.S.A.P."

"On my way."

"Hold on," Bob lowered his voice. He knew this was not the time to say this, but he said it anyway, "The barbeque..."

"Saturday."

"Trail ride B.B.Q. Bring your horses."

"Anyplace special?"

"My place. We'll ride the cranberry bogs."

"Great."

Bob hung up and called his office.

"Louise. B.C.I. Dispatch. This is a recorded line."

Bob heard the riffling of pages and supposed she was reading a paperback book. Early mornings were always slow and if the suspended-from-duty Sheriff Barton didn't mind, Bob didn't let it bother him either. She was near Bob's age and an ex-smoker as of her last fitness test. Her realization that she was not up to par due to riding a desk all day got to her and she quit cigarettes, opting for e-cigarettes instead, and as part of her self-inflicted make-over, she cropped her brunette hair short claiming it got in the way of her exercise regimen.

"Good morning Louise."

"Good morning detective. What can I do for you?"

"I'm over in Abington. Can you get Wally over here for me? We need some help."

"The railroad tracks? Right away."

"Yes. Thank you." Bob hung up. He turned to Wysup and said, "Don't touch anything. Terri is on her way with a crew."

"I have my van right here. I can start..."

"Thanks Frank. I think we can wait for a little more daylight and some help to arrive. Let's go down." Bob led the way back through the brush and the gap in the fence. He met up with Peter talking to the priest.

"Father Crowley," the priest introduced himself as he put out his hand. He was a tall thin man with boney hands and thick oversized glasses. Medium length wispy gray hair threatened to hide his bald patch but failed.

"Detective Schwimer," Bob said as he shook hands and gave the priest his business card.

"I was telling the officer that I didn't hear anything last night."

"I see. The trains make a lot of noise."

"You get used to it and then you don't hear anything."

"What about yesterday, did you see anything going on out here?"

"The only thing that goes on over there are the commuter

trains. One an hour, about every hour of the day."

"I'll bet that makes prayer and meditation difficult?"

"I wouldn't take that bet, even if I was not a priest." Father Crowley laughed.

"A sense of humor helps?"

"Of course. Life is not about pain and misery."

"No, Father. But besides the trains, did anything happen over the last few days? Anything at all?"

"There are occasionally teenagers walking down the tracks. You saw the hole in the fence. As soon as the railroad repairs the fences the kids cut more holes."

"Why?"

"I suppose it's a shortcut, away from adult eyes. They light fireworks, drink beer over in the cemetery." The priest pointed north along the tracks. "They do what kids do."

"Do you ever have any trouble at the school? Vandalism?"

"This is a parochial school, detective. We always have a little bit of trouble. Nothing that we cannot handle."

"We have got to use your front lawn for a little while. We'll try to be quick."

"Detective. Take your time and be thorough with whatever happened over there."

"There's a body," Bob answered.

Father Crowley frowned. "I'll pray for the deceased," he said.

Bob noted that the priest didn't use a term for gender, nor did he ask.

"Is that Terrance?" the priest asked. Bob followed the man's eyes to the suspect on the wall.

"Do you know him?"

"He comes in for breakfast some mornings. We've got a food kitchen. He started helping us in the warehouse boxing canned and dried goods for delivery. He does some maintenance too. It's only two or three days a week, but he came in about a week ago looking for food, and he asked for work. I let him eat in the school cafeteria early, before the kids arrive, only on the days he's working."

"Can you tell me anything about him?"

"No. He's quiet. Doesn't talk much. Polite. He told me he was renting boats all summer and he's out of work now... for the winter. We don't have a shelter here in town..." The priest trailed off and then asked, "Did he do it?"

"I don't know."

"I hope not."

"Maybe it was an accident?"

"Maybe," Bob said.

Chapter 3

An hour later, as the rising sun filtered through the trees, Sergeant Wally Young taped off the area from the granite wall, around the police cars and back up to the stairs and the rectory-building. He was medium height and build, barrel-chested from working out, sandy blonde hair cut high and tight.

As he unrolled and worked the yellow tape he brushed off news reporters who fired questions at him. With military prowess and a down-east Maine accent he ushered the men and women back behind the line. He had a friendly smile often hidden behind a steel gaze. From the parking lot behind the church a crowd of the devote gathered, edging cautiously closer to see what was going on. Cars slowed and lingered on the street as people craned their necks.

Terri Cox, the county medical examiner, crouched stoop-shouldered over the victim's dismembered torso. Upright, she was tall, lithe, with hair almost black with blue highlights. She sometimes dyed her hair black to cover the very few gray hairs sneaking in. Her neck and brow were white from too much time indoors but sunburned cheeks and nose witnessed her weekends working out of doors on her boyfriend's farm, or riding her horses. She placed small numbered cards beside each body part she found. She tagged anything that looked suspicious. As she directed him, Deputy Peter Jackson photographed the crime scene. Frank Wysup stood in the cool morning air killing cigarettes with an uncommon passion and carefully supervising the evidence collection.

Bob stood by the road inside the yellow police tape. Two local officers stood guard at his sides. Between glimpses back up the hill, Bob gave interrupted and broken answers to the reporters who swarmed to him after Wally's rebuke. They asked questions faster than he could answer.

"Someone was killed in an accident this morning," Bob stated.

"Who was it?" A reporter yelled above the din.

"It appears to be an African-American male."

"Do you have a name?"

"Not yet. It won't be released until we notify the family."

"How old?" one called out. Bob shook his head to indicate he didn't have an age.

"Was it race based?"

"It looks like an accident. We don't suspect a hate crime. We are still collecting evidence."

"Was it murder?" a woman reporter for a television news channel asked into a microphone. Bob could see the camera man and the big lens behind her. A boom mike hovered like a giant gnat over his head. He started to think this interview was a bad idea, and getting worse.

"It's too early to say if we suspect foul play." Bob raised his hands to quiet the reporters. His efforts failed.

"Was the vic hit by a train?" A reporter pointed up to the tracks and railroad trestle.

"We are analyzing the crime scene."

"Is that yes or no? Was the victim hit by a train?" another reporter repeated the question.

"We presume nothing as of yet. It's too early."

"Any witnesses? What's their names?" Some of the reporters looked around at the crowd and beyond, trying to find anyone who might have been a witness. A young reporter cornered Father Crowley into answering questions. The priest didn't seem bothered by the intrusion.

"Yes, we have a witness. Someone found the body and reported it to the police."

"Where is he? Can we talk to him?"

Bob stifled a smirk so as to not appear callous in light of the homicide, but he couldn't help finding amusement in the ferociousness of reporters on the scent of blood. "No. We are taking him in for questioning."

"So he's a suspect?"

"No. Not at all. Not at this time."

"But he is here?"

Bob's jaw tightened. "He is in police custody and he is not to be harassed," Bob ordered the news people. He didn't think that would help if any reporter looked into the county cruiser a dozen steps away.

"The victim is a man then?"

Bob ignored the question. "The person does not appear to have *witnessed* the crime itself. He came upon the scene. The state coroner and the county medical examiner are both on-site as part of the investigation.

"What's the victim's name? Give us something?"

"We don't have a name and we won't release one until the family has been told. Please. I'll have more information for you later. Contact the information desk at County B.C.I. A report will be prepared." Bob began to back away from the reporters and their video cameras. "Let us please investigate the incident. There will be a preliminary report issued to the newswire before noontime. Thank you. Now please..." Bob held up his hands to the crowd as the two officers stepped up to prevent the reporters from crossing the tape.

Bob walked over to Jackson's patrol car and consciously opened the passenger's side door, a position of neutrality rather than authority. Sitting down, he adjusted the rearview mirror so that he could see Terrance Silverman in the back seat. Silverman looked back at him in the mirror and quickly looked down. Bob took out his notebook and scanned down the page.

Turning in the seat to face the man, Bob put the notebook down and said, "Good morning, Mr. Silverman. Can I call you Terrance or Terry? Got a nickname?"

"Terrance," the man said nervously. His eyes darted up to meet Bob's and then back flicked to his shoes.

"Do you want to talk to me about this?"

"I didn't do anything."

Bob nodded as he took out a pen. "You are not under arrest."

Silverman shook his hands which were still zip-tied behind his back.

Bob smiled and said, "I think we can take those off of you. I want to ask you about last night and this morning. Can I do that?"

"Sure," mumbled the man.

"About what time did you find the body?"

"Two, maybe three. I don't remember."

"Were you drinking?"

"Yup."

"Where?"

"Stoney's Mill. I think."

"Stoney's Mill? Here in Abington? Just up the tracks?"

"Yup."

"Where were you going to sleep tonight?"

"Island Grove."

"In the park?"

Terrance nodded.

"Stoney's sold you a bottle of J.D. for the road?"

"Bed warmer." Terrance grinned through stained and missing teeth.

Bob chuckled, "Bed warmer. It gets cold out here?"

"Not yet."

"Winters' coming. So you have some money saved up?"

Terrance didn't answer. His face was placid.

"Summer job? Day labor? You didn't rob anyone?"

Terrance suddenly looked annoyed. "I got laid off," he said.

"What did you do? Where were you working?"

"Houghton's Boats."

"A marina?"

"Yup. Long Pond."

"Over in Lakeville?"

Terrance fell quiet again.

"End of the season? Place closed for the winter?" Terrance nodded in answer. "Terrance. You told my deputy something about Raynham. What's that about?"

"I didn't do anything."

"I know that. I wonder what happened in Raynham. Did you get arrested?"

Terrance kept eyeing his shoes.

"Terrance, I am going to call Sheriff Jasperse over there and talk to him. I'd like to know what we are going to talk about before I make that call. Do you see what I mean?"

Terrance winced at Sheriff Jasperse's name. "I didn't kill that kid."

"Someone got killed in Raynham?"

"It wasn't me."

"You didn't do it? Who was killed?"

"Some kid."

"And you were in Raynham?"

"Yup."

"And the police over there thought you did it?"

"I didn't do it."

"Tell me what happened."

"I found the kid. He was already dead."

Bob nodded.

Terrance stopped talking.

"Terrance," Bob said quietly. "You are not under arrest. Do you understand that?"

"Then let me go," Terrance said sheepishly, raising his eyes to Bob's and quickly flicking them away.

"I would like it… It would be a lot easier on everyone if you came down to Marshfield with me and we talked a little more." Bob stopped while Terrance thought about the statement.

"You got food in Marshfield?" Terrance asked, a faint smile cracking his weathered skin.

Bob laughed, "Yeah. We have food. Maybe we can find you a winter job and a place to stay down there too. You know? Being laid off… I'd like to help you."

"Okay."

"Hang here for a while. I've got some things to do and then I'll have one of my guys take you over to B.C.I. We'll get you some breakfast or something."

"Okay. I'm not going anywhere."

Bob got out of the car and went over to Tom and Carol Rivers' car which still idled along the side of the road by the underpass.

He gently knocked on the glass with his notepad and both the man and woman got out.

"I'm Detective Schwimer. Are you Tom and Carol? I don't want to keep you long. A couple questions."

They nodded.

"What's going to happen with the bum?" Carol asked. "Is he under arrest?"

Bob half-turned and answered, "The witness, Mr. Silverman, is going to come in and answer a few more questions. I wanted to confirm a few things with you. What time did he flag you down?"

"About three-thirty."

Bob wrote notes in his pad. "Did you go up to the tracks?"

"No," Carol said.

"What did he say when you stopped."

"He was shooken-up bad. He asked us to call the police. He said there was a crime. Something about a coyote," Tom answered.

"He was babbling. He said something like we were the first ones to stop," Carol added.

"No wonder being three a.m. and all," Tom put in.

"What was he like? His demeanor."

"He was drunk," Tom said.

Carol added, "He seemed a bit scared. He was kinda frantic. But I guess he would be under the circumstances. Finding a body like that."

"Like what?" Bob asked.

"In parts and pieces."

"Did Silverman tell you that?"

"No, not really," Carol said. Bob looked at her until she answered his unspoken question. "Tom said…"

Bob turned to Tom. "You said you didn't go up there to look."

"I had to see… I told Carol to stay back and lock the doors… But the guy's homeless. He was drunk. I had to be sure he wasn't out of his mind."

Bob corrected his notes. "So you don't think Silverman knew there was a police station about five hundred feet down the road?"

"I don't know. I knew it was there. We live in town, but,"

Tom added, "I called in to nine-one-one because I wanted to keep an eye on the, ah… Mr. Silverman."

"Are you Detective Schwimer?" an authoritative voice came from behind Bob.

Bob looked around and found a young messy-haired man in a frumpy business suit. "Yes. Just a minute." Bob turned back to Tom and Carol.

"I want to thank you for stopping and helping Mr. Silverman. I have your phone number and contact info. You have my card. If you think of anything, please call me or write it down and send it in. You can email me anytime."

Tom and Carol nodded and departed with a handshake.

"One more question… Why were you out so late? The bars close at two-thirty."

"We were at a friends' house. We talked until three, at least."

"That would explain it."

Bob watched as they got back into their car. Several news reporters ran over to them and banged on the windows. Bob listened to the reporters ask if the Rivers saw anything, what their names are, are they suspects. He ignored the reporters and turned to the man in the business suit.

"Good morning. My name's Bob. Can I help you?"

"Officer Perry with the Kingston-Plymouth Line. Your dispatcher called me about a body on the tracks?"

"Yes. Let's step this way." Bob headed up the granite steps and across the lawn to the fence. "Officer, we are not really on the tracks." Bob turned to look at the Railroad Police Shield clipped to Perry's belt, his wrinkled suit, and then his face. The man was young. Bob guessed barely in his mid-twenties.

"Bob. I don't appreciate that you have people contaminating the crime scene. Railroads are private property protected under federal regulations."

"As far as we can tell, this may not actually be a crime scene."

"If anyone is on the tracks, it's a crime."

"As you can see my people are outside the right-of-way."

"There's a hole in the fence. I watched your people going through it several times."

"Any day that starts before the sun is up is not going to be a good day, and this day is going downhill fast," Bob said.

"What?"

Bob paused to put on his proverbial politician's hat. "With your permission we would like to photograph and tag evidence inside the right-of-way. You can see that most of the body parts are scattered in the brush and gravel, from the bridge north a hundred feet or so."

"The railroad will institute its own investigation."

"Officer Perry." Bob's voice dropped and softened. "Let's work together on this. Plymouth County has forensic tools and an M.E. lab and a lot of money to run an investigation. It would be an embarrassment to the railroad and to Plymouth County to have it reported that we cannot come to a swift and accurate analysis of this incident. The railroads do not need the bad press and Plymouth County needs the tourism."

"You think this was a murder?"

"Officially let's treat it as a murder and see if we can prove it was an accident."

Perry stood staring into the distance for a moment. He looked around at the Abington Police Officers. He looked at the County Cruisers and the State and County forensics vans. He looked at Bob and replied, "I suppose we can work together."

"Thank you." Bob offered a handshake to Officer Perry.

"I want to be involved with the entire investigation." Perry took the hand and they shook.

"Of course. I won't have it any other way," Bob assured the officer as he looked at the man's hand. It was pale, soft. The young man was probably barely out of college on his first job riding a desk for the railroad.

"The M.B.T.A. runs the passenger trains on the Kingston-Plymouth line all the way into Boston?"

"Yes."

"And the trains are stopped for now."

"Yes. But we need to clear the line as quick as possible."

"A couple hours?"

"It's gonna be rough on the T," Perry said.

"The Boston commute always is." Bob laughed. "I used to

make those trips every single day."

"I'll bet you're glad you don't anymore?"

"Very glad. Hang out with my team. We can always use a fresh set of eyes on any job. If you spot anything speak up," Bob said as he turned again towards the railroad tracks.

Terri worked with Peter, taking photographs and documenting the handling of the corpse. Frank Wysup and Sergeant Wally Young finished bagging evidence and noting them by location and identification.

As the daylight grew, Terri setup a three dimensional scanner. Within an hour she had enough information to create a virtual copy of the crime scene on computers back in her lab. After the scan was completed and everything was stowed for transport to the M.E. lab the team crisscrossed the crime scene again and again, looking for anything they might have missed.

Chapter 4

Bob's cell phone rang several times, but the unrecognized numbers turned out to be reporters, which he at first politely and firmly dismissed, and then stopped answering. He looked down at the reporters outside the police tape. Several were on cell phones and he wondered if it was they who were bothering him. He was about to turn the phone off when Mary called.

"Good morning, baby."

"Can you talk?" Mary Schwimer asked her husband.

"I got a minute or two. It's a mess down here but it's getting cleaned up."

"I know. It always is. Can you make it for lunch today?"

"Probably not."

"Okay. I was hoping we could get together."

"I appreciate it."

"Are we still on for a barbeque Saturday?"

"And trail ride?"

"That would be lovely."

"Who should we invite?" Bob asked.

"Everyone." Mary laughed.

"With or without horses?"

"Riding early and lunch afterwards."

"You got it. We haven't had a B.B.Q. in a while. It will be fun."

"Great. I'm heading to the store to pickup some stuff so I thought I'd grab anything that looks good."

"Good idea."

"I'll let you go. You can tell me all about the job later."

"I don't think you're going to want to know about this one."

"Save the gory details. Tell me 'what' and 'when'."

"Okay, but I can't comment about ongoing investigations."

"Who do I look like? A reporter?"

"Only if you wear a trench coat and carry a flash camera."

"And nothing else?"

"Promises, promises."

Mary laughed and Bob stifled his smile in consideration of the situation at hand and the media watching everything through camera lenses. "Got to go baby. Thanks for the pick-me-up but I've got some bad news to give, and things here are going to get worse...

"Before it gets better?"

"You can read me, Mary."

"It's a gift."

"Call you in a bit.

"Wait."

"What?"

"Dinner with Sheriff Barton tonight, don't forget."

"I didn't. Eight o'clock."

"Come home early if you can. Bye-bye."

"Goodbye love."

Bob hung up the phone and approached Terri as she stored her tools in the M.E. van. She pulled off her white field coat and hung it inside, where she took out a long canvas coat, heavy and functional. He asked her for an update as she pulled off her hairnet and let a long ponytail fall to her shoulders. She pushed the ponytail back up under a baseball hat from her coat pocket. Black letters on the gray cap told the world she was an M.E.

Terri smiled, "Nothing out the ordinary for a body dismembered by a train."

"I need some coffee." Bob didn't return her smile. "How can you be so lighthearted at a murder scene?"

"It keeps me sane," she said with a mawkish grin.

"Are you sure?" Bob asked and Terri tried to mute her laughter as she looked at the gaggle of reporters and news camera's not far away, several reporters were looking at them and walking over.

"Take a look at this." Terri handed him a plastic evidence bag with a wallet inside it. She climbed inside the van and Bob followed her, closing the door behind him, shutting out the reporters. Bob pulled on latex gloves and opened the bag. He flipped through the wallet. A two inch thick stack of bills threatened to fall out.

"Must be five thousand dollars," she said. "That's only part of the weird thing. Look at the I.D."

Bob found a Massachusetts Welfare Department Benefits Identification Card.

"B.I.C.?"

"He's on welfare with thousands of dollars in his wallet," Terri said.

"And our resident homeless guy and first suspect didn't take the money?" Bob looked up at Terri.

She smiled. "This is a premeditated murder."

"Hmmm," Bob hummed. He noted the name on the welfare card. It read, 'John Spears'. "You might be right but maybe it was a suicide or a thrill-kill, maybe a hate-crime. I'll leave the speculation to the reporters. Silverman doesn't seem like the 'emo-neo-nazi-white-racist' type. He's out of work. He flagged down a car to call the police."

"Unless he's covering up something? Hide in plain sight?"

"There's the Raynham thing I need to check on.

"What's that?"

"Something he said. We can hold him long enough for you to do a post mortem. He's so cold and hungry right now a couple days in jail and three squares a day will be like a vacation, minus the alcohol. Terri, I'd like you to have Mr. Spears' clothing and personal belongings analyzed. Let's find out what happened here. Also, have Mr. Silverman's clothing checked. I'll pick him up some new clothing, some winter clothing. I think he will gladly discard his old clothes…"

"Which means we don't need a warrant," Terri interrupted.

"Yes. If he discards the old clothes."

"And if he doesn't?"

"We'll ask nice. Have Peter take Silverman in, will you? I have some calls to make and a bar to visit. It would be best if Silverman didn't overhear. Also, have Peter run John Spears' name through the computer. Let's find his family. They need to be notified."

"Don't we have probable cause on this guy?"

"Maybe, if finding a body is a crime and last time I

checked…"

"Are you sure he isn't involved?"

"I didn't say that."

"Okay. Would you like me to go over the crime scene with you?"

"Definitely," Bob said. "I'd like your take."

Terri grabbed a digital camera off a shelf and slung it over her shoulder. They got out of the van and headed back up the granite steps and through the chain link fence.

"I'll know more after the autopsy and we can take a look at the 3-D digital." Terri pointed as she walked. "So we have the body, dismembered. There were parts scattered along the tracks. Not as many as it seems. The head over there with a leg. The right arm up the tracks a ways. The other leg and arm are broken but attached. There are no drag marks in the grass and dirt, but the gravel on the railroad bed was turned up a bit. I figure the perp carried the body up the tracks from south of the bridge. If you look over here there's footprints where someone moved the body."

"To position it on the tracks?"

"Exactly," Terri said as she took photographs in addition to the one's Peter had taken earlier. "I don't think the body was chopped up before it was dumped. By the way the flesh is torn and ripped it looks like it was struck by a train, maybe more than one. I can't be sure until I get the bone fragments under a microscope."

"Do you have a shoe type or size on the footprints?" Bob asked.

"Twelve. It's a leather sole, like a wingtip or loafer," Terri responded.

"Silverman is wearing boots."

"His boot prints are here too. Size ten-and-a-half. Looks like he walked down the tracks. Jackson found boot prints leading this way from the north, over half a mile along the tracks."

"Could Silverman have been an accomplice? They parked in the cemetery and maybe his cohort drove off without him. He goes down to the street and the Rivers couple drive up and they stop to ask what's going on at three a.m.?"

"Peter checked the tracks and the cemetery. There's a cut in the fence. Like this one. No fresh tire marks. The gates have been locked for days. The caretaker vouches for that. One set of boot prints. No drag marks. Take a look at this." Terri led Bob over to an area of wet gravel along the tracks.

"What is that?" Bob asked.

"Regurgitation."

"Who's?"

"Or 'what'. Could be Silverman's, could be a dog. Could be our murderer's. I'm sending a sample of the bile to the lab. We should be able to get some DNA out of it."

"DNA takes months, but we have time," Bob said.

"Maybe he vomited when he found the body or a dog ate too much of the victim?"

"Probably the former."

"Interesting. You said it looks like someone carried the body from the south. Why?"

Terri looked down across the railroad bridge. She said, "Behind Island Grove, Park Avenue. I think that's the name. Odd name in the burbs. Wally found some tire marks in the dirt. He said there are two sets of shoe prints. And another hole in the fence. He marked the area with police tape and taped the cut in the fence also."

Let's take a look. Bob turned south with Terri when he noticed Officer Perry following on their heels. "You might as well join us," he invited and the young officer smiled and picked up his steps.

"It looks like the priest was right," Perry said.

"About what?"

"The kids cut holes in the fences almost as fast as the railroad can repair them. It's a big problem. From Boston to Rhode Island and the Cape. We have crews out all the time fixing fences."

A quizzical look came to Bob's face, "Were there any crews through here in the last twenty-four hours?"

"I can check with maintenance."

"Do that, please."

"Now?"

"If you can... Can you?"

"I'll call in."

Bob smiled and the officer stopped to talk on his radio.

"You have something?" Terri asked as they continued south on the tracks and across the short bridge.

"Just pieces. We need to know anyone and everyone who might have been here. Maintenance crews qualify."

"If a maintenance person did this, don't they drive the rails? Why would they park on a side street?"

"Depends on the train schedule. They can't be on the tracks when a train is scheduled to come through."

Bob and Terri reached the cut in the fence and they ducked through and under the police tape and walked down to the street.

Terri took her camera off her shoulder. She pointed to the spot on the ground. A half dozen orange cones marked the area. "There was no way to tape off the area. Peter got photos of the car tracks and shoeprints. I'll take a few more." From a hind pocket she took out a six inch yellow and black engineers scale, and took several photos of the prints and tire marks.

"What size?"

"Too hard to tell. Probably the same twelve's we got by the body. That's what I'm thinking anyway. Not even sure it was two people. I am going to take a look at Peter's picts and do some math, but I think the body was dragged across the bridge a couple hundred feet."

"Why not leave the body in the woods? If you were dumping a body..."

"I think they wanted it dismembered."

"And still discovered?" Bob asked.

"Yes. And the woods are not the best place to hide a body you want found."

"I agree. They leave a body on the tracks, where it's sure to be hit by a train and discovered by someone, a teenager, or in this case a homeless person." Bob fell into silent thought and then said, "That's a message."

"What kind of message?" Terri frowned.

"I think we'll find out. What time do the trains come

through?"

"Perry said the morning trains don't come through until six. Abington Dispatch called in to hold the trains until we can clear the area."

"Keep your eyes and ears open anyway. We don't need another victim today."

"That reminds me of a joke. What was the last thing that went though his mind?" Terri looked at Bob's stern expression. "Right. Not now."

Photographs finished, engineers scale retrieved, they started back up the tracks as Perry caught up to them. He was out of breath, "There was a maintenance crew through here. Yesterday morning. They noted the holes in the fences and logged them for repair."

"How many guys on a crew?" Bob asked the officer.

"Four. Sometimes three."

"How many on *this* crew?"

A vacant look came over Perry's face. "I'll find out."

"And their names?"

Perry nodded.

"And their supervisor's name. I'll need to speak to them."

"All of them?"

Bob smiled.

"Okay." Perry stopped again to call in on his radio, while Terri and Bob continued back up the tracks.

When Bob and Terri returned to the dump site Bob said, "Tell me how the body parts were scattered. What kind of distance are we talking about?"

"Not much. We aren't talking about a total dismemberment. From the clothing and the blood, it looks worse than it is. We found a shoe, still missing one of them. The clothing was pretty torn up. Found a sock that probably goes with the shoe and foot. We have a torso between the rails of the tracks; minus the head, a leg at the knee, and an arm. The head and leg were by the rails, less than a dozen feet away. The arm was thirty yards north, but there's probably a stray dog nearby. I photographed some paw prints around the arm. There are teeth marks. Could even be a coyote that tried to drag the arm off except it's relatively heavy."

Terri pushed a few of her long dark hairs back under her baseball cap.

"That tends to agree with Mr. Silverman," Bob said.

"Why?"

"Because of time. Coyotes like quiet. That's why they come out at night. They scavenge."

"And if someone hung around after dumping the body the coyotes would never come down this close," Terri agreed.

"Coyotes are not dumb, but that doesn't rule out Silverman completely," Bob said.

"Return to the scene of the crime?"

"Possibly but probably not. If coyotes moved the arm then what I told Officer Perry is not entirely true."

"About the body being found off the tracks? The right of way? I won't say anything to him." Terri smiled.

"I'm going to try to confirm Silverman's story. I'll see you back in Marshfield." Bob returned to the street where Wally was taking down the police tape. Most of the reporters had left. Bob vaguely recalled a helicopter flying overhead earlier but it was gone now. The scene was oddly quiet. The streets and the sky was clear.

Officer Perry caught up to Bob by the granite retaining wall.

"Four men. Got their names from maintenance, and their H.R. files are being sent to my office. I'll get them over to you."

"Thank you. That's above and beyond. You can fax them to this number. It goes straight to my email." Bob handed Perry a business card. "Where do they work out of?"

"Braintree. There's a maintenance yard. Are we finished here?"

"For now," Bob answered.

"So we can start the trains again?"

"For now. I'll let you know if we need to get back on the tracks and look for anything we might have missed." Bob smiled. The young man returned the smile, shook Bob's hand, and turned to his car. Bob called after him, "You can follow the M.E. back to B.C.I. in Marshfield."

"Roger," the wrinkled suit waved.

It was Bob's turn to smile as he pictured a willing puppy

wagging its tail.

Bob walked over to Wally who was bagging the old police tape and stowing it in the trunk of his cruiser. "You are with me. Follow me to North Avenue for a few minutes."

"Okay." Wally slammed the trunk lid closed.

Chapter 5

Bob, with Wally on his tail, drove north on Plymouth Street. They crossed the railroad tracks, and turned right on Route 139 at the traffic light. They passed the mom and pop stores and a hundred year old printing and paper factory before turning left into the Stoney's Mill parking lot where the railroad tracks again crossed the residential streets. Inside Bob and Wally approached the bartender who was stocking liquor bottles on the shelves.

"Good morning," Bob said.

"Not open. We don't open until noon. Blue laws."

"I think you could make an exception." Bob put his badge and a business card on the bar.

The bartender picked up the business card and looked at it. "Okay. What kind of drink do you want and is this a setup?"

Bob laughed. "No setup. Nothing to drink. My name is Detective Schwimer. This is Sergeant Young." Bob gestured to Wally.

"Harry. Bartender and half-owner." He put the card down and returned to his shelf-stocking task.

"Who is Stoney?" Bob asked.

"No one. Stoney's Mill is only a name. My brother and I bought this place a couple years ago. Rehabbed it inside and out and turned it around."

"There was a homeless guy in here last night."

"Is this about all the police cars down the street?"

"Do you know something about that?"

"I was stuck in traffic at the light. I saw all the cruisers. I live in Hanson."

"Long drive," Bob commented.

"Yeah, but the hours are good; no grid lock at three a.m."

"Not much at nine a.m. either. You work some long hours?"

"Working for myself there's never any time off. My brother and I switch off some days, most days we are both here. It's cheaper for us to mix drinks and open beers than it is to hire a bartender."

"Were you here last night?"

"Most nights and days, and mornings too." Harry finished the liquor shelf and pulled open the top case on a tall stack of boxes. He started putting bottles into a refrigerated cooler under the bar, five bottles in each hand, two hands at a time.

"So you remember the guy?"

"The vagrant? Yes. He's been coming in every night for a week."

"Ever seen him before that?"

"No. I guess he tried the other bars but they threw him out. Probably."

"What do you mean?"

"Clientele. Some places don't want a homeless guy hanging around. Figure they lose money."

"And you don't?"

"He pays cash. Never asked for a free drink."

"Your clientele don't mind?"

"He didn't smell. He keeps himself clean, mostly. Had one or two complaints from some of my regulars. I told them the same thing I'm telling you."

"Did he ever cause any problems?"

"Nope. Not here. He'd come in around dark or a little later. Drink for a few hours. Always closed the place. Almost always. Paid for every drink as it was served."

"What kind of guy do you think he is?"

"He always tipped on his first drink of the night. Maybe he figured it would get him a free drink later on. He never asked for one."

"Did it work?"

"Sometimes."

"He paid cash."

"Sometimes he'd get a free drink from another patron. Sometimes I'd throw him one."

"Isn't that kind of like feeding a stray dog?" Bob asked. He knew the question was baiting but he hoped to learn more about the bar and Silverman, and to see if anything slipped out or came up. Keep the guy talking.

"There's a reason why men are referred to as dogs. This guy, whatever his name is, he always has cash and he always pays. This bar has problems like any other, less than most around here. But that bum..."

"Silverman."

"Yeah, Silverman." Harry said the name like it didn't quite fit the image he had of the man. "He never caused any problems. Sometimes I saw him talking to someone, but never the same person twice."

"He didn't annoy them?"

"I don't think so. A few regulars, but I told them to shut up."

Bob took down the statement in his notepad. "How late did he stay last night?"

"Closing. He was here until closing. Probably for the warmth. He always left when we asked him to. Never had any problems. He sat at the bar over there." Harry pointed. "And he drank whiskey by the glass. Slow. Real slow sometimes. I think he was milking time till closing."

"Did he know anyone?"

"I don't know. Like I said, sometimes some of the regulars would buy him a drink so they could lean on his ear. Talk to someone who cared about their problems. When it's slow and a guy is drunk, I swear, he will talk to a wooden Indian, if I had one." The bartender laughed.

"Did anyone else know him? A waitress or your brother?"

"My brother and... I'm sure Arlene met him. He only sits at the bar. One night we were real busy and that end of the bar was taken. He sat at a table, ordered one drink and then left."

"When was that?"

"Wednesday, maybe Thursday. Wednesday we have the dart league. Probably Wednesday." The bartender stopped stocking beers into the cooler and looked at Bob. "What is this about?"

"Not sure yet," Bob answered.

"The radio said there was a body found in Abington. Schwimer? Is that your name?" Harry asked.

Bob nodded.

"That's what the radio said."

"Yes. Um. Thanks." Bob pushed the business card on the bar-top towards Harry. "Call me if you remember anything else."

"Is the bum dead?"

"Mr. Silverman? No. What time does Arlene come in?"

"She's off work today. Do you want me to have her call you?"

"Yes. Thanks." Bob made a note to follow-up with the waitress before turning and opening the door. "Please call if you remember anything."

"Will do," Harry said as they exited.

Bob walked out to the parking lot and looked over at the railroad crossing that ran behind the bar. He stopped and Wally took another two steps before turning back.

"It's new," Bob said.

"Wha' is?" Wally's Maine accent showed more with fewer words.

"The commuter rail was extended down to the South Shore about fifteen years ago?"

"A'bout that."

"The crossing barriers, lights, and chain link fences still look as new as the day they were installed, unlike the chain link in the brush and woods down the tracks."

"Tha' get maintained. Not much vandalism by the crossings? Kids don't want to hang out he'ah. Besides tha's cameras." Wally pointed up at the crossing cameras and solar panels that powered them.

"There's cameras." Bob repeated. He took his cell phone from its belt holster and called the number on Perry's business card.

"Officer Perry, Kingston-Plymouth Rail Service," the officer answered the phone.

"Perry? Schwimer."

"Yes?"

"There are surveillance cameras at the Route 139 crossing. Can you get me copies?"

"Probably."

"Good. I need them. I also need copies if you have a camera on Plymouth Street."

"I don't think there is one on Plymouth. I looked for one this morning."

"You did? When did you do that? Forget it. See if you can get me those videos; DVDs, AVIs or MPEGs, whatever format. We need, let's say, from noon or when the maintenance crew went by yesterday until four or five this morning? Can you do that?"

"I'll have word back to you in a few minutes."

"Great." Bob hung up the phone and looked at Wally.

"We can corroborate the bartenda's and Silverman's stories?" Wally asked.

"You'll make detective yet, Wally" Bob laughed.

"No thanks. I like prisoner transport and patrol."

Chapter 6

As Bob drove to Marshfield he had Bristol County's Sheriff Jasperse on the phone.

"Hello Bob. What can I do *to* you? *Haw-haw,*" the Sheriff crudely joked. Bob let the remark pass. He knew Jasperse for many years and his respect for the man, and his police work, slipped ever lower.

"Hello Sheriff. I need to talk to you. We got a situation over here in Abington that might be related to a problem you had in Raynham awhile back."

"Oh? What problem?"

"Was there a murder or something in Raynham recently?"

"Raynham? No. No."

"Are you sure? How about a while ago? A couple years or so."

"Give me some details."

"I got a homeless guy over here who said something about Raynham."

"Yeah. Okay. I know that bum. I remember a kid got murdered. It's still unsolved. Young kid. Teenager."

"In Raynham?"

"Yeah. That's what you said. Raynham. Quiet town. Not much happens there, since or before. We solve eighty or ninety percent of our crimes within a few days. Strange thing though…"

"What's that?"

"The kid was fifteen or fourteen." Jasperse paused to remember the case. "The boy was blasted with a shotgun in an alleyway. No leads. We picked up a homeless guy and held him for a long time but we couldn't prove he did it. It appeared like the vagrant was just looking for a warm dumpster to sleep in and he came across the body. The curious part, the reason we held him while we looked for evidence was the boy had twenty bucks in his pocket. Couldn't figure out why the vagrant didn't take the money before he reported finding the body."

"So you held him. The vagrant? Terrance Silverman?"

"Is that his name?

"You tell me?"

"I'd have to look in the case file. Sounds right. We held him, the vagrant that is, for a long time. Months maybe. You know, 'pending investigation', 'suspicion of murder'. We couldn't make anything stick. The guy didn't have any weapons on him. Every bum carries a pig-sticker, just in case. Everyone knows that. *Haw, haw,*" Jasperse guffawed into the phone. "This guy had nothing on him. I mean the kid was killed with a shotgun but if the bum had so much as a toothpick on him we'd have sent him up for the crime. *Haw.*" Jasperse laughed again. "Finally the D.A. said we had to let him go. There was nothing we could do."

"I see. Thanks." Bob cringed at the malevolent laughter. "If I get a chance I'd like to come over there some time in the next couple days or so. Talk with you some more. Any chance I could look at the case file on that kid?"

"Sure. Let me know. I'd love to solve that murder case. If it relates to anything you have going on, we can work together."

"Thank you, Sheriff."

"Hey Bob. Hold on a sec, what's going on over there? What's the sudden interest?"

"We picked up a 'Terrance Silverman' over here. Homeless guy. Not sure how he fits into this but he's a 'first suspect'... ah... 'person of interest'."

"You mean he's guilty. *Haw, Haw, Haw.*" Jasperse laughed again. "If it's the same guy, I'd like to send him up for something. We got room at Cedar Junction for bums."

"Thanks again, Sheriff. Got an emergency call on the radio. Gotta run." Bob hung up before the sheriff finished ranting. Shaking his head, Bob said aloud to himself, "Couldn't even remember the name of a suspect he had locked up for months."

Chapter 7

Bob scrolled through his cell phone contacts and placed a call.

"State Police. 85364. This is a recorded line," A woman's voice answered.

"Captain Rudolph, please. Detective Schwimer calling."

"Hold." It was several minutes before the line was picked up. "Hello Bob. Good to hear from you."

"Hi Donald."

"Have you considered my offer?"

"Oh. The state job?"

"We sure would like to have you up here in Worcester."

"Thanks Don. I'm still talking to Mary about it."

"Don't think too long. You have a good reputation. Your Boston work was impeccable. We want you up here helping us."

"I'll let you know."

"Do that."

"We got a call this morning about a body."

"Yeah." Don fell quiet as he clacked on a keyboard, the sound coming through the phone. "Abington?"

"Yes."

"Got a report this morning, early, from a Lieutenant Singer."

"He said he would call it in."

"So why is county involved?"

"We got called in by Abington's dispatch."

"It was on railroad tracks?"

"Yes, Don. It's beginning to sound like you know more than we do." Bob laughed.

"These databases are pretty nice?"

"Are you sure you weren't in Abington last night?"

Don laughed. "Do you have Frank Wysup with you?"

"Yes and Terri Cox.

"Great. Sounds like a good team."

"An Officer Perry showed up from the T."

"Railroad police?"

"Yes."

"So what can I do for you? It sounds like it should be wrapped up in no time. Probably an accident? Unless you need to find a suspect and a motive."

"It's not an accident."

"Are you sure?"

"The evidence points to a body being dumped on the tracks. You've never seen anything like this."

"A train took care of it? If I had any hope, I'd ask that the guy was dead before being hit by the train."

"Pretty much. It looks like it was staged to be an accident but the way it was executed... The method... The location..."

"What are you thinking, Bob?"

"It looks more like a message goes along with the murder."

"Gangs or the mob?" Don asked.

"Not sure. No drugs but they left five thousand dollars in the victim's wallet."

"That sounds like a message to me. They don't need the money or don't want it. You said 'they'. More than one perp?"

"We found multiple sets of footprints down the tracks. Tire marks, drag marks. There were at least two guys. Men's shoes. Leather sole," Bob answered.

"So we aren't talking Nike-wearing gang-bangers?"

"No."

"And you're calling me because you want to head up the investigation?"

"If it isn't too much trouble."

"It sounds like the ball is in your court already. You must be bored."

"I like my job."

"Really? Sounds like love to me."

"Yes. That, and it has been a bit slow." Bob's face grew grim. "What I haven't said is the body was dismembered."

"I got that in the Singer report. Pretty sick."

"It is. I suppose a train could do that to a body properly laid on the tracks, but the money plus how they disposed of the body..."

"Murder..."

"You got it."

"Bob, I'll see what I can do on this end. If you've got things under control let's say you are unofficially in charge of the unofficial task-force until you hear otherwise. I'll draw up the paperwork and push it through on this end."

"That's all I'm asking."

"Keep me updated."

"I will but what about Wysup?"

"Frank is state."

"He wants to lead the investigation."

"I got a message from him too, but I haven't checked it. You can handle this."

"Can you do anything?"

"I'll put it in. Keep him on the team for now. I'll make sure he knows this is your game. You're in charge."

"Thanks Donald."

Bob glanced at his watch as he pulled into a sub-shop on Route 52 in Hanover. Wally pulled in behind him. It was quarter to noon. He and Wally ordered several submarine sandwiches and cans of soda for take-out. They waited at a table by the window, watching the noontime traffic backing up by the entrance to the Hanover shopping mall. Bob counted twelve, thirteen, then fourteen cars lining up before the first one got across the street. "What do you think Wally?" Bob asked, trying to break the silence.

"I think we will know soon enough."

Bob laughed. "I know you better than that." Wally held the thinnest line of smile on his face. "You're an old soldier. You've seen battle in the Gulf War. You've policed worse battle grounds than Plymouth. What's your gut telling you?"

"If you want me to speak freely, I think we are going to find out this guy is a high-end drug dealer or a mobster or a top of the line car thief or jewelry thief, burglar or something like that and he got bumped off by the competition. He lives on the edge. Skirting the law, pushing the limits. And he pushed too far.

Abington is not far from Brockton and Boston. You know the criminals have been moving out to the suburbs."

"Of course. Why?"

"Because of the money, the welfare card, the location."

It wasn't lost on Bob that his work in Boston had pushed the criminals out of the city and into some of the very suburbs he now worked. Where would they go from here? Back to Boston?

Wally continued, "I don't get the welfare card with five grand in his pocket."

"Money is tight, even for criminals. It comes and it goes. The welfare card means he has something to eat once in a while. Maybe he has kids," Bob said.

"Maybe he's just leaching the system?"

"That wouldn't surprise me. What do you think about the M.O.? Dumping a body on the tracks?"

"That's a pretty nasty way to die. Hope it isn't a serial killer."

"Me too. Another body like that and I'll have to find another career," Bob added.

"That's why you can keep the homicides. I'll stay with domestic violence. At least I can arrest the scumbag right in his own home. Usually with the victim's bruises just starting to appear on her skin."

"Unfortunately a lot of those end up on my desk too." Bob's eyes narrowed and wrinkles formed on his brow.

"Human nature. Stay with the security, money, affection, attention even if it's mostly bad. Ninety-nine percent of the time the woman stays for her kids, or the rush, or the nest, or her own illusions of love, instead of getting out. You asked for my thoughts."

"The truth hurts. I think a lot of homeless guys, like Mr. Silverman, choose to stay on the streets. They are escaping something, or think they deserve that kind of life. Victim of domestic violence, A & B, a lot of times as a kid. Saw more than one army recruit escaping a bad home life. No one deserves that. Any way out is a good way out. I'd take homeless, or the army, or anything, over some of the stories I've heard."

"Any way out before they end up on a table in Terri's lab?"

Wally added.

Bob turned back to counting the cars lining up in the middle of the street, trying to turn into the shopping mall. Ten, eleven, then they moved again. They both let the conversation die a welcome death as Bob's cell phone vibrated in silent mode. The phone displayed Officer Perry's name.

"Perry?"

"Detective? I have the video camera records for you."

"Good. What's the format?" Bob pictured a puppy, a wrinkled Chinese Shar-Pei, jumping up and down. Waging its tail.

"Hi-def video. I can have them sent over to you by email. Sometime tomorrow. I put the requests in and I got a call back from central within ten minutes."

"Thank you," Bob replied. "A question."

"Yeah?"

"Where are you now?"

"I'm going to help Terri in the M.E. lab," Perry replied.

"Good. Thanks."

"It's a joint effort."

"I appreciate the work," Bob said as he continued counting and recounting cars waiting in the street. "Let me know when you email the videos."

"Yes, sir. Goodbye."

"Bye." Bob hung up the phone and relayed the information to Wally.

When they got their food and left the deli, Bob sent Wally on to H.Q. Bob entered the south-bound roadway and quickly changed into the left hand lane to stop at the end of the long line of cars trying to get to the mall. A few minutes later he was roaming the parking lot and debating the use of police privilege. A parking space opened up before he could decide.

Inside the mall he picked up winter clothes; everything from size ten-and-a-half insulated boots to a knit hat, long underwear, wool socks, long and short sleeve shirts; flannel, size: large, and blue jeans (he had to guess on the size of the trousers, so he guessed larger) and a heavy coat. Terrance would be outfitted for the winter if he chose to stay on the streets. Bob knew that putting this expense on the department budget was pushing the limits of the tax-payers tolerance, but he could justify the cost with the extreme nature of this particular murder, and what he had to do to find the answers he needed.

Chapter 8

Bob sat down with Terrance Silverman at B.C.I. headquarters. The man had willingly changed into the clean new clothes and methodically ate a submarine sandwich. Bob met with Wally in the video observation room before the interview. The room was more of a closet with a simple desk sporting three video monitors and a D.V.R. recorder connected to a PC. Small computer speakers broadcast Terrance's shuffling in his chair.

"I want you to stay in here and watch the interview."

"Am I looking for anything specific?"

"Just watch and listen. If you catch anything that doesn't feel right then remember the time stamp and we can review it." Bob pointed to a blank pad of paper on the desk.

"Why the food and clothing?"

"Because he's homeless, which will mean he might be hungry. Hungry enough to eat free food and…"

"DNA," Wally answered.

Bob smiled, "Only if he throws the wrapping papers, napkins, and soda can in the trash."

"But what's with the clothes?"

Bob smiled as he picked up his briefcase and left the room, "I can't give you all my tricks all at once. You've got to learn to walk before you run."

Bob entered the interview room down the hall and sat down opposite Terrance. He took a stack of paperwork from his briefcase and set it on the table. On top of the pile he placed an old V.H.S. tape.

Terrance stopped eating to look at the tape. "You got a video tape?"

"Yes," Bob lied.

"Good," Terrance said as he took a small bite of his second sandwich.

"Why is that good?"

When Terrance finished chewing, he swallowed and replied, "Then you know I didn't do anything."

"Okay." Bob smiled. The V.H.S. tape ruse fooled almost everyone. His sense of the man was just a little more confirmed. Silverman's statement had the sound of certainty in it.

Silverman returned to his sandwich while Bob reviewed his notes looking for inconsistencies.

"Terrance. Tell me again what happened last night."

"Drinking at the bar." Between bites, Terrance answered Bob's questions in short sentences.

"Stoney's Mill?"

Terrance nodded.

"What time did you leave?"

"Closing. They threw me out."

Bob nodded at the terminology Terrance chose. "They asked you to leave?"

"Yup."

"Like every night?"

Terrance stopped eating and looked at Bob. After a moment he nodded. "Sometimes."

"Were they bad about it?"

"Nope."

"So it was just closing time?"

Terrance nodded.

"Harry seems like a nice enough bartender."

Terrance stopped chewing to glare at Bob, but he didn't respond.

"I talked to the bartender for a few minutes this morning."

"He's okay."

"He said he gives you a free drink once in a while."

Terrance nodded as he took another bite of the sub. "I pay for my own."

"Sometimes someone buys you a drink?"

"Sometimes."

"Then what?" Bob waited for Terrance to finish chewing and take a drink of soda.

"Then I drink it."

Bob laughed and Terrance smirked through a full mouth.

"Then what happened *last* night? After you left the bar."

"I walked down the tracks."

"Where were you going?" Bob leaned forward, looking intently at the man.

"To sleep. Island Grove."

"And that's when you found the body."

"No. That's when I found the dog."

"A dog?" Bob asked as he flipped through his notes to the canine prints along the tracks.

"A dog, a coyote, with an arm."

"It was carrying an arm?" Bob knew the statement matched his notes but he phrased it as a question anyway.

"Yeah. I haven't seen anything like that since Iraq."

Bob wrote a reminder to pull the military records on Silverman.

"Recently? You were in Iraq recently?"

"No. Desert Storm."

"I see. So what happened with the dog?"

"Coyote."

"Coyote?"

"I think it was a coy-yot. Couldn't really tell in the dark but it sort of yelped at me the same as I remember them."

"You remember them?"

"Yup. It barked in a yelping kinda way."

"With an arm in it's mouth?"

"It dropped the arm and took off into the cemetery."

Bob checked his notes to confirm what Terri said about Peter finding the arm further up the tracks and the paw prints around it.

"You said 'remember them' about the coyote. What do you know about coyotes?"

"They yelp. I listened to them all summer."

"You listened to them howl? At night?"

"Yeah. At night. Early mornings." Terrance stared into the blank wall behind Bob.

"In Lakeville?"

"Yup."

"Do they have a coyote problem over there?"

"Sometimes."

"What do you mean sometimes?"

"Sometimes people shoot them."

"Yeah? Who shoots them?"

"People."

"You?"

"Nope."

"Then what happened? Terrance?"

The man's eyes darted back to Bob and then down to the sandwich in his hands. "I went around the arm and down the tracks. That's where the body was. Body parts."

"When you saw the body parts what did you do?"

"I felt like I was back in Iraq."

"Did it make you ill, dizzy, sick to your stomach? Anything like that?"

"No. I don't remember. I just went down to the road to get some help."

"The body might not have been found for days up there on the tracks, behind all the brush."

Terrance ate and sipped his soda.

"So you hailed down the Rivers' car?"

"That's their name? I don't know."

"Why didn't you go by the police station?"

"Where?"

"The Abington Police... right down the road on Central Street."

"I don't know. I guess I forgot it was there."

"Terrance? Tell me again about Raynham?"

Terrance stopped eating to think for a moment, like the name must of meant something, but he could not recall why.

"You know what I'm asking about," Bob stated.

"I don't know."

"You don't know about Raynham?"

"Nope."

"You mentioned it this morning."

A sudden realization came over Terrance's face. "Nothing to say. I got nothing to say about that."

"You told me a bit this morning."

"I found a body." Terrance took another bite.

Bob waited while Terrance ate. The man eyed Bob nervously. Finally Bob asked, "And?"

"Nothing." Terrance went back to eating. Terrance looked at the ceiling while he chewed, "There was a motorcycle."

"Yeah?"

"I heard a gun shot and a motorcycle raced down the street. Then I found the body."

Bob waited a moment to see if the man would continue talking. When he didn't, Bob looked back at his notes. He read them and added more notes while waiting for Terrance to grow bored. Five minutes went by. Then twenty. Terrance finished eating and drinking his soda. With nothing to do, the man cleaned up the wrappers, crumpling them and stuff them into the bag they came in. He took a napkin and wiped his faces. With nothing else to do he stared at the wall.

Bob gathered his paperwork into his briefcase and left the room. He went down the hall to the video room.

"What's he not saying?" Wally asked Bob.

"I called Sheriff Jasperse and I'm going to find out some more, but there was a murder over in Raynham a few years ago and he was a suspect." Bob put his briefcase on the desk and took out his notepad.

"And he doesn't want to talk about it?"

"I'm guessing they treated him pretty bad. Lot's of bad memories about it."

"But no charges?"

"No."

"So what are we doing?"

"Letting him stew. I want to see how honest he is."

"I'm getting that he's okay."

"I got the same feeling, which bothers me. Whenever I get to thinking I know something for sure that's the best time to step back and be extra careful. We'll let him get bored for awhile. He'll want to talk again. Coffee?"

"Sure," Wally said.

"Great. Get me one too."

"Cuz you're the boss?"

"That's one reason."

Wally went down the hall and got two cups of coffee and brought them back. They sat silently watching Terrance on the video screen for a few minutes, sipping their coffee. Terrance sat uneasy, shuffling in his seat, like a restless child.

Eventually Bob went back to the interview room. As he closed the door he asked, "What about Raynham?"

"I didn't do it."

"You found a body in Raynham?" Bob sat down and leaned forward onto the desk.

"I didn't do it."

"That's a heck of a co-incidence finding two bodies."

"Not me. That's why I stopped a car." Terrance's voice rose in fear.

"I talked to Sheriff Jasperse. He never solved that murder."

Terrance stared at Bob, then finally said again, "I didn't do it."

"I don't think you did, but I'll be looking into it." Bob sat back.

"Why are you telling me?" Terrance asked.

"Someone finds a body and gets falsely accused they might think twice about reporting anything to the police again. But to find a second body? That's pretty rare." Bob poked and prodded at the man. If he could confirm any of what the man said then he might believe him. If Terrance lied or his story changed he'd remain suspect.

Terrance didn't comment.

"It's more than rare. It's virtually unheard of."

Terrance shrugged.

"Can you see where I might have a problem with that?"

"I saw bodies in Iraq. A lot of bodies. Some of them were my friends," Terrance defended himself.

"I'm sorry about your friends."

Terrance acted as if Bob had not replied. After a moment Bob continued, "Why did you flag down a car? You could just walk away, sleep in the park. No one would know or suspect you."

"I did the right thing. Someone did that to me I'd want it reported. I'd want someone to know. Wouldn't want to get chewed on by a coyote." Terrance started laughing.

"What's funny?" Bob asked.

"I wonder if the guy's father ever told him he wouldn't amount to shit."

"Dog shit? I get it," Bob answered without humor in his voice. He felt like he was losing control of the interview.

"Yup." Terrance laughed again.

"That's it? Just being a good neighbor? You found a body and got accused of murder, and then you found a second body and reported it? Can't you see how I would have a problem with that?"

"Nope."

"No?"

"Nope."

"After Raynham, you find a second body and still report it to the police?"

"Yup."

"Most people spend their entire lives and never see a corpse outside of a funeral home. You found two inside a few years."

"He never did anything to me. Plus there's footprints."

Bob sat back amazed. "So you thought you might be placed at the scene from your boot prints and shoe size?"

"I ain't stupid."

"I didn't think you were. That's pretty good. You had the forethought to know you leave boot prints along the railroad tracks and…"

"And you can follow the prints."

"What did you do in Iraq?" Bob changed the subject.

"I'd have to kill you." Terrance remained jovial.

Bob smiled. "You could tell me but then you'd have to kill me? Right?"

"It's an old joke."

"Very old." Bob laughed. He began to feel better about the interview. "What did you do? You saw lots of bodies? You did some killing? Of course… Stupid of me to ask."

Terrance nodded.

"What unit?" Bob thought that would be a good place to start. Put Terrance at ease talking about something he knew.

"Airborne."

"Yeah? Where were you based?"

"Dhahran."

"That's in Iraq?"

"Saudi."

"What was your specialty?"

"Support."

"Like S.A.W. machine gunner?"

"M249."

"That'd make you a squad leader?" Bob recalled his own service days. Terrance nodded as Bob wondered how an enlisted man, a squad leader, sank to being homeless, out of work, and drinking every night. He didn't express his thoughts, instead focusing on the body. "So you were following your training and reporting the situation?"

"I was a boy scout. An Eagle Scout, if that means anything to you."

"It means a lot to me, actually." Bob sat back in his chair. A look of incredulousness came over his face. The boy scouts added another wonder to this man's fall from the civilized world. After a moment, all Bob could think to say was, "I'm beginning to believe you."

Terrance nodded. "I didn't do it."

"I'd like to keep you here for a couple days. It's warm and we'll feed you. But…"

"No alcohol. I need to dry out."

"Yes," Bob said. "Then we'll see about a job."

"Okay." Terrance ducked his head and smiled shyly as he sipped his soda.

"Hang out here for a little while," Bob said as he got up.

"Okay."

Chapter 9

Out in the hallway, Bob pulled the door closed behind him. Before it clicked shut Frank Wysup and Wally came out of the observation room door. Frank spoke first, "He did it?"

"I'm not sure yet but I get a feeling of 'probably not'."

"No?"

"I'm going to pull his military service records."

"Damn bum."

"I think I would disagree," Bob said.

"If you want to," Frank retorted.

Bob ignored the statement by changing the subject. "How's the autopsy going?"

"I saw the body delivered to the lab. Terri is doing the prep work. I'm heading down there in a few minutes."

"That's a good idea."

"Detective?" Frank asked. "This is my case."

Bob looked Frank in the eyes and smiled.

"This is my case," Frank repeated himself, wondering if Bob had not heard him.

"Check your voice mail, Frank." Bob walked past the man. "Wally. My office."

Wally turned and the two left Frank standing in the hallway.

When they were seated in Bob's office with the door closed Bob asked Wally his thoughts on Terrance.

"I think he's telling the truth," Wally answered.

"About both bodies?"

"About the two bodies and about the army."

"What makes you think that?"

"The way he acts... I transport a lot of criminals between the courthouse and the county lockup. Look," Wally said with his drawl. "I'm not a prison guard. I don't spent 24/7 with criminals but... He doesn't act like any of them."

"That's what I'm thinking," Bob added.

"He's got something going on in his head."

"Yeah. Probably Iraq."

"Definitely Iraq."

Bob's eyes widened.

Wally took the clue to continue, "Dhahran. I was there. I don't remember this guy, but if he was there... I know Dhahran. I got shipped out of there a week before it happened, but I heard the news. They took an Iraqi Scud. Killed 28 of our men. If he was there. If he knew any of those guys, it'd be tough."

"That'd mess you up a bit... What about you?"

"Everyone is different. I saw guys killed. Some handle... This guy... Maybe he's still dealing with Iraq. He knows the war is over but the army is like your whole life. It's like your family. You live, eat, sleep, and work with the same guys for years. Here with police-work, we go home at night. There, you don't go home. Then you get out eventually and find your whole life turned upside down."

"I was in for a couple years but remind me. "

"When I came back from Iraq I couldn't sleep indoors for a week." Wally laughed. "It's funny now, but seriously I had to sleep on the porch to get any rest at all. When I moved indoors I had to open all the windows in the house."

"You said you don't think it's him."

"I could be wrong. Maybe. But he doesn't run from his problems. He doesn't blame someone else. He lives with his problems. Stuffing it deep inside with alcohol on top. Criminals almost always have one thing in common; 'It's not my fault'. They blame everyone else for their problems. It's their drug dealer. It's their parents. It's 'poor me', and 'I never had a chance in life'."

"Terrance drinks his problems down," Bob said.

"I don't know if he bottles things up or he drinks his problems away but I get the feeling he's being straight. That's my gut feel."

"That's exactly what I was thinking."

"He's not a suspect?"

"I think he's a person of interest until we find out otherwise.

I'm not sure of anything yet. Instinct doesn't solve crimes."

"What do you want to do with him?" asked Wally.

"We hold him for a couple days and do a little more digging. You know," Bob smiled, "The detective's exam is next month."

"That's okay."

"I want you along with me on this anyway. we've got a lot of ground to cover."

"Okay." Wally's stoic face neither frowned nor smiled.

"For now just keep your radio on, day and night," Bob said.

"You got it."

"Can you move Terrance to a cell."

"General population?"

"No. Use one of the other interview rooms. There's one with a cot and a TV. Grab some magazines from the break room. If he needs the bathroom, or needs out for any reason, Louise can handle that."

"Ask him to clean up the table. Throw his sandwich wrappers and soda bottles away." Bob took his trash bucket from under his desk and turned it over to empty it on his office floor. He handed the empty bucket to Wally .

Wally nodded. "DNA," he said as he took the bucket and turned out the door for the interview room.

Bob's cell phone rang. He checked the display and answered, "Hi Mary."

"Hey. Missing you since this morning."

"It's been a long day."

"Saw the news. Something about a body in Abington?"

"Bad. Pretty bad."

"Sorry to hear that. Any chance I can get some time with you tonight?"

"We were planning a dinner?" Bob asked.

Mary accepted, "It's a date."

"Don't be late," laughed Bob.

"You don't be late. I'm here all the time. Don't forget we are meeting Alan and Janine." Mary laughed with him.

"I'll be home soon. Just got to follow up with the M.E."

"How is Terri?"

"Like the rest. Up early this morning."

"Tell her I said, 'Hi'."

"I will."

"Have you invited her to the barbeque Saturday?"

"I'll do it again."

"Great. And James, Wally, Peter and Frank. Who am I forgetting?

"Louise and Sheriff Barton."

"How is Alan?"

"Haven't talked to him in a week. Not since the suspension."

"He's not allowed to do his Sheriffing?"

"Not with the State Police Internal Affairs probe and all the news coverage. That leaves me in charge over here."

"It's a good thing." Mary tried to assure Bob. "Acting Sheriff."

"I don't really want that title. I'd rather have Barton back."

"But the corruption charges?"

"He didn't do anything wrong. I'm sure of it."

"You've been wrong before. We all have."

"Maybe."

"They are our friends. No discussing that subject at dinner," Mary said.

"I was hoping you were going to corrupt me later." Bob laughed.

"Maybe. Only if you are bad."

"It's been a long time since I was good. What's the hold-up anyway?"

"Long hours at your job, for one."

"Sorry baby."

"Don't be. You're happy when you are in your element."

"Up to my neck in crime?"

"Yes. So how's that going?"

"I'll tell you about it later."

"Okay. Get back to work, but don't be late for dinner."

"Love you, Mary."

"Love you too. Bye, lover." Mary hung up the phone.

Bob looked at the police radio on his desk. He flipped through his notebook as he picked it up and pressed the button. The radio chirped.

"Peter?" Bob released the button and waited a few seconds. "Peter. Check in." Bob waited longer this time and when Peter didn't respond he picked up his desk phone and pressed zero.

"Afternoon, Detective."

"Hi Louise. How are you?"

"Good. Can I get something for you?"

"Peter. I can't get him on the radio. Can you have him call me?"

"He's in the briefing room. Paperwork I think. I'll page him."

"Thanks Louise." Bob remembered that the radios didn't work very well inside the B.C.I. building. "I forgot about the radio problems."

"I run face first into it almost every day. The maintenance company was out last week."

"What did they say?"

"The usual. Something about overdriving the signal. The transmitter is on the roof and it's supposed to be further away from the building."

"Like on a cell phone tower or a high-rise?" Bob added.

"The NYC police had similar problems during 9-11."

Bob let the conversation drop.

"I'll page Peter for you."

"Thank you."

"My pleasure." Louise hung up the phone and seconds later Bob heard her voice echo through the building's public address system. "Officer Jackson to Detective Schwimer's office." For an instant she made the building sound like a high school.

A few minutes later Peter knocked on Bob's open door. "Detective?" Peter asked.

"Come on in. Call me Bob. Please." When Peter was seated Bob continued, "What did you find out on next-of-kin?"

"I spent an hour on the FBI database. Got some interesting prior convictions and time served, but no family listed."

"None?" Bob asked.

"There's some known associates, known aliases. Even the FBI is not sure what his real name is. No social security number. Probably a mid-wife birth or could be from out of the country.

Could be family members from a broken home. I emailed you some files."

"Okay. I'll take a look. I might need you to be available the next couple days. I told Wally the same thing. Keep your radio on, even at night."

"Yes, sir."

"Peter." Bob smiled and the officer looked nervous. "Try not to be so polite all the time."

"Sorry."

"And don't apologize."

"Sor... I mean... yes, *sir*," Peter stammered.

Bob looked at Peter and smiled.

"Sir? It's just the way I was raised."

"Then you were raised right. Try to relax a little bit sometimes?"

"Yes, sir. "

"Back to paperwork?"

"Yes, um... Paperwork." Peter got up and backed away, out of Bob's office, like cornered prey backing away from a predator. Bob chuckled to himself after Peter was gone.

Bob turned on his computer monitor and brought up his email folder and reviewed Peter's emails. Logging into the FBI Criminal Justice Information database he confirmed what Peter had said. No definite information on Spears. He switched to the Massachusetts Welfare Department website and spent an hour making no further progress. Looking at his watch he weighed putting in another hour of work.

Louise poked her head in his office doorway. "Jasmine is on the switchboard. Are you heading home?"

"Thinking about it," Bob replied. "Can't find any family on the victim."

Louise nodded. "I'm sure there's a family somewhere and they're wondering where he is."

"That's what I was thinking."

"You can't kill yourself for the job."

"I can try."

"You work too many hours as it is."

"I know."

"Today is Sunday."

"It is?" Bob looked perplexed.

"It's a weekend."

"It is." He laughed.

"Tell me that you promised Mary you would be home on-time tonight?"

"I did."

"Then go home." Louise smiled again and turned. As she walked down the hallway she called out, "Good night, detective."

Bob placed several phone calls into the FBI and Boston Welfare office. His calls all went to weekend automated phone systems where he, eventually, was able to leave messages and a phone number. While he waited on hold and between calls he searched the County Recorder website for marriage, divorce, and real estate records. A handful of "Spears" surnames came up but the first name did not match any of them. He wrote down the real estate information and noted the married women's first and maiden names. He spent an hour looking up phone numbers online and calling the family. Every call but one didn't know a 'John Spears'. The one positive hit turned out to be a seven year old child safely playing in the family's back yard.

With his information paths nearly exhausted Bob logged off his computer for the day. Looking at his watch he figured he had just enough time to get home to Duxbury to pickup Mary and meet the Sheriff and his wife Janine.

Chapter 10

Bob and Mary walked into the Blue Lagoon sea-side restaurant overlooking Duxbury harbor. It was decorated in tourist-fisherman. Taxidermy fish hung on the walls alongside nets, harpoons, sea surf fishing gear, buoys, and paintings of square rigged ships and whalers. There were a few Cape Cod schooners and lobster boats. For a welcome change there were no pilgrims.

Mary saw Alan and Janine in the bar and she tugged on the sleeve of Bob's blazer. The two friends saw them and smiled. Bob recognized a welcome relief in the smiles of both of them. The corruption allegations wore hard.

The couple came over. Alan took Mary's hand in greeting. She laughed and said, "How about a hug," as she wrapped her arms around Alan.

"It's great to see you both," Alan said as he released Mary. Janine hugged Mary next while Alan shook Bob's hand. "Are you missing Boston yet?"

"You've been asking me that for five years." Bob laughed.

"And you haven't answered it yet." Alan held Bob's hand tight and reached around to clap Bob on the shoulders.

"Bullshit. What I'd like to know is why you keep asking me that question."

"I told you."

"Never, but I can guess."

"Bullshit." Alan retorted.

"Why ask if you know?"

"Maybe I like your answer."

"No. Maybe you always wanted to be a big city cop and didn't get to."

"Naw. I like living in the country. That's why I'm here. I think you couldn't hack it in the city and came running back home."

"Bullshit. I think the city was too boring and I had to come down here to get some excitement."

"You were lost up there."

Janine interrupted their banter. "If you *gentlemen* are going to cuss like sailors then Mary and I will adjourn to the lounge."

Bob and Alan laughed as they followed their wives to the bar. Bob ordered a double of Glenlivet and Alan followed suit. Mary had a martini and Janine ordered a margarita.

After a couple of drinks, they took a table in the mostly empty restaurant. As they crossed the room Bob saw Peter sitting at a table. Peter waved and Bob went over. Alan followed.

"Hello detective. This is Tim," Peter said as he gestured to a young man at Peter's table.

"How are you, Tim?" He put his hand out and the man shook it. "Call me Bob. You haven't met Sheriff Barton," Bob said to Peter.

"Sheriff." Peter put out his hand. Alan shook it.

"You must be the new hire?"

"Yes sir. Happy to be working for you."

"Then you haven't been paying attention or you'd know you don't work for me. Not exactly."

"I heard. From what I heard you don't deserve what they're doing to you."

Alan laughed. "You haven't been talking to the right people. I like you already. Welcome to the department, even if I never see you again."

Peter gave an embarrassed laugh. "Thank you."

Mary called to Bob, "Over here guys!"

"Dinner calls," Alan said. He shook Peter and Tim's hands once more and then turned to go.

"See you tomorrow, Peter. Nice to meet you, Tim," Bob said.

As they walked Alan asked, "Is he...?"

"Yes. But it doesn't effect the job."

"He isn't even wearing his uniform."

"He's careful and considerate."

"I think he'd have to be... considering..."

The waitress showed them to a table overlooking the water where the sound of the waves rolled from under the pier beneath them. The sun was down and the moon had not yet risen. The only thing they could see on the bay were the lamps illuminating the pier and the occasional red and green lights from a boat motoring across the harbor.

Bob and Mary each ordered the shrimp scampi and Janine had steak. Alan ordered an oyster and muscles plate. They all shared a bottle of the house wine.

"So what kind of cases are you working on?" Alan asked.

"A murder."

"The railroad tracks?"

"Yes."

"It sounds like an accident."

"You read the news."

"Yes. Nothing much else to do now." He suddenly stopped talking, as if embarrassed to have brought up his suspension and the fraud investigation.

"It's murder."

"You are sure." It was a statement not a question. Alan's natural inquisitive nature brought out the questions. The conversation was following the same lines as their work together over the last five years. They thought alike and that helped them work well together.

"Clear as day. Too much is wrong. There's tire marks and shoe prints. It's not a robbery though. They left cash, more than enough to not be on welfare."

"Welfare?"

"The victim had a welfare card in his pocket."

"He's a drug dealer." Alan stated. Bob always liked Alan's intuition.

"Not sure yet, but he was hip-hop. Gold chains, expensive watch, expensive shoes."

"Any track marks?"

"Not sure yet. Terri is working him over."

"There will be drugs in his system. Probably intravenous. The killer wanted to make it look like an accident. Make the vic look like he was high and got hit by a train."

"Who's investigating this case?" Bob asked.

Alan laughed.

Chapter 11

"Good morning" Mary whispered into Bob's ear. He could feel her warm presence hovering over him as he slowly opened his eyes. The first thing he saw was her beautiful face as she kissed him. Mary gave him a quick peck on the lips before rolling away and off the bed. He heard her footsteps receding briskly down the hallway.

"Kiss and run?" he asked.

"Coffee." She laughed.

"Yeah," he moaned. "At least I know where I rank."

"Try not to sound too enthused. You know you always come before coffee," she called back from the kitchen.

Bob looked at the clock on the nightstand. It was six. What day... Monday. He slowly got out of bed and pulled on a robe to chase away the chilled autumn air that crept through the open window. He looked out onto the grassy fields behind their house. He had left their horses out in pasture the night before and the big beasts played, running and kicking. Fall and spring brought cold nights and warm days and that made even the oldest horses feel young again. When they saw him in the window, they stopped to nicker and bugle in anticipation of breakfast.

"It's getting colder," he said.

"What's that?" Mary called from the kitchen.

"Winter is coming."

Mary stuck her head around the corner of the kitchen door with a quizzical look on her face. He looked down the hallway and laughed. Her face changed to mild annoyance as she popped back into the kitchen.

A minute later she came down the hallway with two cups of coffee. He reached for a cup but she shooed him away, nearly spilling the coffee. "Open the door. Let's sit on the patio."

Bob opened the French-doors and escorted Mary to the glass table. She sat the coffee cups on the table and disappeared inside, only to come back with a plate of toast and jelly a moment later.

Bob sipped at his coffee and watched their horses over the fence. They all stood quietly now, watching them closely.

"Do you want breakfast?" he asked them. The young mare, a registered quarter-horse called Bluebonnet, named for her deep black hair that shines blue in the sunlight, nickered at his words. They called her 'Blue' for short. Two other horses, a chestnut colored gelding named Santeba Dodger, and Bob's favorite bay mare, Chicago's Miracle, nicknamed Mira, stood quietly watching.

"Thanks for last night," Mary said as she leaned over and gave him a kiss.

"Dinner was wonderful," he said.

"That's because it felt like a date." She smiled.

"It was a date."

"Do you have time to work the horses this morning?"

"I'd like to put some more training on Bluebonnet but…"

"But you need to find the family of yesterday's victim?"

"Yes. Mr. Spears has priority."

"Why do you always talk like that?"

"Like what?"

"It's just that you talk about your dead victims as if they are still alive."

"They are, so to speak."

"How?"

"It's just about respect. John Spears has some family somewhere. I have to deliver news of his demise so I want it clear that I have respect for him, even in death." Bob fell silent for several moments while they ate their breakfast.

"And…" Mary asked.

After another long pause, Bob answered, "…And if I can keep him alive in my mind. If I can picture who he was, and what he did in life, it helps me frame the conditions of his murder or death."

"So it's an investigative technique?"

"I never thought of it that way… I never thought of it at all."

"Does it work?"

"I guess it does. I guess it puts me into the mental state of the victim."

"Or the suspects?"

"Yeah. Suspects too. In this case a murderer, or two."

"You said last night this looked like a murder with a message?"

Bob nodded.

"What kind of message?"

"If I knew the message it would narrow down the suspects. If we had any suspects at all I might be able to guess at the message."

"So you need to build the list of suspects first?"

"That's a start... After finding the family and talking to his associates."

"What about the homeless man?"

"Silverman? I'm going to keep him around for a while. I promised to find him a winter job."

"So he will be close by if he becomes a suspect?"

"Or if he remembers anything or he thinks of something we missed."

Bob finished his coffee and left Mary on the patio with a kiss on the cheek. He dressed in barn-clothes; jeans and an old gray hooded-sweatshirt, and he went out to the pasture to throw hay to the horses. Five minutes later he was back in the house preparing for work; shower, shave, and putting on dark blue slacks and a white shirt and tie under a dark suit jacket. He grabbed his black cowboy hat off a hook by the door as he went out.

As Bob pulled out of his driveway and headed towards state highway 3A out of Duxbury and towards the Bureau of Criminal Investigations headquarters in Marshfield he called Wally on the radio.

"Yes, Detective?" Wally's Maine, but militaristic, accent came back on the radio. It was an odd combination mixed with the cracking and popping of radio static.

"Come on in when you get a chance."

"Yes, sir." Bob almost didn't hear the response through the static hiss.

"My office."

"Is it regarding the murder?"

Bob winced. He knew the reporters listened in on the police radio frequencies and he wanted the news to know as little as possible, at least until he was ready to consult with the D.A. on charges. Bob deflected the question with one of his own. "When can you be there?"

"Less than an hour."

"Good enough." Bob clicked off the radio and holstered it on his belt.

Chapter 12

Bob flicked on the light switches as he entered the darkened B.C.I. basement level Medical Examiner's lab. Terri blinked and looked up from her examination. She wore a light blue smock and her long dark hair was pulled back and tucked up under a plastic hairnet topped with a baseball cap turned backwards. A protective shield hid her face behind the glare of the fluorescent lights overhead. The ultra-violet examination light she held in her hand flickered as she turned it off.

"Sorry. Do you need that off?" Bob asked. "Aren't you claustrophobic?"

"I am, but I'm not achluophobic."

"What's that?" Bob asked as he crossed the room.

"Fear of the dark."

"If I worked down here I think I would be scared."

"It isn't the dead to worry about. They are harmless."

"True. But the cellar doesn't bother you?"

"It's big, spacious, sheet-rock, paint, modern."

"Windowless."

"Not achluophobic." Terri smiled.

"You said that. What have you got for me on Spears?"

"Just checking for blood quantities on the body. Trying to confirm if he was dead before he was dismembered," Terri answered as she pushed up her face shield.

"And?"

"And it looks like he was." Terri turned on an x-ray panel and hung several negatives from the clips. "This is the cranium here. You can see the hole. But look around the edge. See that massive fracture?"

"Yeah."

"You see the radial fractures around the point of impact? He was struck with a single hard blow from a round flat object. He was hit hard enough to cause comminuted skull fractures. There are pieces of bone here, here, and here." She pointed to the x-ray. "It's an intercranial hematoma. He was probably unconscious with the blow and died within minutes of the impact. Measuring the size of the hole, the area where the fractures start across the skull and where the center piece is missing, that's it by the way," She pointed at a small flat line of bone turned sideways to the x-ray. "At least I'll find out when I go in, but it looks like he was struck with a hammer... hard, very hard. It came down from the top. You can see crushing of the spinal column in the neck. There and there."

"It couldn't have been a rock or something after the train..."

"No. Too much blood around the wound. The impact point of the skin is not granulated or tenderized. He was alive when he was struck with the hammer and dead when cut up by the train. The way the skull was laying on the ground a blood pattern would have run down towards the ground but that isn't the case. The blood pattern ran up across the skull from the position it was found. Take a look at these pictures from the crime scene." Terri picked up a pile of photographs and showed them to Bob.

"Or the coyotes nosed the parts a round looking for something edible?"

"Maybe."

"And you think he was killed before being hit by the train?"

"Yes, and possibly not by Mr. Silverman. This hammer came down at a high flat angle. Mr. Silverman is short. No taller than five-foot-six or seven if I had to guess."

"How tall is the victim?"

"His welfare B.I.C. says he is... Um... *was* five-ten. That's about average for a male of African American descent of his age. Whoever did this was either tall or had a situational height advantage."

"The victim could have been sitting or lying down and the murderer comes up by surprise?" Bob asked.

"Sitting maybe. In order to fracture a skull that hard takes some muscle. The impact was pretty intense. Swinging a hammer sideways wouldn't do it."

"Then the murderer could be short? As short as Silverman?"

"I guess."

"And if the victim is sitting down would the murderer have to be a strong person? Muscular?"

"Maybe not as much."

"Terri. You are saying that we are looking for a tall or short, muscular or skinny, male or female with a hammer?"

Terri laughed. "I guess so, if you say it that way."

"What else do you have?"

"Whoever did this made some serious efforts to have the body dismembered. I did some research. This is my first train hit. It looks like trains don't usually do this much damage to bodies. They hit hard and fast, break a bunch of bones and throw the vic to one side or the other. Rarely they go under the train. Even then they don't actually do much to dismember a body. Worst thing you get is hamburger in a human skin package. All the muscles are torn-up, bones broken but very little separation of body parts. The skin and tendons are elastic and hold everything together."

"So what happened?"

"It's almost like the body was positioned on the tracks for maximum damage... and they were successful. We found body parts tens of feet away from the impact point. But it's 'parts'." Terri pointed to a diagram of the crime scene she had drawn on a white board. "The left lower leg was here. The dismembered arm was down the tracks. The torso with the broken arm and leg was beside the tracks as if tossed aside. The cranium was still between the rails."

"Gruesome."

"That's not the word for it. This guy was not cut up with a saw or an axe. It looks like the train did it, but they must have positioned him on the tracks to maximize dismemberment."

"Who could even guess how to do that?"

"Lucky maybe, if they even cared about it."

"The effect on the news is enough." Bob was not sure what he could do with that information, nevertheless he stored it away in his mind. "What else?"

"Time of death." Terri walked over to her desk and picked up some papers. She led Bob to an examination table with the body parts spread out on it. "On scene I found the joints, elbows, knees, et cetera, were locked with rigor mortis. It was set in pretty well, so that indicated he died less than three days ago, and more than a few hours after we found him. Initially I figured more than six or seven hours."

"That's not a good estimate."

"I'm getting there. Wait for it... To narrow it down, I took a torso core-temperature reading, and ambient air and ground temperature readings. I also contacted the National Weather Service and received hourly air temperature readings from the Polk County station outside of Boston, and the Plymouth harbor weather reports. The body temperature drops to ambient at a non-linear predictable rate. From that information the time of death can be determined."

"If he wasn't running a fever at the time of death?" Bob interjected.

"True, but that isn't likely and we may be able to determine if he was sick after we talk to his family or friends. How's that going anyway?"

"Not good. But you're good with the Boston weather and temperature correlation to Abington?"

"Close. It's a little further inland than Boston, not on the water, and has more trees."

"Is it close enough?"

"I'd guess."

"Don't guess."

"Yes. It's close enough."

"What does the t.o.d. look like?"

"I arrived on scene at five-twenty-three and took readings at five-forty-six. From my calculations, he died eighteen to twenty hours before we found him or roughly eleven-thirty the previous morning, plus or minus an hour."

"And assuming the train-dismemberment didn't change the calculations of core body temperature cooling."

"Yes, but the University of Glasgow did a study five years ago on body part thermal variations over time and the overall error rate for a human torso is less than five percent in twenty-four hours for the range in ambient air and ground temperature.

I've already accounted for that in the calculations."

"How did they do that study?"

"Using swine."

"Ex-boyfriends?" Bob looked curiously at Terri.

She nervously clarified, "*Pigs*. Swine. Not people."

"Of course." Bob smirked.

"According to Officer Perry, and verified on the Kingston-Plymouth Railroad website, that line is used twenty-eight times a day. I didn't think that information was good enough so I researched it myself. From the average speed at crossings and on open stretches, I calculated that trains run through Abington about twenty minutes after departing Boston and fifteen to twenty minutes from the end of the line. The schedules say twenty-eight times per day on weekdays and sixteen times per day on the weekends. Eight inbound to Boston's South Station and eight outbound from South Station. It's a single line of tracks so the outbound and inbound trains have to share the line and pass each other on spurs. On weekends, they run approximately an hour to an hour and a half apart. I sent a spreadsheet to your email. Inbound departure from the station is seven-twenty-four, nine-sixteen, ten-twenty-nine, eleven-fifty-four, one-thirty-four, three-fifty-nine, seven-fourteen, and ten o'clock. Outbound departures are…"

"Do I want to ask how you memorized that?"

"I'm a genius. Outbound trains run at least twenty minutes before or after the Inbound through Abington starting at nine-oh-two on Sundays. Sometimes as long as an hour later. Not exactly but that's close enough."

"Where did you get all this info?"

"I called some friends in Abington."

"That's better than Perry's information?"

"The tracks run behind their house." Terri's smile revealed the gaff.

"No. You didn't get that exact info from friends."

"I also downloaded a schedule off the M.B.T.A. website."

"I knew you were lying."

"You always do. I have a terrible poker face."

"So Spears was dead by eleven-thirty Sunday morning, give

or take an hour and dismembered by an afternoon train?"

"That's assuming he was killed by the tracks."

"And the drag marks and shoe prints on the side street; Park Avenue. So if he was killed someplace else then the time of death changes?"

"A lot or a little. Could be…" Terri agreed. "It depends on where and how the body was stored and when it was exposed to outdoor air."

"So we don't have an accurate time of death?"

"No. But it's a target."

"A big target?"

"I'll admit that."

"I don't see someone dumping a body at noontime on a Saturday. I can imagine he was dead long before being dumped, and the killers dumped the victim Saturday night, maybe not long before Silverman arrived. But long enough for a train to come through."

"Like the last outbound train from Boston?"

"No other trains use that line?"

"None. No maintenance crews were down the line checking the tracks after ten o'clock Saturday, according to Officer Perry. The last one that came through was in the early morning. If the body had been there early, they probably would have seen it and reported it."

"But our time frame is opened up and maintenance was in the area Saturday morning."

"Does that make them suspects?"

"Probably no. Preliminary t.o.d. is eleven-thirty? If they were through before ten, well… We'll find out. Where is Officer Perry?" Bob asked.

"I asked him to assist with the autopsy and he agreed. He took one look at the body parts, turned white, and he booked it out the door." Terri laughed.

"He left?"

"Banged a huey and ran."

"Ran?"

"*Sprinted* might be a better word. He had his hand over his mouth. I thought he was going to toss his cookies."

Bob laughed. "He is supposed to send over some surveillance videos. If he calls, keep him up on the details but otherwise I don't think we need his assistance. I'd rather keep the investigation inside the team. The media is hot for a story and we don't need any leaks or misinformation. Did Peter send out Terrance's clothes for analysis?"

"The bum?"

"*Terrance*," Bob said as he looked at Terri.

"Yeah. *Terrance*. The clothes go out first thing this morning. Labs are closed on Sunday. Peter brought down his clothes yesterday and we bagged and tagged them. That's them over there." Terri pointed to evidence bags on a table. "I took a long look at them last night. Found some plant matter, hairs, stuff like that. Putting together a package for the lab, victim and prime suspect both. Should have something back in twenty-four to forty-eight hours. Looking for gun-powder residue, skin tissue, blood analysis, dirt, clothing fibers, organic material. The usual stuff."

"Terri. I have the greatest respect for you. Have the lab look for *unusual* stuff too, okay?"

"Everything?"

"*Anything*. A full examination. I want DNA off the body. Terrance's DNA and anything and everything else he came into contact with. We might as well make use of the new state grants."

"Okay. DNA testing will take longer."

"I know. That's okay. We have time. You haven't talked to Terrance have you?" Bob asked.

"No. Not really. He's in an interview room now. I saw him on the way in. I gave him a new stack of magazines this morning. Cleaned out my living room. Hope he likes Plant World, Gardening, Equine-Knows, and Small Farm magazines."

"James must not have liked that."

"James is too busy running the farm to be reading about farming. They are old issues anyway."

"How is he?"

"He has a radio-alarm clock that Wally got for him. He slept in a holding cell last night and was more than happy to have a place to stay. He's got some DTs this morning. He keeps asking for something to put in his coffee."

"Terri? How's James doing? Your fiancée?"

"Boyfriend."

"You two are getting married. Even if you don't know it yet."

Terri smiled wide, which Bob took for an admission of guilt. "We've talked about it."

"Yes?"

"Things are good. The farm isn't going so well. It's a tough living. I've told him to go back to school or get back into high-tech. He loves working the fields. Can you believe that? Most of these farmer's kids can't wait to get to the city, and my boyfriend leaves high-tech and wants to grow crops." Her right fingers toyed with her left ring finger. She didn't wear a ring, but Bob wondered if she had been trying them on at jewelry stores, or if she had one that she only wore at home.

"But?"

"But he is happy with it. He likes it. They are sending high tech jobs overseas faster than manufacturing. India and China are filled with software engineers."

"Who work for nothing?" Bob asked.

"And risk the company's IP, source code, everything."

"If farming makes him happy, I guess that's okay," Bob added.

"At least I make a decent living. Is now a good time to ask for a raise?"

"No." Bob laughed. "Talking about work, what else do you have on Mr. Spears?"

"Um. Glass."

"Glass?"

"Broken glass. Take a look." Terri led Bob to another table where a workbench magnifying light glinted off shards of glass and parts of a broken glass tube on an examination tray. Several items of Spears' personal effects were on the table; wallet, keys, a Rolex watch, a gold necklace and several rings.

"Crack? Meth?"

"I've got a tiny bit of residue for the lab to test but that's a crack pipe if I ever saw one."

Terri and Bob leaned over the table looking at the broken glass and the personal effects.

"So he was a user?" Bob asked.

"I'll test his internal organs but from the visuals, I doubt he was an addict. From his lungs I can see crystal-meth, maybe. No tobacco use. But his liver and kidneys don't show any evidence of excessive drug use. "

"Because bugs don't carry thousands of dollars in their wallets?"

"And thousands of dollars means he was either a dealer or a mule." Terri's dark eyes narrowed, wrinkles appeared at the corners of her young eyes.

"Mules don't carry cash in their wallets. Envelopes, money belts, suitcases, whatever, but not their wallets. That's personal. Mule money in a wallet would get you killed."

"And Spears is dead." She pointed to the body parts laid out on the exam table.

"Good point. A non-addict mule? Probably not."

"So he's a drug dealer."

"No. I'm thinking he was more of a pusher."

Terri's face went blank as she realized the difference. "He was trolling for addicts? Getting people hooked?"

"Supply and demand. A dealer can't wait around for new business to show up."

Bob stood up straight. He walked back over to the table with the torso. "Get me those lab results as soon as they come in."

"Got it. Wait. How do we know he wasn't some high-priced lawyer with a small drug habit?"

"Welfare card."

"Oh yeah."

"What's that smell?"

"Which smell?" Terri smiled.

"I'm sure you are used to all of them."

"I know it gets pretty rancid down here. I'm used to it. But everything is frozen or just starting to thaw out. I kept him in the freezer overnight... Most of him... What we have of him..." Terri was lost for words.

"I get it." Bob saw a little humor in her stammering. "You said he doesn't smoke?"

"Not cigarettes. Probably smokes some crack or crystal meth. I'll find out from the test lab."

Bob pulled on vinyl gloves and leaned over the corpse. He lifted the tattered sleeve of the shirt to his nose and breathed in deeply.

"Cigarettes." He straightened up and returned the sleeve to the table. "If he was in the bar he could have been around smokers."

"Not many people smoke anymore. Not as many as used to," Terri added.

"Most drug users smoke," Bob said.

"Either way, he was around cigarettes."

"Frank was smoking up a storm yesterday."

"He wasn't near the body. When we finally got busy with the removal I wouldn't let him smoke. He didn't like that too much but he dealt with it."

"Which means the killer smoked?"

"No. It just means he was around a smoker."

"So what does that mean?" Terri asked.

"I don't know if it means anything or nothing. Can you tell me anything else about Mr. Spears?"

"Yes. Fibers. The first thing I did with the body back here in the lab was lay out all the parts." She pointed to the table, actually more of a very large tray that slid into human sized refrigerators. "While I was examining the parts I found a fiber on the shirt sleeve, possibly hair, probably human. It was stuck in the crack of a broken button on the sleeve."

"They struggled? A punch goes wild, the cuff catches a hair."

"That's all I could imagine." She took a glass slide off the table and slid it under the microscope. "Take a look."

Bob peered through the eyepieces and adjusted the focus. "Gray."

"And probably human."

"Okay. So we can temporarily add 'gray haired' or 'older' to a suspect's description... if it comes back as human hair."

"Okay."

"What about his name?" Bob looked down at the paperwork on the table beside the examination trays.

Terri looked confused. "The victim?"

Bob nodded.

She looked at the body and then at the paperwork on the table. She read, "John Spears."

"Light dawns over Marblehead. Just testing you."

"I knew that."

"I just wanted to be sure you knew."

"I'm no chowdahead."

"We are dealing with a human being. I just don't want you to forget. Not till the case is closed."

"I'll never forget this case." Terri scanned the body parts spread out on the tray.

Bob caught her gaze, looked her in the eyes and said, "I don't think I will either... What about fingerprints?"

"Got some. Most of them."

"Good. Email me the files when you get a chance. I want to run them past the C.J.I.S. database. Let's confirm that Mr. Spears is who his welfare ID card says he is."

Bob pointed to the right foot on the examination table. The shoe was gone but a black sock was still in place. "I think that solves our suspect's height issue. Or rather leaves it open for further investigation."

"Why?" Terri was perplexed by Bob observation.

"Look at the curl in those toes."

"Yeah?" Terri peered closer as she swung an examination-light over the foot.

"The sock is clenched into the toes. That explains why the shoe is gone but not the sock."

"We found the shoe not too far away. Expensive. Testoni Norvegese. Fifteen bills a pair." Terri moved to retrieve the shoe but Bob stopped her.

"I believe you. Top shelf. How many mules wear fifteen hundred dollar shoes?"

"None."

"We don't need the shoes. Look at the toes. Mr. Spears was

kneeling down when he was killed."

"Are you sure."

"Sure enough," Bob said. "When you are on your knees, sitting on your ankles, the weight curls your toes back. It helps keep your balance."

"That means he was executed."

Bob nodded agreement. "What else was he wearing?"

"The shirt is white silk by Armani... he wore Valentino slacks.

"Expensive tastes. You have my phone number." Bob turned to leave.

Terri asked him, "Where are you going?"

"I've got some research to finish and then I'm going to find Mr. Spears' family and give them the news. Would you rather do it?"

"No. I'm about to analyze some of the victim's brain tissue. Would you rather do that?"

"No," Bob answered. "Talking about brain tissue, do you have any plans for the weekend?"

"Brains and plans? That's a weird allegory. Got something planned?"

"Mary and I are having a little barbeque. It's an end-of-summer traditional thing. You remember from last year?"

"Oh yeah. You already told me. Jim and I will be there. Saturday or Sunday?"

"Saturday."

Chapter 13

Inside his office Bob found printed out copies of each page of information he had discovered in the FBI C.J.I.S. and Welfare department databases. He opened his email inbox to find that Officer Perry had responded to his requests. An email listed twenty different mpeg video files attached, each one labeled with the date and time spanning Saturday through early Sunday morning.

Bob double-clicked one of the files at random. It opened with Winamp. The video started with several cars crossing the railroad tracks in late afternoon shadows. He could see a several-hundred-foot-long section of the railroad tracks and the state Route-139 roadway. He recognized a corner of Stoney's Mill Tavern and parking lot. No one walked along the road or the tracks. He fast-forwarded several times and watched more and more cars cross the tracks. At one point the guard lights flashed and the barriers lowered to block traffic. Several cars stopped behind the barriers on both sides. A minute later, a high-speed commuter train sped across the intersection. Thirty seconds later the barriers rose and traffic resumed.

Bob closed the video and opened one labeled between two and three o'clock in the early morning. The same street and crossing lights and barriers were there, only cast in darkness and reflecting scant light from street lights perched on telephone poles and parking lot lights at Stoney's Mills tavern. Bob fast forwarded in fits and stops. An occasional car left the tavern parking lot or crossed the tracks. Eventually he saw a man dressed in a trench coat come out of the parking lot and cross the street by the tracks. The man staggered as he walked.

Bob knew it was Terrance from his build and posture; on the short side, head hung low. Terrance walked down along the railroad tracks, just as he stated in the interview. In a moment he was gone into the darkness of night. Bob saved the images to his hard drive and looked back at the email Perry had written him.

> *Got the videos from Surveillance. They are high definition video. That crossing has the newest equipment. MBTA wants to be able to recognize faces and read license plates. You should be able to see your hobo-suspect trespassing on the railroad tracks. Let me know if I can do anything else to help. My boss is breathing down my neck about this case.*

Wally walked into the office with a knock on the open door.

"Hello again, Sergeant," Bob said looking up.

"Detective."

"Not the best of mornings yesterday, was it?" Bob handed Wally one of the copies of victim information he had printed. Wally's face presented the faintest smile of agreement.

"I'd like to go over this paperwork with you and then we'll take a ride."

"Victim's family?"

"Looking for family, but fact-finding also."

They sat in Bob's office and read through the criminal justice reports. After a moment of silent reading, they put the pages down.

"What do we know?" Bob asked.

"No relatives. No spouse. No parents. No kids."

"I'm pulling records from the Boston welfare office. He's got a list of priors but only a few known associates," Bob replied.

"We've got fingerprints?"

"So we can prove if the ID is fake. Drug dealer's tend to like stolen IDs."

"Not if he wants to collect his welfare. A stolen ID of a criminal carried by a criminal? Not the first time." Wally's normally stern face cracked into a smile.

"He may not need the welfare. Prostitution, drugs, five grand in his pocket. Probably makes a decent living."

"No DNA record. His last prison release was before the mandatory DNA sample-testing. Fairly petty crimes and he always copped a plea to lesser charges so…"

"No felony means no justice system DNA records. Which means we can't prove Spears is even his real name. We'll check on his address. See if the name matches or any alias comes up." Bob read aloud the list of particulars from one of the sheets. "Full Name: John Weston Spears, Alias: Johnny Spears, Alias: Spearman, Alias: Wes. African-American, five-ten and a hundred-sixty-five pounds, brown hair and blue eyes, twenty-five years old. Last known address in Worcester."

"Blue eyes?" Wally asked. "The victim is black."

"It's not uncommon," Bob answered.

"It's not very common."

"Maybe. Maybe not any more or less than Caucasians or any other race."

"Blue eyes would make him stand out. Anyone who saw him would recognize him from his eyes."

"So finding his family and friends, associated ex-cons, should be a bit easier."

"He's a transient," Wally said. "Picked up for theft, trespassing, drug dealing, prostitution, pimping, and more in Rhode Island, Connecticut, Massachusetts: Brockton, Worcester, Taunton. Did some prison time at Walpole State, several county lock-ups. No records in the town of Plymouth."

"No Boston or New York City arrests."

"No federal convictions or federal prison time. Nothing for Danbury, Devens, up-state New York, New Hampshire or Vermont."

"Which means he thought small cities or towns, Worcester, and Brockton, even Plymouth, were easier to blend in. We've got nothing on him here. Didn't even know he existed until he was dead. We can check school records. High school and middle schools here in Plymouth, plus Worcester and Brockton. I'd like to know where he grew up. I'll bet he worked closed to home."

"The Department of Education should have some records."

"Let's find out." Bob turned to his computer and pulled up the Massachusetts Education Department website. He called the information line on the website and the call went straight to an automated service. After being directed to hit several buttons Bob was prompted to leave his name and phone number. He knew they were as over-worked as all the other state agencies but he left his name and contact information and why he needed John Spears' records.

"I hope 'detective' is a trump card with them, but I might have to pull some strings," Bob said to Wally as he hung up.

"What do you think about suspects?" Wally asked.

"I think the list is going to get longer before it gets shorter. We need to get close to Mr. Spears. I'm sure lots of people on both sides of the drug war like to see drug-dealers and pimps in the cemetery. Let's start with his associates." Bob scanned through the pages to the mug shots of Spears and his listed associates that he pulled out of C.J.I.S. "Elizabeth Harding with various aliases, a Pamela Jones and a Sally Anne Jones."

"Alias for the same person?" Wally asked.

"No. Look at the photos." Mug shots showed the two women had the same eyes but their jaw bones and cheeks, and skin-tone were slightly different. They wore their hair in the same style: medium length, straight, plain, bottle-blonde.

Wally looked at the images, "They could be mother and daughter."

"Says they're six years apart. They don't look that much different. Probably the drugs and the hard lifestyle. I'd bet money they're sisters. The older sister takes care of the younger one."

"Teaching her the trade?"

"When parents are locked-up or dead sometimes the eldest kid has to make do."

"And sometimes this is the best they can do?"

Bob nodded. There was another photograph. "Thomas Simmons. Alias: Tom, or Tommy; Sim, Sims, Simmy."

Louise walked into the office and handed Bob several sheets of paper, "Off the fax. Boston Welfare…"

"Thank you, Louise."

"All for you," she said with a frown.

"How are you?" Bob could tell Louise was flustered.

"The phone doesn't stop ringing…and not just the office line. They keep calling in on nine-one-one."

"Who does?"

"Reporters. News-stations. Radio stations. Crank callers. What did you tell them yesterday?"

"As little as possible."

"That's why. They are hungry and fishing for information."

"It must be a slow news day. Just handle the emergency line and call Jasmine back in... if she wants some overtime."

"Thanks, Detective." The barest smile touched her lips and Bob raised a hand. He smiled back as he looked at the fax pages.

"The last known address from Welfare doesn't match the FBI records. I just left a voice mail over there last night. Actually I didn't expect a response so quickly."

"Sounds like you need to send someone a thank you note," Wally said.

Bob looked at the fax cover sheet and read, "Janice Bellaggio. She's my favorite person of the day. I'm going to Spears house. I want you with me. Let's meet after lunch. You got things to do till then?"

Wally nodded.

Chapter 14

Bob sipped iced tea. It was late in the season but many restaurants still offered it. Alan had a whiskey and water, a drink that never went out of season. The two men sat together for lunch at Meg and Kev's in Brant Rock, Marshfield. The place is a 150 year old red salt-box converted into a restaurant. They were seated at a table on the second floor by a window that gave them a view of the marina, Brant Watchtower, and a view of the ocean. M&K's offered three meals a day, no alcohol before noon, and good food. It was a tourist place, but they stayed open all winter catering to marina traffic and the lunch crowd. Bob recalled that near here, about a hundred years ago, Reginald Fessenden sent the first two-way radio-telegraph signals to Scotland. The four hundred foot tall radio tower was torn down long ago, but the foundation still stood with a dedication.

"What have you found out on the case?" Alan broke the silence.

"Not much yet."

"It's still too early. I should know that." Alan grimaced.

Bob realized the man was going stir-crazy sitting at home, too young to retire, too good a detective to sit idle.

"Wally and I are just starting to run down the leads. Talk to witnesses, known associates, drug addicts, bartenders, neighbors. We are just pulling the lists together now."

Alan's eyes lit up. It was the kind of work he was born into. His father had been Sheriff before him. Bob knew he should not discuss the case with Alan. He knew he should not be even associating with Alan until after the Internal Affairs investigation was completed, but he felt the friendship was more important than politics. Alan had not done anything wrong, as he himself had told the lawyers several times.

"I really don't have anything yet. Very little has come out of the M.E. lab. I'm on my way over to Plymouth after lunch."

"You probably shouldn't be telling me anything anyways. It's just hard being on the outside looking in."

"So how are your horses?" Bob asked, hoping to change the subject. The animals were one of the main reasons Bob had likened to Alan, and vice-versa, on their first interview. Bob knew why; a person who cares for animals cares about a great many things. Concern is a necessary part of detective work.

"Good. Riding a lot. Now that summer is over Janine and I'll be trailering to Sandy Neck beach. Beautiful riding down there."

"We've been," Bob added.

"Yes and you two are welcome to join us."

"When are you going?"

"Maybe next weekend. You have a get together this weekend at your place?"

"We do and you know you are invited, but the way this case is going we might have to postpone that."

"Let us know..." He fell silent. They both drank and ordered club sandwiches.

Bob said nothing.

"You know we shouldn't be doing this." Alan continued flatly. His eyes gleamed but narrowed, judging Bob's reaction.

"Fuck 'em," Bob said.

Alan laughed, "I knew I liked you from the moment we first met. Hey, did I ever tell you the time I saw a twelve point buck on the dunes at Sandy Neck?"

"Yes, you did."

"Let me tell you something else," Alan said. He had a dark look in his eyes and Bob knew immediately what was on the man's mind... what was probably on his mind for a few weeks.

"It's not necessary."

"Yes it is," Alan said sullenly and Bob knew that if Alan talked about his problems it would suffice as a form of therapy. He let the man talk.

"The whole thing is trumped up. The town council is led by a new police lieutenant. He's an outsider, came here from some big city in the mid-west."

Bob nodded.

"So this guy, Ward, has the town council bamboozled into thinking he is wonderful. He's got all new ideas on raising revenue, and fixing things that aren't broken, and arresting repeat offenders. So far he's stayed off the toes of the council members themselves, but he's eyeing bigger things. He's announced that he wants to run for Sheriff next year.

"So what does this have to do with you?"

"He's got friends in high places and..."

"And they called an audit of the department finances?"

"You know that much. Look. There's no money missing. It's just I wasn't careful enough with the receipts. State I.A. is going to find a couple hundred bucks unaccounted for over the last ten years. It was all spent in good faith but this guy is going to make a trust issue of it during the election."

"And that's it?"

"That's all. He's playing politics. He knows I'm close to retirement..."

"That's good enough for me. I've known you long enough and well enough... Let's talk shop."

"Shoot." Alan looked vastly relieved to know he'd salvaged their friendship.

"I want to talk to you about a case. Not the railroad, but one you might remember."

"Go for it."

"Do you remember a drowning in Long Pond..."

Chapter 15

With the stack of faxed papers stored in his briefcase, and the briefcase in the backseat of Bob's car, Bob drove to Plymouth. He met Wally near the Plymouth Rock waterside display, where the sergeant had parked the cruiser. Wally joined Bob in his car.

It took them ten minutes of driving and then locating the walk-up tenement located in the lower income part of town, away from the tourist areas by the marina and the Mayflower and Plymouth Rock. None of the buildings had street numbers on them and street signs were sparse, but Wally knew the area from serving domestic violence and fugitive warrants, and his work in Plymouth transporting prisoners to the courthouse. Children played basketball on a portable hoop at the end of the street. They yelled and shouted as they played.

They sat in the car for a minute looking around. Wally recognized the faces of residents who peered out of windows, or from porches, and balconies along the row of apartment buildings. He could not recall any of their names and when he smiled, or slightly raised a hand to wave, some waved back, while others turned around and disappeared into their flats.

"Anyone you know?" Bob asked.

"I recognize several."

"This part of town, knowing a cop could be a good thing, but knowing a cop too well is trouble."

"I don't take anything personal." He paused. "Like Iraq, or Afghanistan."

"What do you mean?"

"Stability only comes when the people trust the police and the government."

"Police Academy 101."

"That too."

"Were you an M.P. in the Army?"

"No. But it was a police action. The gulf war; Desert Storm, not Iraqi Freedom. Not much different than the invasions."

"Or Vietnam?" Bob asked.

"Too young to have been there. Missed it by several years."

Bob had parked the car outside a nineteen-sixties apartment building painted a drab gray. The paint was peeling to reveal faded yellow-ocher beneath. Harvest yellow it was once called, and all appliances came in that same shade. They got out of the car and looked around. The street was quiet. Even the kids down the block stopped playing to watch Bob and Wally.

They found the apartment number on the fourth floor. Bob pointed to Wally to stand clear to the right of the doorway while Bob took a position on the left. Wally had his hand on his service weapon, a Glock. Bob reached across the door and knocked three times. When no one answered he knocked harder and called out, "Spears? Is anyone home? Sheriff's office."

They listened to the echoes reverberate down the long hallway. No one answered the door but from the floor below they heard a lock click and a door open. Returning to the stairwell and walking down one flight, they found an old man with sickly yellow skin looking out of a doorway. He was deep into a case of liver disease.

"Hello?" Bob said. The man nodded. "I'm Detective Schwimer. Can I ask you something about your neighbor?"

"The Spearman?"

"He lives upstairs?"

"Nothing but problems with that guy. Is he under arrest?"

"I'm looking for his family. Was he married? Did he have a girlfriend?"

"He had a lot of girlfriends. Women coming and going at all hours. Some guys too. I figured he was dealing drugs but I try to mind my own business. In this neighborhood…"

Bob nodded.

"It's a dangerous part of town. Sometimes it's better to keep your eyes open and your mouth shut. Used to be a good place, but that was twenty years ago."

"Did you recognize anyone who visited Mr. Spears on a regular basis?"

"Who?"

"Spearman."

"No. No. A lot of trash. White trash. Guys in BMWs and Mercedes. Business suits but you knew they were trouble. Bankers, probably, or ambulance chasers. Maybe one guy used to come around a lot. Haven't seen him in awhile. He was trouble too."

"What was his name? Did you know him?"

"Simmons. Forgot his first name but knew him since he was a kid. Black guy. Good parents. Broken home. His life went down the same path as the neighborhood. Too bad. He lived here with his dad off and on. His mother was a drug addict and a prostitute, at least that's what I heard."

"Thomas?" Bob knew the name from Spears' known associates list.

"Yes. That's him."

"Does the dad still live here?"

"No. He died. Decided to clean up the neighborhood ten years ago. Got stabbed."

"Mom?"

"Dead or in jail. It's a hard fast life."

"Do you know where this Simmons guy lives now?"

"Down on Fifth Street. The flop house, I think."

"Thank you." Bob turned to go.

The old man called after him, "Is this about the body they found by the tracks?"

Bob ignored the question and asked one of his own, "Do you have a number for the landlord or manager?"

"Yup. He lives on the first floor. Apartment B, I think."

"What's your name?"

"Martinez... Mark Martinez."

"Mr. Martinez, what about you?"

"What about me?"

"Cleaning up the neighborhood."

"Me? No way. I'm no hero."

"Thank you." Bob and Wally turned and walked down to the first floor.

The landlord opened his door and stepped out into the hall

as Bob and Wally approached. He brushed long greasy hair from his splotched and hairy face. A pot-belly stretched a brown tee shirt, making him look pregnant. "I figured you were coming to see me. I saw you go upstairs."

"Yeah?"

"Surveillance system."

"So you know what your tenants are doing all the time?"

"I mind my own business, if they mind theirs."

"I see. My name is Schwimer." Bob smiled and handed a business card to the man.

"You're a cop. I don't even have to read the card." He looked at the card anyway.

"Yes. What's your name?"

"Ford."

"Mr. Ford, I'm investigating a murder."

"Spears?"

"Yes."

"He hasn't been around for a couple days... Figures..."

"He's deceased. Can we take a look at his apartment?"

"Deceased?"

"He died."

"I'll get my keys." The landlord went back into his apartment for a minute.

"He didn't ask for a warrant." Wally whispered to Bob.

"We could get one if we needed too."

Ford returned jingling a large key ring. "Let's open it up," he said.

"What figures?" asked Wally.

"Huh?"

"You said 'figures' about Spears being deceased."

"The guy paid his rent. On time. Every time. Best tenant I've got."

As Bob and Wally followed the landlord Bob asked, "If you keep copies of the surveillance videos of the hallways and entrances we might want to take a look at them?"

"You won't find anything but your welcome to them. I only keep a few days worth on the system." The landlord led them up the stairs to Spears' apartment.

"Do you keep backups?" Bob asked.

"Only if there's trouble." The landlord unlocked the door, pushed it open and went inside.

Wally put a hand on his shoulder and the man turned. "Please. Let us first. Police investigation."

The landlord stepped back. Bob and Wally entered the apartment with their hands on their service pieces. They quickly determined the apartment was empty. Bob pulled on a pair of latex gloves. Wally did likewise.

They found a sparsely furnished, clean, ultra-modern apartment that contrasted the dark dirty hallways and exterior of the building. The apartment was spotless.

"Either Spears is a germ-freak or someone cleaned this apartment," Bob said.

"After a crime." Wally entered the living room.

Bob went to the dishwasher and opened it. It was empty.

"Someone hiding stolen drugs in a dishwasher?" The landlord commented from the doorway.

Bob smiled and returned to the door. The landlord took a step back. "Thank you. We'll be changing the locks and sealing the door. Has there been any trouble in the last few days?"

"No. Not much."

"Anything from last week or weekend?"

"With Spears? No. I don't think so."

"Thank you. Please wait out here."

Bob turned to the apartment again. "I remember a case in Boston where the killers scrubbed the murder scene from top to bottom and when they were all done they forgot to turn on the dishwasher. Dishes that still bore their fingerprints."

Wally entered the kitchen and said, "Luck like that was once in a lifetime. Looks like yours is used up."

"You take the kitchen and living room. I'll check the bedrooms."

"What are we looking for?" Wally asked.

"Anything family related. Letters, photo-albums."

"Drugs?"

"If you find them."

"Like this?" Wally pointed to an ashtray and beer bottle on

the breakfast table.

The ashtray had a joint laying across it, unlit. Bob looked at the beer bottle. It was still half-full.

The landlord called in from the doorway. "Spears was a spotless guy. Very clean. I liked him for that. You should see some of the ways people around here live."

"Did Spears have any roommates?"

"No. Lots of visitors, none permanent."

"Could you tell me who any of them are?"

"Nah. I mind my own business. Don't want to know."

Bob lowered his voice as he asked Wally, "Would a clean freak leave half a beer on the table and an unlit joint in an ashtray? This isn't the crime scene. The killers would have cleaned this up."

"What does it mean?"

"It means that wherever Spears was murdered, he was in a hurry to get there."

"And?"

Bob turned to look at Wally.

"There's always '*And*'." Wally protested.

"And... it means Spears knew the killer or killers..." Bob paused to think. "Or he knew someone associated with the killer."

"He rushed off? Got a phone call and had to leave quick? Didn't want to be late for his own funeral?" Wally didn't laugh at his own use of the old cliché.

Bob nodded, his lips drawn, his eyes narrowed. "You finish here. I want to look around."

The apartment had two bedrooms. One was a guest bedroom. Unused. The dresser was empty. The closet was filled with movie production equipment; video cameras, digital still cameras, lights, tripods, reflectors, power cords, DVD cases, blank DVDs. The other bedroom was obviously Spears'. There was a California-king bed and an armoire. No desk or dresser or book shelves. The closet and armoire were filled with high-end clothing. Charvet, Armani, Borelli. A shoe caddy sported rare (and expensive) Nikes, as well as handmade wingtips and cordovans. Bob looked for papers, photo albums, letters, postcards, or even receipts, and he found nothing. Where family photos would hang on many walls, he found expensive post modern art instead. A small trash can was empty. The bathroom was spotless but the medicine cabinet held toiletries. A small glass vial filled with gray rocks stood on the top shelf. Bob took a Ziploc bag from his jacket pocket and sealed the vial away as evidence. He found hair in a used brush that he also bagged for DNA comparison. Bob moved to the desk in the living room, catching up with Wally.

"Anything else in the kitchen?"

"Like the landlord said, spotless. Even the trash was empty. New bag. Nothing in it."

"We'll ask the Landlord about maid service. Spears had the money."

"No maid service." Ford said from the doorway.

"Thank you," Bob replied.

There was a computer on a desk in the living room. Bob turned it on, hoping there was no password required. He was disappointed. He'd have to contact I.T. forensics and might need a warrant for that. He knew he could pull the hard drive and read it with a USB adapter, but anything he found might be compromised in court without proper paperwork and procedures. Looking through a victim's place for clues to next-of-kin was one thing. Searching a computer was another league. The drugs would be enough to secure the warrant, despite the victim's current state of health. Opening the drawers to the desk he found a check register that was three years out of date. Besides pens, a calculator, some unopened utility bills, and a few homemade music CDs, the desk was bare.

The sound of bad canned rap-musac grew and Bob turned around.

"Take a look at this. Spears?" Wally said. The panel television showed a black man having sex with two women.

"That explains the video equipment in the other room. Hobby or business?" Bob walked over to the entertainment center. He looked at row after row of porn movies, all Hi-Def DVD. Multiple copies of the same DVDs, most with titles like 'The Spearman Strikes Again', 'Playing with Spears. Volume

Five', and 'Spears Spanking Specials'.

"Business. And not all hetero either." Wally showed Bob a DVD cover.

"Our list of potentials just got longer."

"How so?"

"A closet full of video equipment. I could guess that prostitution; sex for money, or sex for drugs, becomes porn. DVDs and internet. Amazing technologies. Someone doesn't get paid what they think they're owed. A father's little daughter turns up in some late night internet porn and daddy wants revenge. Maybe even a husband, or a boyfriend."

Wally turned off the DVD player and TV. "Someone catches something and *sorry* isn't good enough."

"That too." Copying the text from several DVD boxes, Bob wrote down the screen names of the porn stars and the DVD production and distribution companies.

"Wally, call in a locksmith. I want this apartment sealed until we can clean it out. We'll need a day or two. Is that okay with you?" Bob asked the landlord.

"Yeah. If he's dead I'll need to get it rented."

"When's his rent due?"

"Paid till the end of the month."

"Good enough. No one goes in or out of here." They left the apartment and Wally placed a call to a local locksmith while Bob pulled off his latex gloves and taped the door shut with an evidence sticker.

An hour later, after the locksmith sealed the door, and Bob and Wally carrying the only two keys, they left the building and the landlord behind.

Chapter 16

Bob fetched Bluebonnet's halter from inside the barn and he set a worn and tattered western saddle and training bridle on the fence. It was an old saddle for he didn't want a good saddle ruined if she rolled onto it, or banged it into the fence.

The horse's poked their noses through a half-dozen flakes of timothy hay he'd thrown over the fence for breakfast. He let them eat for ten minutes. Blue watched him suspiciously, snatching bites and then raising her head again to keep her eyes on Bob. She knew what was coming next. It had been a week since Bob rode her last when she'd dumped him in the dirt for the second time.

Her training was taking longer than he'd expected, yet he was unwilling to hire someone to break her to the saddle. He preferred to train his own horses. They tended not to end up with hard mouths or spur-hardened sides. A more gentle and willing horse was often the result, although he could, and would, be more stubborn than the horse when necessary.

The horse had a long way to go in her training. Blue was dominant. In a wild herd she would vie for the job of boss-mare. At pasture in the west she might be made the bell-mare with a cowbell hung around her neck so that the other horses would follow her to pasture, to water, to shelter, or home. In Duxbury she ruled the stable, occasionally biting the other horses to push them forward or away. She was only three and with no other more dominant mare to challenge her, she ruled over the other horses.

He took the halter and hid it behind his back as he passed through the gate, closing it behind him. Blue had her head up. She'd stopped chewing and stood staring at Bob. The other two horses didn't care.

She stepped away from him as he slowly glided sideways

up to her. He kept his eyes off her, watching her in his peripheral vision, telling her he was not a threat and would not hurt her. He slipped the halter under her neck. He raised the noseband around her mouth and nostrils and tipped the crown billet over her poll. He buckled the crown and the horse gave to him, lowering her head slightly.

He led her to the gate and the saddle. He'd saddled her thirty times and this time was no different. She took to the halter most times, except when she wanted to play and ran off around the pasture. Sometimes he spent his whole hour just trying to catch her or trick her into giving to him and returning to be haltered. Those time he would never use a carrot or apple. Treats are a reward and bad behavior could not be rewarded. The people he got the horse from had her for two years and he believed they had spoiled her rotten.

To catch her he would get a lunge whip or a long-line and chase her, pushing her away, as she would push the other horses. He played the part of the boss-horse. He acted as lead stallion, boss mare, and head wrangler at the same time.

She would do what he asked and if she didn't want to stand to be haltered he pushed her away, immediately and suddenly, so it would be his idea for her to run off. Then he pushed her ever further away. In a round pen it was easy. In the arena or pasture he ran. He would run, and chase, and crack the whip, and throw the end of the long line at her. He made her sweat as he sweated. Most horses gave in quickly, tiring of the game, and becoming interested in whatever came next that the boss-horse asked for. Bluebonnet didn't give in easily once she'd decided that play-time would be more entertaining.

Today she walked with Bob easily and willingly to the gate. He tied her arm-long and eye-high to the fence. She looked curiously at the wool pad as he lifted it easily and slowly onto her back. Next came the western saddle. She'd seen it before. He lifted the saddle high enough to get the offside stirrup and girth over the horse. The flank cinch was removed as it tended to make Blue buck. That was another tool that she would have to learn to accept if he was to rope off her someday. He pulled the wool pad up into the gullet to take pressure off her withers. Then he slowly let down the girth. He'd saddle-broke her with his English jumping saddle and quickly progressed her to the heavier, more utilitarian western rig. Eventually she would ride with a broken-mouth shank bit like a tom-thumb, or pelham polo bit that was easy on her mouth but had leverage if he needed it.

One of the most dangerous parts of training a young horse came next. He stood beside her, patting her shoulder. Leaning down he reached under the horse for the girth hanging down from the other side. He grasped the wool and nylon strap and lifted it under her, happy that she didn't jump over him or kick him in the head. He fastened the girth and snugged it up slowly, letting her breathe and adjust to the pressure.

He retrieved her training bridle, an English bridle with a full-cheek snaffle bit that would not pass through her mouth when she opened it. He looped the reins over her head and with the halter still on, he slipped the noseband over her nose and played at the corners of her mouth with his thumb until she opened up and accepted the bit into the space between her molars and incisors. The vet had come out and removed her wolf teeth as the floating teeth would bang into the metal bit and cause her pain. Wolf teeth were rare in horses and rarer still in mares.

Bob tied up the reins to the saddle horn so they would not drag on the ground or fly about while he lunged her. He untied the rope and led her to the small arena beside the barn. He'd stationed a long-line and lunge whip within easy reach. He removed the lead strap after he clipped the long-line to the bit. Then he fed out the line as he pushed her away with the whip. She moved easily into a trot and then a canter. Bob let her run and play, throwing her head with stubborn spirit, but keeping her on a circle defined by the length of the long-line.

He smiled turning from the center of her circle and pushing her along with the whip. He stopped her occasionally with a, "Whoa," and turned her to canter the other direction, after moving the long-line to the alternate side. After thirty minutes she sweated.

Bob brought her to a stop. He unclipped the long line. And lowered the reins. Feeling the time was right to ride her again, he checked her girth. It had loosened slightly as the saddle settled on her back so he retightened and re-buckled it. He stepped up into the stirrup. She immediately jumped right and away from Bob. He swiftly stepped down as she left him and he landed on his feet.

She ran a handful of paces and then stopped to look at Bob. He sidled up to her and tied up the reins once more. He clipped the long-line to her bit and put her back to work trotting and cantering for another twenty minutes.

He then made a second attempt at getting on her back. This time she took his foot to the stirrup and tolerated the shifting of the saddle under his weight as he stepped up. She didn't run off. He swung his leg over her back and sat easy on her as he petted her neck and whispered sweet nothings. He kept his right foot out of the stirrup but planted his left foot deep. Better for a quick step-off if the need arose. He asked her to walk with a bump of his calf against her side. She did so willingly, as she'd done several times before.

Pleased with the progress, Bob raised his right foot and felt around for the stirrup. He found it quickly and then asked her to trot. She picked up a right-diagonal gate and Bob posted to her stride. He cared not that she was going left around the arena. Correctness would come later.

He was feeling confident about the ride when Blue decided to start bucking. Bob knew it the moment she slowed her pace and started to arch her back. He bumped the reins and kicked her onwards. Instead of moving out she tucked her legs under her and jumped straight up into the air. After the one good buck she rounded her back and bumped up and down switching between her front legs and her back legs.

He sat back, leaned back, pushed his feet down and forward, and continued to tug and release the reins as he held onto the horn with his other hand. A couple rough landings jarred his spine. Normally a horse will quit after a few seconds but Blue was feeling good and enjoying herself. Bob stayed on her for a solid eight seconds before he found himself pitching forward and losing his balance. He plunged sidelong into the dirt. No graceful landing on his feet this time.

"Are you okay?" Mary couldn't stifle a laugh. She stood at the fence as Bob picked himself up from the dirt.

"Yup," Bob answered.

"Are you going to get back on her?"

"Yup," Bob said as he walked to the horse, which stood quietly looking at him. He dressed the reins and checked the girth before putting a foot into the stirrup and lifting himself back atop the horse. She stood still. He bumped her with his calf and she walked off. He made her walk two full circles before stopping her at the gate.

"You aren't going to trot her again?"

"Nope," Bob said with a smile.

"I wish you'd hire a trainer."

"Nope."

"She's dangerous right now. A trainer will get her so you can ride her and not risk your neck."

"It's not the horse's fault."

"I think you are just as stubborn as that horse."

"Yup," Bob said as he dismounted the horse. Mary laughed and went back to the house.

Chapter 17

Bob and Wally walked up the sidewalk from their parking spot on Fifth Street. They headed toward the flop house described by the landlord as where Simmons was supposed to be living. Wally knew the neighborhood so they had no problem finding the decrepit green and white trimmed Colonial with the peeling paint, an overgrown front yard, and a broken front-window sporting rain-slogged cardboard over the opening.

The door bell button was missing; bare wires hung out of a hole in the wood siding where it had once been. Taking the same positions beside the doorway as they had done at Spears' apartment, Wally knocked this time, his right hand again resting on the grip of his Glock.

"Come in." A voice rang out. Wally carefully turned the knob and pushed the door open. He knocked on the door again as he pushed it open.

"Come on in. Jesus. No one eva knocks. What'sa problem? You a cop or sometin'?" The voice came from a room off a long hallway. In the background the noise of a television blared out a commercial for adult-diapers.

"Hello?" Bob called out as he took a step inside. This time he took no chances. He placed his hand under his coat, fingers wrapped around the grip of his own service weapon. The heady odor of marijuana smoke hung in the hallway. "I am a Sheriff's office detective and I'd like to talk to you." A shuffling of feet and furniture clattered from the parlor to the right.

The same voice came again. "Okay, okay. Just a minute."

"Now would be good," Bob said loudly.

"Yeah?" A black man poked his head around the doorway.

"I'm looking for Thomas Simmons."

"What you want?"

"Are you Mr. Simmons?"

"Yeah," Simmons said from the doorway.

"Do you mind coming out here where we can talk?"

"Yeah. I ain't hiddin anything." Simmons left the doorway and shuffled into the hallway. He was bare-chested and wore dirty tattered jeans. Bob recognized him from Spears known associates mug shots and he saw the tattoo on his left arm that declared love and peace. The man had been arrested once for drug possession. At the moment, he was stoned to the line.

"My name is Schwimer. This is Young."

"So what?"

"Did you know a John Spears?"

"He arrested or something?"

"No. I'm trying to locate his family."

"He win the lottery or have a rich uncle die?" Simmons perked up.

"Not exactly. We are trying to locate is family. Parents? Siblings? Did he have a wife or girlfriend? Anyone here in town?"

"That's info and that's ex-*pen*-sive." The man leaned against the wall and put out his hand.

The corners of Bob's lips turned slightly upwards and his eyes relaxed as he took a twenty dollar bill out of his wallet and offered it to Simmons. "No, No. In-*fla*-tion. Re-*ces*-sion. You gotta do better than that." Bob took another twenty out of his wallet.

"That's better. Let me think... Yeah, he got a girl. Gotta couple of 'em. That's the Jones girls, a few others." Simmons took the money with a smile. The bills disappeared into a pocket.

"Jones girls? Were they around him a lot? Got some first-names?"

"Yeah. Regular girls, Pam an' Sally-Anne, not recently though."

"Pam Jones and Sally-Anne Jones?"

"Yeah."

"Do you know where I can find them? Got an address?"

Simmons laughed. "Sure I have an address. I even gotta time. Corner of Main and Third some-*times* and the Stop-n-Go other *times*."

"Do you mean the truck stop over on Route 24? They are

working girls?"

"Sure. They work. Lot-lizards." Simmons laughed.

"Lot-lizards... Yeah. I've heard that one. You didn't like them?"

"I like everyone."

"Are you everybody's friend?"

"That's right."

"Anyone else?"

"Huh?"

"Is there anyone else you seen over Spearman's place. Anyone regular?"

"Yeah. Not sure." Simmons put his hand out.

Bob's jaw tightened and wrinkles formed at his temples as he took another twenty from his wallet.

"I remember now. Beth Hardin'. Haven't seen her much. Hear she working the diner, got a regla' job as a waitress over there. Turnin tricks on the side. She's trying to go straight. Got a kid in college."

"Spears have any family. Brothers or sisters?"

"Nah. None I heard of. What happen to the Spearman? You never said."

"No. I didn't," Bob frowned.

"He's dead. I know it."

"Yes. He's dead." Bob admitted.

"Damn. Man. He was one o' the good guys."

"A good guy?"

"Yeah. You know. Not 'good' in a law 'n order way but just a good guy."

"It's a tragedy."

"That's who got hit by the train, idin'it? I saw it on the news."

"What did Mr. Spears do for work besides pimping these girls?"

"Don't know. Odd jobs."

"Was he selling drugs?"

"I'm not snitching on anyone. I'll say he knew how to party."

"Any drug dealers want him dead?"

"I told you, he was a good guy. Everyone liked him."

"Everyone except someone he owed money to?"

"You just don't get it." Simmons laughed again and waved Bob and Wally away.

"What about porn?"

Simmons laughter stopped abruptly.

"You starred in some videos with him?"

"Yeah. It ain't illegal."

"Did he owe you any money?"

"Nah. He always had cash."

"Because of the porn?"

"Porn is big-business. *Big-business*. Spears was loaded. He hit the internet market right. Don't know how he did it."

"How about the girls? Were they regulars? Did he owe them anything? How'd he treat them?"

"Great. He treated everyone great."

"Straight up guy?"

"You know it."

Bob turned slightly and moved towards the front door.

"He didn't have a bad bone in his body. He did what he had to, to make money but he neva' got a girl on drugs or forced 'em to work. Porn or street. He never stole from anyone, even as a kid, and he paid his debts. He had good parents. A good upbringin."

"Got it. One thing…"

Simmons started to put his hand out but Bob said, "No. This one's paid for. What kind of person was Spears?"

Simmons pulled his hand back and folded his arms. "What's that mean?"

"How did he live? What was he like?"

"Clean freak. Terrible. Couldn't put an empty beer can down on the coffee table. Had to take it into the kitchen and put it in the trash. He didn't even smoke butts and if I wanted one I had to go out on the balcony. And I had to put the butt in the trash can."

"You hung out with him anyway?"

"Free beer and great parties."

"Free drugs?"

"I'm not saying nothing about nothing but…"

"But what?"

"But nothing."

"We aren't here for you. You can say anything you want about Spears. We can't use it against you."

"A promise from a cop?"

"It's all hearsay. I just want to know what you saw. As a witness."

"Okay. Some drugs. Weed."

"Anything more."

"Sometimes."

"Sometimes what?"

"Sometimes coke."

"Crack?" Bob asked. "Meth?"

"No. Maybe. But I wasn't always around. Thought he was too smart for crack or meth."

"Thanks."

"Anytime. Anytime." Simmons straightened and started to count the bills he'd crumbled and stuffed into his pocket as Bob and Wally turned away.

When they were out of earshot Bob said, "A straight up guy, makes and sells porn movies, who carries a crack pipe, doesn't test as a serious addict, but supposedly doesn't get anyone hooked on drugs? A functional addict?"

"Carries five-grand in his wallet."

"And a welfare card."

"Unless the crack pipe was planted on him?" Wally added. "Does that bring us back to Silverman?"

"Maybe."

"Where to now?"

"The diner. Simmons confirmed the names of the Jones girls that show up as Spears' associates. Let's follow every path. One of them is going to lead to a murderer."

"Or two." Wally reminded Bob.

"Or two… But there's something about Silverman I need to look into also."

"What's that?"

"His employment on Long Pond. Boat rental."

"What are you thinking?"

"There was a Houghton that had a daughter raped a few years ago. If I remember right they rented boats on the lake. Yeah. I'm sure of it because the accused rapist turned up dead in the water."

"What's the connection?"

"Probably nothing. Probably coincidence. But if Silverman worked for the same boat rental place… That would be interesting… I'll need to confirm that anyway."

"See if his story checks out?"

"He's got cash. Paid for his own drinks. Abington Police don't know him so he wasn't panhandling in town. The money came from someplace." Bob took his radio from his belt and called Peter. No response came. He called Peter again and listened to growing static as he adjusted the squelch and gain. Still nothing.

He took out his cell phone and called the phone-to-radio number at B.C.I. He waited for his call to be patched through to the radio transmitter. He heard the line click and he said,

"Peter? Pick up."

"Bob? I heard your call on the radio but you didn't answer," Peter replied almost immediately.

"I'm on my cell phone, patched through. Peter, I need you to run down some names for me. We are at a dead-end here in Plymouth, for now. Can you check on a Houghton rape case about four or five years ago? Long Pond, Lakeville area. Find out the name of the suspect and call me back."

"Yes sir," Peter answered. "Are you thinking Silverman is connected to the Spears murder?"

"I'm not sure. Can you scan the case summary and email it to me? Also, Wally and I are heading over to the T.R.S. Stop-n-Go on the Holbrook-Stoughton line. I'm going to try to find an Elizabeth Harding, a Pamela Jones, and a Sally-Anne Jones. Take a look through the C.J.I.S. for me. We are running down the John Spears leads but still no next-of-kin."

Peter took a moment to write down the names as Bob repeated them to him. Bob heard Peter typing into a computer.

"You want a second set of eyes…" Peter asked.

"Yes. See what else you can find on Spears and these girls and a Thomas Simmons and get back to me right away, will you please? Also, Harding is supposed to have a college-age kid. Find out what you can on him. See if he has an alibi for Saturday night."

"Sure thing." Peter clicked off the radio.

Bob and Wally made the drive up Route 3-A towards Boston. A couple minutes later Peter called back over the radio. "Tim Rickman."

"That's it," Bob said. "What do you have?"

"Nothing much else."

"Let me know when you have the rest. You can try me on Wally's radio or ask Louise to patch the radio through to my cell."

"Over and out," Peter replied.

Wally turned to Bob as they drove. "Tim Rickman?" he asked.

"Rickman died of an accidental drowning after he had been accused of rape by Houghton... Amelia Houghton. Her father was probably Terrance Silverman's boss. I just want to take another look at that case. We've got to talk to Henry Houghton to verify Silverman's job anyway."

"Connection to Spears?"

"Probably none. Just scratching an old itch."

"One that bothers you?" Wally stated as he opened Bob's laptop and started searching the criminal database.

"It always has."

"What's the connection with the Harding kid?" Wally changed the subject back to Spears.

"I'll bet those girls were working for Spears. We have to look at them and any adult kids. Maybe they didn't like mom's line of work."

"You think the kid, Harding's kid, wanted some revenge?"

"Elizabeth Harding is supposed to be a waitress at the truck stop where she turns tricks, or used to. The Jones girls are working the lot now, according to Simmons. Spears was probably pimping these girls," Bob replied.

"Motive? Revenge? Spears ripped someone off? Some

trucker's wife got the clap or HIV?"

"Everything is as clear as a red tide."

"Bob. You know the truck-stop is just over the county line from Abington? Holbrook, isn't it?"

"Yeah?"

"Could be Spears was attacked on his way to the truck stop, if he was pimping girls out of there."

Chapter 18

As Bob and Wally pulled off Route 24 in Holbrook and looked for the T.R.S. Stop-n-Go the radio chirped and Peter's voice came back again over the speaker.

"Detective Schwimer? Bob?"

Bob clicked the microphone. "Go ahead, Peter."

"I've got something on the names you gave me. Elizabeth Harding, and the Jones girls are convicted prostitutes. They've been picked up a few times and spent some time in the county lock-up."

"I got that. What else do you have?"

"Elizabeth Harding did some jail time for stalking and harassing a lawyer here in Plymouth. Name's Laurence Smith. Defense attorney. Seems he botched Harding's prostitution case and she didn't appreciate it much. She got picked up for harassing him a few times, but he never pressed charges."

"Do you think that this Larry Smith might have been a customer of Spears' girls? A john? That would explain him defending Harding."

"Maybe. Might be worth looking into."

"Yeah. I know he's a lawyer but run his name through C.J.I.S. too. Until we can start eliminating suspects we need to check every lead."

"I already did that. Came back clean."

"Good job, now run it through the bar association. Let's find out what kind of lawyer he is. Call over the courthouse and talk to the judges. Tell them it's for me, a favor."

"Okay."

"Anything else come up on Harding or the Jones girls?"

"The Jones girls are gone. One's in jail for drug dealing, intent to distribute, got kicked up to federal court. That was Sally. She's doing twenty years mandatory minimum. It's on appeal but she's inside waiting, and the other, Pamela, was picked up for prostitution in New Jersey. Plead down to trespassing and kicked to the streets. Looks like she moved to be closer to her sister's prison." Bob motioned to Wally to find the information in their copies of the C.J.I.S. report. A moment later Wally had the Jones and Harding reports.

"The Jones girls are off the list. Eliminated," Wally said.

"Unless Pamela jumped on a plane. Came home to murder Spears and go back. We can check flight records, but New Jersey is driving distance." Bob looked at the sheet on Harding but his mind wandered to Silverman and his summer employment. "What did you find out about Silverman and the Tim Rickman drowning?" Bob asked Peter.

"Elizabeth Harding and Justin Harding's names come up in the Department of Education reports. The Rickman file is in the archives. Cold storage. There's a connection. The only thing I've got is that Tim Rickman was accused of raping an 'Amelia Houghton' girl over in Lakeville. Rickman was then found dead in Long Pond. Justin Harding was Tim Rickman's friend in high school and Justin is the only son of Elizabeth Harding."

"It's a small world. Elizabeth is a prostitute of Spears and her son was friends of a dead rapist. That makes Justin a suspect."

"A suspect in both Spears' and Rickman's deaths?" Wally asked.

"Could be," Bob replied. "Rickman brags about the rape. Justin gets mad at someone he considered a friend. Instead of coming to us, he takes matters into his own hands. Got a mother on the streets turning tricks, maybe he lives outside the law, or just on the edge. Maybe he hates it and takes his anger out on a rapist?"

"And Spears?" Wally asked.

"A couple years go by. Got away with one murder. Maybe he sees his mom wanting to get out."

"And killing Spears is a nice way to do it?"

"Not very nice, but it solves his problem. The pimp is dead. Mom goes clean."

"Only problem is that the Medical Examiner ruled

Rickman's death accidental," Peter said.

"Frank Wysup? He moved to State Coroner's office since then. A good murderer can still make it look like an accident. Harding's kid was just a teenager then, can't imagine he was very good at first degree homicide. Still... Nice company these guys keep."

"That's what I was thinking." Peter continued over the radio. "Twenty-something son finds out, or has been suppressing his feelings about, what his mom's been doing for a living..."

"And he can't hurt his mom so he decides to knock off the pimp." Bob finished Peter's words. "Peter? Get a current address on Justin Harding. Run his name through a background check also. Wally and I just got to the diner."

"Got it," Peter said.

"You already got the info?" Bob asked.

"No. No. I'll get it."

"Okay. Thanks." Bob put the radio down.

Wally rippled the papers and asked, "Justin Harding and Tim Rickman were friends? Rickman was twenty, or twenty-one. What was he doing hanging out with a teenager?"

"And Rickman turned up dead? Two bodies..."

"Justin is connected to both, but Rickman's death was ruled accidental."

Bob saw the diner and turned into the parking lot.

"The accidental death of a rape suspect is always suspicious. We've got a reason to visit Houghton for the Silverman-employment tie. Maybe they can offer something else on Amelia Houghton's rape or Justin Harding's connection."

"That's three bodies," Wally added.

"Right. Silverman found a murdered kid over in Raynham. I talked to Jasperse about that. Heading over there tomorrow or the next day."

"I just thought of something."

"What's that?" Bob asked.

"What if Rickman was tied into the Spears pimping business and Rickman tried to get Amelia to come on board?"

"He starts out slow and soft and she's an innocent girl and won't budge, so things get forceful?"

The air grew heavy and the sun seemed to dim. Both men grimaced and went quiet. Bob pulled up along the side of the white concrete building at the truck stop. Behind the building twenty columns of diesel tractor-trailers, two rows deep, idled as drivers took rest breaks, showered in the motel, or ate in the diner. Several trucks lined up at the fleet-refueling pumps and others cued-up at the truck wash. A handful of RVs dotted the lot with one getting propane tanks refilled and another having its tire pressure checked.

Bob got out of the car. The air was still and filled with the stench of exhaust.

"Stay here," he said to Wally. "If Peter finds out anything let me know. I'll talk to Harding and then we'll head over to Houghton's place."

Wally nodded. Bob pulled his suit jacket down over his sidearm and closed one button. Bob walked toward the diner passed open garage bays where mechanics in filthy overalls worked on trucks.

Bob nodded to several mechanics taking a cigarette break, while leaning against the wall or sitting on oil drums and old tires.

"Hi guys," he said as the mechanics sized him up by his expensive, but worn blue business suit. Bob thought he might pass as a salesman. They nodded.

Bob stopped, looked around and grinned. He asked, "Where's a guy find some company around here?"

The mechanics laughed. One of the mechanics answered with a thick Boston-Irish accent. "Go inta da din'ah and aw'sk for the Truck'ahs-Spesh'awl-Spesh'awl."

"The Special-Special?"

"Nah. The Truck'ahs-Spesh'awl-Spesh'awl." The mechanics all laughed.

Bob waved as he walked away.

Inside the diner, he approached the dirty yellow counter and sat down on a green vinyl stool. The room looked every bit of a fifty-year-old diner, the same one he remembered as a teenager. The walls were bare but he recalled there once were Elvis and Temptations posters and neon signs blaring "Route 66" and "US

Route 1". The checkered black and white linoleum floor was permanently stained to a medium gray. Bob was thrown into déjà vu. He was sixteen years old, new license, old car, just left the drive-in in Quincy and stopped with his friends for hamburgers and sodas. This was the same building, only long neglected.

A woman in a greasy apron walked along the counter filling coffee cups and wiping the counter with a filthy rag.

"What can I get yah?" she called at him in between smacks of her chewing gum. She didn't even look up.

The waitress was every bit the image of the stereotypical truck-stop-diner-waitress he had seen in movies since he was a kid. Even the gum-smacking was perfect.

He smiled at her and said, "Coffee and the truckers-special-special."

The waitress stopped her wiping to look him in the eyes, then she laughed. "You ain't a trucker."

"Traveling salesmen don't count?"

"What are you selling, because from your clothes it looks like a load of crap." She laughed raucously louder this time.

"You don't believe me?"

"Ha." She got a coffee cup and filled it from the pot. "What are you really here for? You a cop trying to bust a prostitute?" She pushed the coffee at him.

Bob laughed along with her. He looked at the name tag on the woman's apron. "Mary. That's my wife's name."

"Does your wife work here?"

Bob smiled. "Is there an Elizabeth Harding working here?"

"You are a cop."

"Yes. I'm a cop, but I'm investigating a murder... Is she here?"

"A murder? Who's?"

"I just need to talk to her for a few minutes."

Mary's laugh dissipated. "Okay." She turned her head back over her shoulder and yelled, "LIZ? GET YOUR BONEY-BUTT OUT HERE."

A moment later, a heroin-skinny woman peered cautiously around the door to the kitchen.

"This cop wants to talk to you," Mary said.

"I've got a job here. I can't afford to lose it," Elizabeth said to Bob as she disappeared back into the kitchen.

"I'm not here to arrest you or harass you. I just want to talk to you about something."

"What? Rape, robbery, murder?" Mary interrupted with a laugh.

Bob pondered her curiosity. *'Humans and animals both cannot help but stop and look behind them, even when they're losing ground to a predator, like horses in training,'* Bob thought. *'Chase them down until they accept I'm not leaving.'*

Elizabeth was looking with doe-eyes at him through the small round window in the swinging door.

"Thank you, Mary. Can I talk to Elizabeth now?"

Mary scowled and walked away.

"Yes. It's about murder." Bob's voice grew softer in the midst of the staring from the nearly filled restaurant.

"Justin? Is Justin okay?" Elizabeth came out of the kitchen and approached Bob with trepidation. Her sunken eyes closed into worried slits.

"I'm sure he is. This is not about Justin."

"What happened to Justin?"

"Nothing. He's fine. It's about Spears." Bob watched Elizabeth's face. He looked for the recognition that came from the name. It didn't happen, as if Spears no longer existed in her world.

"That's what the news was talking about? Murdered by the railroad tracks. What about him? It's not like I've seen him, but I knew him."

"He was killed and his body was dumped. I was wondering when you saw him last?"

"I don't know. A week ago. He got me in some trouble a few years ago but I've been trying to rebuild my life. My son, Justin, he's in college and I'm doing what I can to keep him there. I had some hard times."

"What college?"

"Huh?"

"Your son is in college? Where?"

"Boston Tech and Science."

"Can you remember exactly when you saw him? Spears? When you saw Spears last time?"

"It was a week ago. Monday, Tuesday last week. He comes in every couple days trying to sell drugs, and get his money from his girls."

"His working girls?" Elizabeth nodded as Bob continued, "I got a problem. I can't find any of his family members. No father. No mother. No wife. No ex-wives. No girlfriends. Do you know any of his family?"

Elizabeth shook her head.

"No?"

"No," she repeated.

"Who's his girls?"

"I don't know anything." She closed her lips tight, as if she had said too much.

"But they come around here?"

She didn't answer.

"Do you know if anyone was out to kill him? Did he rip anyone off?"

"No. No. Look, I've got to get back to work."

"Is that, 'No' as in, 'He didn't rip anyone off', or 'No', 'No one was out to kill him'?"

"I've got to go." Elizabeth began to shake and she turned and fled into the kitchen. Bob let her go. He sipped the bitter coffee for a moment and left a few bills on the counter. He knew where she worked. Perhaps a visit with Justin might be useful. As he got up to leave a big man in a cook's apron came out of the kitchen. He looked at Bob and a look of anger crossed his face. "What did you say to her?" the cook growled.

Bob took his badge from his belt and showed it to the cook.

"That doesn't scare me."

"I'm investigating a murder. A pimp running girls out of your parking lot doesn't bother you? What about the Board of Selectmen or the Zoning Board?"

"Okay. I just don't like my girls getting upset." The cook relaxed a little.

"Can I ask you something? It has to do with a murder

investigation."

"What?"

"What's Elizabeth's work hours? Has she been coming to work regular? Not missing any time?"

"She's good. One of the best waitresses this dive can keep. She works seven days a week. Got a kid in school and she's off the drugs. If I could get her off the prostitution... She's got college tuition to pay."

The cook gave Bob a strange look, but Bob just smiled and said, "I'm with homicide, not vice. Her hours?"

"Open to dinner. Seven a.m. to six p.m. Ten hours. An hour off for break."

"I would think someone working seventy hours a week would be too tired for murder?" The cook didn't answer Bob's question. He turned around and went back into the kitchen. "But she might be crazy enough with exhaustion to do it?" Bob answered to himself.

Chapter 19

Bob and Wally stopped in a fast food place at the Westgate Mall in Brockton. After retrieving a late lunch from a drive-up window they continued down Route 24 to Lakeville. Peter's voice came over Wally's radio. Wally handed the radio to Bob who talked through mouthfuls of hamburger and wrangled the wheel at the same time.

"What do you have for us, Peter?"

"I tried you on your radio."

"It didn't make a sound. What's up?" Bob thought Reginald Fessenden might be rolling in his grave.

"Not much more or different on Harding and the Jones girls; prostitution, drug possession."

"Serious enough for murder?"

"Everyone is a suspect until proven innocent," Peter said.

"Now you are starting to think like a homicide investigator. What did you find on the kid?"

"Justin Harding. Twenty years old. Sophomore at Boston Tech. Hasn't missed any classes. Good Grades. B-student according to his teachers in high school and college. Dormitory monitor says he's been in his room studying since starting classes. No car. He couldn't have driven down to Abington. Sounds like he couldn't have done it?"

"The mom being a prostitute and drug addict is motive. He could have borrowed a car. Keep looking into it. He was studying all weekend?"

"That's what it sounds like."

"We need to confirm that. I might send you up there to ask around. Follow him for a bit."

"To Boston?"

"To the college. Maybe talk to him in person. Check out his alibi."

"Here's something else. From the Rickman files Justin Harding was questioned as part of the Amelia Houghton Rape case and the Tim Rickman drowning. He was a character witness to both. The school confirmed that Rickman graduated as a senior from the same high school when Justin was a freshman. I talked to some of his teachers and they remember Rickman too. They said the two were friends."

"Harding? Okay. I think I remember him. Just a baby-face kid. A senior and a freshman... Thirteen years old? I'd think they barely knew each other existed. That Houghton name keeps coming up. How did Justin know Amelia? What's the file say?"

"Detective, your name is on the report."

"It was years ago, Peter. Remind me."

"Something about the teachers. I guess you interviewed a couple of them?"

"I remember the interviews but not the content. Who said what?" Bob slowly began to recall the Amelia Houghton case.

"Just that they hung out together. No sports. Not bookworms. Some minor infractions for smoking together in the bathrooms."

"Burn outs?"

"Emos."

"Is that the name now?" Bob asked.

"Yeah, but not into the goth thing. Pretty sure."

"Just cigarettes? Drugs? Anything like that?"

"Skipping class. The schools only record violations, not many details."

"Are there names? Teachers' names? Other kids?"

"Yeah."

"Call them up. Talk to them. See what they remember."

"Looks like I already talked to a couple."

"Print out a copy of the report and follow up with them. Peter? Pull the case box from the archive for me. Original records. I want to go through it page by page. And Peter, thanks for your help." He handed the radio back to Wally, stuffed another bite of hamburger in his mouth, and looked at his watch. They were coming up on Route 495.

"We are almost there. Exit 140. I remember the Houghton

place. They also have a winter place in Fort Lauderdale. Let's hope they haven't left."

"What if they've closed up for winter and gone south?"

Bob grunted through another mouth full of food then changed the subject. "Rickman raped Amelia. I knew it but I couldn't prove it."

"Why?"

"There just wasn't enough evidence."

"The D.A.?"

"Keller wouldn't touch it. Rickman used a condom or something. Dumped Amelia in the lake before fleeing and he shows up at a bar five miles away. No one can place the exact time in the bar, and Amelia getting dumped in the lake washed off any evidence; DNA, hair, blood. Cover-up the crime. It didn't help that Henry... Mr. Houghton, her father, got her clothes changed and into the laundry before he found out about the rape. Thought she was upset about falling into the lake."

"She wouldn't talk?"

"I can't blame the girl," Bob said.

Wally sighed. "We teach our kids to play sports, dress like pop-stars, say no to drugs, think about careers, but not how to defend themselves from rapists. A month of army basic training wouldn't hurt a single teenager in this country."

"There's always the stigma for the victim. Amelia had to go back to high school. All those kids knowing what happened."

"Or worse, rumors about it."

"Should never be..." Bob fell silent as they turned down the lake road. He slowed as he looked for the small sign that adorned the rental office and storage yard, a half mile before the docks.

Wally rolled down his window and breathed in the cool autumn air. "So Rickman turns up dead and the case is closed. Took a bad spill in a boat, whacks his head and off into the drink. No investigation?"

"Not much of one. The coroner did an autopsy. The body was in the water for days."

"What did the D.A. say about that?"

"There wasn't a lot of interest from Keller. There wasn't a lot of interest from anyone, including the family. Rickman's own family."

"Like the family knew Rickman was trouble?"

"Maybe. They had money. Could of bought the best lawyers in the state. Good lawyers and scant evidence doesn't make good convictions. I remember the family wasn't too happy. The mother was a wreck. The father didn't seem surprised his son was dead."

"Kinda odd?"

"Who knows. In Boston I've broken the news a dozen times to family members. You get all kinds of reactions. I'm sure they go the spectrum and sometimes all at once."

"And Amelia and her parents?"

"I figure Rickman getting whacked was karma. The rape case was closed. I wonder how closed it was for Amelia? Let's keep this on Silverman for now. Let's just verify his employment, any problems he might have had while working here."

"And?"

"And let's let dead dogs rest in peace."

"So why are we here? We could verify employment over the phone."

"In person, we can read the person better. See if they're lying about something."

"What's that about dead dogs?"

Bob pulled into the driveway and they got out of the car and headed up the gravel path to the porch. The boat rental office served as a home and workplace for the family business.

"Mr. Houghton?" Bob asked as a man answered the door before they reached the bottom step.

"Yes." Henry Houghton, a thin man with gray at his temples looked out the door. He had deep set dark eyes that looked tired. His head hung forward.

"I'm a detective with the sheriff's office."

"I know who you are." The man started to close the door, but Bob stepped up onto the stoop and put his hand out to stop it.

"Now hold on. I just need to ask you a couple questions about a Terrance Silverman you hired this summer."

"That's none of your business." Henry spat, his eyes narrowing, his head rising.

"There's been a murder and he's a suspect. If I can talk to you about it maybe he can be eliminated as a suspect and we can release him."

"That's not my problem." Henry tried to force the door closed but Bob put his foot in the door jam. "Now. If this is about your daughter, that's not why I'm here. I'm sorry about what happened to your daughter, but I believe Silverman is innocent of this murder and I'd like to clear him of the crime."

"If you believe he's innocent let him go. You believed Rickman was innocent. You protected him."

Bob was silent for a moment. The man's eyes bored holes through his face. "That's not what happened and you know it," Bob said.

Henry shoved the door against Bob's foot. "Doesn't matter. He got what he deserved. I made..."

"I'll get a subpoena if I have to." Bob pushed back on the door, holding it, but not forcing it open.

Henry yanked the door open. He looked Bob straight in the eyes and calmly said, "You do that. You go ahead and talk to your judge-friends and your lawyer-friends and you get a subpoena and a warrant and anything else you think you need because that's the only way I'm talking to a cop after you let that rapist touch my daughter."

"We never let Rickman *do* anything."

"If you want to talk to me you better consider reopening that rape case and finding out the truth."

"Rickman is dead. There's no point..." Bob regretted his words immediately.

"No point? Amelia's honor is not important?"

"Of course it is, of course she is important, but the resources are..." Bob grimaced at the words he let escape his own mouth.

"Are what? *Unavailable?*"

"No."

"Then what are they? *Unnecessary*? You are dammed right they're unnecessary. One more dead criminal means lower prison costs and more justice. I know people too. I've got grease.

You can't push me around. Go get your subpoena." Henry slammed the door closed on Bob's foot.

"...are tied up with this murder." Bob softly finished his statement.

Wally's thin line of a mouth threatened to smile.

"Don't do it," Bob said as he limped back to the car.

"What?"

"Laugh."

"I wasn't."

"You were thinking about it."

"That was a little funny."

"In ten years, maybe."

"Let's take him in for assault."

"No. Don't worry about it," Bob replied as he reviewed the conversation in his mind. "Something Henry said isn't right, but what?" He took out his notepad and wrote down what he could remember.

Peter's voice came over Wally's radio again, breaking Bob's train of thought. "Detective Schwimer?"

"I need to get you one of these that work," Wally said as he handed over his radio. Bob looked sarcastically at Wally and took the radio from him.

"Go ahead, Peter," Bob said.

"The phone company traced Spears' cell phone. I'll transfer the files to your folder on the network drive. I also emailed you a copy of the report summaries from the Rickman-Amelia Rape."

"Great, Peter. Thank you."

"It should be there now."

Bob turned on his dashboard laptop. The wireless network connected automatically. Within minutes he was looking at cell phone relay-tower records that had pinged Spears' phone. In a second file he found the victim's call records.

"What do we have?" Wally asked.

"It looks like Spears, or his cell phone anyway, was in Abington Friday night. He stayed late, three a.m."

"After closing time for the bars."

"Then he goes back to Plymouth and in the evening on Saturday he is back to Abington, probably dead by then. We need that cell phone. Looks like it stayed in the area until the battery died sometime on Sunday. It wasn't found with the body. And if it got dumped on the road or fell out of a pocket it could be anywhere within three miles or more. At least there's phone numbers we can track. The last call came in Saturday morning." Bob looked to the west at the sun sitting low in the sky. He turned to Wally. "You live over near Abington?"

"Yeah."

"Let's head back to the station and pickup your car then follow me over to Stoney's Mill. Let's talk to the bartender again and the waitresses. Maybe someone remembers Spears. Maybe Spears and Silverman knew each other at the bar."

"There's a handful of bars and restaurants in Abington. Could be coincidence?"

"I love coincidences." Bob's eyes brightened as he recalled Silverman working for Houghton. It didn't ease the pain in his foot.

Chapter 20

Bob and Wally, driving separate cars, pulled into the Stoney's Mill parking lot, less than a mile north of the body recovery scene and right next to the railroad tracks. Inside the bar, Bob recognized the bartender.

"Hello Harry," Bob said as he limped into the tavern.

"Detective. How are ya?"

"Good. Not very busy tonight?"

"Weeknights and work-nights." Harry looked at his watch. "It's almost seven. We get a boost between four and six and everyone starts going home for dinner about now. What happened to your foot?"

"Nothing. Took a bad step."

"Did you find anything out about the homeless guy?"

"Yes. In fact I have a photograph I need you to look at." Bob showed Spear's mug shot to the bartender.

"Nope. Don't recognize him."

"His name is John Spears."

"Don't know the name either."

"I'm looking for his associates. If you didn't see him then you probably wouldn't know that. I'm trying to put the two together. Spears was in Abington Friday night."

"He was here? At the bar?"

"I'm not sure he was in your bar but Silverman was here."

"The homeless guy?"

"Yeah. Just trying to find out if they knew each other."

"I was off Friday night. My brother, Seth, was bartending. Arlene over there worked Friday till closing." The bartender called her over. Arlene was closing in on her fifties but had her hair in a long Farrah-Fawcett cut and wore Daisy-Duke shorts with the cropped-top shirt of a seventies-teenager. *'Probably helps with tips,'* Bob thought. She had the body for the clothes.

Probably a jogger.

Bob turned as she came over. "Hi Arlene."

"Hello. Schwimer? Right?" Arlene said to both Bob and Wally.

"Yes," Bob answered.

"You seem surprised." Arlene laughed. "I have a great memory."

"Have we met?" Bob asked.

"No, but Harry told me the police wanted to talk to me about the bum."

"In fact I have to ask you about another guy. Do you recognize this man?" Bob showed her Spears' photograph.

"Oh yeah. He was here the other night. Friday."

"What can you remember of him?"

"Not much. He didn't talk much and I'd never seen him before. Beer drinker. Got plastered. Personally I think he was doing lines in the bathroom. He came in quiet and calm and left wired to the hilt. You'd think he was drinking coffee by the gallon instead of beer. He wore a nice jacket. Expensive black leather."

"Do you remember who he was with? Did he have any friends with him?"

"Yeah. He had an old guy with him."

"Old guy?" Bob asked.

"Yeah. Tall. Gray. Wrinkly. Creepy. Smoker."

"Do you remember anything distinguishing about him?"

"He wore a sports jacket, gray or beige, like in the old movies. Definitely not my type. Either one of them," she laughed. "You know they both left pretty pissed off. There was some loud yelling and arguing. It was close to closing by then so I asked them to leave and they did. It was weird. First they're fighting and arguing and then they shut-up real fast and leave quiet and quick. That one guy wired for ten-thousand volts. I heard some tires squealing in the lot, but I figured good riddance to them. They didn't even tip."

"Thank you, Arlene. Do you remember who else worked Friday night? Do you think they would remember these two guys?"

"Seth worked the bar, Harry was off, but they sat at my tables. They sat at the booth over there by the bathrooms. The other girls might remember them coming in or the fighting. Janet works tomorrow night. Sue-Ellen only works Friday and Saturday nights. You can swing by and ask them."

"Can you give them my card and have them call me?" Bob said.

"Sure. Would you two like something to drink? Water? A soda?"

"No. Thanks again." Bob dropped a couple of his business cards and a twenty dollar bill on Arlene's drink tray.

Back outside in the parking lot Bob stopped under a light pole. "Wally. We have to talk to those girls. A gray-haired man, and Terri finds gray hairs on Spears' body. They were arguing. Whatever they were arguing about is probably the motive for murder."

"But Spears left and went back to Plymouth. He wasn't dead for at least another eight or nine hours."

"They had an argument. The two of them went home and stewed on it. They both got themselves angry enough to meet again, someplace. Angry enough to commit murder."

"If we find that second meeting place we have a crime scene for the murder," Wally said.

Bob nodded. "Spears apartment was clean. Very clean."

"Too clean? Spears buddy, Simmons, and his landlord both said he was almost a germaphobe."

"Mysophobia... I'll take another look at Spears' phone records to see who he has been talking to."

"Are we done for the night?" Wally asked.

"Yeah. I guess so."

"You'd better call Mary." Wally reminded him.

"I'll do that."

Chapter 21

Bob awoke to the slowly growing realization that his foot still hurt. He sat up in the bed just as Mary brought him a cup of coffee and ibuprofen.

He took the cup and pills and said, "I love you."

"I love you too. I figured your foot was still bothering you."

"He got me pretty good." Bob laughed as he got out of bed. He swallowed the pills and sipped the coffee.

"I don't think it's funny. You should have arrested him."

"He has enough troubles. I can't blame a guy for not trusting the system. He seemed pretty happy that Rickman was dead but it seems he wants more. Apology for dropping the rape investigation was not enough."

"The suspect was dead. You didn't do anything wrong."

"I know. Just no evidence and Rickman five miles away at the time."

"Don't let it bother you. It was years ago. You did your job, best as you can, as always."

"Yeah. Maybe," Bob said as he put the coffee cup down and he took her in his arms.

"Maybe nothing. Quit that talk. It won't help you if you run for Sheriff next year," Mary said as she hugged him back.

"I haven't really thought about that."

"Sheriff Barton is done. Even if he beats the accusations he's already lost any re-election. You're second-in-command and you are doing the job anyway."

"I like detective work."

"You can still do detective work."

"Not as much. More paperwork, schedules, meetings, prisoner transfers, fugitive searches, domestic violence warrants. public relations."

"You have deputies for that. You can hire another detective or an assistant."

"Budgets to write and follow." He kissed her neck.

"You're good at numbers." She giggled.

Bob stumbled. "Why didn't you ever become a cop? You're good at it."

"Don't change the subject."

"If I become sheriff but keep doing detective work then I'm not doing my job. I love detective work. If I run, and if I got elected, I'd be required to do a job that isn't what I really love to do. It's the Peter Principle."

"The pay is pretty good,"

"Exactly. It has never been about the money. That's all I'm saying. Besides, the state police still want me to make a move."

"But it would be nice..." Mary didn't finish the sentence.

"I know."

Bob released her and went to the bathroom. Mary returned to the kitchen, calling down the hallway as she went. "I've got breakfast when you are ready."

"Thank you." Bob's voice resonated through the door.

A few minutes later they sat down together in the breakfast nook over looking their pasture and their horses.

"What's for today?" Mary asked. Bob had told her about the investigation over dinner.

"I'm going over to Taunton. I want to check on Silverman's story some more. Have to talk to Sheriff Jasperse."

"What about Spears' family? They haven't been notified."

"Looks like we are coming up short on that... for now. Still looking for some family, any family. His landlord and friends know what happened. We'll keep looking maybe one of his friends will get the word passed along."

"Just a matter of time before the newspapers find out his name?" Mary sipped her coffee.

"True. These things happen. Some people have no family to speak of." Bob looked at his watch. "Gotta go. Make some phone calls. Should be in the office in a couple hours anyway. What's on your schedule for the day?"

"Substitute teaching today. Got a call earlier."

Chapter 22

After feeding the horses, followed by a shower, a shave and a change of clothes, Bob left for Taunton, the Bristol County seat. With his briefcase and notes on the seat beside him, the center console mounted laptop booting up, he sat and warmed up the car. Mary came out to hand him a travel cup filled with coffee.

"Be careful," she said.

"Always," he smiled.

They kissed goodbye through the window and Bob backed out of the driveway.

As he drove away he called Frank.

"Morning, Bob," Frank said.

"Good morning, Doctor."

"What are we finding out on Spears' murder?"

"No next-of-kin. Wally and I interviewed some of his associates. We checked out his apartment yesterday, which is why I'm calling."

"What do you need?" Frank asked. Bob heard him taking the short breath of a cigarette puff.

"I need you to put a team together and clean out his apartment. Wally has the keys. We sealed and locked it yesterday."

"Evidence?"

"Everything smaller than a bread box. If it doesn't become evidence we'll hold it for next of kin, if we can find any. Use Terri, Frank, and Peter. Let's box up Spears' apartment. I want everything right down to luminal on the walls and furniture."

"Think it might be a murder scene?"

"It's spotless. Spears is reputed to be a clean-freak, but maybe someone tried to wash away a crime. Check out a cargo truck from the lot. Bag and tag everything. There doesn't seem to be any living relatives that we can find and the landlord will throw everything away if we don't take it. I want you to treat it like a crime scene. It just might be one."

"Should we get a warrant?"

"Unless the landlord complains, I don't think we need one, but we might as well get the paperwork done. I spoke to the landlord, and he seems okay with us being there. Probably wants to get it rented again quickly, but put new police-tape on the door before you leave. We may have to go back."

"So you don't know if it's a crime scene or not?"

"That's what I want you to find out," Bob said.

The drive to Taunton was long, and made longer by morning commuter traffic. The highways and two lane state-routes lined with pitch-pine, sugar-maples, birch, and white-oak trees turning bright in their fall colors, partially blocked farms, cranberry bogs, and suburban developments. The change was early and pretty. Bob thought it might be a sign of an early winter except for the warmer days. He loved the fall air, cold at night and warm during the day. Today was especially warm. *Indian summer* they called it when he was a kid. He had left his heavy wool coat at home but he would not need it.

When he arrived in Taunton, Bob stopped at a coffee shop and refilled his travel mug before heading over to the Sheriff's office. He sat in his car for several minutes while he reviewed his notes from the previous two days. There was not much on Raynham and his talk with Silverman had not revealed any details.

He finished his coffee and climbed out of the car with his briefcase and cowboy hat. He walked swiftly across the parking lot to the County Sheriff's building.

As he opened the door to the lobby he was hit by a blast of hot, steamy air. He turned to close the door but a breeze took it from his hand and slammed it shut. A female officer behind bullet proof glass looked up. Bob smiled and mouthed the word, *"Sorry."* She looked back down at her desk, seemingly consumed in work.

"Good morning. I'm Detective Schwimer with the Plymouth County Sheriff's office. I have an appointment with Sheriff Jasperse."

"I'll check. Please sign in." The officer didn't look up as she flipped her hand towards a clipboard on the counter. She continued to type on her computer before getting out of her chair and disappearing into the back offices. While he waited Bob pondered the older, run down look of the Bristol County facility compared to the newer Plymouth B.C.I. offices he shared with his team. He wondered if it was a reflection *of* the Sheriff, or a reflection *on* the Sheriff.

Several minutes later Sheriff Jasperse opened a door and gestured for Bob to come in. "Good morning, Bob. What can we do *to* you?" Jasperse used his tired cliché.

"Hello Sheriff. I'd like to see that Raynham murder file and talk with you a bit." They walked down a plain powder-blue hallway and into an office. Jasperse sat in a large comfortable looking, but heavily worn, leather chair and motioned for Bob to join him at the desk. Bob pulled up a rickety office chair and took a file that Jasperse handed him.

"I pulled the file yesterday; the Joel Richardson murder. Started reviewing the details. Not much there."

"You had Mr. Silverman for a long while."

"The bum? Yeah. Like I said, we couldn't prove anything. The case has gone cold. *Unless,*" Jasperse leaned forward. "You said you picked him up over there, but you didn't say what for? Did he kill someone else?"

Bob lowered his gaze. "I'm not sure he killed anyone just yet."

"Ah, yeah." Jasperse eyes narrowed and his lips pulled back into an evil grin. "Looking for evidence. But you did say there was a murder? You're keeping me in the dark here. I almost called you about a dozen times yesterday. I've been watching the news and they said something about a body in Abington. You think it's related?"

"Maybe. What do we have here?" Bob thumbed through the file. Inside he saw police incident reports, a coroners' report, rap sheets, mug shots, crime scene photographs, personal information on the boy and his family.

"Everything I have is right there. That's your copy. You can keep it. You know the basics. A kid, Joel Richardson, was found dead, from a shotgun blast, in the alleyway beside a bakery on Main Street. The bum and the body were found in the alleyway the next morning when the cook showed up to open the store."

"What else was in the alleyway? Any trash or anything? Crates and boxes? Cars?" Bob asked as he scanned through the incident reports.

"There was an old shopping cart, some empty wine bottles, probably the bum's, some rags and trash spilled over from the dumpster. The photographs are there. It probably looks the same now as it did back then."

"And a couple cans of spray paint." Bob read off the incident report.

"Yeah. If it says there." Jasperse pointed to the papers.

"Do you think Richardson was a tagger and got caught? Maybe the cook or a shop owner caught him painting graffiti? Do you think that might have been a motive?"

"I talked to the shop owners. They all had alibis for that night. I mean that could have been a motive but of course a lot of people knew that kid. He came from a nice family but he wasn't loved. It was weird, Bob." Jasperse paused in thought and then he laughed in his crude and cruel heehaw laugh. "You'll see a rap sheet on the kid, Joel, in there, but it was petty stuff like throwing rocks through windows and slashing tires, maybe some graffiti. Never enough witnesses or evidence to charge the kid. His parents always picked him up and accused me of not liking the kid. The stuff he did…it was all kid-stuff anyway. Who doesn't get into a little trouble as a teenager? Figured he'd out grow it. So I asked around and talked to the store owners. Most of them knew him by sight, because they'd kicked him out of almost every store in town for causing problems. Never thought anyone in Raynham had a bad enough bone to murder an innocent kid."

Bob scanned through the pages, "Animal cruelty? Doesn't sound too much like he was innocent." Bob remarked.

"Okay. Well… But to be murdered like that? I don't see it."

"He had family in Raynham?"

"Yes. Parents and a sister, I think."

Bob continued to read through the papers. "Who is this

Mulligan couple?"

"Who?"

"Betty and Shawn Mulligan? Do they own a horse ranch?"

"Oh, yes. They caught the kid shooting BBs at their horses one time. Claimed they had some feral cats disappear from their farm."

"That could be a motive."

"BBs? Nah. I talked to them but they didn't seem the type."

"BB guns are a short way from a .22 caliber rifle or even a shotgun. Kids that torture animals are a short stretch from *killing* animals, or even people. Alexithymia. They often grow up to be psychopathic or sociopathic."

"I just don't see it, *Haw-haw*. You think he'd shoot their horses with a real gun?"

"I'd like to talk to the bakery owner…"

"See if he did it?"

"Maybe."

"You don't think it was the bum?"

"You didn't charge him. It would be a good frame except Silverman didn't have a shotgun. What about the storeowners? Any of them got a registered shotgun?"

"The bum could have hid it someplace after the murder." Jasperse laughed again.

Bob considered of the improbability of a homeless murder suspect hiding a gun and returning to the scene.

"…Or the store owners," Bob said. "Or the Mulligans, and who knew how many others might be suspect, even Joel's parents or siblings could be suspect. Do you mind if I do a little poking around, Sheriff? I'd like to go over to Raynham and check this out."

"No. You got my permission. I'd like to close that case. It's been bothering me. A kid killed in a town alleyway, and no witnesses, and no suspects, and no motive. Or not much motive that I can see."

Bob kept quiet about his suspicions as he thanked the Sheriff. "I'll let you know if I find out anything more. Goodbye, Sheriff." Bob shook the Sheriff's hand and left the office.

Chapter 23

The phone rang four times before Louise picked up Bob's call. He had tried to call Peter on the radio during the drive. No response. He also radioed Louise with similar results. He called Louise on the phone.

"Plymouth County B.C.I. This is a recorded line."

"Good morning Louise."

"Morning Detective."

"I just wanted to let you know I'll be in much later. Maybe." Bob heard Louise clanking the keys on her computer.

"Okay."

"Forward any calls to my cell phone."

"Reporters have been calling in again. A couple showed up this morning in a van."

"Just hand them a copy of the press release."

"Done. They want more details."

"Do what you can. Have one of the officers intervene if they get too persistent."

"Will do. They are hounds."

"Thank you, Louise. Any problems other than that?"

"No. Terri was asking for you."

"What did she want?"

"She didn't say."

"Okay. Can you run something down for me?"

"Absolutely."

"I need you to take a look at the Spears' cell phone records on the network drive. Peter put them under my folder."

"Got it. I'm there now. What am I looking for?"

"Try to get me a name and address for every caller from Thursday through Saturday."

"Done by E.O.D."

"Thank you." As he hung-up the phone Bob made a mental note to call Terri. He closed in on the Raynham town center and his stomach told him it was nearly noon.

The street was lined with a mix of two and three story pre-1900s granite block buildings and a few art-deco and more modern buildings. He drove up and down the main road looking for the bakery and the alleyway where Joel Richardson was killed. He finally located the store across from an empty parking space. He got out of his car with just a notepad and a pen, leaving the case folder in the car.

The alley was not much different from the crime scene photos Jasperse had given him. The adjacent buildings were single story red-brick construction. He entered the alley. Wind blown trash filled the corners, a dumpster on wheels and a pile of broken down cardboard boxes and pallets blocked the access. Someone had painted over graffiti along the walls. The new red paint didn't match, but for an alleyway, Bob thought it looked perfect. A little more graffiti on top, and they could rename the area *Roxbury*.

He went into the bakery and ordered a sandwich and asked to speak to the owner. Taking a seat by the window he waited for his food until an older woman approached him.

"I'm the owner." She spoke noncommittally, almost as a question.

"Hello." Bob turned and moved to rise but the woman waved him down as she sat across from him.

"Can I help you?" she asked.

"I'm a police detective. I was wondering if you knew anything about the murder that took place in the alleyway here. The boy? Joel?" Bob noted a frightened look that crossed her face. As quickly as it arrived, her fear changed to relief.

"Oh that. I haven't thought about that in awhile."

"That's okay. I'm a bit taken aback at the moment. I was expecting the owner was a man. A *Steven*?"

"That's my husband, Steve. He died last winter. He would have been able to tell you something. I took over the business after he passed. It gives me something to do."

"I see." Bob wrote in his pad. "Can you tell me anything at all?"

"He talked to the police. There was an investigation. We

were both home that night. I didn't even know anything happened until Steve called me. He usually opens up the kitchen at three to start heating the ovens and baking for the day. A homeless… umm… person… told him about the body."

"Did Steve tell you any more? Did he talk about it?"

"No. No. He didn't even go look. Too smart to go down a dark alley at night with a stranger. He called the police and they took care of it."

"So he didn't tell you anything about the body or the crime scene?"

"It was all taped off by the time I got here to open the store. That tape stayed up for a month."

"And you never went down the alley during that time?"

"Heavens. Never. It's a crime scene."

"Thank you. Ah?" Bob handed the woman a business card.

"Judith."

"My name is Bob. My cell phone number is on that card."

Judith looked expectantly at Bob and nodded. "Do you suspect Steve had anything to do with the murder?"

"No… and not you either. I'm just following up on the old case. Seeing if anyone remembers anything differently."

"For something to help solve the crime?"

"That's it exactly." Bob smiled. "How do you take your trash out? Isn't that your dumpster?"

"Oh, I have a waitress do it. I refused to go over there. I paid a couple guys to move the dumpster anyway. It's out back now instead of in the alley. The one that's there is the neighbor's. He blocks the alley. Can't say I blame him."

Just then a waitress brought over Bob's sandwich. Judith retreated to the kitchen while Bob ate his lunch.

After lunch, Bob questioned the other business people along the street. Either they didn't know about the murder or they could add nothing more to the file.

Chapter 24

Under a growing cloud of failure, Bob drove up and down unmarked county roads for forty minutes before he found the Mulligan ranch. The house was set up over a hill from the road, and the gate, which was overgrown with brush and weeds, was chained closed, but not locked. The address on the rusted mailbox was faded with time.

The place looked like an old pasture or cornfield gone fallow. He could barely see the red barn from the road, but once he found the gate and started up the gravel drive he knew it was the right place. Set back in the pasture, tilting over on rotting wood posts, was a large sign that read; Sunset Ranch, Horses for Sale, Training, Lessons, and Boarding. The paint peeled from the wood.

He got out of his car in order to open, and then close the gate. It was horse property and he obeyed the unwritten rules. He continued over the rise and down a shallow gently sloping valley of green grass pastures and cornfields towards a white two-story farmhouse.

The barn stood detached from the house. An old corn silo tilted at an angle, threatening to topple over. Turn-out pens held corralled horses which ran up and down the fence-lines, whinnying and snorting. Dust created a magical haze over the farm as it rose from a John Deere tractor dragging a rake across a riding arena.

A woman in blue jeans and a white palm-leaf cowboy hat led a prancing horse from the barn to one of the turn-out pens. She quickly turned to look at Bob's car as he slowly drove down the hillside, then she snapped her attention back to the misbehaving horse that she walked in-hand. She closed the gate to the pen and removed the horse's halter. The horse ran and bucked, spun and stopped to snort, before prancing around the perimeter of the corral.

Bob parked his car and got out as the woman walked over, the halter and cotton lead line coiled in her hand. She took off her hat and wiped sweat from her face with her sleeve. She looked at Bob with a flat expression, then smiled as if it was an afterthought. "What can I do for you? Interested in lessons or training?"

"No, but thank you." Bob returned a smile to her. "I'm Detective Schwimer with the County Sheriff's office. Call me Bob." He left out which county he represented. He knew right away that she was the type of person who told you like she saw it.

"I told you that was a dead horse," the woman said nervously.

"What was a dead horse?"

"What do you want?" she asked.

"I'm looking into the Joel Richardson murder a few years back."

"What's that got to do with us?"

"I didn't catch your name."

"Betty Mulligan. This is my place." She looked relieved.

"I was just looking into this kid's life and trying to find out what kind of person he was."

"Joel Richardson?"

"Yes."

"I didn't know his last name. I remember him. A piece of shit," Betty said.

"Yes?" Bob asked.

Betty stayed silent. Bob stared at her until she grew uncomfortable.

"You asked about his character." Betty smiled again and Bob thought of crocodiles.

"Yeah. You seem to remember him pretty good. How well did you know him?"

"I knew him."

"You had some problems with him?"

"Nothing a good spanking wouldn't have helped if his parents were right in the head."

"Oh yeah? What did he do?"

"You're with the sheriff's office? You got our complaints, some of them in writing."

Bob didn't recall any letters or complaints in the file Jasperse had given him. He would not doubt if they had been thrown away. "That was before the murder. Could you expand on them a little bit?"

"What's the point? The kid's dead and the world is better off without him."

"Better off? What exactly did he do to you and your husband?"

"It's not what he did to us."

Bob stayed silent until she continued on her own.

"We caught him shooting pellets at our horses from up on the hillside. Usually he'd be doing it during a lesson and the horses would spook. My students got real shook-up. Caused more than one or two falls, and if you don't know, falls off horses lead to major injuries and lawsuits. Called the police. They didn't do anything. Do you know how hard something like that is on this business? I'd put up an indoor arena if I could afford it. Got a couple hundred grand to loan me? Having a kid shooting BB guns at our horses for the kicks of watching someone get thrown off."

"I have horses of my own. It doesn't sound too funny to me," Bob agreed with Betty.

"It ain't," she said.

"Did he ever do anything else?" Bob turned at the growing noise from the tractor as the driver steered it out of the arena and into a spot by the barn.

"My son used to go to the same high school and he said Joel was always starting fights. Not with my son, but with other kids. Not always winning them but asking for them anyway. Got so bad Joel was expelled."

Bob noted the comments on his pad. The tractor idled and stopped behind them and the driver got out.

"Then we had a few of our house cats go missing. We'd put them out during the day and bring them in in the evening, just like clockwork, but then not long after we first chased that kid off our property one didn't come back. A few weeks later, a second one didn't come back. Then a third. I just now realized that after that kid died the cats stopped disappearing. We keep the cats in the house, now, anyway. Back then, one of our dogs went missing. It was just a puppy and prone to running off with our other dogs. We got more than a few acres here. Didn't come back. Shawn even saddled up and road the fence line in the dark but couldn't find a trace of him. He *did* find a break in the hedgerow with the barbwire cut through. We went back out the next morning, in the daylight, and sure if there weren't tracks in the tall grass, where someone had walked across the field, right in and out of that break in the brush. I always figured it was that kid. Him and his friends, maybe. Not sure he had many friends."

"So you think it was Joel?"

"I don't think it wasn't," Betty frowned. They both turned as Shawn walked up from the tractor.

"Wasn't what?" Shawn asked.

"Police. Asking about the Joel-kid's murder in town."

"Got what he had coming to him," Shawn said.

"Sounds like you both had motive?"

"Us?" Shawn laughed. "Us and everyone else in this town. Everyone we talked to knew that kid, and the ones that knew him since he was little said he was born-bad. Genetics or bad upbringing, it doesn't matter. If you are looking for motive you will find ten motives at every crossroads between here and Raynham Center."

"I don't see a kid getting killed as very amusing," Bob stated flatly.

"No." Shawn's voice fell to a grim baritone. "Having animals killed isn't very funny either. You want copies of my vet bills from having infected BB-gun pellets dug out of horses? I had a milking cow with seven broken ribs because that little shit thought it'd be funny to tip her over one night out in the pasture. She gave up milking after that. You want to see the bill for a new milking cow? I had to send that girl to slaughter and buy a new one."

"Is this about money?" Bob asked.

"No. It's about life. It's about work and value. It's about God's green earth and giving something back to the land and to our kids and the future."

"And Joel's murder makes the world a better place?"

"It's a shame a kid got killed. Worse he went bad enough to deserve it. I don't like where this is going Mr. Detective whatever-your-name is."

"Bob Schwimer." Bob motioned to hand Shawn a business card.

"Keep it." Shawn waved Bob away. "I think you better leave. If you want motive you could throw a rock in any direction and hit ten people with motives. You could drive ten miles and walk into any gas station, shopping mall, insurance office, or anyplace else and find someone with a motive on that kid; broken windows, stolen or vandalized equipment, break-ins, missing pets, graffiti. A little of that might be teenage pranks, but when it all happens, and to everyone... You know people still shoot coyotes around here. I think you better leave and don't plan on coming back either."

"I'm going to need to talk to your son."

"No," Shawn said.

"No way," Shawn and Betty said almost in unison.

"It can wait. What's your son's name?" Bob asked grimly.

"I think you better leave, and I mean now." Shawn turned and walked towards the barn.

Bob saw a shovel leaning up against the wall. He centered his balance. His right elbow instinctively bent just so, his fingers opening near the flap of his coat, just above the hip. Shawn turned and stopped before reaching the weapon. Bob knew then it would be better to leave now than have to arrest both of them for assault and battery on a police officer, resisting arrest, interfering with an investigation, or anything else he could think of. He realized he couldn't get much more from the Mulligans at the moment and maybe time for them to cool would help. He could always drag them in later and put their feet to the coals if he needed to.

As he drove up the dirt driveway, he wondered if he could have handled the interview a little bit better, or if he should go back and arrest them anyway.

Chapter 25

"Can I help you?" the high school administrative assistant asked as Bob walked into the office. Bob closed the glass door to the mauve and brown office and looked up. A dozen desks set in cubicles filled the center of the room and doorways lined the wall opposite the glass windows, allowing the red haze of the autumn sun to fill the room. The effect was pleasant and warm.

"I'm a police detective. I called a little while ago to speak to the principal."

"Oh. Yes. Mrs. Pendleton let me know you would be coming in. I'll tell her you are here." The woman got up from her desk and went into a back room.

Bob turn towards two teenage boys sitting in chairs along the wall. They held their heads low. Long strands of hair hung down over their face. Bob stood at the receptionist's desk flipping through his notebook while he waited. Finally he took a seat near the boys. He barely settled himself down when Principal Pendleton came out.

"Detective Schwimer? Barbara Pendleton. Good to see you. Come inside so we can talk." Barbara was a woman in her mid-forties. Her hair was auburn and her skin pale as if from a lack of exposure to sunlight. She had thin lips, and a sharp business manner. She wore little makeup and didn't need it.

She walked to a large table in her spacious, albeit windowless, office. She gestured to a chair. "I already paged John Mulligan and a friend of his, William Stevens."

"Thank you. I'd like to keep this informal, with their parents not informed as of yet. As I said on the phone I'd like to talk to them as witnesses to the behavior and psychological state of Joel Richardson. I only have a few questions for them."

"That's fine. They are waiting outside. Shall I have them come in?"

"Yes. Please."

Barbara pressed the button on an intercom and asked for the boys to come in. She got up from her desk and opened a file cabinet, from which she hunted for, and found, several folders. A moment later the two boys who Bob had seen sitting sullenly in the outer office walked in the door.

"Please close the door," the principal said with a smile and one of the boys complied with her request. "Have a seat. Please. Boys, don't look so glum. You are not in trouble. This is Detective Schwimer." She gestured to Bob and then to the boys as they sat down. "And this is John Mulligan and Will Stevens."

"Good afternoon, boys. As you know, Joel Richardson was killed a couple years ago." They nodded their heads. "...and the case has gone cold. There are no suspects, and no leads, and no evidence, so I am just talking to everyone who knew him and I'd like to find out what kind of kid he was."

The boys nodded again but stayed silent.

"Will? Is that the name you go by?"

"Yeah." He mumbled.

"What was Joel like? How did you know him?"

"He was okay."

Bob's face smoothed into calm concern as he saw a nervous anxiety rise in both of the boys. He decided to lighten the mood with humor.

"*Okay*? I heard he was a troublemaker." Bob laughed. The fear left Will Stevens' eyes and both boys relaxed.

"He was a jerk," Will said casually and John Mulligan nodded agreement.

"Yeah?"

"He started a fight with me a couple times." Will looked at John out of the corner of his eye as he hesitated to continue. Then he said, "He beat me pretty good a few years ago, I mean a few years before he died, but I worked out and the next two times he started something, I finished it."

"Coward." John smirked and Will laughed. Mrs. Pendleton's thin lips turned down and the boys stifled their mirth.

Bob noted the change instantly and moved to avert it. "It's alright. You can speak freely. No one here is in trouble. Right?"

Bob looked at Barbara.

She nervously said, "Of course not. No."

"You said Joel was a coward? What's that mean?" Bob asked John with his best attempt at an easy smile.

Will answered the question for John. "The last time we fought he came at me with a bat, but John saw him coming up behind me and warned me."

"Yeah," said John. "We got him good."

"You both fought him?" Bob asked.

"Yeah. Just that once and only until we got the bat away from him."

"Fair fight?"

"Yeah." Both boys mumbled as they dropped their heads again.

"So what was he like besides the fighting?"

John answered, "He killed my dog. I had some cats disappear and I know he was the one killing them."

"Did you ever see him doing something like that?"

"No, but people said he did," Will said.

"He did it. My parents caught him shooting our horses," John answered simultaneously.

"Yes?" Bob asked, as the boys confirmed what Shawn and Betty had claimed.

"Yeah."

"Do either of you guys know who might want to kill him?"

"No," they said in unison.

"Are you sure?"

They shook their heads.

"Did he have any enemies?"

They kept their heads down.

"Did he have any friends? Anyone he hung out with?"

They shook their heads again.

"Is that 'No, he didn't have any friends' or 'No, you don't know if he had any friends'?"

"I'd say it was both." Will smirked as he looked at John.

"Did he do drugs?"

"I think he was a pot head," Will said.

"Did he sell pot? Was he a dealer?"

"No." Both boys shook their heads.

"Did he owe anyone any money?"

They shook their heads again.

Bob looked at his notes and then at the principal. "I think that's enough."

Barbara smiled and dismissed the boys. "You can go on back to your classrooms. Please leave the door open on the way out. Thank you, boys."

"Thank you, Mrs. Pendleton," Bob said when they had left the room. He stood up to shake her hand.

She looked warmly at Bob and took his hand in hers, "The pleasure is mine. Anything I can do to help in this tragedy."

"Can I ask you a question?"

"Of course." She smiled again.

"Did you know Joel? Did it bother the children when he was found dead? Did it bother you?"

Her smile sank from her face as she let go of his hand. She rose out of her chair. "Me? Of course. To think of a child murdered. I knew him but only briefly and mostly by reputation from the middle school. It bothers me and I can say it bothered many of the children and families. I knew him from church. He was an alter-boy. He was always up at the alter, dressed in his nice robes and lighting candles and helping with the body and spirit. Oh. I mean the sacraments."

"I know what you meant. I was raised catholic." Bob laughed.

"I would have thought..." She faltered.

"That I was Jewish? No. My mother is Catholic and my Father is Jewish."

Barbara stood looking at Bob, lost for words.

"The whole family, both sides, said it would never last. They are married 40 years this winter."

"That's wonderful," Barbara said as she appeared a little more at ease.

"I'm half-Jewish and half-Catholic. I'm going to hell in two places, I'm sure," he joked. Barbara laughed at the joke and Bob looked back at his notes. "What did you hear of Joel's reputation from middle school?"

"Oh, I don't trust such things. Children need to be taken one at a time and given their full opportunities to make mistakes and atone for them. Reputations are cursed things. I believe the bible has a few things to say about casting stones. Children can wear on the teachers. Boys find it endlessly funny to tell the same jokes over and over again. They will steal a teacher's markers from the marker-boards every day for a month and then replace that teacher's lunch with fifty markers and think it's hilarious. They make noises in class. Hit other kids. Write graffiti in the bathrooms. There's an infinite list." The principal took a step closer to him. "They can be quite a trial but they cannot be guilty of all the things they're accused of by adults with strained nerves."

"I think I know what you mean." Bob laughed.

"Do you have children?"

"Oh. No. Not that we didn't try. My wife and I..."

"That's too bad," The principal said. "I have a couple boys but they are grown now."

"One more question. I was told that Joel was expelled. Is that correct?"

"No. Not at all. I believe he had been suspended a couple times for the fighting but he was not expelled."

"No?"

"He did miss a lot of school near the end. I could see that people might think he was expelled." She gently put a hand on Bob's forearm.

"Thank you again," Bob said as he moved away from the unwelcome touch.

"Call if you need anything. Anything." Barbara coyly waved after Bob as he turned and walked out of the office wondering what *her* reputation was.

Chapter 26

The concrete driveway to the Richardson's house was cracked and grass grew up through it. Fallen leaves flew into the air as he turned the car into the drive and approached the dilapidated Victorian house. There were no cars in the driveway and the window shades were drawn closed. A converted carriage-house stood behind the house and the driveway wrapped around the building. Bob stopped at the edge of the drive where it was joined by a stone and gravel walkway leading to the front door. While getting out of the car Bob saw movement in a second floor window.

The once stately centennial home bore peeling paint and wooden molding showing signs of rain rot and needed maintenance. The door opened to greet Bob as he climbed the squeaking stairs to the porch. The failing state of the home belied the distinguished clothing of the woman at the door. She stepped a Prada heeled foot into the doorway. She wore an Isabel Marant green blouse and a matching knee length skirt. Her long dark hair was pulled back and up into a clip and her makeup unsuccessfully attempted to cover dark circles under her eyes. She presented him with a fake smile as she closed the door behind her. Bob detected the permeated odor of alcohol.

He smiled and introduced himself before she could ask, his police identification in his hand.

"Did you find him?" she asked. Her weakened determination holding up her smile instantly fell from her face. The well manicured woman dressed in fine clothes was gone, replaced with the empty husk of skin and sticks that is the parent of a murdered child.

"Who, ma'am?"

"Joel's murderer?"

"No. Kathy? Is it Kathy Richardson?" Bob asked politely.

The woman nodded.

"We are working on it," Bob thought it a lie, but supposed it may be true in a sense. He'd only intended to drive to Taunton to find out about Silverman, but here he was in Raynham interviewing suspects, and witnesses, and the family of another murder victim.

"What do you need?" Kathy asked.

"I wanted to talk to you about the case. I wanted to talk to you about Joel."

"Where's Jasperse?"

"He knows I'm here."

"Who are you? You work for Jasperse? That worthless..." Kathy let her statement drop.

"Can we go inside and talk? I've uncovered some things." Bob lied again.

"I have an appointment with a developer. I have to meet someone about a project."

"It will only take a few minutes. We would like to solve your son's murder. We would like to put an end to this case." Kathy's eyes grew wide with uncertain expectation. "I'd like to help bring some closure for your son."

Kathy sighed, hung her head and turned and dragged her feet into the house. Bob followed her into the hallway and immediately heard footsteps above. He looked up into the dim vault over the entryway and saw someone through the banisters flit through a doorway, then the door promptly closed.

Kathy turned and saw Bob looking up, "That's Angelee. Joel's sister. She was sick today so I kept her home from school."

Bob smiled. He wanted to talk to her also. "I hope she feels better."

Kathy merely returned his smile and gestured to the dining room. Bob looked around the hallway and house. The Victorian offered several large rooms connected, one to the other, to meet the needs of hundred-year-old European-tradition. They passed from the entryway through a small parlor where a guest would be invited if they were to stay for a visit. Kathy led Bob through the sitting room where people would enjoy tea and pass the time. Finally they reached the dining room at the back of the house. As they walked Bob noticed that the house was in disarray and that ancient traditions were lost.

Unopened mail and paper lay strewn across table tops. Dirty clothing, expensive clothing, was tossed into corners. Sweaty sneakers sat on upholstered chairs. The furniture was undusted and the windows were filthy. Bob looked into the kitchen beyond a doorway, the swinging doors long removed for modern lifestyles. The sink overflowed with dishes. The countertops were filthy with food and more stacks of unopened mail. Framed family pictures hung crooked on the walls or lay broken on the floors. Kathy appeared to maintain a mask of order and professionalism for her job, Bob thought. But the inside of her house was like a window to her heart; broken, damaged, destroyed.

Kathy walked to the end of the room and stood behind a chair. She motioned for Bob to sit. He took a chair as Kathy sat down before a place set with dirty breakfast plates.

"Mrs. Richardson? Kathy? I have been talking to several of Joel's classmates and teachers at school."

"None of that is true." Kathy spoke so quickly and dismissively it caught Bob off guard. He paused and looked at the woman. Her mask was replaced. The grieving parent was gone, hidden once more.

"Yes…" He paused. He wondered how to approach this woman, a woman who was obviously in denial of her deceased son's personality, and possibly, his demise.

"Kathy. What was Joel like?"

"He's wonderful." She beamed, as if a switch was thrown and she suddenly recalled all the fun and love she shared with the boy. "He is great. He smiles all the time and he gets good grades. He has never been in trouble. He works so hard to be a good boy."

"Yes?" Bob took out his notebook and jotted down her words. She exhibited a delusional image of her son, speaking of him in the present tense, as if he was still alive, as if he was at school or out playing and would be home soon.

"He helps his dad in the workshop. He loves to go shopping at the mall. Do you know his dad takes him shooting at the rod and gun club? They shoot trap. Sometimes they go hunting for ducks. One time they brought home a big goose. It was tough as nails but I picked up a goose at the store and baked it for them and didn't tell them I switched it." Kathy laughed. "He even goes fishing with Angelee. They go over to the lake and rent boats. He is in boy scouts. He got his Eagle Award. Did you know that?"

"No. I didn't. Was that Long Pond?"

"I suppose." Kathy's lips turned up pleasantly. "I really have to go to work now. Joel will be home soon. You can stay and talk to him."

"There's just a couple more things. Mrs. Richardson, is your husband available?" Bob watched as Kathy instinctively reached for her ring finger. Pale white skin gave evidence to her missing wedding band.

"Ummm. No. I mean he's at work but he will be back soon. He's working very hard. He's been spending a lot of time at the office lately."

"Thank you, Kathy." Bob noted that he should check the courthouse for divorce filings. "Can I speak to Angelee?"

"I must get to work. She's upstairs. She's very sick."

"No momma." A tall, thin teenaged girl with brunette hair and her mother's voice stood in the doorway. She wore designer bleached jeans and a pop-star tee-shirt topped with a beret. "I'm okay. I'll talk to the officer."

"Good. You take care of everything here. I have to go. Thank you officer for stopping by." Kathy stood and smiled and quickly disappeared into the kitchen and out a back door. Bob barely got to his feet before she was gone. A Mercedes drove past the dining room window and around his car.

"She's not well." Angelee's voice startled Bob.

"Yes. The death of a child is hard on people. It affects everyone differently."

Angelee sat down where her mother had just been. Bob settled himself back into the chair and handed the girl his business card.

"I'm Detective Schwimer."

"Angelee."

"How are you?"

"Okay."

"Are you well?"

She nodded her head.

"I'm looking into your brother's murder."

"I know." Angelee looked at the business card and then thrust her hands into her lap.

"So you know why I'm here?"

"You want to know whether Joel was a jerk. Whether those stories the kids tell are true. You want to know if there was anyone who wanted to kill him."

"Yes."

Angelee sat still and quiet. Bob pondered which question to ask first. Angelee seemed like she wanted to talk, but he had to be sure he kept his questions vague. Let her talk. She appeared to be a smart girl. She probably could not be manipulated. Bob knew if he was open and honest he would find out far more about Joel than Kathy was willing to admit to him, or even to herself.

"I only know a little bit. He got into some fights in school. Did you hear about that?"

"Yes. He was tough."

"He wanted to be tough."

"Do you think someone wanted to kill your brother?"

"Probably."

Bob was surprised to hear her say that. "What do you mean?"

"You know."

"No."

"You heard the stories."

"A little. A few. But I'm surprised that you would think they are true. That they might be true?"

Angelee looked at her hands in her lap.

"Do you know who?"

"No, but..." Angelee paused and looked out the window.

"What happened?" Bob asked. Angelee's face grew reserved, insecure. In that moment she looked like her mother, as though she gained thirty years in an instant.

"It's okay. I just want to help you and help your mother. I

think when we find out what happened to Joel we can stop this person. You can help me put away a murderer."

"He was mean. He was vicious." Angelee stopped. Bob waited. He did not want to rush the girl. Years of experience told him to shut up and listen. She would talk when she was ready. He looked at his notepad and wrote down what she had just said.

Angelee looked up and stared out the window. Clouds passed over the house and the dining room grew dark. Her face tilted slightly left, her chin up as if she steeled herself for what she was about to say. The tone of her voice fell. "When I was young, seven or eight years old, Joel wanted to go 'fishing for puppies'."

Bob's eyes narrowed at the phrase, but he let her continue uninterrupted.

"I didn't believe him, but I wanted a puppy real bad. He said we could catch a puppy in the lake and that's where puppies came from. We rode our bikes down to the lake. It took all morning but we made it. Every time I wanted to quit and go back home Joel promised me a puppy and how we were going to have a puppy to play with." Tears came to Angelee's eyes and she sniffled. "We found a boat tied to a dock and Joel loaded all the fishing gear. Then we rowed out into the lake. Joel rowed. I just sat there. I told Joel he was lying and that I wanted to go back home. Then he picked up a bag... his backpack from school that he had brought with us. It was moving. It was whining and I knew he had a puppy inside the bag. I told him I wanted the puppy, but he refused to let it out of the bag. He opened the zipper just enough so it poked its nose out. It was a small black puppy. It pushed its head through the opening but Joel stuffed it back inside the backpack. He was laughing. He tied a rope to the straps and he tied the backpack to the boat anchor." The girl started sobbing, tears streaming down her cheeks.

"That's okay," Bob said. "You don't have to tell me."

"Yes I do." Angelee screamed at Bob as she stood up from the table and banged her fists down. "I see that puppy every night. I have nightmares every night." Angelee stood sobbing and weeping. She slowly sat back down. "He handed me the rope and then he dropped that poor dog into the water. He threw the anchor over the side. He told me, 'if you want a puppy you have to fish it out.' He told me to hold onto the rope, to pull the puppy back up and I could have it. The rope burned my hands. I pulled and pulled but it was too heavy. I tried and tried to save that poor dog and Joel just laughed. He sat there and laughed at me while I begged him to help me pull the dog back up. I couldn't do it. Do you understand? I couldn't pull the rope. It was too heavy."

"I know, Angelee." A tear came to Bob's eyes. "I know. I know." He wanted to hold the girl to take away the pain of guilt for something she didn't do. Right now he only wanted her to be a little girl of eight with a puppy to play with and not the sister of a psychotic brother who tormented her.

"It's over. It's okay. It's not your fault. Angelee? It's not your fault." The shallow words fell from his lips before he could think. His brain was fuzzy. He couldn't concentrate. He couldn't recall what his training had told him to do in times like these. What he did remember seemed empty, his words sounding hollow and disheartening.

"He laughed for a long time. Then, when he pulled the rope back up... When he pulled the bag and anchor back into the boat he laughed as he opened the bag. The puppy was dead. He threw it at me and asked me... he asked, '*how much fun did I have dead-puppy-fishing?*'"

Bob sighed as he wrote down the cruelty. He waited a very long time staring at his notebook and listening to Angelee's breathing. When she settled down and her breathing returned to normal he looked up. She met his eyes. Her cheeks were streaked.

"Are you okay?" he asked.

She smiled through her sorrow.

"Did he do anything like that before?"

Angelee shook her head.

"Did you see him do anything else like that? Shooting horses or cats?"

She continued to shake her head and sat silent.

Finally, she said, "Chris Douglas."

"Who is that?" Bob asked. "Douglas?"

"That was a friend of his in boy scouts. They weren't friends for long, a year or so, but he knew Joel better than anyone."

"What can he tell me?"

"I don't know. They were friends. They went camping together. They hung out together. He was by the house a lot."

"When was that?"

"A few months before Joel died. A year maybe, I guess... They had a fight. A couple fights, then Chris stopped coming around."

"Do you think Chris...?"

"Joel was bad. Evil. Any friend of Joel's had to be evil too."

Bob looked at Angelee closely. She had opened up to him. Far more than her mother was capable of, but it had cost her dearly. He was not sure she could or would talk much more. "Thank you, Angelee."

She nodded.

"Can I call you if I have any other questions?

She nodded again.

"I have one more question. Joel was never an Eagle Scout?"

Angelee laughed. It was good to see her smile, even through the tears that left streaks on her face.

"I'll show myself out." Bob got up to leave and Angelee went upstairs.

As he sat in his car Bob called Sheriff Jasperse.

"Hello Bob. *Haw-Haw*. What did you find out about the kid?"

"Some interesting things. I went over to the bakery and the high school. Not much there. Just some confirmation of what we already know."

"Yeah?"

"Talked to the Mulligans. Friendly bunch."

"They weren't too happy with me either. *Haw-haw*."

"They acted pretty happy that Joel was dead."

"Yeah? So what?"

"In some investigations that would be considered suspicious."

"Okay. What'd they say?"

"They said there's enough people in town that wanted this kid dead..."

"Probably true."

"So why did you think Silverman did it?"

"We've been down that road, Bob. I couldn't prove who did it."

"Here's something interesting... Joel was out to the lake, maybe Long Pond. Drowned a puppy. Probably the Mulligans' dog. If Silverman had been working out there a couple years ago they might have crossed paths."

"Okay. But why kill him in town? And with a shotgun?"

"Don't know yet. I'm still leaning towards Silverman being innocent."

"So?"

"I need an address. Can you run down a name for me?"

"Sure thing."

"Chris Douglas. Get me what you can on him. Should be a teenager. About Joel's age. Did you know him? Did you talk to him before?"

"Naw. The name never came up."

"See what you can find on him."

"Give me a few minutes and I'll have something for you."

"Thanks Sheriff." Bob hung up and waited, paging through his notes, but not reading the words. It didn't take long for Jasperse to call him back.

"Got it for you. Chris Douglas. Seventeen years old. No criminal record. Twelve East Green Lane, Raynham. Nothing suspicious about the boy. Keep me in the loop," Sheriff Jasperse said.

"Will do." Bob started the car as he hung up the phone. As he backed down the driveway, he saw Angelee in an upstairs window and he waved to her. She waved back and Bob smiled. Maybe she would be okay. Maybe he could have social services check on her and her mom. Maybe Kathy's illness kept Angelee sane. Wasn't there some kind of Japanese thing about 'reason to live'?

Chapter 27

Louise called Bob's cell.

"What have you got?" Bob answered.

"Names and addresses. Some Stop-n-Go, some public telephones, a few business numbers. Two numbers came from an internet based call-forwarder. They promise absolute privacy for phone calls."

"Smart johns?"

"Numbers that lead nowhere. But that's not all. He got text messages. I traced the records to off-shore IP masking websites. Whoever was talking to Mr. Spears was smart. They hid their cell-phone numbers and IP addresses."

Bob frowned. "What do the messages say?"

"There's no record of the contents. We have time, date, origins and destinations. The origins were aliased and we know the destination."

"Did Spears send any texts?"

"Not that I can tell. Going back further I have a couple phone calls to and from a DVD Production Company."

"Spears' porn business."

"Uh-huh," Louise agreed.

Bob rang the doorbell at a house on East Green Lane. He looked at his watch. School should be dismissed by now and the boy might be home. He listened to a television making a lot of noise. He knocked and rang the bell. The noise on the TV stopped. A moment later the door opened and a dark-haired, skinny boy of around seventeen or eighteen stood there in a Led Zeppelin tee-shirt and black jeans. He wore new neon-green sneakers.

"What?"

"I'm Detective Schwimer. Are you Chris Douglas?"

"Why do you want to know?"

Bob smiled at the teenage rebellious remark. "I'm looking into the Joel Richardson murder and I heard you were friends with Joel before he died."

"Not really."

"You weren't friends?"

"No."

"Okay. I must have my information wrong. Are your parents home? I'd like to ask you a few questions."

"I guess. I didn't do anything."

"I didn't say you did. Can you get your parents?" Bob smiled. Guilty people never 'did it', he thought.

The boy turned around and yelled, "MOM!" as loud as he could.

A moment later, a short middle-aged overweight woman in a flower-print house-dress came to the door. She had bleached blonde hair and her makeup must have required the use of a masonry trowel. "What's the matter?" she asked.

"He's a cop," Chris answered.

Bob handed her a card. "I'm a detective investigating the Joel Richardson murder. Chris knew Joel and I just wanted to ask your son a few questions, if that is okay?"

"Of course. My name is Lilly. Come in." She led them to the living room. "Ask anything you want." She pointed to the couch. Chris sat down and picked up a video game controller. Bob stood in the middle of the room and looked around. The room was tidy, middle class. The television displayed a first-person-shooter game. Chris continued his game with the volume turned off. Mrs. Douglas left through the doorway to the den.

"Okay," Bob said. He turned and took an arm chair. Leaning forward he looked at Chris. Chris stared at the screen, his fingers flicking on the game controller buttons.

"Can we talk?"

"Go ahead. I can hear you."

"I'd like your attention."

"Yeah. Go ahead."

"I'd like your FULL attention."

Chris clicked a button and looked at Bob. His eyes grown wide. A look of annoyance came over him but he put the game controller down.

"Thank you," Bob said. "How long did you know Joel?"

"Just in scouts."

"Boy scouts?"

"Yeah."

"When was that? What years?"

"About three or four years ago."

"How old were you then?"

"Twelve or thirteen."

"So you joined the scouts and met him there?"

Chris nodded.

"Did Joel join before you or after you?"

"He was there before me. I only joined because my parents made me. I didn't like it."

"I heard you are an eagle scout?"

"No. I didn't like scouts."

"What didn't you like about it?"

"Joel. The other kids." Chris sat back and looked up at the ceiling. "The leaders."

"The boy leaders or the adults?"

"The adults. They wouldn't do anything."

"Do anything about what?"

"Joel."

"What about Joel? What kind of person was he?"

"He was bad. I thought he was okay at first. We liked the same music. He liked to tell jokes and punk on kids. He was always doing something funny."

"So what changed?"

"I guess it started with the cow-tipping. He thought it was funny to knock over sleeping cows at night. We'd be on a scout camping trip and he was kind of an unofficial leader. He woke me up and a couple other kids one time, and he led us to a cow-field. The cows sleep standing up and he thought it was funny to deck the cows and knock them over."

"Yeah. I know what cow tipping is."

"It was kind of funny. The first one. Seeing a cow fall over on its side. I guess it was funny then but not really."

"What else did he do?"

"He would tie up kids in their sleeping bags and piss on them." Chris frowned. "He was a jerk. He was a bully. I quit scouts after that."

"What about the leaders?"

"I guess they were okay. I think they knew he was doing stuff but they wouldn't do anything about it. His dad was one of the leaders so I think they just covered for him. They didn't do nothing."

"Nothing?"

Chris looked down at his hands. "They would talk about it. They would say stuff but it was meaningless. I don't think they ever singled him out. He should have been the one kicked out."

"That doesn't sound right."

"Are you saying I'm lying?"

"No. I'm agreeing with you."

Chris's face screwed up tight in thought and then relaxed.

"What about drugs?"

"Not me."

"Joel?"

"I saw him huff paint a couple times. Thought it was stupid."

"Anything else?"

"He always wanted to smoke pot, but no one at school would sell him any. No one liked him."

"I think I've got a pretty good picture of who Joel was as a person."

"Do you know who killed him?"

"I know who probably *didn't* kill him."

Chris gave Bob a weird look.

Bob smiled and said, "Thank you. I'll show myself out." As Bob closed the door, he heard the volume turn back up on the video game.

Chapter 28

The dashboard clock glowed in the evening dusk as Bob called Sheriff Barton. It was late. The days were growing shorter.

"Hello Bob."

"Hi Sheriff." To Bob, Alan would always be known as 'Sheriff'.

"What can I do for you?"

"Do you remember hearing anything about a murder in Taunton about three years ago?"

"Give me the particulars."

"A kid, fifteen years old was shot-gunned in an alleyway. The owner of the adjacent store found the body and a homeless guy hanging about."

"I'm not sure I remember. What's the concern? Is this related to the railroad thing?"

"Only peripherally. The homeless guy is the same in both cases."

"So he's suspect number one?"

"Maybe. I don't get that feeling from him."

"Feelings can lie. I've had my intuition busted a few times myself."

"Not this time."

"That's the worst time. When you *know* you are right, watch out. So tell me what did Jasperse say?"

"He locked up Silverman for a few months. The guy hates homeless people. Couldn't pin the crime on him, no shotgun, no gunfire residue on his clothes or his hands. Silverman reported the crime to the store owner and the police. Same story both times."

"That story was *what*?"

"He found the alleyway a safe place to sleep for the night. Probably had no place else to stay. No homeless shelters in Taunton."

"What did Jasperse tell you about the kid?"

"Nothing. It's like he didn't even try to investigate the victim. I did it myself today."

"What did you find out?"

"The kid had a lot of enemies. He killed a puppy, probably cats too. Shot horses, cow-tipping holsteiners, tagging, vandalism."

"Kids' stuff?"

"Kids' stuff to start, but I think he was psychotic. He was on his way to life in prison."

"But someone got him first. Who do you like for the murder?"

"I talked to the mother, the kid's friend, his sister, his school principal, the surviving store owner, and the owners of a horse farm. I'd say out of all of them, the horse farm is my favorite."

"They would own a shotgun."

"They would. They had no love lost on that kid. Said that I could throw a rock and hit a dozen people with motive. That might even be true. The problem is I can't prove they did it."

"So you wait." Alan advised. "You can put some pressure on them. Drag it out. Did they appear to be in a hurry to move? Flee town or anything?"

"Not yet. It was years ago."

"It's out of our jurisdiction, but if you care you might be able to work with Jasperse to lean on them a bit. Start asking questions around town. Questions that you know will get back to them. Find out what they're like and make some off-the-cuff accusations, they don't even have to be related to this case. Just make stuff up."

"And see if they get tweeky."

"You got it."

"And see if they make a mistake."

"That's the idea."

Bob ate an unhealthy but great tasting dinner of steak and baked potatoes that Mary reheated for him. He sat in front of the computer and Googled the words; 'Raynham', 'murder', 'crime rates', and 'news'. Mary kissed him after delivering the plate and then she retired to bed.

Besides the standard town fare regarding budget cuts, tax increases, and tax protests, Bob found nothing about the Richardson case. No MySpace or Facebook pages left over from when Joel was alive, and none in-memoriam. He made a note to ask the mother, or Sheriff Jasperse, if the family had kept it out of the newspapers. He searched Joel's name and his parents in every combination with and without the words; 'body', 'murder', 'death', 'died', 'dead', 'Raynham', and 'Bristol County'. The most he found was the parents' construction and real estate businesses, completely unrelated to Joel. He narrowed his search on the parents and found their business incorporation documents with the state, plus marriage records from twenty years ago and year-old divorce records. He imagined that the loss of a son forced a fair marriage into the bad category.

He repeated his search with Chris Douglas' name and found nothing at all. He replaced 'Chris Douglas' with 'Mulligan' and found their horse training and lessons business and nothing related to Joel.

Growing frustrated he changed gears and typed in the words; 'railroad' and 'Abington'. Among trains schedules and model railroad clubs, a handful of South Shore newspapers reported the accident in the Sunday late editions. By Monday the Boston newspapers had picked up the story. A couple news-bloggers had commented on the death being suspicious. By Tuesday the national news services had decided the story was not worth any more space on their database servers, but the local papers proclaimed "Railroad Death is Murder-Insider Says" Bob wondered who the insider was; Peter or Wally? Probably not. Terri? No. Frank? Not if it was "unnamed". One of Frank's or Terri's team? The railroad's Perry? Local police? He considered whether it mattered, and decided it didn't.

He pushed the keyboard away and opened the boxes labeled 'A. Houghton rape' and 'T. Rickman drowning'. He spread the contents of the boxes out on his desk, careful not to cross the files; the rape on the left to indicate the earlier incident, and the drowning on the right for later. He spent a bleary-eyed three hours reading the reports, interviews, and original notes in his own handwriting. He returned to Google, Bing, and news search engines. He found nothing on the rape or the drowning. If any newspapers had covered the story, their online reports were long cleaned to make way for newer material. The only news story he found was a long dead Google cache of the body in Long Pond. The html link had no images, advertising banners or media, and it was a straight-forward typewriter courier font of less than a dozen lines;

```
       Thursday - A body recovered from
Long Pond this morning is believed
to be that of a local worker that
drowned during an outing. A small
fishing boat was found on the south
end of the lake. The registration
numbers on the boat match those of a
boat reported missing from a rental
business. Empty liquor bottles and
fishing gear were in the boat along
with illegal fishing lights and
lures. It is believed the deceased
was night fishing and may have
accidentally fallen into the lake
and drowned.
```

Bob sighed, sat back, and tried to think. Realizing he'd discovered almost nothing, and retained less from all the study, he pushed back his chair and stretched.

He closed his eyes and rested them for several moments before opening the crime scene file-folder that held the Rickman murder scene photos. There were photos of the body in the water, photos of it being pulled out of the lake, a photo of the missing boat with the distinctive "Houghton's Boats" lettering on the sides. There were docks, and boats in the water, boats on trailers parked outside the blue dock-house, a couple cars and police cruisers in the parking lot, a white pickup truck parked facing the boat launch with two trailer hitches on it, a rear hitch and a second one poking from the front bumper.

Bob stared at the photos until his eyes went blurry. He let

"what-ifs" wander through his mind until his lips turned down and wrinkles formed at his brow. Then he smiled wide and sat back, stretching his arms and legs.

He got up from the chair. He quietly slipped into the master bedroom where Mary was fast asleep. From the top shelf of his closet he retrieved a small wooden humidor that he carried into the kitchen. He broke the seal and refilled the tiny water reservoir. Selecting one of the higher end stogies from the box, he nipped the end off with a cutter, and went out on the porch. He lit the cigar from a red and black barbeque lighter that he returned on the rack.

He took a long drag and looked out to his pasture. The horses were standing upright, heads up, ears forward, and focused on Bob. The cigar, the lighter, or the heavy fragrance captured their attention in the pasture. He called softly to them and his favored mare, the bay Chicago's Miracle, nickered back in the dark, expecting a treat or a late snack. Bluebonnet raced the fence-line back and forth. The sound of her hooves came like a drum beat. Santeba Dodger stood frozen, watching.

Bob heard the French doors to their bedroom open behind him. He knew Mary had awoken.

"Didn't mean to wake you, baby." Bob turned towards his wife.

"I wasn't asleep."

"Why not?"

"Something is bothering you."

"It is?"

"You only smoke cigars when you're stuck."

"I wouldn't say I'm stuck. Just thinking about the case... Cases."

"Do you want to talk about it?"

"No."

"Good. I have a better idea." Mary took Bob's hand and placed it inside the folds of her robe and upon her breast.

Bob grinned and tamped out the cigar.

Chapter 29

Russell Waldon looked at the five dollar watch on his pencil thin wrist as he picked up the community telephone in the common room of the half-way house. At exactly eight-ten Wednesday morning he dialed the number to the Boston parole office. A woman's voice, deep and commanding, answered the phone, "IPO."

"I need to check in with Officer Turbins."

"Who's calling?" The woman demanded.

"Russell Waldon."

"Hold." The line went dead for several minutes.

"Officer Turbins."

"This is Russell Waldon checking in." Russell waited to hear his rap-sheet read off to him, as Turbins did every morning at eight-ten-ante-meridian sharp.

"Russell P. Waldon?" Officer Turbins paused and Russell heard papers being shuffled and shifted. "Nineteen years old. No surviving parents. Convicted of Massachusetts Statutes part I, title 1, chapter 265, section 13B, violation of the age of consent for sexual relations with preteen minors of both male and female genders. Part IV, title 1, chapter 272, sections 2, 4B, and 7; enticing a person for prostitution under the age of consent, living off the shared earnings of a minor prostitute, and support from shared earnings of a prostitute.

"Served four years in the juvenile offender facility in Boston. Paroled June 12th. Mandatory prison release due to teenage convict coming of age at nineteen years. Remainder of eight year sentence to be carried out in supervised release program. Subject to registration as a convicted sexual offender. Is this correct?"

"Yeah," Russell answered sullenly.

"You will answer in the affirmative with a 'yes', or in the negative with a 'no'. Is that clear?"

"Yes."

"Is this information correct?"

"Yes."

"Are you still employed?" Turbins asked as if he expected that, eventually, every parolee lied about one of the questions.

"Yes. The supermarket. Bagging groceries."

"Any problems at work? If I call the manager..." Turbins threatened.

"No problems."

"Associating with known criminals?"

"No."

"Drug usage?"

"No."

The phone went dead. Russell put the receiver down, his morning absolutions completed. He looked at his watch as he picked up the phone again and dialed.

"Hi," Russell said excitedly and then he lowered his voice so that the other residents would not overhear him. Speaking in nearly a whisper he asked, "Larry? Can we get together tonight?"

"I think we can do that," an older, more mature voice answered. "Spears doesn't have you working?"

"I work only for you, Larry. Besides I haven't seen Spears in a couple days. Maybe I can give you a couple free-bees."

"I don't mind paying."

"That's sweet," Russell said. "I have to go to work. I miss you."

"I'll see you tonight."

Russell climbed the stairs two-at-a-time back to his room to get ready for work. From a distant corner of the house someone yelled, "Stop stomping around."

A few minutes later Russell peddled his bicycle down the tree-lined boulevard of row-houses that led to the center of Plymouth. The half-way house was in the middle of a low-income area; full of rental houses and rooming houses for blue collar workers. Except that one by one the local blue collar industries of a hundred years ago died. First ship building, then rope and hemp factories, and finally fishing. The workers moved on to other towns, or else they took jobs in Boston, did the seasonal-tourist work, or hired onto construction companies. The town filled with executives who commuted into Boston. Several of the run down Victorian style homes were being renovated. Several others sat empty, victims of the housing crash.

As he passed in front of an abandoned and overgrown Romanesque house set close to the street a white van suddenly pulled out of the driveway right in front of him. Locking its brakes, the van stopped fast, tires squealed on the asphalt. Russell jammed on the bicycle's brakes and skidded to a stop right by the side door.

Russell yelled at the driver as the door slid open and two men in white coveralls jumped out of the van. They grabbed the skinny teenager off his bicycle before he could react. He started to kick and lash at his attackers. He clawed at the hands that held him and he twisted wildly as they pulled him into the van.

Pinning him to the floor, the taller man crushed down on his chest, pressing the air from his lungs. The attacker stuffed a rag into his mouth. It smelled bad and tasted worse. Long fingers wrapped around Russell's throat as he gasped for breath and beat at the man's long powerful arms. His fingers pulled at the vice like grip at his throat. The smaller man slid the van's door closed and jumped into the driver's seat. As Russell fought in vain against the man, he realized the attacker was wearing a stocking mask and gloves. As darkness closed over Russell P. Waldon, he heard someone say, "Make sure he's dead."

The tall man bound Russell with ropes, tying his hands behind his back and tying his legs together. He handcuffed Russell's hands and feet to metal rings bolted into the floor of the van.

"I told you we shouldn't do this. It's too soon," the smaller man said from the driver's seat.

"We got the wrong guy last time. We were supposed to get Waldon," the tall man said.

"I still don't see how we got the wrong guy. Waldon is White. Spears was black."

"He showed up for the meeting, instead of Waldon."

"We could have aborted."

"It was too late. We were committed. What would we do?

Slide open the van door, jump out with masks over our faces. Take a look at Spears and say, 'Ooops. So sorry matey. We meant to bugger the other slime, not you,' and jump back in the van and drive off?"

"Why would a pimp do that? The meeting was all arranged."

"Who cares? He's dead. One less leech on society. His girls will have to find another pimp to beat them and his addicts will find another drug dealer."

"I still think this is too soon. We could have waited six months or a year, like we did with the others."

"The only person who will miss this pervert will be his parole officer."

"It's too soon."

"Shut up. We have him. Now let's get rid of him."

"What if someone finds the body?"

"That attorney will find the body himself and dispose of it. That's his problem."

"I think we should bury him."

"No. I want to send a message to that scumbag lawyer. His turn may be coming soon."

"That isn't part of the plan. We've never done anything like this before. The coyotes were supposed to take care of the pimp. Now it's all over the news."

"The police don't know anything."

Chapter 30

Mary got out of bed and went into the bathroom and then to the kitchen. Bob slowly awoke to the smell of brewing coffee. He climbed out of bed and opened the shades to the sliding-doors and he looked out over the field behind his house. Their horses ran to the fence whinnying when they saw him in the window. White dew frozen into a crystal blanket shimmered on fallen leaves as forewarning of the coming winter. He opened the door and walked with bare feet out onto the deck. The air changed during the night. It smelled clean. The sun rising through the trees warmed his face.

Mary came out onto the deck with a cup of coffee which he gladly took in exchange for a kiss. They smiled at each other, staring into each others eyes. He saw the young girl he fell in love with years before and his smile widened.

"How can you do that?" Mary flushed red at his gaze.

"What?"

"Every once in a while, for no reason at all, you look at me like we haven't seen each other five or six times a day, every day, for the last ten years."

"It must be love." Bob laughed.

"You are so full of crap."

"Yup. But you knew that when you married me, but I still love you."

"I still love you too. Can't figure out why."

"Because we are so cute together."

"Cute?" Mary laughed. "Of course I am, but you?"

"I think I'll make breakfast today."

"You make breakfast? Did we get remarried and I slept through it?"

"Am I getting cuter?" Bob asked as he took her into his arms.

Mary leaned into his hug and she whispered into his ear, "Definitely. Last night was wonderful."

While Mary showered, Bob opened the cabinet under the stove and found two frying pans. He retrieved a mixing bowl and several plates and a cutting board. He opened the refrigerator and took out fresh fruit, syrup, eggs, bacon, sausage, and the half-eaten angel-food cake Mary had made over the weekend. He sliced an apple and banana and placed them with some blackberries on top of a slice of the cake. Drizzling strawberry syrup over the top he finished the quick and easy treat and took the plate with flatware into the bathroom.

"Is that you?" Mary asked from the shower.

"Yes." Bob left the plate on the vanity and went back to the kitchen. When Mary arrived, a few minutes later she wore a wide smile on her face. The eggs were finishing up in the pan while the bacon slowly grew cold. They sat across from each other at the table.

"What's going on?" Mary's smile faded. Bob always sat beside her, sharing 'comfortable space' as she called it, unless something was bothering him.

"This murder case."

"What have you found out?" she asked, her face growing grim.

"Spears, the victim…"

"Yeah?"

"He was a pimp and a drug dealer. Silverman found the body and he found the Richardson kid's body in Raynham."

"You've told me that much. What else did you find out? Do you think he committed both murders?"

"At first I was sure he was innocent. The last couple days it was not so clear. After yesterday I'm pretty sure he's innocent but something doesn't seem right. Jasperse, that Sheriff, tried his hardest to make the Joel Richardson murder stick to Silverman but he couldn't find enough evidence. Actually he couldn't find any evidence."

"Nothing?"

"Not much. Yesterday I found out more about Joel

Richardson and his murder than the entire case file Jasperse had."

"He isn't a very good detective, is he?"

"He's a sheriff, detecting is not his thing, but that's not illegal. I suppose he is a decent enough top-cop. I've never wanted that job. I'm sure he was not trying to frame Silverman. He probably just wanted some easy answers and some polish on his badge."

"You are making excuses for him."

"Am I?"

"You know from Boston that there are no easy answers. How many times have you given me *that* speech and I don't work for you."

"Detectives that look for easy solutions aren't doing their jobs."

"So what exactly do you think?"

"Other than Joel being a junior felon-in-training and Spears being an ex-convict I don't have much."

"Criminals."

"Bad guys."

"So they were murdered. Eliminated?"

"Yes. If I can find a common enemy, but one was a drug dealer and the other a High Schooler. Not even from the same county."

Mary's brow wrinkled slightly and her eyes grew narrow. "What else are you always telling me?"

Bob laughed, "I don't know."

"Any connection, any similarity is a starting point..."

"Take what you know and go from there." Bob finished Mary's statement. It was a proverb that had slipped his mind, but in his early career he found it useful when leads ran out or the evidence was limited.

"Back to basics," Mary said.

"And I, basically, have three dead bodies; John Spears, Joel Richardson, and Tim Rickman."

"Rickman?"

"He was the rapist from Lakeville that was found dead in Long Pond."

"Three criminals. What else?"

"Joel was never caught or prosecuted and Spears had been in and out of the system for years."

"And Rickman?"

"Couldn't prove he raped Amelia."

"Drugs?"

"Maybe for the kid, and yes for the drug dealing pimp. I'm not sure on the rapist. So I guess that answers the next question. Prostitution for one and not the others. The kid was a violent, animal killing thief, and vandal. Spears was a drug dealing pimp, apparently a non-violent one."

"And all deaths were in Massachusetts, different counties."

"But two had a link to the pond. One didn't. Silverman rented boats for Houghton's Boats. And the pond is where Tim Rickman was found."

"And the boy? No connection to the lake?"

"His sister and mother claim they went fishing there sometimes, and that Joel had drowned a puppy."

"Hideous. Could a child be that cruel?"

"I don't doubt it."

"Rickman rented boats. Same as Silverman."

"You remember that?"

"I read the newspapers. That was the guy who worked for the Houghton's before the rape. Plus you talk too much." Mary laughed.

"We couldn't convict Rickman, but I don't think Amelia Houghton was lying."

"So three criminals dead. Two murdered and one an accidental death. Do you think there's a serial killer out there?"

"Rickman was drowned. The investigation appeared he slipped and banged his head and fell out of a boat. He was in Silverman's job renting boats for Houghton, before the rape."

"Sounds like a big circle."

"A circle of coincidence with no real suspects, evidence, or proof."

"Was Rickman murdered?"

"I wonder."

"The autopsy was bungled?" Mary asked.

"I'd like to know."

"Find out."

"I could ask the D.A. to petition the courts for an exhumation order. Keller would go along. He trusts my judgment. Terri could perform a second autopsy."

"Did Frank Wysup do the first one?"

"You know too many of my co-workers." Bob laughed. "I don't think Frank would appreciate being second guessed.

"Does it matter?" Mary cleaned up the plates on the table.

"The case comes first. A second set of eyes might see something he missed. I think it's too soon for that anyway. I've got one murder to solve and the kid's murder might be related. When I wrap these up maybe I'll take another look at the Amelia rape and Rickman drowning. Something about that case has been bothering me."

"It's been on your mind for four years."

Bob looked at Mary and she winked at him. "What bothers me is that everyone in Raynham and half of Bristol County is a potential suspect for Joel."

"Sounds like Jasperse had a job-and-a-half trying to figure that one out."

"...And you still want me to run for sheriff? I'm never home now. I'd have to put a bed in my office."

"Only if I can sleep over." Mary smiled and then grew serious. "You know Sheriff Barton is retiring."

"He's still the Sheriff in-title anyway. He's as good as retired... with the scandal."

"He is our friend."

"He is our friend no matter if the corruption is true or not, and I'm sure it isn't." Bob got up and refilled his coffee cup. "The worst thing I've heard from I.A. is petty cash not accounted for."

"How much?"

"Alan told me a few hundred. I heard a little more. Still a pittance. Ten dollars a month average. Going back fifteen years or so."

"Less than a couple thousand dollars all totaled up? You hear about charity workers stealing hundreds of thousands and even millions over decades. Sounds like he didn't account for a few receipts."

"That's what it sounded like from the start."

"What do you think is going on?" Mary pushed her cup over and Bob refilled it.

"I think he is being pushed out by the county commissioners; forced to retire one way or another."

"And you don't want that job?"

"Not if that's the kind of politics I'd have to play. I like to solve knives-to-the-back, not receive one."

"What about the Statie job?"

"I'm thinking about it."

"They have a good pension plan," Mary prodded.

"We have a good one here too. We would have to move to Worcester. That means no more dinner cruises in the bay. No more walks on the beach. No more weekends on the Cape."

"We never do those things anyway and it's closer to skiing," Mary said.

"It *is* closer to skiing." Bob repeated as he looked at his watch. "Hey. I gotta go."

"I'll feed the horses," Mary offered.

"Thanks baby."

Bob drove straight to his office at B.C.I. He parked in the lot and was walking towards the building when a Harley Davidson motorcycle roared up the street and pulled into the lot. As it raced past, Bob saw Terri riding behind the driver. She held tight to the sissy-bar with one hand and waved to Bob with the other, smiling broadly as her long hair lashed the air wildly from under her helmet. The motorcycle stopped in front of the door. Terri slid off the back, removed her cherry red full-face helmet, and leaned over and kissed her fiancée before turning to Bob.

"Good morning," she said.

"Hi Terri, James. Nice bike." Bob walked over to them.

"Is that so? She's got guts. Picked it up last year." He revved the throttle a couple times and then cut the engine, setting the bike on the kick-stand.

"Jim, you've been treating Terri all right?"

"Don't answer that." Terri laughed.

"Of course I am. Two treatments a day." James laughed as Terri struck him in the arm.

"We are trying for a baby," Terri admitted as James gave her a hug.

"Terri says you have some mean coffee in here. Never been inside a police station, before I met Terri." Jim took off his World-War-Two style German army helmet and hung if from the handlebars. Terri handed Jim her helmet and he strapped it to the sissy-bar.

Bob put his hand on Terri's shoulder and said to James, "We have some of the best coffee our budget can afford. Come on in. I'm buying."

Terri retrieved coffee mugs and Bob poured. James grabbed the sugar and creamer and set them down at a small table.

"How do you like your coffee?" Bob asked.

"Regular. Both of us," Terri answered for James.

"How's the farming business?"

"Not well... hmmm... well enough," James said.

"What's wrong?"

"Harvest time and we got caught in a price gap. I cut the fields two weeks ago..."

"It's okay." Terri sat down beside James and put her hand on his arm. He put his hand over hers and smiled. "Bob pays me pretty good. Next year will be better... We had to sell the crop in the field last spring. We couldn't afford to buy the land outright and with the price of corn down we lost a little on current price when we figure in equipment purchases. If we had waited to sell..."

"No one knew corn was going to rise. The only people farming these days are the big corporations or families that have owned the land forever." James changed the subject, "Terri says you guys are working on a big murder case."

"She did?" Bob asked and Terri blushed.

"I didn't say anything. Just what's been in the news."

"It's okay. I talk to Mary a bit too."

"How is she?" Terri asked.

"Good," Bob said. "She's well. We need to have you both over for dinner."

"Sounds like fun. What do you think about the murder? That guy who got chopped up?" asked James.

"JAMES. Stop it." Terri slapped at James' arm.

"I'm just curious," James protested.

Bob interrupted their banter. "We don't really talk that much about the cases. Only what gets said to the news. Now if you two were married then maybe there'd be an exception."

"Bob," Terri yelled.

"I've asked her. She won't give me an answer," James admitted.

Louise's voice came over the P.A. "Detective Schwimer. Call on line one."

"I'll have to take that call. So, Terri, I think we both have work to do. Good to see you, Jim."

Behind the closed door of his office, Bob picked up the phone and pressed the line two button. "Good morning?"

"Hi Detective. Officer Turbins at the parole office asked me to call you because Russell didn't show up for work today. He's always on time, sometimes he's a couple minutes late, but he always comes to work, except that one time he was sick, but he was sick bad and the half-way-house-mom vouched for him. I called over there this morning and she said he left for work on his bicycle after calling his parole officer so I called the parole officer, Officer Turbins, just like I'm supposed to when a parolee doesn't show up for work and he said he expected something like this, but I think he is a negative person anyway, so he asked me to call you and see if you would go check on him. I would check on him but one of the ladies, a cashier, sees him riding his bicycle into work almost every morning and she didn't see him this morning but she did see a bicycle on the sidewalk, not like chained to a fence or a tree but laying down next to a driveway, so he asked me to call you and I'm calling you."

"Sally." Bob laughed as he recognized the voice of the local supermarket manager. "Who didn't show up for work?"

"Russell."

"Russell who?" Bob picked up a pen.

"Waldon. He's a parolee and he works here but something

might have happened to him."

"And Officer Turbins told you to call me so I can check on him?"

"Exactly what he said."

Bob sighed. He knew the parole officer from the Boston office, and the man never missed an opportunity to have someone else do his leg-work. Anytime a parolee went missing, even if they went to the bathroom for too long, he was calling the local police departments to check on it for him. Asking a supermarket manager to call him directly was a new low. Bob-himself would kick it down a level.

"Okay Sally. I'll check on it and I'll call Turbins and find out what's going on." Bob picked up the radio on his desk. "Louise? Can you please get Peter for me?"

The radio crackled and hissed. No one answered. Bob put the radio down and picked up his desk phone.

"Yes, Detective?"

"Trouble with my radio. Can you get Peter for me? Patch his radio through to my desk phone."

"Ten-four, Detective."

"Louise? Call me 'Bob'."

"Ten-four." Louise clicked off the line and a moment later a call went out. Bob's radio merely popped.

Peter responded a few moments later. Bob's desk phone rang.

"Peter. I need you to check up on one *Russell Waldon*. He's a parolee who failed to report to work this morning. He's been staying at a half-way house downtown. Pull his information out of the C.J.I.S. and talk to the house-manager over there. See if she'll let you checkout his room."

"Yes, sir."

"Peter? One more thing. On your way look for a bicycle laying down on the sidewalk. If you find one it's probably Waldon's. Let me know what you find. I'm going to catch up on paperwork."

"Lucky you."

"Oh yeah. When you are done there go take a statement from Sally Sonders at the supermarket." Bob's cell phone rang. It was Frank Wysup. "Hold on a second, Peter." Bob answered Frank's call.

"Detective. Where are you on the investigation? I'm finding out more from the news."

"Apologies, Doctor." Bob used the formal term to ease the frustration he could hear in Frank's voice. "I was out of the office yesterday following up on some other investigations."

Frank didn't respond.

"I've got something I need checked out. Peter's got the details. Where are you?"

"Terri's lab. Downstairs."

"Good. I'll send Peter around to pick you up. Thirty minutes?"

"What's the rush?"

"A missing parolee."

"What does that have to do with Spears?" Frank asked.

"Probably nothing but humor me for a while. You've done just about everything involved in police work. I can use your help. Pickup some slack with Sheriff Barton gone."

"Alright."

"Thank you, Frank. Does Terri have the lab test results back?"

"Not yet."

"We should have something soon."

"Stay in touch." Frank hung up the phone.

"Peter?" Bob asked into the desk phone."

"I heard. I'll pick him up on the way."

Bob put the receiver down and read the display on the phone. He had a dozen messages. Filtering through a plethora of calls, he wrote notes into his computer, filled out forms, and processed court orders, adjusted the duty roster for the entire department, handled prisoner transport documentation, read domestic-violence warrants, and reviewed apprehension orders.

The most curious of all his voice mails was a call from a young girl.

"Detective? It's Amelia. Don't call me. I'll call back later."

Bob checked the time the call was recorded. Five o'clock. He picked up his phone and dialed Louise.

"Detective?"

"Please call me Bob."

"Yes, sir," Louise said with a laugh. "Sorry! Habit."

"It's okay. Did you take a call from Amelia Houghton this morning, about five?"

"No. I don't start till six now. New schedule."

"Has she called back?"

"Let me check the log... No. I see the five o'clock call and that's it."

"If she calls back give her my cell phone number, would you?"

"You got it. I'll put it in the records and put a post-it on the call-monitor. Any time day or night?"

"You know I'm married to this place?"

"How does Mary feel about that?"

"She knows. She tolerates my other marriage as long as it's not to another woman."

"Sounds like a great woman. Hey? There's a dozen reporters up here looking for information on the Abington body."

"Can't you shoo them away?"

"I've been doing it since Sunday. Your turn."

"You're right." Bob hung up and went to the lobby. He gave a short briefing to the few gathered reporters, five all totaled, representing mostly local newspapers but one Boston daily. Sharlene Cimmino recognized Bob and waved to him.

When he finished the briefing and asked the reporters to depart, Sharlene came up to him. She wore a dark burgundy knee length dress, tight-fitting in all the right places. It complimented her shoulder-length auburn hair and eyes.

"Hello Detective."

"Cimmino? Sharlene?" Bob put out his hand.

"You got it. So you moved down here after Boston? Thought I hadn't seen you in a while."

"Yeah. Quieter. Short commute. It's nice."

"Is this week starting to feel like Boston again?"

"Are you looking for an exclusive?"

"My editor wouldn't be annoyed by one."

"I'm sure he wouldn't. No exclusives. Okay? I told you all I can for now."

"You can make an exception... For old times sake?"

"The old times weren't all that."

"No?"

"Maybe a little."

"Do you eat dinner?"

"Maybe a little."

"But no exclusive?"

"No."

"Call me if you change your mind. I could put a good spin on it. County Sheriff is up for reelection next year and it looks like there'll be a vacancy." Sharlene handed Bob a business card.

"I won't," Bob said as the thought danced in his mind. "Barton is a friend of mine. I wouldn't end-run him."

"Are you giving me that exclusive?"

"No. And don't print that. Anything," Bob said as he waved Sharlene away.

She smiled at Bob, turned, and walked briskly away.

Chapter 31

Back in his office Bob turned to the regular sheriffing paperwork but it didn't hold his attention. Several times an hour he opened his notebook and reviewed his interviews or wrote down a new thought or remembered remark. He fidgeted until lunchtime and wished a hundred times he had gone with Peter, just to get out of the office.

He finally decided to walked down to Terri's lab on the basement level.

"Hi Bob. How did the interviews go yesterday?" Terri said.

"I hope your test results went better... Anything from Spears' or Silverman's clothing? Anything else you've found?"

"Nothing from Spears apartment. No blood. Some DNA from the hairs you gave me. Probably Spears. Clean freak?"

"He appeared to be so."

"It's his hair for sure. Matches the body."

"So we have the right guy. No stolen ids. I figured that anyway because of his associates. No one has seen him in days. Not uncommon for a drug dealer or pimp to disappear for days."

"Silverman is a different story. The most interesting is that the lab reports back aquatic-seeds, sagittaria heterophylla, or sometimes called sagittaria rigida, or arrowhead, on Spears' shirt sleeve and the same seeds were in Terrance's coat pocket. Terrance also had some seeds stuck in the stitching of his gloves."

"That puts Silverman at the railroad bridge."

"Which we know already... Also there were some gray fibers... human hair we had tested that were not from Silverman or Spears. Closest thing the lab can tell me, pending an exact DNA match, is they came from a Caucasian male."

"Found in the sleeve button?"

"Yes." Terri cocked her head.

"Not Silverman?"

"Middle aged and Caucasian, but the initial DNA test says no." Terri picked up some papers from her desk and handed them to him.

"Do you think the seeds were cross-contamination from Silverman?" Bob asked.

"Probably. You might want to talk to Silverman again. I'll bet he found the arm and turned it over or picked it up. Arrowhead doesn't grow in Abington. The closest pond is Island Grove but that's groomed. The city goes in there and cleans out the pond every spring and periodically through the summer. Herbicides, I believe."

"It would turn into an overgrown swamp if they didn't?"

"Yup."

"Where does Arrowhead grow?"

"Big ponds, lakes."

"Like Long Pond?"

"That's what I'd think."

"And Silverman worked the lake all summer," Bob said as he looked through the reports Terri had handed him.

"Is Long Pond maintained?"

"I think the state is using herbicides but I wouldn't be surprised if the landowners were releasing carp. They eat the weeds, but its illegal. Carp are an invasive species and there are some big fishing tournaments on Long Pond. So what else do we know about Arrowhead?" Bob continued to flip pages of the report.

"Arrowhead is emergent. The roots grow in the soil, underwater, and the leaves and flowers only appear above the surface of the water."

"And Terrance spent the summer renting boats to tourists on the lake... Cross-contamination," Bob said.

"Also there were no fingerprints on the body. Nothing on the neck or clothing. I'm not terribly surprised. Remember I found a white fiber under a fingernail?"

"No."

"It turns out, it's a thin, light polyester. Most likely from a canvas tarp, jump suit or lab coat, like a mechanic or a house painter wears. Terrance had nothing like that and his background doesn't fit."

"Could they have used a tarp to carry the body?"

"And take it with them when they left?"

"Anything is possible." Bob leaned back against a lab table. "Let's assume they were smart. They would wear jumpsuits? Something to cover their clothing? They would wear gloves, so no fingerprints on the body or clothing. Hairnets or hats, baklavas rolled up like a hat."

"Anyone sees them, they look like house painters or handymen."

"Smart."

"Except one hair got away."

"Still the murderers could be mechanics or someone who worked in a machine shop?"

"Or Silverman could have sidelined as a boat mechanic? Wore overalls when working."

"Gray hair and a white thread? At least two people from the shoe prints."

"I'll guess the lack of fingerprints and the jumpsuit means someone went to a lot of trouble to make sure they didn't leave any traces of evidence." Terri's eyes grew worried.

"But they made a mistake with the hair?" Bob asked.

"Possibly, or it was planted for us to find."

"We could say the same about the seeds."

"That would be smart," Terri said.

Frank Wysup and Peter Jackson walked into the laboratory. Bob and Terri turned to them. "What did you find out on that Waldon kid? A skipped-out parolee?"

Peter answered, "Don't know about that yet but I found a photograph of Waldon with another kid. Looks like a teenager, high school, maybe. According to the house-mother Russell is the kid on the right. Matches his mug shots." Peter held out the photograph sealed in an evidence bag.

Bob looked at the picture. It was a photo-booth strip with four images. Two boys, both dark haired, Russell shallow faced and skinny, the other with rounded features, probably not from fat, were goofing off; giving the camera the finger, putting two fingers up behind the other's head, but the last picture was of the two boys kissing.

"Homosexual?" Bob asked.

"Just kid's. Who knows. They might of thought it was funny," Peter answered. Frank just shook his head.

"Run that down to the schools. Ask the superintendent and show it to some of the teachers. Make a copy and leave out the last picture. I want to know who that other kid is. Find out some details. You can ask the teachers about the homosexuality, if they know the kids. See if you can identify the boy on the left. That picture is inflammatory considering Waldon is a convicted pedophile. Scan it into a computer and edit out Waldon. Let's just try to find out who he's with. We don't need to be spreading rumors."

"Got it," Peter said.

Frank spoke up. "We found something else. There was a phone number."

"Did you trace it?"

"I called it from the half-way house telephone. Russell knew our train victim."

"Waldon had Spears' phone number?" Bob asked.

"Appears that way," answered Frank.

"Let's talk to the district attorney and get a subpoena on the telephone records for Waldon. If Waldon is a pedophile parolee and Spears was a pimp... Let's get a team back over there. Look for blood. Everything. Just like we did Spears' apartment."

"What's the justification? The D.A. will want to know," Frank Wysup asked.

"We are investigating the criminal activities of a reputed pimp and drug dealer, now a murder victim and a parolee who has, we can assume, skipped town. We can put them together by the phone number. That means Russell is potentially a male-prostitute and a person of interest in the murder of Spears. Keller will go with that and he should be able to get a judge to sign it. Let's try to find Mr. Russell Waldon. He just became my first suspect. Murder then jump parole."

"You think he did it?" A puzzled look came over Frank's face.

"Anything is possible," Bob answered. "Frank, can you take care of the paperwork and run it through the DA's office and the court? Let me know what you find out. I'll call Keller now and let him know you are going to get those search warrants." Frank and Peter both nodded. "Terri. How soon can you run those gray hairs through the FBI database?"

"I need final results from the lab, they can processes through the FBI. DNA takes weeks or months. I don't expect anything for a long time. It depends on their back log."

"We have time, if Mr. Waldon is a one-off killer. He won't kill again, unless he has a good reason. When you know, you let me know."

"The half-way house search will take all day," Frank said.

"We have time."

"By tomorrow Waldon could be halfway to Mexico."

"We'll find him. Get on that warrant and search his place. Let's find out who he knows and where he might be going. Ninety percent of the time the rabbit runs to a familiar hole. Let's find his family members... Associates."

They stood there looking at Bob. He sighed and said, "Go... Now."

Frank, Peter, and Terri gave a collective smile and turned to leave. As they went, Terri to her office, and Frank to a workstation upstairs, Bob put his hand on Peter's arm, holding him back. Peter turned but Bob waited until the others had left the lab.

"One more thing, and I'm guessing here, check with Homeland Security and pull an FBI Uniform Crime Report for Plymouth County."

"What are you thinking?"

"Let's agree that I'm interested in crime statistics."

A confused smile entered Peter's face. Bob added, "You might as well pull a report for all adjacent counties too. Bristol, Barnstable, Norfolk, even check out Dukes."

"Dukes? Martha's Vineyard?"

"And Nantucket."

Terri overheard the conversation from her office across the room. "What are you not telling us, boss."

"Every few years I like to see where we are. All the suburban growth causes crime to go up, we push it down, and I just like to keep track of it."

"He's lying," Peter said to Terri.

"I know, but he isn't going to tell us until he's sure," Terri replied as Bob laughed and walked away.

Before he closed the glass doors he said, "Peter? I want to know who's in that photograph also. Get me a copy, please."

Chapter 32

Bob heard his office door click closed. It startled him to find Peter had come in.

"What is it, Peter?" He looked up from his computer.

"Detective?"

Bob saw a dark look on Peter's face. He motioned to a chair and they both sat down. Bob waited for Peter.

"Detective. It's not my place to say this." Peter stopped. Bob patiently waited for the young officer to continue. "I can get fired for this."

"Depends on what you did."

"I didn't do anything."

"Then I don't see how you could be fired."

"Chain of command. Blue wall."

"There's no blue wall around here, Peter." Peter looked at Bob as if he was joking. "Seriously, Peter. If another officer did something you need to tell me."

"It wasn't an officer." Peter fell silent again.

"Are we going to play twenty questions?"

"I won't be fired?"

Bob leaned forward in his chair, leaning on his desk. "If this office was the kind of place that fired people for reporting crimes, would you really want to work here?"

"That doesn't help."

"Peter. You came in here. Something happened. I'm going to guess that it's either very wrong or illegal. What was it?"

"You see I'm not sure if I saw what I saw. If I am wrong I'm blaming someone for something they didn't do."

"And if you are right?"

"Then it's illegal."

"But you can't prove it, whatever *it* is?"

"No."

Bob sat back again and waited. Peter didn't continue. Finally Peter said, "When we were cleaning out Spears' apartment I thought I saw something."

"And?"

"Um... Wally and I were packing up the DVDs and the computer, and um... And Frank was in the bedroom packing up the video equipment. We ran out of box-tape so I went into the bedroom to see if Frank had any. I saw him put something in his pocket."

"What was it?"

"I don't know. That's the thing. I don't know if he really did put something in his pocket. I mean it could have been his keys, or a tool or something, or nothing at all. He was leaning over, half into the closet and he just kind of moved his arm under his coat and back out. It was probably nothing."

"Probably?"

"Maybe."

"Did he say anything?'

"No. He looked up. I asked for box-tape. He pointed to some on the floor."

"That's it?"

"It's nothing."

"If he did take something it's evidence."

"Why would he do that?"

"I don't know." Bob sat looking at Peter. "I'll find out. If it's nothing, we'll forget about it."

"If it's nothing I've falsely accused him of stealing."

"No you haven't. This is just between us. Okay?"

"Okay. Thank you Detective." Peter stood up and left very quickly.

Bob and Wally went up the road to the rooming house where the rest of the team was boxing up Russell's room. The house mom, Denise Ward, was visibly upset but Bob allayed her fears. After talking to her for a few minutes he went up to the room. Several boxes sealed and marked as evidence stood piled in the middle of the barren room. Terri and Peter filled boxes with clothing and Frank and Wally carried them down to a waiting cruiser. Only a bed and decrepit dresser remained. The closet was empty.

The house mom followed them into the room. "He didn't have much. Just a few clothes. I offered him some books. We have a nice library downstairs."

"No visitors?"

"None. No one ever asked for him until your deputy came along. Even the parole office never called. Russell had to call them every morning."

"Was he any trouble?"

"Never."

"No drugs? Alcohol?"

She shook her head.

"No calls?"

"The phone is for outgoing calls only. I limit my guests to five minutes. I have a timer by the phone downstairs."

"Any cell phones?"

"Not allowed, but they have 'em."

"What's his day like?" Bob asked.

"Gone by eight after calling his parole officer. Home by seven or seven-thirty most nights. Supposed to be home before dark. That's my rules, not the parole office. He'd go out on the weekends sometimes. Said he was at the mall or walking the park downtown."

"Do you know if he had any friends?"

"None. None I know of."

"I'm just the caretaker here. I try to keep the kids in line. No problems or trouble or they are out. They go back to jail. I've done it before and all my guests know about it. They don't play games with me."

"That's good to know." Bob smiled and looked at Terri and Peter. "Any blood?"

"Nothing. Just like Spears."

"Any papers? Phone books?"

"Mostly receipts. Some poems."

"Let's take a look back at the office."

Frank came up the stairs and looked around the room. Bob turned to him and asked, "Where are we at?"

"Done," Frank said. He took a cigarette out of a pack.

"No smoking in the house," the mom said.

Frank gave her a dirty look and put the cigarette away.

In his office Bob returned to the ever growing stack of paperwork that required daily attention. He'd been ignoring the work for days. Work schedules, patrols, warrants, escorts and reports called to him. Several hours later he rubbed his eyes, and closed his management applications in favor of the Firefox browser. From Google he looked up 'Abington murder' and clicked the news link. Nothing. 'Plymouth County Death,' same results. 'Eastern Massachusetts' returned dozens of the Boston greater area crime reports. 'South Shore' recalled a Brockton Fairgrounds attack.

Lakeville had an archived news report of the Rickman drowning. Over fix years ago Raynham reported the Richardson shotgun attack standing out from petty vandalism, burglary, theft, and robbery all-over and unrelated. There were vehicle thefts, a car jacking, and a short string of bank robberies. Repeating the searches for Cape Cod brought nothing except off-season house break-ins and woods and field fires suspected as arson. He worked late yet he felt he'd produced nothing.

Chapter 33

Bob tossed in his sleep. He spoke though his words were unintelligible. A phone rang. Default ring. An unknown number. Suddenly awake, he answered the call.

"Detective?" The diminutive voice of Amelia Houghton came over the line. "Detective?" she said again softer this time.

"Yeah. Just woke up."

"It's Amelia."

"Yes, Amelia. I recognize your voice."

She fell quiet as if waiting and listening.

"You called the office yesterday," Bob said as he looked at the clock. It was four in the morning. He felt Mary sit up in bed. She was awake.

"My father..." She hesitated.

Bob turned on his nightstand light, and grabbed a pen and paper.

"My father thinks Rickman was murdered."

"Did he say that?"

"No."

Silence followed.

"Do you think Rickman was killed?"

"Yes. But..." She didn't continue.

"What did your father say?" Bob prodded.

"When you came out a couple days ago it brought it all back." Bob heard her starting to cry. "He started saying things he hadn't said in years. Things I forgot about," she sobbed.

"Amelia? It's okay. Tell me what he said."

"Before he died, my dad said Rickman should be drowned. Drowned in the lake. Then afterwards, and now, he keeps saying stuff like how Rickman got what was coming to him. How he was no better than fish food. Rickman got what he deserved and it was karma. Like that..."

"Did he say he killed Rickman? Did he say anything about

actually committing a murder?"

"No."

"Did he say anything else?"

"Just like bible stuff."

"Like what?"

"I don't know."

"An eye for an eye?" Bob asked, knowing it might be considered leading a witness.

"No. Just things like, 'protecting your family,' and 'it's not *Thou shalt not kill*, but *Thou shalt not murder*.'"

The words reconfirmed Bob's thoughts that maybe Rickman had been murdered. Was Henry justifying the action as self-defense? Was he feeling guilty for killing a man, a man found innocent, or rather not proven guilty for lack of evidence? Had Houghton convinced himself Rickman was guilty? What parent would not value their child's word over that of a hired-hand? In the eyes of the law the rape didn't occur. At the least, the rapist was not Rickman, if it had occurred. Although Bob believed it had occurred when it did, and nothing had changed his opinion. Did Henry Houghton take justice into his own hands and now the guilt of his actions haunted him? Without evidence, was the tiniest bit of self-doubt growing to consume the man?

"What else did your father say?"

"That's it. That's a lot."

"Yes. It is."

"Are you going to arrest him?"

"Do you think he murdered Rickman?"

"Maybe."

"I will look into it. I'll figure out what happened."

"Okay."

"Thank you Amelia." His next words felt stale in his mouth, "If you think of anything else, please call me again." He hoped she would.

"You cannot tell him I called you," she pleaded and hung up.

Bob wrote several notes of the conversation on his pad before turning off the light and going back to sleep. He fell quickly into snoring that Mary, still awake, listened to for an hour. Then he started tossing and yelling in his sleep.

"Wake up," Mary said. "Hey. Wake up. It's just a dream. Bob, it's just a nightmare." Mary shook him as he slowly awoke.

"What happened?" he asked as he awoke to a cold sweat.

"You were yelling, 'I didn't rape your daughter. There was not enough evidence.'" Mary tried to soothe Bob's shivering arms.

Bob rubbed his face and thought for a moment. "I was drowning. I was a lifeless body in a lake. I haven't had nightmares since I was a kid."

"Now you've had one now. Who did you supposedly rape?"

Bob recalled Amelia's phone call and Tim Rickman drowning in Long Pond. "No one. What else was I saying?"

"I don't know. Something about, 'reopening the case', and you 'made certain', or 'made sure'."

"Made sure what?"

"I don't know. You didn't say what it was. You said something about, 'What does it mean?' and 'Rickman got what he deserved.'" Mary shook her head. "You said it all stiff. Like you were interviewing a suspect."

"Huh?" Bob asked.

"You said it," Mary said with a laugh. "It was just a dream. If this Spears' murder is bothering you, maybe you should talk about it."

"It's not Spears. It's the Rickman rape investigation four years back." Bob stared at the light and shadows of the darkened room.

"And?" Mary asked.

"Mary!" he exclaimed as he sat up in bed. Realization reflecting in his voice. He turned on a light and blinded them both. "Henry Houghton said, 'Rickman got what he deserved. I made...', but he didn't finish the statement. He was pushing the door closed on my foot. I got distracted. What did he make? I made... *something*. I made *certain*? I made *sure*?"

"I made *sure Rickman was dead*," Mary calmly answered. "Houghton killed Rickman."

Bob looked at her incredulously.

Mary continued, "I always thought he did it. I figured the

Houghton's killed Rickman."

"Why?"

"You couldn't prove Rickman raped Amelia. Houghton wanted revenge. Rickman was found in the lake. Houghton rents boats on the lake. It's motive. Rickman used to work for them. They live right up the road from the docks. It makes sense. Houghton figured if you can't, or couldn't, prove Rickman raped Amelia. That the water washed away evidence... then you wouldn't be able to prove Rickman was murdered. Or at least who murdered him."

"The autopsy said Rickman drowned."

"It was a mistake in the autopsy. I always figured Houghton murdered that guy anyway."

"You never told me that before."

"I never told you I thought Rickman raped that little girl either."

"He had motive, of course, and opportunity."

"And means." Mary laughed.

"And he had an alibi. Amelia. I wonder how strong her word is. They live together and work together... Maybe... circumstantial?"

Mary smiled. "You are always so concerned about the evidence you don't see the case. Rule of law. Got to have proof."

"I get suspicions and I act on them. The investigations produce evidence and then we pursue prosecutions."

"Just like that? All lined up like ducklings marching to the water?"

"Yeah. No..." Bob was embarrassed. Mary was the only one who ever had that effect on him.

"What is it then?" she asked with a sweet laugh as Bob's face grew red.

"I think you are right. He wanted me to reopen the rape case. Maybe we should reopen the Rickman-drowning also. If Rickman was murdered, we might be able to prove Houghton did it. I need to call Keller."

He turned in his bed and reached for the phone. Mary put her hand on his arm.

"It's five in the morning. The D.A. is asleep," she reminded him. "Let's go back to sleep for an hour."

But Bob didn't sleep. He got out of bed and wrote notes on his computer. He sent emails of his suspicion to D.A. Keller, and to Terri, and Captain Rudolph.

As Bob drove to the office he speed-dialed Keller on his phone. He switched to the speakerphone as he waited for the district attorney to pickup. He grimaced as a Vivaldi ring back tinged loudly. The call went to voice mail and Bob looked at his dashboard clock. It was ten after seven.

"David? It's Schwimer. Did you get my emails? I want to reopen the Tim Rickman Rape case from four years ago and I'd like to have the team review his accidental drowning in the lake. I'm not sure it was an accident and if this goes where I think it might, we'll want to exhume Rickman's body. I think we should revisit the autopsy on him. Call me back." Bob hung up the phone and became lost in thought. He arrived at the office before he realized it and he walked on autopilot into the lobby, until he saw Terri and James Sullivan.

"Good morning, Bob," they said in unison.

He greeted them saying, "Good morning. No coffee today. We have work to do. Terri?"

"What's going on this morning? I got some early emails from you."

"The murder case. You read them?" Bob said as he looked at James.

"Anything new on the pimp?" James asked.

"No," Bob said, not wanting to discuss that case at the moment. "Terri, we need to talk. Good morning James." Bob leaned in and shook James' hand. James took the hint and said goodbye and headed out the door, pulling his motorcycle helmet on as he went.

Bob and Terri were buzzed through the lobby door by Louise and headed into the break room. Bob stopped in the doorway. "None for me. I've had four already."

"So you were up sending emails early."

"And you must have been up early to be reading them."

"I'm a night bird. Working days makes me crazy. I prefer the silent darkness."

"Are you sure it's the 'days' and not the 'silent dead' that makes you crazy?"

"Yes. Wait. What?"

Bob laughed, "You said it. I didn't say it."

"Wait," Terri beckoned as Bob walked away.

"Meet me in my office," he said over his shoulder. "Find Peter and Wally first. I want them there too."

"What about Frank?" Terri asked.

Bob stopped and turned back to Terri. "Let's leave him out of this for now. I want to exhume Tim Rickman's body and Frank was the M.E. back then. I'd rather keep him out until I can talk to him in private. Maybe he missed something but I don't want him getting upset about this. We are all human and people make mistakes..."

"Okay. But... Tim who?"

"I'll explain everything. This was before your time. Closed-door meeting. If you see Frank, don't tell him anything... for now."

"If he finds out he's out of the loop he'll be furious."

"So make sure he doesn't know."

Twenty minutes later Wally and Terri walked into his office.

"Where's Peter?" Bob asked.

"He's taking prisoners to the court house."

"Forgot he had Transport today. Close the door. Terri, where are you on the Spears case?"

"Mostly wrapped up. Waiting for some test results." She pushed the door closed.

"You have time?"

"I need to go through the Spears and Waldon evidence again, but I can make time," Terri said.

"Okay. I want you to work on a cold case."

"What's up?"

"Have a seat..." When they were seated around Bob's desk, he opened a folder. One by one he leafed through dozens of pages of interview notes and evidence lists as he told Terri and Wally about how Tim Rickman couldn't be prosecuted for Amelia Houghton's rape. How the evidence was limited due to the girl's clothes being washed, how she was dumped in the lake, that a condom could have been used, that Rickman claimed to be at a bar at the time, that people in the bar swore he was there, but none could point the exact time he came or left or even if he was missing for a period of time, and finally how Rickman was later found dead in Long Pond.

"I remember that case," Wally said. "We couldn't prove Rickman did it and Rickman turns up dead? And Rickman worked for Henry Houghton renting boats, same as Terrance Silverman, our number one witness in the Spears' murder."

"Exactly my connection," said Bob as Terri looked on curiously. "I had virtually forgotten about that case until you and I went down there the other day. We went to confirm Silverman's summer employment. Simple as that."

"And he assaulted you. I knew we should have arrested him," Wally added.

"We didn't. And I'm glad we didn't and I'll tell you... Over the last few days something has been bothering me about Houghton's reaction to our visit. Then as I recalled the case some more I realized we needed to take another look at it; both the rape and Rickman's drowning. Terri, you know Frank was the M.E. and part-time coroner back then, just before we had that budget boost from the state." Bob closed the Amelia file and opened one labeled 'Rickman'.

"I remember coming on board and wondering why Frank was so grumpy. Figured he was just old."

"No. He was upset. He lost his dual responsibilities."

"And lost pay?"

"No. He kept his pay scale. He just wanted the work. Had a hard time giving up ownership of both jobs."

"I see, but this Rickman thing was before my time," Terri said.

"Shortly before, but not by much."

"And as M.E., Frank did the autopsy on Rickman and determined it was an accidental drowning?"

"Yes."

"Which is why he isn't here." Terri looked at Wally.

"Rickman drowning was suspicious too, but, as in the rape,

we couldn't prove Rickman was murdered. No witnesses. The autopsy report stated that Rickman probably slipped and fell overboard. He banged his head as he fell, probably on the side of the boat. He goes unconscious and drowns. Either he stopped breathing or he sucked water into his lungs. It's in the report. Either way he drowned."

"So why the sudden interest now? Do you think Rickman was murdered?" Wally asked.

"When we talked to Henry Houghton about Silverman, to verify his summer employment, Henry slammed the door on my foot. I had a dream about that last night."

"Bob. You've never said anything about dreams before." Terri's lips turned down. "Are you saying you had a premonition?"

"Not a premonition. It was more of a realization. I don't have it on tape. It's not even in my notes, but just as Henry slammed the door on my foot he said something. Do you remember what he was saying?" Bob asked Wally, who shook his head. "He said, 'Rickman got what he deserved. I made...' *something*. I don't think he finished what he was going to say. It was like he was admitting something but caught himself. He stopped himself before he could say it out loud, or maybe he was just caught in the heat of the moment. I remember it clearly, 'I made...', but what would someone say? What would you put there if you were him. I made, *'pancakes for breakfast'*?

"I made *certain Rickman was dead?*" Terri asked.

"Exactly. That's what Mary thinks he was going to say. I think he came close to admitting that he killed Tim Rickman. When I saw his face in the doorway I could see that four years haven't changed a day since Amelia was raped. Henry Houghton is still consumed with anger. I think he wanted revenge for his daughter's rape and he had a great place to hide a body and make it look like an accidental drowning." Bob closed the file for effect.

"Which is exactly what Frank determined?"

"That's what the autopsy says." Bob slapped his hand down on the cover.

"So you think it wasn't accidental?"

"I don't know. It could be… or it could be murder and the autopsy is wrong. People make mistakes."

"You said that in the hallway." Terri leaned on the arms of her chair, scowling, her eyebrows hooked and her gaze locked on Bob.

"I did. People make mistakes. Including me. Which is why we are here."

"You want to dig up Rickman and I get to perform a second autopsy." Her voice rose, almost gleefully.

"You might. Try not to sound too excited. He's been dead for four years."

Her smiled widened.

"That's not supposed to be a good thing," Wally added. A tinge of a smile grew on his square-set face.

Bob said. "I've got some calls into the D.A. and I want you two to handle the second autopsy. Wally you are leading the exhumation detail under the direction of Keller and myself. Terri, you get to cut. Don't say anything to Frank until I can talk to him first. That's not a question, it's an order."

Bob's phone rang, interrupting the meeting. Bob looked at the display. It was Sheriff Jasperse. "Hold on a second guys. Let me take this," he said as he picked up the phone. "Hello Sheriff."

"Hello Bob. I've got something for you."

"What's that?"

"I forgot to mention it. Didn't remember until I just got the results back. I got a call a few weeks ago about some bones found in a manure pile in Lakeville."

"Manure?" Bob asked.

"Yeah. They said it was an old horse they put down a few years ago."

"Who's that? Where?"

"That's what I forgot. You were asking about them a couple days ago."

"The Mulligans."

"Yes."

Bob grimaced that whatever Jasperse was about to say was probably pertinent to his visit to them.

"I'll back up for you. I got a call a couple weeks ago about these bones found in a manure compost pile. Someone over in Lakeville. Not anywhere near the Raynham place. A resident was spreading manure around his garden and came up with them. We sent the bones out for analysis and contacted the landscape company. It took some doing but they tracked the manure back to a horse farm in Raynham. I went over and interviewed them, the Mulligans: Shawn and Betty. We are going to take them in for questioning. I just wanted to let you know because you were asking about them. I thought I'd see what you found out on the Richardson murder. You asked about the Mulligans and their name is in the file."

"I met the Mulligans a couple days ago. They were less than helpful. They said something about a dead horse," Bob recalled.

"I let it pass. Focus on Richardson." Bob slowly realized that Jasperse was not being his usual crass self. He was professional and direct.

"The Mulligans told me the bones were from a horse they had put down. I let them slide while we waited for the FBI. Figured they weren't going anywhere. I guess the manure breaks the body down pretty fast and it doesn't hurt the gardens too much. So I had some DNA tests run. You know that new budget from the state. Got more money for our department than we've seen in years. Anyway the bones come back as human. So just for kicks, after you came out here a couple days ago I was thinking about the Joel Richardson murder, reviewing the file, and I contacted the lab again and had it run the DNA through the state database for missing persons."

"Joel was found in a city alleyway."

"He was. But they were one of a dozen of suspects in his murder. So after one murder, how much harder is it to kill again?"

"I can imagine." Bob recalled how he once put down a rabid dog that tried to attacked his horses. "Put it out of our misery."

"What's that?"

"Nothing. Go on."

"I didn't think it was Joel, of course not, but it got me thinking of who else might be missing or disappeared in town. So the state comes back with nothing. No match to any missing persons. This is a couple weeks ago. I kicked it to the D.A. and they're sitting on it. I forgot about the case until you came over, back burner. Just as a wild hunch I had something called fast-string matching done with the DNA. Something about short tandem-repeats," Jasperse continued.

"Then I had the state send the DNA over to the FBI. They compared it to the FBI crime records which came back negative. Got the preliminary report yesterday, but then this morning I get another phone call. The FBI ran the DNA through their missing persons list. It takes a little longer to do that. It turns out the bones are from a missing kid out of Barnstable County. Disappeared this past spring. I called Sheriff Anderson over there this morning and he said he would notify the family.

"Turns out they don't technically live in Barnstable. He wanted to talk to you. The kid and his family are from Plymouth County, your area. Some kind of mix-up with the Assessor's office records. They have the family living right on the county line, paying taxes to both counties."

"That's interesting," Bob said. "Who's the kid?"

"His name is Samuel Swanson. Teenager. Chubby, five-six, brown and brown."

"Who's the family?" Bob grabbed a pen and took some notes.

"The Swansons, out of Bournedale. Right on the county line. You ever heard of them?"

"No. Wouldn't have if they stayed out of trouble."

"I guess that's where the mix-up came from with the Assessor's office. You got some troubles with the 911 system?"

"Because of the county line?"

"Yeah."

"I've heard of it happening, but not around here. I'll look into it. Got some first names for me?"

"Cinda and Mark. So if you take care of the family I'll take care of the investigation over here. Looks like the Mulligans have a lot of explaining to do." Bob liked this new business-only side of Sheriff Jasperse.

"Keep me informed," Bob asked as he remembered the Mulligan's lack of cooperation with the Joel Richardson murder."

"I will. I just thought to call. Thought you ought to know cuz of your interest in the Richardson murder. You know I'll betcha cash they have a shotgun over there."

"Too bad shotgun shot can't be traced," Bob added.

"Bob, the internet is an amazing place. I just found an article on ballistics for shotguns."

"I never would have thought that could happen. Thanks Sheriff. You might be able to close two murders."

"True Bob. Talk *at* you later."

"Hold on Sheriff. Did you let Barnstable County know?"

"Yup. Talked to the Sheriff just before calling you. Anderson. That's his name. Know him from the Sheriff's association."

"I'll give them a call and let them know I'm heading over."

Jasperse hung up the phone as Bob brought up Google. He half-turned his chair towards Terri without taking his eyes off the computer screen.

"Get to work on that exhumation order for Rickman. Try not to have too much fun with this."

"I love my job."

"If the DA calls, I'll have him talk to you. Let him know what's going on. Wally, you are going with me to Bournedale."

"Okay. Can I ask why?"

"We got something on the Mulligans. Enough to hold them and question them. Let me do some research and we'll go."

"You are holding out again," Terri said with a laugh.

"There's another body," Bob replied grimly. Her face fell flat.

"Sorry."

"Don't be. You think it's cool anyway."

"That's just me."

Terri and Peter left the office and Bob looked up Cape Cod newspaper articles about the missing boy. The disappearance was in the crime section, alongside of a hay field fire and a barn fire. Bob tracked down the FBI missing persons report on Samuel Swanson and reviewed details on the family. After printing out copies of the report he turned back to the Cape Cod newspapers. Doing article keyword searches on the internet, he wrote several notes to himself on the printed pages.

He picked up the phone and dialed, waited, spoke to a receptionist, and he finally heard, "Yes?"

"Sheriff Anderson?"

"Yeah."

"Detective Schwimer with Plymouth."

"Good morning... ah... afternoon detective. I can assume this about the Bournedale boy?"

"Yes, sir. What can you tell me about it."

"If you talked to Jasperse, probably not much more than he told you. Samuel Swanson disappeared last spring. We looked everywhere for him. No trace. No family or extended family heard from him." Bob heard Anderson shuffling papers on his desk. "Some extended family was glad not to hear from him. No reports of hitchhikers being picked up on the roads, no reports of kidnappings, the dogs traced him to his bicycle missing from the garage and the trail ended there. He just got on his bike one day and rode away. No one has seen him since."

"Never found the bike?"

"Nope. If you find it, it's a silver Nishiki mountain bike."

"You said some family was glad he was gone?"

"Yeah. Relatives in the mid-west. Iowa. Knoxville. He spent a summer there two years ago. They said he was trouble. Running off. Hanging out with trouble makers. Causing problems."

"Two years ago? That would make him ten?"

"No last year. Eleven. That's right."

"That's still pretty young for wild."

"Some grow 'em young. We ran that down. They hadn't seen him. No one else had either. None of the trouble-maker-friends, unless they're lying. So it's not a runaway case. Jasperse said you are putting together a serial killer case."

"I don't know about a serial killer. I wouldn't call it that. We've got a handful of crimes that appear related."

"And it involves this Swanson kid and the Mulligan farm?"

"At this point *definitely*. Sheriff, If you don't mind I'd like to go over and talk to the parents in Bournedale."

"Do you want company?"

"I'd like you to send me over what you have on the kid."

"I can do that. I'll email the entire case-file right now."

"Thank you, Sheriff."

Chapter 34

Bob stood in the middle of a circle of dust. Bluebonnet trotted around him counter-clockwise on a long-line. He turned round and round to follow her, keeping his shoulders and eyes square to her croup. The morning sun was just starting to show through the trees, casting long shadows of the horse that circled around him.

He set aside an hour three or four days a week to train or ride their horses. He roped steers one or two Sundays a month and sometimes team-penned with Mary for fun. He felt the horses grounded him, to become intentionally distracted from his job and experience nature, return to a more base level of life and living.

He loved it. He'd worked for two years as a mounted cop in Boston, riding details by Fenway Park and the Red Sox games, Quincy Market, Faneuil Hall, and Boston Commons. He spent many cold nights patrolling near the Boston Gardens, the old name for the ever-name-changing home of the Boston Bruins and Celtics.

That was before the soulless number-crunchers disbanded the country's oldest Mounted Police unit. He'd moved to homicide after that, and then moved to Duxbury and their own private little horse farm.

He had named Bluebonnet after one of his favorite actors in one of his favorite movies; a western about the open range. An easygoing man who should not be mistaken for a wilting flower, much like the horse in front of him. Blue was tough and stubborn, but he knew there was a kind and willing horse somewhere inside her. It would take time.

He raised the lunge-whip in his right hand whenever she threatened to falter and drop down to a walk. He lowered the whip or bumped on the line with his left hand if she picked up her feet and appeared on the edge of cantering. Like working the gas on a car, he pushed her to the speed he wanted, keeping her moving, keeping her mind occupied with her job. And she had to work. All horses did better with daily exercise. Make them earn their keep, he told Mary. Give them a job. A job they are suited for, and they will thrive... and they did.

Mary suggested that he had been neglecting the horse's training for the last week; that Blue was still green and would be so for many more months. She thought that if he worked the horses he would be able to clear his mind and regain some perspective on the murder cases. Bob thought Mary correct. She also reminded him not to risk getting bucked off again, for a while.

He let Blue slow with a soft verbal, "Easy," and a slight shift of his shoulders and turn of his head to the right, taking pressure off her and letting her slow down a gait. She walked around in three circles.

Bob put his eyes in front of her, turned his entire frame to adjust and said, "Whoa."

Blue immediately stopped. Instinctively she recognized humans as predators. Through training, Bob made her see that he was not to be feared, but was to be respected.

He said, "Reverse," in a sharp and clear voice. He switched the whip from right hand to left. The nylon long-line switched to his right hand.

Blue knew the command. She turned to Bob and around to face his right and she started walking again.

"Trot," he ordered and the horse complied.

"Whoa!" someone yelled and Bob was caught by surprise. Blue spun around at the sudden new voice. Bob wondered why she had not sensed the person sooner, as most horses will.

"Whoa!" the command came again as four young men jumped over the fence into the arena. They spread out around him, encircling him.

Bob dropped the long-line and let his right hand move to his waist. He realized that he never carried his firearm when working horses. That would have to change.

The men laughed as Blue ran free, dragging twenty feet of

line behind her. Bob looked from one man to the next. They wore black t-shirts, one with the sleeves cut-off. Various logo's stated their interest in martial arts and street fighting. One man, the biggest and thick-necked, wore a tight t-shirt stating 'Ultimate Boxing'. Tattoos emblazoned his black skin. Bob guessed that he sported over 220 pounds of muscle and sinew. The man's arms hung as if muscle bound.

All but one wore fighting gloves, meant to hurt the target and protect the weapon. The smallest man had his knuckles taped-up. He was skinnier than the others, almost scrawny, and maybe Asian or Pacific Islander. He bore close resemblance to a rat; a rat with Bruce Lee muscles.

Bob knew that his regular work-outs and his horse training kept him fit and strong, but he knew he was no match for these four thugs.

The big one said, "Back off."

"Glad too," Bob replied with a cocky grin. He backed away from the men but they continued to encircle him. They punched the air, warming up for the main bout.

"Got a sense of humor."

"I think so." Bob pondered a break for the fence and watched for a spot to open. He wondered if he could clear the fence and get to the house before they caught him. He thought about going for the barn, which was closer. A metal hay-fork would give him a lethal defense.

"Back off."

"I understand that part." Bob raised the whip and cracked it in the air.

"Look guys. He's got a fly swatter."

Bob knew the horse whip stung as he'd accidentally hit himself once or twice, but the whip was only a mild threat and these thugs seemed to have experienced worse in the ring. Bluebonnet ran a full circle of the arena, distracting the men for fear of getting run over.

"I'm telling you to let off," the big man said as he watched the horse run by.

Bob knew they were not talking about horse training. He wondered what interest this guy had in police work... besides being on the wrong side.

"Who hired you?" Bob asked.

The scrawny guy ran in behind Bob and punched him in the kidneys. Bob's back arched as he twisted sideways.

He saw one of the middleweight fighters coming in for an attack and he struck his fist upwards and under the man's chin. The jaw slammed closed and knocked his whole head backwards, as a gloved fist connected with Bob's left eye.

The big one stood aside and watched his men do the dirty work. He was probably saving his own strength for when Bob was beaten down, and he would deliver the coup-de-grace. Bob felt blow after blow land on his sides, back, gut and face. He blocked one or two attacks and he landed a lucky punch. An attacker struck a crippling kick to Bob's inner thigh. He went down. Blood filled his eyes. Anger wracked his mind. Pain flooded his body as kicks and punches viciously met their targets.

He heard a gunshot and realized he was still alive. *Mary*, he thought. He heard the slide of a shotgun rack another round into the chamber.

"Gun!" one of the thugs yelled.

"Get out!" Mary ordered. "Now."

Bob looked up to see the thugs running for the far fence. As one of them topped the fence Mary let loose another blast. Bird shot peppered his backside. The man fell forward off the top of the fence, landed on his face, and was helped up and away by his friends.

Mary ran to Bob's side as he slowly got up.

"What did they want?" Mary asked.

"I don't know," Bob said as he reached for the shotgun. Mary handed it to him. He pumped another round into the chamber and watched the woods at the back of their pasture. The men were gone. Probably parked on the next street over and soon they would be miles away.

"I'll call 911," Mary said.

"No. Too late. Thank you for the rescue." Bob let Mary slide an arm under his as she helped him walk to the house. His right leg cramped as they went.

"They were going to kill you."

"No. I think they were sending a message." He felt around his mouth with his tongue at a loose tooth. He spit blood into the grass. They went into the house.

"You know," Mary said impishly as he settled into a kitchen chair and she wet a dish towel. "Every time you train that horse you end up in the dirt."

"Not the horse's fault."

"Not this time."

"Not the other times either."

"She's stubborn," Mary said.

"She'll eventually understand her job," Bob replied

"If you live long enough."

"That's another matter..."

"I wish you'd hire a trainer. Get someone to buck her out for you. At least that." Mary started to wipe the dirt from Bob's face.

"I'll consider it." Bob took the towel from her.

"No, you won't." Mary laughed.

Chapter 35

Bob's desk intercom clicked in his office as he limped up the hallway. He walked slightly hunched shouldered from bruised ribs. He heard Louise's voice and he quickened his step. Missing the call, he went past his office to the lobby beyond.

"Hello Louise," he said as he opened the glass door. Louise sat at the reception desk behind a bullet proof window facing the lobby. Her graying brunette curls shimmered as she turned to greet him.

"Hello Detective. I just got a call in from a woman over on Eighth Street, says she saw a kid get kidnapped yesterday. Might be that Russell Waldon kid that Sally Sonders called in about?"

"You don't listen in on my calls, do you?" Bob joked.

"I just pay attention to details. It's my job."

"And you are good at your job." Bob watched Louise surreptitiously put her hand on a Dick Francis mystery novel and push it further under the computer monitor. She pealed a post-it note from the corner of her monitor.

"You are embarrassing me."

"That's not my intention. What have you got?"

Louise read the post-it, "She's ah... Pearl Hoffman. Got a phone number and address. She just called in so you should be able to reach her."

"Thank you. Can you get a hold of Wally? Give him the address and have him meet me over there." Bob turned to the photocopier but Louise interrupted him.

"I have a copy in the log already. That's your copy."

"You are looking for a raise, aren't you?"

Louise laughed and waved him away.

Bob met Wally at Pearl Hoffman's address on Eighth Street. They talked on the sidewalk, beside their cars. Bob could tell

Wally was trying to withhold his questions about the black eye darkening on his face and his overly stiff movements. He told the Sergeant what happened.

"Anything broken?" Wally asked.

"Pride."

"It builds character."

"I've got enough of that."

"*Back off*? That's all they said?"

"I think we are getting close to something someone doesn't want uncovered."

"What? The murders? Who?"

"When we know who, we'll have them. Russell Waldon getting kidnapped means he didn't murder Spears."

"You said they wore boxing shirts?"

"There's probably hundreds of boxing gyms, martial arts studios, and fitness clubs on the South Shore."

"Hospitals."

"There'll be a report if they're dumb enough to get a doctor to pull that birdshot out of the guy's back."

"What'd they look like?"

"One guy had a shirt with the logo for Ultimate Boxing on it. Big guy, a black guy, lots of tattoos."

"A black guy did it?"

"Not funny," Bob said and after a minute of dark silence he added, "A little Asian thug too."

"That narrows it down." Wally laughed.

"Still not funny."

"It's a little funny."

"Someone hired them. All they said was to back off. It's like they were told to rough me up a bit and tell me to leave things alone."

"But we don't know which thing to leave alone."

"And I'm not going to leave any of them alone."

"You're going to find them."

Bob grinned through the stiffness and pain. "Do you want to know what we're doing right now?"

"Absolutely."

"Recognize the area?" Bob asked.

"Half my domestic violence calls."

"Anything else..."

"Simmons. Just up the road."

"It's a small world and..." Bob pointed to a house. "We got a witness to an abduction."

An elderly lady wearing a peach sundress stood on a porch across the street and waved them over. As Bob climbed the steps to the porch the elderly woman held the screen door open and shooed them inside saying, "In. In. Quickly." As she let the screen door slam she said, "This neighborhood isn't as safe as it once was. I don't want the neighbors to see me conspiring with the police." Bob and Wally smirked.

"Oh. It's nothing to laugh about. I could be in serious trouble." She went to a window and peered out.

"I'm sorry to frighten you. That's not our intent," Bob said.

"Oh. They don't bother me that much. I have a shotgun."

Bob introduced them both while Wally looked around for the named firearm.

"I'm Pearl. My friends call me *Minnie* as in Minnie Pearl. What a wonderful hoot she was. Do you remember her?"

"Yes," Bob said. "Minnie? What can you tell us?"

"Oh. Today is beautiful. Beautiful morning. I love the autumn, don't you?"

"Yes. But to the point, did you see some criminal activity the other day?"

"Oh yes. I see everything. I see a lot from my front window. I stay inside because of it, but I see it all. It used to be I could sit on my front porch and have days and days go by and nobody would do anything illegal. Nothing. For days. Then, someone would mow their lawn before seven a.m. Oh, did I catch them. Sometimes the kids would play in the street. It's very dangerous you know. I was very glad to see they made that illegal. I used to go talk to the parents. I know everyone. Everyone. But that was before things changed. Before Harold died."

Bob looked at Wally, his face grim. "Was Harold your husband?"

"Harold? He's gone several years now. There's not a day I don't miss him."

"Sorry for your loss."

"Think nothing of it. It was a blessing in disguise."

"Was he very sick?"

"Yes. For too long. Would you like some tea or coffee?"

"No, ma'am," Bob said. "Do you remember a kid on a bicycle yesterday? Something about a white van?"

"Oh yes. I was sitting right here by the living room window and watching the people speed off to work. I saw that pedophile boy riding his bicycle down the sidewalk, just like he is not supposed to, just like every morning a little after eight o'clock."

"Did you say pedophile?" Bob interrupted her.

"Oh yes."

"How do you know he's a pedophile?"

"Everyone knows that. He's a registered sex offender. It's on the internet. Don't tell me you don't have the internet. So many of my friends don't know how to use a computer. It's a shame really."

Bob was both shocked and amazed by Minnie. "Go on..."

"Well, Um... I teach some of the old folks down at the retirement center. I teach them to use Google and setup email accounts. That's how they keep in touch with their kids and grand kids."

Bob tried as hard as he could to stifle his laughter, "Continue about the pedophile riding his bicycle on the sidewalk."

"Oh. Just like every morning. You should arrest him. It's illegal. I looked it up."

"What happened to him?"

"Well, let's see... He was riding in front of the Delvechio house across the street and a white van pulled out of the driveway right in front of him. I thought they were going to run him over but they stopped. I was so scared I got up and yelled but I don't think they heard me. It's a good thing because two big men jumped out of the van. They grabbed that pedophile kid and pulled him off his bike. Then they dragged him into the van and drove off like crazy. They left his bicycle lying on the sidewalk."

"Is the bicycle still there? We couldn't see it."

"Oh. No. No. I went outside to watch the van go down the street but it was gone around the corner on Main Street. Just then my tea kettle started whistling and I went and made some tea. I guess I lost track of the time because the bicycle was gone this morning and that's when I decided to call the police."

"You waited until you saw the bicycle was missing."

"Oh yes. When I saw the bicycle was gone. That didn't seem right."

"Why not yesterday, when the van raced away?"

"Well, I guess, it wasn't something *that* odd."

"A kid getting kidnapped wasn't odd?" Wally asked.

"I understand," Bob interrupted Wally. "I'm glad you called us. Could you identify the men if you saw them again?"

"They were pretty far away and they grabbed him really fast. They wore white clothing and white hats. I remember because the van was white too. I thought they might be painters. That old house is run down. I saw them a few days ago driving up and down the street and they stopped right in front of the Delvechio place and they got out. They weren't wearing white then. One wore a t-shirt and jeans and the other wore a suit."

"What kind of suit? A jumpsuit? A business suit?"

"Business… They only stayed a few minutes so when they came back this morning I figured they were going to paint that old place. It's been empty and abandoned so long I was glad to see that someone was going to fix it up."

"What about the van? Did it have any markings on it? You didn't get a license plate number, did you?"

"Oh. No. No. It was too far away. It was just white. My old eyes don't work as well as they used to. My mind is sharp as a whip though. I knew there would be trouble when that child molester moved in down the street."

"What happened to the bicycle?"

"It was gone. Someone must have taken it. I was going to call the city to have it taken away as trash. Maybe someone stole it. I didn't see."

Bob handed Minnie a business card, "That's my number and my email address is on there. Thank you for calling us. If you think of anything else please let me know."

"I will Detective, and thank you. You guys do a great job. You and Sergeant Young."

Chapter 36

Sergeant Wally Young pulled his patrol car into the parking lot of Stoney's Mill. He was dressed in his street clothes, being off-duty and on his way home. He knew Stoney's Mill and a few times a year, when he was bored with the other taverns and bars, he stopped in for a few beers before going home. Tonight he was curious of the bar and the far table where Spears and the unknown suspect had sat drinking and arguing. As he approached the tavern his chapped lips told him he was thirsty and his growling gut told him he was hungry. It wouldn't hurt him to get a bite to eat and try a few samples of the latest micro-brews before heading out for a serious bout of drinking later.

The bar was packed but he didn't recognize anyone. He bought a beer from the bartender. It must have been Harry's brother, but Wally didn't introduce himself. He left a good tip and dropped himself into a dark booth by the restrooms. The Spears booth was occupied. As he lifted the bottle he heard whispering from behind him, that last booth. It wasn't the talking that caught his attention. It was the whispering. People without something to hide never whispered. Probably just gossiping or telling a dirty joke, Wally thought. Then the words came clear as a level of excitement rose in the voices. He listened intently.

"What did we do?"

"What do you mean?"

"What are we doing? This is crazy."

"Two problems were taken care of. Not a bad bit of work."

"The problem is appearances."

"Appears pretty good to me."

"Not to me. What about the police?"

"They don't know anything. The more we handle these problems ourselves the things are."

Wally could have agreed with the guy. People needed to handle their own problems instead of running to the police all the time, as long as the solution wasn't illegal. He wanted to hear more about this shady business deal, maybe he was hearing a bit of the gossip people never tell a cop, even a cop who is a friend or relative. The men's voices sank to an even lower whisper than before.

The waitress came to check on Wally's beer and he ordered a second one. She moved to the other table where the two men ordered another round of drinks; sapphire gin and tonic and a black velvet whiskey straight-up. Wally knew now the table was occupied by an older businessman and a roughneck man, probably a redneck.

"We got a bonus," The redneck continued when the waitress left the table.

"No, we didn't," the businessman disagreed. "There's too many questions. Too much interest."

"Let them ask and let them talk."

"You don't have anything to lose. I've got a child. I have a business."

"I have a lot to lose. I have a farm and family and a business of my own."

"It was supposed to be one transaction a year. Never more," the businessman said as a glass landed hard on the table.

"So they can call it an investment in the community, rogue reactions, whatever. It isn't if it's good for everyone."

"It's not an investment."

"We call it an investment and that's what it is."

"We all agreed as a group. We are all supposed to agree as a partnership. We all get a vote. We can't have this publicity." Wally heard the businessman nervously stirring the ice in his glass.

"Look, you came into this operation with open eyes. You knew what we do and how we do it and you got your own profits," the redneck said.

"Profits too late are not a profit."

"Quiet. We don't need... You called this little meeting. I never should have come. Listen, we are going to have a meeting in a few days. All of us are going to..."

A cell phone rang. The phone rang a second and third time while someone fumbled to answer the call.

The redneck raised his voice as everyone does on the phone, "Hello? Okay... Yeah... I'll see you soon." Wally heard the phone land on the table. "That's the old battleaxe. I've gotta go," he said. "See you in a few days. Remember the big meeting."

Wally was struck with an idea. He whipped his cell phone from his belt and clicked the camera button. As the man walked by his table, Wally snapped a picture. He watched the man leave the bar as he saved the image on the phone. It was blurry. Probably unidentifiable.

The man wore a flannel lumberjack shirt and jeans. He was probably late-thirties to late-forties and stout, football player stout, but not tall enough.

Wally waited several more minutes, sipping his beer and listening intently to the older man in the booth behind him stirring the ice in his glass. A few minutes later the older-businessman spoke. "Yes, honey... I'll be home soon... I had a meeting. Just got out and headed back now."

The waitress brought Wally his beer. He thanked her and handed her a twenty dollar bill. While she moved to the next table and placed the drinks down, Wally got up and walked to the restroom. He palmed his cell phone and snapped a picture of the businessman. He looked quickly and then away as he walked by. The man wore a business suit, expensive... maybe a lawyer, or a high commission sales executive.

In the restroom he looked at the images. They were fuzzy and dark but the lab might be able to clear them up. He smiled as he realized that Bob might be interested in a little business corruption. It might break the routine of murders and kidnappings. It might even get him a raise.

He waited several minutes in the restroom, biding his time to make it look good. When he finally left the restroom the Spears' booth sat empty. Disappointed in a lost second look at the man, he was excited still and his appetite for food sank. He realized his thirst was undiminished. He ordered another beer.

Chapter 37

Bob filled Wally in on the details he had studied from Sheriff Anderson's email. "It turns out this Samuel Swanson kid disappeared last June and the interesting thing is that there were a lot of Barnstable County fires over the last year." Bob turned the wheel onto the cloverleaf for Route 3 to Cape Cod, the Pilgrim's Highway. As he righted the wheel and accelerated he continued, "It looks like the fires stopped right around the time this Swanson kid disappeared."

"So you think the kid was an arsonist?" Wally asked.

"He spent last summer in Knoxville, Iowa. The uncle and aunt said he was a lot of trouble over there and they weren't too broke up that the kid disappeared. They didn't tell the parents that, of course, but they admitted it to Anderson. Do you want to guess how many unexplained fires they had in Iowa last summer?"

"Another troubled kid causing trouble. Let me guess," Wally said. "A drug dealer and an arsonist both dead. We've got horses and puppies being killed on a farm where one of the bodies shows up. We've got a drug-dealing-pimp-pornographer murdered and the body is made to look like a train accident..."

Bob added, "Or maybe they thought the coyotes would take care of it."

"And a shotgun murder in Raynham three years ago."

"Which leads back to the Mulligans' farm. Plus we have a dead rapist from four years ago floating in the lake." Bob nodded.

"Is this looking more like vigilantes?" Wally asked.

"Careful ones. Adult sociopaths killing teenage sociopaths? What's the annual murder rate here in Plymouth?"

"The town of Plymouth? Zero. Eastern Plymouth County? Almost zero." Wally turned and looked out the window. "Last murder case we had locally was what, two years ago? A jilted husband and a bottle of whiskey… case closed."

"And for all of Plymouth County?"

"Except the greater Brockton area? Less than one per year. Including greater Brockton, maybe ten or fifteen per year, still just about the national average for a city."

"I'll bet Bristol County and Barnstable County are not too different. How many crop fires do we have?"

"Woods fires?" Wally asked.

"Or fields or bogs."

"Cranberry bogs don't burn unless it's on purpose."

"Those days are gone. No one burns a bog anymore." Bob continued, "My grandfather caught himself on fire one time, back in the seventies, burning a cranberry bog. Got gasoline on his pants."

"Nasty." Wally frowned.

"He was using one of those antique blow touches. The one's you see in the Three Stooges."

"Nothing funny about that."

"So we have kids setting off fireworks in the woods. An occasional dumpster fire. But hay fields? Corn fields? Barn fires? There were two articles about arson in the same newspaper that reported this kid missing. Several more fires reported in the weeks before."

"Arson."

"How many woods or field fires normally? None? One? Due to lightning strikes or teenagers having a bonfire? I counted seven on Cape Cod. Fields, woods, and barn fires since last spring. The last fire was at a grain and feed store. They all stopped the day Samuel Swanson disappeared. The family thought he might of run-away. He was in and out of trouble for the last three of his thirteen years."

"And they all stop the day this kid disappears?" Wally asked. "Sounds just like Joel Richardson. Dogs stop disappearing the day he was killed."

"The Mulligans are the first suspects now for Joel and Samuel."

"I hate to think this…" Wally mused.

"What?"

"Why not let them go. Sounds like they did the world a good turn. Two or three fewer psychopaths in the world..."

"Five or six, maybe more? I've considered the same thing," Bob said. "I even thought it in Boston when drug dealers kill drug dealers. The only problem is if someone takes to being a judge and executioner on their own, who judges them? Who stops the killers when an innocent person gets in the way by accident?"

"I get it. It was just a thought."

"One I think of myself."

"Do you still think there's a connection to the lake?"

"Houghton's and Silverman? The Mulligans don't have any connection to the lake. I think Silverman was in the wrong place at the wrong time, both in the Raynham alleyway and Abington. Lakeville renting boats is just a coincidence."

"And Rickman was murdered for revenge?"

"If there's a vigilante out there who is murdering kids, then who killed Spears and Rickman?"

"I'm not sure, but we have the Rickman drowning case reopened. The D.A. will pull an exhumation order. I'll bet there's a connection and I'll be damned if I don't find it. You kill a rapist, then a couple sociopath kids. What's a drug dealer to them? Nothing. No problem. They got away with the murders. Across county lines. Doesn't draw in the Plymouth Sheriff's office. Why not abduct a pedophile. Scum of the earth. Must be okay if the others were okay."

"Almost like they got permission. Then it's alright."

"Pushing the line. Except it isn't right. They got cocky. The Mulligans."

"And who else?"

"I'll bet my badge there's more to all this... The Mulligans aren't acting alone. Houghton's first on the Rickman list, but there's a connection. There has to be. We just have to find it."

"The way they're taking badges around here you should be careful." Wally joked at Sheriff Barton's departure.

Bob didn't laugh.

They turned off the highway and up the road to the

Swanson house. The family lived in an old bedroom community surrounded by woods, some working colonial-era farms, others defunct. Bob hated talking to parents of missing children. It was a part of his Boston job he didn't miss. Living in the country had its advantages; Lower crime than in the city, fewer missing persons, half of which were drunks or homeless, not as many shootings and murder.

"... except people moving out of the city to escape the crime are bringing the crime with them."

"What's that?" Wally asked.

"Nothing," answered Bob. He didn't realize he had spoken aloud. "I think we should stop into that feed store that burned on the way back."

"What's with them?"

"I just want to see how bad the damage was and where they are on rebuilding. It wouldn't hurt anyway."

"Good will and sympathies?" Wally asked, but Bob didn't answer.

"You know," Wally said, continuing their earlier conversation. "If they murdered one kid a year, they might have actually got away with it. What bother's me is how does a kid missing from Barnstable County end up in a Bristol County manure pile?"

"Could have been friend's with Joel. The Mulligans could have had a barn fire, but I'd guess they would have mentioned it in their tirade. Maybe, or maybe they have friends who were an arson victim."

"We will find out," Wally added as they pulled into the Swanson driveway.

A woman in a flower print house-dress answered the door when they knocked.

"Good morning," Bob said.

"Good morning?" she replied with a question in her voice.

"I'm Detective Robert Schwimer. This is Sergeant Young. Are you Cinda Swanson?"

The woman started visibly shaking. She nodded her head and her fear stole her voice. Bob saw her eyes starting to roll backwards. He stepped swiftly into the doorway and caught her by the arm.

"It's okay. Mrs. Swanson? It's okay. Wally..." Bob called as her knees started to buckle. Her face flushed pale white as her blood stopped flowing. Wally grabbed her other arm and together they kept the woman upright.

She recovered her senses as quickly as she had fainted, and she found her feet once more. Bob and Wally slowly took their hands away.

"Are you okay?"

"Yes, yes." She looked at Bob and Wally.

"You are the police?"

"Yes. County Sheriff's office. You almost fainted."

"I'm sorry. Sorry."

"It's okay. Are you okay?"

"Yes. I'm so embarrassed."

"There's no need to be," Bob assured her. "Can we come inside?"

"Yes. Of course." She stepped back to let them enter.

Bob watched the woman closely. He knew she nearly fainted because she knew why they were there. Probably the last time she saw any cops was when her son disappeared. He spoke his next words carefully. "We need to talk to you about..."

"Sammy." Mrs. Swanson finished Bob's sentence. "Come in."

"Thank you," Bob said as Wally nodded and stepped inside the house. They stood in the entryway as she did not indicate where they should go. Cinda's shaking slowed and she looked at them with trepidation.

"This is not easy," Bob started again. With these words Cinda began to shake even more and then she cried in dismay. Not the slow tears of a sad movie. She sobbed. Tears lined her cheeks and she sniffled at the droplets running to her lips. The sob sank deeper until a moan rose from the depths of her being. Wally was prepared to catch her if she fainted again.

"I'm sorry," was all that Bob could say between her long howls. He immediately felt both foolish and lost. No words came to him. He put out his arms and she fell into him crying into his chest. Wally crossed into the living room and took a box of tissues off the coffee table.

"Tha... thank you." Her sobs continued as he handed her a tissue. She stood back, her face flushed red. She wiped tears from her eyes.

"Is your husband here?" Bob asked.

She shook her head and patted a tissue to her tears as she said what Bob couldn't, "Sammy is dead."

He hated himself for her words, and wondered why he didn't let the Barnstable Sheriff Anderson, or even Jasperse, himself, come here. "The sheriff over in Bristol County found your son's remains. We, ah... Sheriff Jasperse has some suspects in custody and they're being questioned." Bob fell silent.

He had given this same talk dozens of times in Boston and he never knew what to say. He knew what the parents of a missing child always wanted to hear; that their son or daughter was found in some distant city, alive and well and staying with relatives, or riding on a bus toward home, or better, waiting in the police car in the driveway. In his years as a Boston cop he delivered good news of a found child on a single occasion, and the family was very upset to hear their minor daughter was picked up for prostitution, instead of being happy to hear she was alive.

"I knew he was dead," Cinda said as her shaking subsided and her tears dried. "Mark insisted he was alive. I knew it."

"I'm sorry." Bob repeated himself as his face flushed red with his own embarrassment at his continued loss of words.

"What happened to him?"

"Sheriff Jasperse is looking into it."

"He was just a boy. He was my baby."

"I know. I'd like to ask you about him. I'd like to know who his friends were, who might have wanted to hurt him. Can you give me any of that information? I know this is hard."

"A detective asked me that last spring."

"Barnstable?"

"I guess so."

"We are from Plymouth County. I'll be in touch with the sheriff over there... over here... But we'd like to help with the investigation. It seems your property sits on the county line."

"I know. We've been paying taxes to both counties for years. Neither county provides us services, too far from town, but both collect taxes. It's frustrating."

"I can understand, but let me assure you, you have our attention."

"That doesn't matter," Cinda said. "I have a notebook." She turned and left the hallway. Over her shoulder she said, "Why don't you sit in here."

Bob and Wally walked down the hall into a den where they stood waiting for Cinda to return. The room was decorated in antique Americana quilts, painted tables, embroidered wall hangings. The common theme was fishing boats and harbor views, mostly of Cape Cod. Cinda returned with a large spiral bound notebook. It overflowed with scraps of paper and photographs. She handed it to Bob. Cinda sat on a couch while Bob and Wally took overstuffed armchairs and leaned forward onto the edge of their seats.

Several photographs fell out as he opened it. Picking them up he realized he was seeing Samuel Swanson for the first time. The boy was eight or nine in the pictures. He wore untucked tee-shirts and long shorts. What struck Bob most was the lack of any expression on the boy's pudgy face. He placed the photographs on the table and flipped through the notebook. The writing was in a woman's script and it appeared to be a diary written in reverse. Sort of a biography of the boy. As Bob read the entries he realized it was written as much about the boy as about Cinda. One of the passages read:

> *Mid-February Sammy and I went out walking in the snow one day. He has always hated the snow and I had to promise him hot chocolate when we got back. We had a great time making a snowman in the back field and having a snowball fight. I told him we would go skiing in the spring but forgot he didn't like skiing. He chastised me pretty bad but I let it pass. He left for several hours that afternoon. I remember because there was a barn fire in Barnstable County on the news that night and Sammy was talking about*

it.

Bob looked up at Cinda, "Can I keep this? I'll make a copy of it, but I think this is a good start for figuring out what happened to your boy."

"Of course. I wrote everything I could remember about Sammy in there from his birth to his disappearance."

"That will be very helpful. Thank you. Did he have any friends from school or the neighborhood?"

"None. He didn't make friends easily."

Bob nodded. He looked at Wally, who fidgeted in his chair, looking very uncomfortable. He turned to Cinda and looked her in the eyes. "We won't take too much of your time. I'll look this over and I will get back with you. Here's my card if you need to call me, Sheriff Jasperse will have more information about..." He paused to frame his words. "...for making arrangements."

Bob handed her a card from his shirt pocket and Cinda took it without a word. She saw them to the door and closed it, not responding to their farewells.

As they got into the car Wally said, "I hope the rest of the day is better than that."

"Is this your first time with a grieving parent?"

"In twenty years as a cop I've never done that and I hope I never have to again."

"It gets easier," Bob lied.

"When?" Wally asked

"I'll let you know. That's just what the psychologists keep saying in all those police magazines."

Chapter 38

They drove in silence over the unimaginatively name Bourne Bridge that spanned the Cape Cod Canal, and into the center of town. They ate bagel sandwiches at a little deli. Bob was lost in thought and Wally gave him his space.

Finally, as they headed back to the car, Bob spoke again, "I've been doing this job for over ten years and I've never had something like this."

Bob stopped and stared into space. "I've had lots of dead bodies, lot's of cases of drug dealers, prostitution, revenge killings, turf wars, rapists, and all manner of scum. I've seen things so horrible I can't even mention them to my wife. Even when the ghosts come back to haunt me I can't tell her a word of them."

"I know," Wally added. "I saw a car accident once that cut a girl in half. I couldn't hold it in. It was killing me. My wife asked over and over what was wrong and in a weak moment I'd give everything in the world to take back, I told her." As they got in the car he said, "I swear to this day that was the beginning of the end of my marriage."

"I've never seen anything like this in my entire career. All that trash. Adults acting like children because they can. I've never seen vigilantes, adults, full-grown, intentionally kidnap and murder children."

"Do you know in prison even pedophiles have to be segregated or someone will off-them?" Wally said.

"We've got someone out here killing children. Children who drown puppies and burn barns."

"Richardson and Swanson."

"It starts with a rapist, twenty years old. Then a teenager. Then a child, barely teen-age." Bob started the car.

"Spears wasn't exactly a child, mid-twenties."

"Russell Waldon is an ex-con child-molester, nineteen years old. Almost a child himself." Bob turned the car out of the parking lot and towards the canal.

"Remember when people had a fuss over the courts trying children as adults?"

"Yes. Now they want death penalties for minor-aged murder convicts." Bob finished Wally's thought.

"Even cowboys have to cull the herd once in a while."

"We are not cowboys. Do you approve of vigilantes?" Bob knew Wally well enough that he wished he hadn't asked that question.

"No. But I understand them," Wally answered anyway.

"I can't say I understand them. I can understand they feel justified." Bob turned the car into the Bridger's tack and feed store. Masons had patched new cinderblocks along the top row of a wall. Half the roof was missing over the loading docks. A sign in the glass door at the front indicated that the retail store was open for business during construction.

Bob and Wally walked in with the bell jingling. A woman's voice called from the back, "I'll be right there."

They waited by the counter and a moment later a woman with sandy brown hair hanging over a sun splotched neck and shoulders, walked stiffly up between rows of shelves.

"I just love this weather," she said with a big smile.

"Yes, ma'am," Bob agreed.

"What can I help you with?" she asked.

"I'm looking for Cody and Jan Bridger, the owners."

"I'm right here and Cody is in the back helping with the reconstruction."

"That's terrible about the fire," Bob said.

Jan looked at Wally's uniform and Bob's plain suit and asked, "Fire investigator, police, or insurance company?"

"No, No. I'm Detective Schwimer, Bob, and this is Wally Young. I do want to talk to you about the fire. Arson? Is that what the fire investigator determined?"

"That's what we figure but we haven't heard back from the fire department. The insurance company says they won't pay for arson and…" She paused and stared past Bob a moment and then said, "I'll let Cody tell you. Just a minute…"

She turned and walked back down the rows of shelves and through a door to the warehouse area. Bob watched where she went. Several minutes later she returned with a middle-aged man in tow. He wore a green and black plaid cowboy shirt, jeans, and cowboy boots.

"Are you with the police?" Cody asked as he looked at Wally.

"I'm a detective looking into the fires down here." Bob saw Cody's eyes widen. "Seems there was a bit of arson in the area and your store might have been hit by the same people."

"Have you arrested anyone?"

"Not yet. We'd like to talk to you. See if you suspect anyone."

"So it's a dead end? We called you last spring."

"I remember. I had my team work with the fire chief. That's why we are following up with you today." Bob lied and Wally smirked. "Did you have any angry customers last spring?"

"No. I told your people it was Samuel Swanson."

"Samuel Swanson? How do you know?"

"It was him."

"Are you sure?"

"He was hanging around the day before the fire. Ask anyone. All those fires stopped the very day he died."

"Died?"

"Yes," Cody said, nervousness creeping into his voice.

Bob stared at Cody for a long moment. He didn't say a thing. Cody appeared ready to say something else when Bob turned and looked around the store. He saw a missing person's poster hanging in the window. It was tattered as if it had been taken down and put back up several times. Layers of Scotch tape filled the corners and the paper was yellowing in the sun. Bob walked over and tore the sign down from the window.

Cody followed him. "What are you doing?"

"This says Samuel Swanson is *missing*. What makes you think he is *dead*?"

Cody stared at Bob but he said nothing. Bob let the man squirm for another long moment, gazing at him as only an inquisitor knows how. When Cody didn't answer he said, "You clearly said that Samuel Swanson is *dead*. We didn't know he was dead until today."

Cody's eyes turned to the right and his eyelids flickered rapidly. "I heard it on the news."

"It hasn't been in the news... Don't make any vacation plans." Bob turned to Wally and said, "We've got everything we need here."

Chapter 39

Back in the car, Bob looked at his cell phone. Peter Jackson had called and left a message. Bob's phone had not even rung. He played the message on the speaker phone so Wally could hear it.

"Hi Detective. I got some news for you. You won't like it... You know that Waldon photo with the other kid, the one we cropped and I showed to the school superintendents? I just finished the rounds. Over a dozen schools. No one knows who he is. Most of the schools agreed to copy the photo and send them to all the teachers to look at. Maybe something will come of it. Can you believe that kid didn't show up anywhere? I must of gone to fifteen schools in all the surrounding towns... Let me know what's next. Bye."

Bob closed the voicemail.

"Bob?" Wally said.

"Hold on a sec." Bob dialed David Keller from his contact list. The receptionist picked up the phone.

"District Attorney's office."

"Hello. This is Detective Schwimer. Can I speak to the D.A. please?"

"Hold," she said, responding before Bob could thank her. A moment later the District Attorney answered the phone.

"Hi Bob."

"Hello David."

"Are you calling about the Rickman Exhumation?"

"Yes and no. How's that coming?"

"Talked to Terri a little while ago. The judge signed the order and it turns out the victim's family was wealthy enough to purchase a tomb instead of burying him. They are very upset about it, but we can pull the casket out tomorrow morning, if you want to do it that early. No need for a backhoe."

"Did the family fight it?"

"They tried too, on the basis of 'leave the dead' alone. In this case he was an accused rapist, so it's even more sensitive, but Judge Awahd had already signed the order. It didn't take much convincing, considering he plays golf with Henry Houghton every second Wednesday."

"The judge plays golf with Houghton?"

"Yes."

"Henry Houghton is our primary in the Rickman murder."

"I guess the judge didn't know that. He's a straight up guy. He thought he was doing Houghton a favor, collecting evidence for the rape. But if he knew Houghton was a suspect in a murder he'd have thrown in a search warrant for his house and business if I asked him to."

"You know him that well?" Bob said.

"Anything you need. Especially if it comes to who the judge associates with. He doesn't play around," David said. The D.A. started rapping a pen on his desk. Bob heard it through the phone.

"If that gets public he won't like the attention."

"He's toughed-out worse."

"I'll bet. But I need to talk to you about the arsons in Barnstable county last spring."

"Out of the jurisdiction, isn't it?"

"There was a kid murdered in an alley in Bristol County a few years ago. Joel Richardson."

"Also out of our jurisdiction. Barnstable and Bristol Counties. Are you assisting the investigations?"

"Heading up the task force. We are going to have to expand it. Hold on, David. I want to get Captain Don Rudolph with the Staties in on this call."

"Okay. I'll hold. Have my secretary ring me back when you are ready."

Bob scanned his cell phone contacts and a few moments later he had David and Donald on the conference call.

"Bob?"

"Hi Don. I've got D.A. Keller on the line. I wanted to talk to you both."

"Hi David."

"Captain Rudolph. So Bob?" David asked. "You mentioned the Barnstable County arsons and a murdered kid in Bristol County?"

"The kid was murdered in Bristol County, Raynham town center exactly. It's possible they tie into the Spears murder over in Abington."

"How?" Don asked.

"You know that Spears was a drug dealer. He's the vic in the railroad case. Our first suspect was the homeless man, Terrance Silverman, who was working out at Long Pond renting boats. Same place as that girl was raped a few years ago.

"I went over and talked to Henry Houghton about Silverman and he insisted that we reopen the girl's rape case. Between investigating Spears background, I also went over to Bristol County to follow up on something Silverman said about accusations of murder over there. It turns out he found the body of a teenager, a Joel Richardson, in an alleyway. Sheriff Jasperse held Silverman for awhile but they couldn't find any evidence."

"I remember that case," Don interrupted. "I told Jasperse several times to let that guy go. It finally took threats of a court order."

"Not surprising. The murder case is still open but pretty cold. I found out what seems like the victim, Joel, was a sociopath." Bob continued, "Drowning dogs, shooting farm animals, et cetera. So I interviewed some of his associates and victims. There is no shortage of people who would not have been upset with this kid's demise. The Rickman drowning and the Spears murder, a pedophile kidnapped off the street a couple days ago, plus this psycho kid's murder in Bristol led my team to research some crime rates. Wally and I were just looking into the Barnstable County arsons that suddenly stopped last spring after Samuel Swanson disappeared."

"Suspect number one for the arsons," David interjected. "What's the time line?"

"Rickman was murdered, or rather he died under suspicious circumstances, but both Amelia and Henry Houghton have alluded to murder... That was four years ago. Amelia thinks her father may be involved. Some of the things Houghton has said might amount to an admission of guilt, and he has motive; revenge or retribution."

"Amelia was the rape victim," Don stated.

"Joel was murdered via shotgun three years ago. There was nothing two years ago that we can find but the arsons started last fall. Then in the spring this Swanson kid disappears and the Barnstable arsons stop immediately. Four or five months later, Spears is murdered. Not long after that an ex-con prostitute and convicted sexual predator appears to jump parole. I'm thinking he killed his pimp, but it turns out he was probably kidnapped."

"Next on a list? Someone doing our jobs for us," Don said.

"Vigilante justice may be swift, but it's far from just," Bob said. "It's only a matter of time before innocents get hurt or killed. We have to stop these people. Collateral damage might be okay in war, but not in peace."

"Agreed. What can I do?" David asked.

"I need suspects. We need to link the crimes. I think there is a conspiracy here. It's not just one. It's a group. At least two people and possibly more... And they're killing kids and ex-convicts."

"Not just ex-cons. He is going after sociopaths?" Don added. "Arsonists, animal abusers, rapists and drug dealers, a sexual predator, prostitutes."

"It sounds like he, or she, or they, are moving up to bigger game. Take out a kid in Bristol County, a rapist, another kid playing with matches, and now a pimp and drug dealer, and then a pedophile."

"Not kids. Future murderers... The pedophile is still missing and Swanson turned up dead? Where? When?" David asked.

"A little while back, not sure how long, a couple weeks ago maybe. Sheriff Jasperse said someone found bones in a manure pile in Raynham. Jasperse just got a DNA match from FBI missing persons. Came up with this Swanson kid. The landscape company claims the manure came from the Mulligans. It turns out they, the Mulligans, are potential suspects in the Joel Richardson murder."

"What else?" David asked.

"While Wally and I are over here in Bournedale breaking the bad news to the parents, we decided to talk to the feed store owners in Bourne. Their store about half burned down last spring. Arson, of course. Wally and I were just over there talking to the owners and they said something interesting. Cody Bridger said the fires stopped after the Swanson kid *died*. He used that word. *Died*."

"He said that?" Don asked.

"Yes, not 'disappeared' or 'went missing', but 'died' and is 'dead'."

"Let me guess; the news of Swanson's body being found has not been made public?"

"The information is hours-old. No one has that information except for us and Jasperse. Jasperse has known about the bones for weeks but he had no name for them. Here's the connection. The Mulligans own a horse farm and the Bridger's own a feed and tack store. If we can prove they know each other, through the horse business..."

"I think you are going to ask me to subpoena phone records?"

"You read my mind, David. Can you work with the Bristol and Barnstable D.A.'s and Sheriff Jasperse and Anderson and get the Bridger's and Mulligan's phone records for me?"

"Will you and Wally attest to the Bridger's statement?"

"Of course."

"It's flimsy," Don remarked.

"Worse than the Rickman case?" Bob asked.

"A lot worse," David replied. "Bob, you know, but Donald might not be aware yet... We already got the exhumation order for Rickman. We got lucky. Judges are supposed to examine evidence, not suspicions. He wants to help his golf partner solve the rape case. I spun that angle on him. Trying to get a judicial opinion on the rape, collecting evidence, DNA, et cetera. We can prove that either he was murdered or confirm it was an accident."

"You didn't put that in writing?"

David's voice sank deeper. "Just the rape part. We get the Rickman cause of death as a bonus. Can you find anything more solid on Bridger?"

"I can work on it. I've got the guys going through Spears' and Waldon's personal effects. There's a tiny chance that Waldon off'd Spears and disappeared but I have a witness that watched Waldon being kidnapped off the streets. Waldon's story matches the witness, right down to the vehicle and clothing."

David spoke his mind, "If you are going to link the two kids to each other and a drug dealer you will need more than hunches and a feed store owner's misstatement. Can we wait for Jasperse? Let's see what he finds out on the Swanson kid. I'm guessing the Mulligans are being interviewed?"

Don said, "Why don't you go be a fly on Jasperse's wall. Maybe the Mulligans will slip-up in the interview."

"Phone records would help."

"I'll see what I can do," David said. "A search warrant and phone records for the Mulligans shouldn't be hard with the Swanson body on their property. I'll make some calls."

"Thanks David," Bob said.

"Thank you, David," Don echoed the sentiment as the D.A. hung up the call.

"Donald? Don't hang up," Bob said.

"What?"

"I have to talk to you."

"I have to talk to you too. Frank Wysup is pretty upset that he's been excluded from the investigation."

"He is not excluded. He's more in the way than anything else."

"Frank is pushing me to put him in charge."

"Is that what you want?"

"Damn it. No, Robert." Don's frustration sounded in his voice. "You've got a handle on it but now this looks like a multi-jurisdictional mess. We have to formalize the task force."

"You are taking care of that."

"Yes. And you are heading it up, but Frank wants the job. He is a good coroner, but I don't think he is the man for this job right now. He has connections and I'm not sure what he's up to. He could bring in some favors." The line went quiet for a moment. Then Don continued, "Bob. If you were up here working for me directly I wouldn't have these problems. I could put you right in charge and…"

"It sounds like you don't trust Frank."

"I'm not saying that. Dammit, I'm offering you a job."

"Don't change the subject. Why not Wysup?"

"Do you want to step away?"

"No, but you didn't answer my question."

"I shouldn't tell you. There have been some issues in the past but he was Plymouth County M.E. before Terri came along. He might still have some old longings for the work. With you bringing up the Rickman exhumation he's going to feel his work is being questioned."

"It's not a matter of that," Bob said. "We just want to see if anything was missed. People make mistakes."

"I know that. Just be careful. Frank's got some powerful friends. If he really wanted to, he could get us both fired."

"He's that good?"

"No. He's that well connected. Just keep him in the loop. Make him feel like he is part of the team."

"I'll make it happen. But there's more you should know. Frank was seen taking something from Spears apartment."

"You mean he stole something?"

"Maybe. I got an officer who thinks he saw Frank put something in his pocket while they were packing up the place."

"I don't like the word 'think'."

"Me either. I haven't said anything to Frank but if he took something it's probably evidence. I just can't figure why else he would take something."

"This is bad. I can't do anything with it."

"I know. That's why I've let it drop. I can't prove he took something based on a supposition of a witness who watched from a bad angle for less than a couple seconds."

"Get me more and I can get Frank removed."

"I'll see what I can do."

"What about Perry?"

"I've got the Railroad Police on the CC list. I left him a couple voicemail messages but he isn't returning my calls."

"Why?"

Bob laughed.

"What's funny?"

"He offered to help Terri with the Spears' autopsy. She said the last time she saw him he turned green and ran out the door."

"Keep sending him reports anyway. I've got the M.B.T.A. hounding the Commissioner to get this out of the news. No one wants to ride a train that dismembered a guy, or worse, that they think is haunted."

"I'll take care of it."

"You do that. One more thing. You've been spending time with Alan Barton." Don formed his words as a fact.

"He's a friend."

"He's a suspect in a police misconduct case."

"And?" Bob felt his defenses rising.

"And you need to stay away from him. At least until that case is resolved. I don't need the grief and it has already brought up questions about you." Donald hung up the phone.

Bob started the car.

"Bob?" Wally turned to Bob, still quietly sitting beside him, listening to the conversation.

"Yeah." Bob was lost in thought as he navigated the car towards to the highway.

"That feed store guy looks familiar."

Bob looked at Wally but didn't speak.

"I think I've seen him before."

"Can you remember?"

"That's the problem, and I've been thinking about it while you were on the phone."

"Keep thinking about it."

Chapter 40

Wally spoke up as they drove back to Marshfield, "What's next?"

"I guess I'm going to pay Jasperse another visit. Can you help Terri with the Rickman autopsy? Make arrangements for transportation. Keller said tomorrow is a possibility for the exhumation. It's an above-ground crypt. Unlock a gate and a door and haul the casket out. You are in charge."

"Sure."

Bob dropped off Wally at the B.C.I. He stopped into his own office to call Jasperse about the Mulligan's interview and check his messages before heading over to Taunton. A few minutes later as he walked out the door he met Frank Wysup walking in. Frank glared at Bob. His head held back, looking down his nose.

"Why are you reopening the Rickman case?"

"Hi Frank," Bob answered with a smile.

Frank stepped back at the remark. "Uh?"

"I said, 'Hello'."

"Hello. Um…" Frank grunted. His demeanor didn't improve.

"Yes?" Bob asked.

"I would like to know why you are reopening the Rickman drowning."

"What are you doing in Marshfield? Don't you have an office in Dedham?"

"What? I'm following up. I used to live over here. Hanover. Randolph now. I saw you pull in and I needed gas anyway." Frank pointed to his car for no particular reason.

"Oh. Yeah. You moved to Randolph." Bob walked past Frank.

"What about Rickman."

"What about Rickman?"

"Are you questioning my work?"

"Frank, I took you on this case because Captain Rudolph asked me to include you."

"You are questioning my work."

"No. Terrance Silverman worked for Henry Houghton and he insists we reopen Amelia's rape."

"You are not reopening the Rickman case."

"No." Bob lied, "I just want to collect some DNA samples for the rape case."

"Oh." A look of surprise came over Frank's face. "Why? The suspect is dead."

Bob continued his deceit. "Maybe Rickman wasn't the rapist?"

"Why was I not informed?"

"You were. It's in your copies of the case progress reports."

"Why are you keeping me out of the Rickman case?"

"I'm not keeping you out. I just want a fresh set of eyes on the evidence."

"You think I'm old?"

"No Frank. I think you are good."

"Then why?" The surprise in Frank's voice belied his suspicions.

Bob chose his words carefully. "Because you are too close to the Rickman-Amelia rape case."

"I was M.E. on the drowning and you were the detective on both."

"And I need new eyes on the old evidence. I'm not so sure Rickman really did rape Amelia." Bob continued his falsehoods.

"That case is closed."

"I'm reopening it." Bob turned and walked away.

"What if you find something?"

"What am I going to find?" He turned back to the taller man.

"What if I made a mistake or missed something?"

"I'm sure you didn't miss anything. I'm sure you got it all right."

"You know the state is trying to force me to retire. This could be all they need. I need this job. I don't want to retire."

"Did you do anything wrong?"

Frank stepped back. A look of wonder entered his old gray

eyes. "No. Nothing."

"Then you have nothing to worry about. Look Sheriff Barton is trying to save his own job right now. Terri is working twenty-four-seven on Spears. Wally and Peter have enough to do with their regular work. I'm swamped with Spears and several other cases I'm working on. No one down here is trying to torpedo you."

Bob turned and walked to his car. A wrenching feeling filled his guts. He hated to lie but he wondered what Frank would do if they found serious problems with the Rickman autopsy. Frank would be forced to retire and after a dozen or more years of working Bob was starting to think about his own retirement someday, a thought he didn't enjoy, especially if he was eventually forced out himself one day.

Bob headed down Route 3 and west on Route 44 to Taunton. He squinted into the setting sun as he passed the familiar old dairy farms and new housing developments. Eartha Kitt told him, "How good it is," in French, from his cell phone and he thought about Mary and the blessings he and his wife enjoyed. He knew he was in the heart of his work, and he knew he sometimes did not give her the attention she deserved. He pulled into a gas station off a Middleborough rotary and picked her up a pre-wrapped rose and teddy bear as a tiny gesture of his love. It was cheap, chintzy, but it was the thought that counted.

He called her and let her know it would be a late night. The street lights were just turning on as he pulled into the Taunton Sheriff's office. He parked and crossed the parking lot to meet Sheriff Jasperse returning from dinner, a doggy-bag in hand.

"What do we have?" he asked the Sheriff as they shook hands.

"A body, two suspects, circumstantial evidence."

"Two bodies."

"Two bodies?"

"Joel Richardson. The Mulligans had motive."

"Oh-yeah. *Haw-haw.* And opportunity. I'm sure they own a shotgun."

"Did you find any shotgun shells in the alleyway?"

"No. We dug some pellets out of the body."

"You said on the phone there's some new forensics on shotgun pellets?"

"Yeah. We'll grab every gun and round of ammo they own for testing. Rifles and shotguns. We'll run the gambit. We might have even saved some pellets as evidence. There are manufacturer's lot codes on the shells. I'll bet we could pull something out of the lab." Jasperse took his radio from his belt. He called for a deputy. A few seconds later the officer reported in.

"While you are at the Mulligans' box up all their firearms and ammunition. We might have a second murder on these two. *Haw-haw.*" He released the button and clipped the radio back into its belt holster.

"No admission of guilt or confessions?" Bob asked.

"No confessions yet. The day is not over." Jasperse laughed.

Bob frowned again as he realized he would have to kowtow to Jasperse, at least until Donald got the task-force paperwork finished. The Sheriff's jovial and crass self was back. Gone was the professional he had heard while talking about the Swanson child. "How can I help?" he asked as the sheriff led him to a viewing room.

"Just take a look at our tapes and see if we missed anything."

They walked to an unmarked door adjacent to the interview room. Wall mounted monitors showed the Mulligans sitting in the next room. A technician sat in front of a computer displaying the same images as the monitors. The couple was alone but locked in. They fidgeted and moved in their seats. Occasionally they leaned close to each other and whispered. It was a bad idea for the two suspects to be locked up together. Bob knew they could conspire and create a story.

"This is video?"

"Yeah. Recorded this afternoon. We still have them. Wanted to consult with the D.A. and with you before we officially file charges."

"You are holding them for questioning?"

"Yeah we have forty-eight hours. It's mostly circumstantial

but I think we can make a case against them. *Haw-haw.*"

"Not like Silverman?" Bob asked sarcastically.

"Heck No. *Haw-haw.* Take a look at the video. This is great." Bob's point was lost on the Sheriff. Jasperse picked up a remote. He rewound the D.V.R. to a specific time stamp and turned up the volume to maximum. When Shawn leaned over to whisper to Betty the microphones picked up every word.

"They don't know anything," Shawn said softly, his voice faintly audible.

"There's nothing to know," Betty said. "Now shut up. You dumb..."

Jasperse turned the volume back down. "We know there is something to know."

"I didn't like them," Bob said. "They came off tough and concerned for their animals but something just doesn't seem right. I'll say that I am liking them more and more... for the murder."

"Do you want to go in and talk to them?"

"No. Not right now. Let me take a look at what you have. Maybe a new set of eyes and ears will give us something. You still want to close that Richardson case?" Bob asked.

"Of course. We are going to let them stew for awhile. Take a look at my notes and there's a couple parts of the videos I wrote down for you to look at."

"That's a start." Bob smiled.

Several hours later, as Bob headed out of Taunton, he phoned Mary. She picked up right away and asked, "Bob?"

"Hi baby. I'm heading back now. Should be home in an hour."

"Dinner's in the fridge. How did it go in Taunton?"

"Good enough. It seems the Mulligans know something about the Swanson kid but they're not talking."

"Not surprising," Bob said. "The body was on their property. If they don't know anything. It's touchy. They admitted to each other that we don't know anything."

"And that's evidence that they do."

"A good lawyer could make it into nothing, a scared remark

from frightened suspects who are falsely accused."

"What about Joel's murder?" Mary asked.

"Nothing. The Sheriff brought it up but they are stone cold. They were talking a bit early on in the videos, but they must have smartened up. There's enough inconsistencies in their stories to raise my interest, but a good lawyer could mince that also."

"Sounds like a waste of time."

"I hope not. You may be right."

"I'll see you soon?"

"Don't stay up. I've got some notes to finish in my office."

"Have something to eat first. You promise no all-nighter?"

"It's part of the job."

"It doesn't have to be."

"I'll try, but no promises."

"I know you love your job."

"Love you more, Mary."

"Yes?"

"Definitely."

"Love you too." Mary hung up the phone and Bob dialed Captain Rudolph's cell phone number.

The call went to voicemail. "David, Bob. I'll be sending you some paperwork tonight. I just finished reviewing Jasperse interview tapes on the Mulligans. Remember they are suspects in the Raynham kid's murder too, like we talked about. Call me when you get this. Make sure I'm not leaving anything out." Bob hung up and focused on the drive home.

Chapter 41

Bob knocked on Henry Houghton's front door and then rang the bell. He knocked several times more because it was still early, before 6 a.m., and he knew the man was home. The white Ford pickup truck was in the driveway. The same truck in the photographs he had in his hands.

Eventually, some random noises came from the house. The lock turned and the door opened. Henry Houghton said, "What the fuck do you want?"

"Glad to see you Henry." Bob smiled.

Henry pushed the door closed but Bob was ready. He leaned his shoulder to the door, hard and fast. The door gave way from Houghton's hand and flew open. Bob stepped into the doorframe before the man could recover.

"What the hell."

"That's what I came to ask you about."

"You better have a warrant."

"Do I need one?"

"You might."

Bob saw the .38 caliber Smith and Wesson hammerless revolver in Houghton's left hand held low by his leg, turned away from Bob. The muzzle of the weapon came around, but not quick enough. Bob smashed the man in the face with his left fist, stepping his shoulder into the punch and straightening his arm as he did so. He caught the cheek, just beside his nose. Henry's head swiveled like a barstool. His brain took the sudden acceleration of his skull poorly, and the man collapsed. Bob's right hand took the revolver away as he fell.

When Henry awoke, he was sitting at the kitchen table. Amelia had made coffee and put a cup in front of her father. The revolver was on the counter top, unloaded. A stack of photographs, enlarged to ten by eight, sat on the table.

"Good morning," Bob said. "Have some coffee. You are

going to have a hell of a headache."

Henry nodded and froze in half-bob, putting one hand to his cheek and the other to the side of his head.

"I took the liberty of reviewing some old case files, at your insistence. My foot still hurts a little, by the way, and I wanted to ask you something."

"What?" Henry groaned.

"You see these pictures? Don't answer that. It's rhetorical. My guys are pretty good about doing what I ask them to do. When I tell them to take pictures of a crime scene you would be amazed at what we find.

"What crime scene?"

"The docks. Where you launch your boats. Where one of your boats was stolen from and, um, excuse me Amelia..."

"It's okay," she replied and she left the kitchen. Bob heard her settle into the living room, where she could hear everything anyway.

"...not too terribly far from where Rickman turned up dead."

"Rapist." Henry spat.

"See this truck, your truck? The only one you have registered in Massachusetts. You see that it's turned around facing the boat trailer, but it isn't hitched-up. Why is that?"

"I don't know."

"I don't either."

"So what?"

"So Amelia was raped mid-summer. One of your boats was stolen at the end of the summer, early autumn, September. That was when Rickman was found floating in the lake."

"And?"

"And the season is over. You close up the docks, put the boats into storage, and go to Florida, just like every year."

Henry didn't respond.

"Let me help you along with this. The boat storage is here, at the house and office. Half-a-mile from the docks, close to the freeway. You pull all the boats out, one by one, drive them up from the lake on that trailer, forklift them into the shelters and go get another one. Right?"

"Yeah."

"You have the truck unhitched in this photograph. The trailer is at the head of the boat ramp, like it was just dropped there in a hurry and the truck is pulled in front, facing the trailer, like it was parked in a hurry."

"There's a ball on the front bumper."

"Yes. I saw that. When people move a lot of trailers around they can drive them easier looking out the front windshield and pushing the trailer backwards."

"You made detective quick," Houghton said sarcastically.

Bob laughed. "Good. That's good. The headache must be subsiding. Humor is the best medicine."

"Who the hell cares which way I move the boats around."

"My problem is the truck is not hitched up to the trailer and you are spending your days running boats up to the shelters, and you wouldn't be driving the boat trailer backwards down the road for half-a-mile, would you?"

"Maybe."

"Do you?"

"Does it matter?"

"Yes. It does matter. Because if your truck is hitched-up to pull boats out and drop them off, why would you unhitch? To go into town, go shopping? Drive into Boston for dinner?"

"Maybe."

"But you didn't do any of those things. You spent two days pulling boats out of the lake. You said so right here." Bob pointed to a photocopied page of his old notebook. "It normally takes you three and sometimes four days. I imagine you were in a hurry to get closed up. The Miami Sun was calling and it wasn't the newspaper?"

"So what?"

"So I have a horse trailer, a bumper pull just like the boat trailers."

Houghton sighed impatiently.

"My wife and I go horseback riding some weekends. Sometimes two days in a row."

"Good for you."

"Yes. It's fun. When we go two days in a row I leave the trailer hitched up. You know what a pain in the neck it is to run those cranks up and down, and to get the ball lined up just right and all? Then clamp the hitch down over the ball and lock it. Then you got to connect the electrical plug and hook up the chains. And of course there's the trailer breaks that need to be tested and adjusted. So if I'm going to be using the trailer for a couple days I just leave it hitched up. I don't have to block the wheels or back it beside the garage. You understand?"

"If you got something to say, just say it."

"So I think you'd do the same thing with all those boats that have to be moved. And I'm wondering if you went for a drive. Say, to meet someone and you didn't want a boat trailer following you around. Someone might remember a boat trailer that says 'Houghton Boats' on the side of it. I noticed your truck doesn't have the same logo. You might want to put one on there. It's great advertising and virtually free."

"Commercial taxes."

"Right. Commercial vehicle registration taxes. Tax evasion. I don't work for the Department of Taxation. I'm more interested in murder. So my point is that someone might remember a truck and trailer that comes to pick up someone, say, someone drunk, or inebriated, or even hit over the head in a bar parking lot, especially when a boat trailer says 'Houghton Boats' on the side.

"You accusing me of killing Rickman?"

"And that's the problem."

"I don't see a problem. I see grasping at straws."

"I agree with you. I got nothing," Bob said matter-of-factly.

Henry smiled slowly, painfully slowly, and then he laughed. "Then get out. I didn't do anything but that rapist sure got what he deserved."

"Okay. Put a cold steak on that cheek bone. You can keep these pictures. I have extras."

Chapter 42

Laurence, "Larry" as his law business friends called him, Smith Esquire, walked out to his garage expecting an easy last day of the workweek, which involved a short court appearance for a client, finishing some paperwork and a little research for next week. He thought about the weekend, and why, maybe, Russell had been ignoring his calls. He felt slighted. He opened the car door and looked up to find the garage overhead door open to the driveway. He couldn't specifically remember closing it the night before but thought he must have done so out of habit. As he slid sideways along the side of his BMW sedan he found the trunk of his car was also open. The lid just slightly ajar.

"What the…" he exclaimed. "I know the trunk was closed yesterday. I must have been robbed". He slammed the lid down in anger. "Christ. What's missing?" Larry fumbled with his keys to reopen the trunk. As the lid popped up the sight of a body in his trunk made him instantly lightheaded.

"What? How?" he said as he slammed the trunk closed again and looked around the neighborhood. "Anyone see?" he asked himself. He opened the trunk again, and picking up an ice scraper, he poked the body.

"Hey? Hey? Are you alive?" It didn't move. He closed the trunk and went back inside the house, fumbling with his cell phone. He had the number to nine-one-one keyed in and his thumb was on the send-button when he stopped himself.

Larry slowly walked back to the garage. In a daze he pressed the button to close the overhead door. He slid sideways between the car and the wall once more until he stood facing the trunk. He paused for several minutes before inserting the key into the lock. Opening the trunk slowly, he looked at the body. Blood rushed to his head. His ears rang. His vision grew dim. The body lay still. A dark hood was tied over the head. Reaching down with shaking hands he untied the rope and pulled back the hood.

It was a dark haired boy; a teenager. He looked peaceful, like he was sleeping. Then Larry realized who the boy was.

"Christ. Russell. That's why you didn't show up."

He dialed nine-one-one again on his cell phone and he stopped once more with his thumb over the send button. "I'm being set-up," he realized.

Ten minutes later Larry was racing down Route 44 to State Route 3 with the body still in the trunk, but now with a shovel and a pickaxe.

"Barnstable County," Larry said aloud and to himself; a habit he never had before that morning. "Uh-huh. Over the canal on the Sagamore Bridge, near the National Guard Base, wasn't it closed? Rural, ditches, woods, swamps. There's got to be someplace to get rid of a body. Got to call the secretary. Got to cancel the clients. I'm too sick to work. Too sick to call in. She'll call me. Uh-huh. Just wait for her to call me and then tell her how sick I am. Can I trust her? No. Trust no one. But someone knows. Russ didn't climb into my trunk by himself."

Larry saw a highway patrol car going the other direction. He forced himself to slow down to the posted limits and watched in his mirror as the cruiser disappeared into the distance behind him. He let out a long breath he didn't realize he was holding. He turned the wheel slightly and eased the sedan around the interchange onto Route-Three heading south. After crossing the Sagamore Bridge, marked by a cheery 'Welcome to Cape Cod' sign, he swung off onto Sandwich Road along the canal. He looked for side roads, dirt roads, ditches or a tidal pool.

The sun was rising steadily and it threatened to be a warm bright day. He cursed his luck as he realized that if he found the body in the evening, or if it was raining, even cloudy, he would have had some cover or protection. He stopped the car at the red light of a crossroads. As he waited he continued to argue with himself.

"Yes. I'll go home. Hide the car in the garage and wait for darkness. I can find a place to bury the body. Google has good satellite images of the ground and even topographical maps. I can find a wooded area and go back tonight. I've got a GPS. I can find the perfect place. There's a dozen ponds and lakes on the

South Shore. Wasn't a body found in Long Pond a few years ago? Didn't a kid disappear from near here a while back? If I get caught I'd be pinned for all of that." Larry laughed until he realized it was not funny. "But someone knows. They know, but it's not a problem. The police would have been at my house if they had been called. There's still time to call the police. I can report the body. No. How would that phone call go; *'Hi. I found a dead ex-convict-pedophile-homosexual-prostitute in my trunk and I have no idea how he got there. Will you stop on down and take him to the morgue like a good bunch of chaps?'* I can't do that. What of my reputation? If they find out about the tryst, I'll be disbarred. An ex-con, pedophile, and a prostitute."

A blaring horn brought Larry from his thoughts. He looked in the mirror. A tractor-trailer truck stopped behind him was blasting its air-horn. He looked up at the streetlight as it turned from green to yellow. He stomped on the gas peddle and spun the wheel into a u-turn, back towards the bridge. When he looked back in the mirror, the truck driver was shaking his middle finger out the window at him. He smiled and relaxed. "The Massachusetts salute." He laughed. "I have a plan. You don't go to court without a plan. You don't bury a body without a plan." He laughed again. "I'll have to remember that for the next Bar Association meeting. Everyone will think it's a joke. *'You know what they say: You don't go to court without a plan and a witness, and you don't bury a body without a plan and a shovel.'* They will lose it."

Larry drove back to his house and parked the car in the garage. He called his secretary as he looked in the rear view mirror, watching the garage door close behind him.

"Larry Smith Defense Attorney," Sheila answered the phone.

"Sheila? It's Larry." He forgot to make his voice sound sick. Speaking slower and deeper than before he said as hoarsely as he could, "I won't be in today. Had some bad fish last night."

"I told you not to go fishing last week." Sheila laughed.

"Funny. Please cancel my calendar and call the courthouse. There's the Peterson thing."

"I'll explain it to the judge," Sheila said.

Larry hung up and continued talking to himself. "Best to keep it short. Now Google-Earth and wait until dark," he said to himself. "Isn't internet activity traceable? The library..."

Chapter 43

When Bob got into the office, he found the dispatchers' fax machine overflowing and spilling sheets on the floor. Louise was behind her glass door reading a book. She leaned back and opened the door.

"That thing's been running for an hour. I tried to sort the papers but it kept going. There's a stack on the table there." Louise pointed across the room.

"It will probably be running all morning."

"My just rewards!" Louise laughed. "I go and sort them every ten minutes. I'll text you when it stops, if it does. You are in early. Must be a good case."

"Are there ever any good ones?"

Louise's eyes screwed up as she realized what she said. She mouthed the word *sorry*. Bob smiled and went back to gathering the sheets as he pondered the virtues of email, and why the faxes didn't get delivered there instead.

"I'll take these from here..."

"Wait, wait, Bob," Louise called to him and handed him a stack of mail. All envelopes opened. One sealed in an evidence bag.

"You will want to look at that one." She indicated to the bag.

Bob opened the evidence bag and took the letter out by the edges. Louise always opened all mail first as part of department policy. She screened the letters and sent them to the appropriate departments. This was the first time he had ever received a letter in an evidence bag. As he read the letter he realized why Louise had done that.

> That guy in Abingtan was murdered its a consperasy they R killing pple stop them.

The letter was not signed. He placed it back into the evidence bag and he looked at the postmark. It was dated two days ago and canceled from a West Bridgewater post office. The hand writing on the envelope was the same crude script used on the letter itself. The writer appeared either barely literate, or intentionally hiding his writing style. He handed the evidence bag back to Louise who was off her call.

"Send this to forensics. Fingerprints, anything else they can tell me."

"Got it." She smiled.

"And nice job."

"Thanks." Her smile widened.

Bob turned back to the fax machine and the papers on the table. The cover sheet indicated the fax was the Mulligan's phone records, going back five years, since before the Joel Richardson murder. Someone else had worked just as late and hard. Bob could not remember when he had seen a phone company, or any utility respond as quickly. The fax was cc'd to the Bristol County and Plymouth County District Attorneys.

In his office, Bob sorted the pages and cut the stack to a random page just before the last Thanksgiving, nearly a year before. The Mulligans made scores of calls, hundreds in some months. There were peak call volumes over the Christmas holidays and again over the summer. Most phone numbers never repeated.

Consulting the reverse phone book, courtesy of Homeland Security's Law Enforcement regulations, he spent his time finding the names of businesses and residents from all over Bristol and Plymouth Counties among hundreds of phone calls. The thirty-first number on the list brought up the name C. Bridger of Bournedale. Bob checked the number a second time and Googled it. The Feed and Tack store came back in the results. Scanning through the pages, he found a handful of phone calls to the store every month and a half dozen calls to Cody Bridger's cell phone.

Bob added a note to his pad, 'They raise horses. Explains phone calls. Creates an association.' Bob made another note, 'The horse business, horseback rides, pony parties, hay rides.'

In April, he saw a spike in phone calls to the Bridger feed store. An occasional spike in calls might mean they were trying to purchase a specialty item; a tool or a new saddle delivery, but a new phone number appeared in the records that repeated often. It was a cell phone that belonged to Jan Bridger. These calls were incoming as often as outgoing. Bob checked the dates. By May, the calls to the store and home dropped off. Then spiked again in August.

"Just before Spears was murdered," Bob said aloud as he circled the numbers and made notes.

"What was?" Terri walked into his office.

"Huh?" Bob looked up.

"What was just before Spears' murder?"

"Phone calls."

"Sounds like you have some suspects in mind?"

"More than a couple. Four would be a better guess."

"Who?" Terri sat down, curious as to Bob's side of the investigation.

"Cody and Jan Bridger plus Shawn and Betty Mulligan."

"Bridger?"

"Bourne. The Bridger's own a tack and feed store that burned down and the Mulligans had the body of a local arsonist kid in their manure pile. I've got two dozen phone calls to the feed store just before the kid disappeared."

"So they had something on order and were calling to check on the status. That doesn't mean anything," Terri said.

"Coincidence that the calls stop right after the arsonist goes missing? Look," Bob said as he pointed out the calls circled on the pages. "The cell phone calls end completely after Samuel Swanson disappears. In fact. There's no calls at all to the store or the cell phone in May and June. July there's two calls. It could be coincidence but..." Bob pointed to August.

"I'll guess from those circles they were busy again."

"Busy planning a murder."

"I'd say that's a good guess."

"But..."

"What?" Terri's eyes narrowed as she focused on the sheets.

"I can't be sure any of the calls were about murder. Keller wants more proof. All this says is that they know each other and might even be close friends."

"What else do we have?"

"Just that Cody Bridger said Swanson was dead when we still had not told the media, or anyone else, we found the body."

"So he was, as far as the public knows, still missing?"

"Phone calls are not what I would call proof."

"Arson is motive."

"Might be, but I need more. A witness. A weapon. DNA would be nice."

"Manure does a number on evidence. Cooks it."

"The FBI and the Bristol Crime Lab didn't have much more than bones and some rotted clothing to go on," Bob added.

"It still sounds like you could make a case. A body in a manure pile? How does anyone start trying to explain that?"

"They don't. They clammed up."

"Nothing?"

"They said enough to admit that they know something, and we don't."

"Not very smart of them."

"They were on video and audio, whispering, but it's there. Clear as day."

"Juries eat that up."

"They do, but lawyers can be persuasive. Hopefully one of the suspects will talk. We'll dangle a carrot out there and see who bites. Get one of them to testify for a reduced sentence. We can't threatened a death penalty, but life in prison is bad enough to trade testimony for five or ten years."

"I have some pissa news for you," Terri said.

"Pissa?" Bob laughed.

"Sure."

"I'd love to hear it."

"The Rickman body should be delivered by this afternoon."

"Planning on a working-weekend?"

"Are you paying overtime?"

"No."

"It's a good thing I love my job, Bob." Terri smiled.

"Or what?" Bob laughed.

"Or you'd have to wait until Monday or Tuesday for me to get the job done."

"I appreciate your dedication."

"Your gratitude is enough." Terri laughed sarcastically.

"I'm going to get a search warrant on the Bridger's property. Jasperse already has one on the Mulligan place."

"They both run horse businesses. The phone calls could be a work related?"

"Could be, but the fires stopped in April."

"All of them?"

"Every one. Fields, silos, woods. Checked it out."

"What about August?"

"The Bridgers and Mulligans were talking a lot."

"Spears turns up dead on Sunday and Waldon was kidnapped a couple days ago. Do you have phone records for September?"

"No. The current billing cycle is probably not finalized, but with the speed Keller had these records to me, I expect them by noontime."

"You can help me sort through these." Bob gestured to the stack of phone records. While Terri sat down and started scanning the pages for specific numbers, Bob called Keller to get a status on the Bridger's phone records.

"Hi Bob," David Keller said as he answered the phone.

"David."

"Bridger's records are coming now. Talked to Anderson. Seems Barnstable County had a little more trouble getting the judge to sign a search warrant on the feed and tack store. Then the phone company was being a little more difficult. Mulligan was easy by comparison. A body tends to do that."

"You were working late?" Bob asked.

"Yeah. You?"

"Stayed up till almost three."

"You had me beat. We must have had the judge up late too because Bristol told me that the Mulligan warrant came through at midnight. Not too difficult considering probable cause for murder. The Bridger's just came in, but the phone company..."

Donald chose not to repeat himself.

"Whatever you can do," Bob said, trying to sound bright beyond his exhaustion.

"You got your second wind?"

"Third. I think. Thanks again, David."

"I'm only doing this because I trust you to not make me look like an asshole." David laughed.

"I'll try not to let you down," Bob said.

Bob called Mary. She didn't answer and after the long leave-a-message message, he said, "Looks like we are swamped over here. I'll have to work. Terri, Frank, and the others too. Let's cancel the barbeque. Call me when you can. Love you."

By noon Bob and Terri had traced the better portion of the phone records. By two, the fax machine was spitting out phone records for the Bridger's tack store. Terri gave her leave when the Rickman body arrived by ambulance. Bob worked on the Bridger's phone records. He stayed late, calling Mary to tell her not to expect him until ten or midnight.

When he finally quit he had a list of names he recognized. Some were explainable and others would require investigation. He looked out the window, leaned back, and stretched. Terri's car was still in the parking lot. He stopped by her lab.

"Hi Terri," he said as he pushed opened the lab door. She flinched. "Sorry," he said as she looked up from the decomposed thoracic cavity of Tim Rickman's chest, spreaders holding the rib cage open.

"What are you still doing here?" Magnifying glasses made her eyes buggy.

"Same as you. Working."

"Did you find out anything on the Bridgers?"

"I got a list of names I recognize. Some calling patterns that can't be easily explained."

"Like the Mulligans?"

"Henry Houghton seems to like to call over there," Bob said as he gestured to Rickman's remains on the examination table.

"They run a boat rental business? What does that have to do with farm and feed?"

"Not much, but it gives me a reason to darken his door one more time. Hopefully you can come up with something from Rickman." Bob pointed to the corpse as Terri returned to her work on the body.

"Your name came up," Bob said after a moment.

"What do you mean?" She looked up, pushing the magnifying glasses on to her head.

"Your name came up on the Bridger's phone records."

"A tack and feed store? I don't even know who they are. Wait, James has a phone. It's in my name."

"That's what I figured. Where do you buy tack?"

"Catalog's mostly. That had to be James. The farming thing."

"And?"

"And it's a good thing I have a steady job."

It wasn't the answer Bob expected or hoped for. He wanted Terri and James to be successful, and if farming was James choice, he wished the man well. He looked back at his notepad. "Here's another interesting one, 'Frank Wysup'."

"Frank? Didn't know he had anything to do with farming."

"He hunts."

"I forgot about that."

"Fishes too."

"So maybe he gets equipment there?

"Hunting season is coming up. They sell clothing and blinds and tree stands. It's nothing."

"What about Wally and Peter?"

Bob looked at her quizzically.

"Seems like you have everyone you work with as a suspect, so I wondered if they ever called in to the store."

"I haven't finished yet. They don't own or ride horses."

"Or fish."

"Or hunt." Bob pointed to the disinterred remains. "What have you got?"

"First thing was a complete photograph array of the body." Terri turned on a computer monitor. Images of the body appeared. "See here and here on the forearms? That's bruising. It's hard to see on the photographs. Take a look here on the corpse." Terri walked back to the examination table and pointed out darker discolored spots on the embalmed and decayed skin of the limbs.

"And?" Bob asked.

"And I'd guess he either fell down a few times or he was working and bruising up his arms, or he was fighting with someone before he fell in. If he had taken the hits when he fell into the lake his heart would have stopped before the bruises formed. He'd have been dead."

"Can you prove anything?"

"Not yet."

"Can you *disprove* anything?"

"Falling down is probably out. There's nothing in the original investigation to suggest he was overly clumsy."

"That would be bad for someone working on a boat rental dock."

"Looks like defensive bruises from fighting?"

"If we can prove it. He could have gotten bruised a dozen different ways."

"I ran a full body x-ray," she said. I wanted to see if there were any broken bones that Frank had missed. The only thing I found was a dislocated shoulder and the skull fracture."

"Skull fracture?"

"Hence, 'his heart would have stopped before the bruises formed', if he fell in the lake at that moment. What's interesting is that Frank didn't mention anything about the shoulder in his report."

"Could he have missed it?"

"Possibly. I looked for x-rays with the original autopsy report. None."

"I thought that was standard procedures."

"Maybe. Every lab is different. If there was no reason to suspect foul play, Frank could have skipped it. The body was in the lake for a day or more before being found."

"Could Rickman have pulled his shoulder in the fall?"

"I'm going to take a closer look at it. I might be able to get some information out of the lab work. I'll send some tissue over for analysis. They will be able to tell me if the shoulder was dislocated when the body was pulled out of the water. Someone grabs an arm and hoists…"

"What about rigamortis?"

"The water acts different with every body. Sometimes it speeds up the decay processes and sometimes it slows it down, even preserves it. There's a scuba diver from Lake Placid that found a body. 'Lady in the Lake' case, wealthy lady that founded a school. Killed herself forever ago. A scuba diver reported that the body felt like soap or wax. It's called adipocere through saponification."

"What does that mean?"

"Skin turns to wax. It's sometimes called grave wax, and it's actually a process of the human fatty tissue. It's the same process used to make soap from fat, lye, or any alkaline base. It wasn't believed to happen naturally in water until that woman's body was found decades later. I guess the water was alkaline. With acid rain problems in the lakes we'll probably never see it here."

"Back on subject; what about the skull fracture?" Bob picked up Frank's report that Terri had pulled from the archives.

"I'm getting to that. I'm going to put him on ice until tomorrow. I'll know more later."

"Terri, don't work too hard this weekend. I've still got some leads to follow up on and we have time."

"BBQ?"

"No. Thought we should postpone it a week or two."

Chapter 44

As the sun retreated over the suburbs, Larry Smith crept back into his garage with an armful of maps. He pressed the button to open the overhead door. As it rattled upwards he climbed into the car and started the engine. Backing out of the garage, he heard a noise from the trunk of the BMW. Larry froze. The noise came again and then silence followed for minutes afterwards. Larry shut off the engine and he sat there, listening and shaking with fear.

"Hello?" he called. No one answered.

"Hello? Are you alive? Russell?" he asked again.

No answer came.

Adrenaline pumped through Larry's veins. His heart raced. He scrambled to retrieve his keys from the ignition as he got out of the car. With shaking hands he fought to put the key into the trunk lock. The trunk popped up. Russell moved, looking around in a blinded daze. Suddenly, Russell sat upright and swung the shovel as hard as he could. Larry froze in awe as the weapon collided with the side of his face. He spun, dazed from the blow, falling to his hands and knees. Russell climbed from the trunk, falling to the ground beside Larry who held his bleeding face.

Fighting to his feet Russell raised the shovel again, bringing it down on Larry's head. Dropping the shovel, Russell ran down the driveway to the darkened street. He ran without thinking and without direction. He ran on weak and cramped legs that steered him haphazardly.

Larry shook off the daze of the attack and stood up. Russell was gone. He stood staring down the street for several minutes until a car drove by. Realizing the odd position he was in, he got back into the BMW and pulled it into the garage. He pressed the button to close the garage door. He waited. Sweat mixed with blood, staining his shirt, as he waited for the police to arrive.

Chapter 45

Sally Sonders unlocked the employee entrance at the rear of the supermarket and turned on the lights. She walked through the echoing and disserted warehouse past an extra high pile of shelf stocking trash; cardboard boxes and plastic. Past the pallets stacked high with dry goods, she reached her office and turned on the lights to the warehouse and store front. She turned on her computer and while she waited she looked back out the doorway into the warehouse and at the pile of trash. As she brushed her bobby-cut brown hair from her eyes she frowned, trying to remember if she asked someone to take the trash out the night before. Deciding she must have forgotten, she left her office to wheel a stacked and strapped pallet of cardboard to the dumpster. As she approached the gated dumpster pen she heard something banging beyond the gates. She stopped to listen. The noise came again.

"Mrs. Sonders," a voice cried.

"Who's there?" Sally called.

"Sally…" the voice came again.

"I'm here." She pulled open the steel gates that secured the dumpsters.

A crashing noise came from beside the giant metal bins and she saw someone fall to the concrete. With uncertain steps she approached. When he looked up Sally recognized the man despite a swollen eye socket and dark bruises on his face and neck. His lip was split open.

"Russell," she exclaimed and hastened to his side.

"Help me," his hoarse voice begged.

"I'll call an ambulance." Sally rolled him on his side and looked at his bloodied and bruised face.

"No. They tried to kill me."

"Who? Who did this? How could they do this to you? Such animals. Why? Why? Do you know who did it?"

"Help me."

Sally helped Russell get to his feet by putting her arm under his arm and across his back, she let him lean on her as they went inside the supermarket and into her office. She set him in a chair and leaned him on her desk. Taking alcohol wipes from the emergency first-aid kit she cleaned his face. He asked for water and she took several bottles from the warehouse and opened them for him and let him drink. When he'd recovered a little bit of his strength she asked him what happened.

"They tried to kill me. They grabbed me off my bike." Russell stared at the floor.

"I have to take you to the hospital." Sally looked at the handcuffs that hung from one of his wrists.

"No. I'll be okay."

"I need to get those off of you." She pointed.

"What?" Russell looked at the handcuffs that hung from his wrist as if he didn't realize they existed.

"I called Officer Turbins when you didn't come in to work. No one knew where you were."

Russell gave a broken sarcastic laugh. "I'm lucky to be alive. I'm sure he'll be glad to know I'm alive. He'll say, '*That's no excuse for not reporting in.*'"

"I'll explain it to him for you." Sally stifled her laugh. "I'll call the police."

"No. Not yet. I have to call Turbins."

"I'll call him for you."

"Sally?" Russell looked up.

"Yeah?"

"What's this?" Russell opened his clenched fist. Sally immediately recognized the broken fingertip of a latex glove.

"Let me take that." Sally smiled as she picked up the fragment of latex glove that Russell had somehow held onto over the last few days. She put it in an envelope and sealed the flap. "That is evidence of your kidnappers. The police might be able to get DNA or fingerprints from it."

Russell stared at her, failing to comprehend what he had done. She handed him another bottle of water and retrieved a steak from the butcher for his bruised face.

"I'm calling an ambulance."

"No. No. I'll be okay."

"I don't think so. You're so beat up."

"No. I won't go." Russell again refused.

Sally acquiesced and gave him food and more water after cleaning his cuts.

Twenty minutes later, as Sally prepared the store for opening and employees began arriving, Joe Patten Junior ran into Sally's office.

"Russell? Are you okay? Sonders' just told me someone tried to kill you."

"They kidnapped me and left me for dead in the trunk of a car."

"You've been missing for days," Joe said.

"Days?" Russell asked.

"Yeah. What happened?"

Sally walked in and cut off any answer Russell could have given. "That's enough Joe. Go stock the deli shelves. Russell is going with me to the police department."

"Police?"

"Yes. I've decided."

"No."

"They need to know you were attacked and that this isn't your fault." Russell tried to speak again but Sally raised her hand to stop him. "I won't hear it. You are going."

At B.C.I., Louise escorted Sally and Russell to an interview room where they waited for almost an hour. As Sally grew impatient, and Russell fidgeted with his now-warm steak held to his eye socket, Frank Wysup entered the room and locked it closed with a key. Russell noticed the door had a deadbolt lock meant to keep people in, not out. The key lock prevented anyone entering or leaving. He watched Frank put the key in his pocket. Before any greetings were spoken Frank sat down with a note pad and pen and stared at Russell.

"What happened?" Frank demanded across the table.

"I don't know," Russell said, his voice echoing in the nearly empty room. Their words reverberated off the walls and ceiling with a ring.

"You've been here before. You know how this works." Frank's voice dropped an octave and he spoke slowly, methodically. "What happened?"

"I was kidnapped. I'm a victim."

"You are a parolee. Maybe you decided to go partying for a couple days and now you need an excuse. Maybe you killed Spears and needed an alibi. Officer Turbins is coming down from Boston to pick you up. You are going back to prison."

"Wait a minute," Sally Sonders exclaimed. "Russell was attacked and beaten and left for dead."

Frank turned to her. "Who are you?"

"I manage the supermarket."

"I didn't ask what you do for a living. I asked who you are."

"My name is Sally Sonders. I'm Russell's boss."

"Are you a relative? A lawyer?"

"No. I'm his boss."

"You will have to leave. You can't be here." Frank got up and unlocked the door. He held it open for Sally to leave.

"I'm here to help Russell. Where's Detective Schwimer?" Sally slowly got up from the chair.

"You are interfering with a police investigation and I'll arrest you if necessary."

"No. I'll go. I'll wait in the lobby."

"Second door on the left," Frank said as he closed and locked the door again. Frank sat back down and glared at Russell.

"I didn't do anything. Two guys jumped me on my bike. They dragged me into a van. That's all I remember."

They both looked up as Bob pushed on the door. Finding it locked, he rapped on the tiny glass window with his knuckles.

"Frank, come out here." Bob demanded as Frank unlocked the door. Sally Sonders stood in the hallway waiting.

"Sally, stay with Russell will you?"

"But..." Frank protested.

"Frank, I'd like to talk to you down the hall. Bob led Frank to the video room down the hall. After the door was closed, he turned to Frank with steam in his eyes. "What are you doing in there?"

"You said you wanted help on this case."

"You know we never interview a suspect or a witness alone. You know that Frank."

"Yes, but…"

"Are these cameras running?"

Frank looked sheepish. Bob grunted and turned the D.V.R. and computer on and waited for it to boot up.

"What did you find out?" Bob asked.

"Nothing," Frank answered. "I just arrived."

When the computers were ready and the cameras recording Bob said to Frank, "You get in there and sit down and I'll ask the questions."

Frank scowled but said, "Okay."

Bob put four bottles of water from the break-room into his briefcase and with his briefcase in hand the two men returned to the interview room. Bob introduced himself and apologized for making them wait. He passed around the water bottles and retrieved a folder from his case. He looked through his notes on the Waldon boy, while deciding his direction of questioning.

After a moment, as Frank was about to speak, Bob said, "Sally says you were kidnapped?"

"Yes." Russell looked askance at Frank.

"You look pretty beat up. I think we should get you to the hospital."

"No."

"Are you sure?"

"No. I won't go."

"Let me take those off of you." Bob gestured to the handcuffs still hanging from the one wrist.

"Okay."

Bob fumbled with his key ring for a minute. He checked his Smith & Wesson, and Hiatts spare keys but they didn't work.

"Let me do it," Frank said as he leaned in with his spare keys. Frank removed the cuffs and put them on the table.

"Let's get those into evidence," Bob said.

"Why?" Frank asked.

"Those are police handcuffs."

Franks eyes narrowed as he looked closer at the handcuffs. Sally sat quietly. When she moved, her hands shook. She could barely hold the bottle to take a drink of water. She was so nervous she spilled some on her blouse.

"Are you okay, Sally?" Bob asked.

"Yes. Yes." She nervously daubed at the water with a napkin from her purse.

Bob turned to Russell, "You were kidnapped? That was Wednesday?"

"I think it was Wednesday. What's today?"

"Saturday. Tell me what you remember?" Bob opened his notepad and flipped to the account that Pearl Hoffman had given him of the kidnapping. He drew a line across the page and started a new section.

"I called Turbins and checked in like always and I left for work. I was halfway there when a white van pulled up. Two guys jumped out and dragged me in. One guy, the big guy, strangled me. I thought I was dead."

"A big guy? What did he look like? Do you remember?"

"No. Not really. There was a big tall kinda skinny guy and a short stout guy. Maybe not short, but shorter. They had something over their faces and they had painter's clothes on."

"What did they have over their faces? Baklavas? Ski masks?"

"Something fuzzy looking that changed their faces."

"Panty hose."

"Yeah."

"Their clothing? You said painter's clothes? A jumpsuit or coveralls?"

"I guess so. White van, and white clothing."

"Was the clothing like a jumpsuit or more of a lab coat, like a doctor would wear?"

"I don't remember."

"One piece or two piece, top and bottom?

"I don't really remember."

Bob jotted notes down on his pad. "Do you remember anything else?"

"The only thing I remember after that was running down the street. I was running to the supermarket. It was dark but I was late for work and I don't want to go back to prison."

"That was last night?"

"I guess so. What day is it?" Russell repeated his question.

"Saturday," Bob answered as he realized Russell was in near complete shock. "We need to get you to a hospital."

"No. I won't go."

"I insist."

Russell passively nodded. "What time is it?"

"It's almost ten. So between Wednesday and last night things are hazy?"

"No. Not hazy. Wait. I kinda remember a small space, like a coffin. I had a shovel and I remember trying to dig a hole to get out."

"Dig a hole? Was there dirt? Where you buried?" Bob looked at the boy's clothes. They were sweaty and worn but not filthy.

"No. I think it was the trunk of a car. It kept moving and I think I was hallucinating."

"Possibly," Bob said. "Can you be sure of any of this? Think about it."

"Yeah. I think it was a car trunk."

"So you got kidnapped in a van and somehow escaped from a car trunk?"

"I guess."

Bob stared at his notes for a moment then said, "I have another question for you."

Russell looked up, first at Bob and then at Sally.

"Were you working for John Spears? Spearman?" Bob asked.

Russell shook his head but Bob knew he was lying. "Don't worry about it. Okay? We aren't after prostitutes. We know Spears was a pimp. We found his phone number in your room when you disappeared. Were you working for him?"

Russell nodded.

"You aren't under arrest."

"Huh?"

"You aren't under arrest. I spoke to your parole officer. Okay?"

Russell nodded.

"Do you know what happened to Spears?"

"No."

"When was the last time you talked to him?"

"I don't know."

"You didn't read the news?"

"I never read the news."

"Spears was murdered."

Russell sat expressionless.

"Did you hear me?" Bob watched his reaction. "Spears was murdered."

"I didn't know."

"And we are trying to figure out who did it. I think who ever was after him is after you. Anything you can remember will help us catch who did this."

"Okay. I'll try," Russell said.

"I want to take you over to the hospital. We'll have an officer assigned to protect you. You aren't under arrest and I am going to talk to your parole officer again and make sure it's okay. You are safe here." Bob smiled and Russell stared at his hands. "Are you hungry? I'll get you something to eat and drink. Just relax and tell us what happened. Anything you can think of will help us catch whoever did this."

Russell looked down and mumbled, "Okay."

"I'll get you transported over to the hospital."

"Okay."

Bob opened the envelope that Sally had given him. He slid the latex glove fingertip into an evidence bag. He watched Russell as he did it. The boy showed no emotion.

"What can you tell me about that?"

"Nothing."

"Sally said you handed it to her. That you had it clenched in your fist."

"I guess."

"Do you remember that?"

"A little."

"Did the kidnappers wear latex gloves?"

"I don't know."

Bob shuffled through his papers and found the photo booth

film strip. He placed it on the table for everyone to see. Russell flashed his eyes to the photo and quickly away. Frank and Sally both leaned in to look at it. "Who is this boy you are with?" Bob asked.

Russell looked at the image as his eyes became larger. "I don't know." He stiffened as he gripped the edge of the table, his hands turning white.

"You recognize this picture."

"No."

"You don't need to lie. This picture was taken from your room." Bob frowned and sat back in his chair. "I cannot protect this boy without your help."

Russell refused to answer.

Sally sat upright and stopped shaking. She looked from Russell to Frank and then Bob. "I know who that is. His name is Joe Patten. Joe Junior. He works at the supermarket during the day and he's home-schooled and takes classes at night. He has his own car. Drives over from Bridgewater."

"What else can you tell me about him?" Bob was looking at Russell.

"Nothing. We hang out after work," Russell said.

"Do you remember where and when this picture was taken?"

"A month ago. Maybe more."

"Is he in danger?" Sally's voice rose an octave.

"Maybe," Bob answered. He waited for Russell to speak again. The tension grew and even Frank fidgeted, making Bob him a liability at the moment.

Finally Russell said, "He's a good kid. He's funny. After a couple years in lock-up it was good to have a friend to joke around with."

Frank leaned forward and said, "You are not supposed to have contact with minors. You are a convicted pedophile."

Bob put a hand up to Frank and said, "That's enough." Turning to Russell he said, "Try to relax. I can't speak to any prostitution you might be engaged in, but for this, the kidnapping, you are not in trouble. I just want to make sure you and he are protected." Bob gestured to the photo. To Frank and

Sally, he said, "Let's go." He gathered his files and the photo and evidence bag.

Frank continued to glare at Russell as they left the room. Bob asked Sally to wait in the lobby. When Bob and Frank were alone Frank said, "He doesn't remember anything."

They started walking towards Bob's office.

"True, I am hoping he can come up with something more."

"We know he was a prostitute and an ex-con-pedophile. Maybe he picked up a bad john. He admitted he was delusional. He probably dreamt everything. Could have been on drugs."

"No drugs were found in his room. A blood test will confirm it. This is related to Spears."

"I don't think he was kidnapped."

"We got a witness who saw the attack and the latex glove is evidence."

"That could be anything or nothing."

"Or there could be a fingerprint in the glove. These guys were wearing white suits and Terri found a white canvas fiber on Spears. It's the same type of thread used in painters' jumpsuits."

They reached Bob's office and each took a seat.

"What about Swanson?" Frank changed the subject.

"What about him?"

"You think those fires were arson?"

"The news kept saying lightning strikes, and things like that. I'll admit that takes some of the glamour away from the arsonist. Maybe this Swanson kid kept setting fires until he could be recognized for his... um... work," Bob replied.

"Like when they stopped publishing criminal names in newspapers."

"Exactly. Takes away the spotlight. Less likely to have copycat crimes. Maybe this kid got the attention he was looking for, but from the wrong people. Since Swanson disappeared how many fires have there been? None."

"That doesn't mean anything. Could be coincidence."

"I like *coincidence*," Bob said.

The two men sat quietly for a moment before Frank asked, "You think this convict was a botched murder attempt?"

"Yes," Bob said, "Did you see the finger bruises around his

neck? Someone tried to throttle him permanently."

Frank's forehead wrinkled. "What I don't understand is why he was left in the trunk of a car instead of buried or drowned or dumped in the trash."

Bob's eyes brightened. "Who would put a body in the trunk of their own car and drive around with it for three days?"

"A killer with no dump spot."

"Or the killers put the body into the trunk of their next victim."

"As a warning?"

"Spears had all the hallmarks of vigilante justice and a message of warning. Waldon escaped with his life, but I think the killers are getting bold. They are pleased with their own success and are stepping up their activity."

Frank asked, "Do you think it's like those Mexican drug cartels leaving bodies hanging from bridges?"

"Not as gruesome as that, but close. Whoever had the body in his or her trunk has been warned, and if the killer knows about this Joe Patten kid, and the killers are targeting kids in their teens and twenties, then we have to protect him. My guess is the lover of a ex-con is the next target. Maybe we can stop these guys."

"Let's hope so," Frank said as he took a cigarette from a pack in his pocket. "What if we let them off?"

"Let them continue killing?" Bob asked. He was surprised to hear that suggestion from Frank.

"Yes. They are killing psychopaths. Future murderers."

"I can't judge that... I could imaging that a puppy killer might, or even a drug dealer. An arsonist might kill someone on accident. A prostitute? I think they're hurting themselves more than anyone else."

"What about this message? Who's next? Do they deserve it?"

"I don't know about deserve. A gay teenager? The owner of the car he escaped from? Why would they deserve anything? It's not illegal to be gay and I don't enforce morality. Anyone else? A john? It may be illegal, but I see a victimless crime. Yes, we arrest people and prosecute them, and they pay a fine or get five days in lockup and then they're back out, working, supporting a family, and sometimes engaging in immoral or illicit activity. Maybe that's too lenient, but I wouldn't want them murdered. Would you?"

"Killed? No. But you admit the penalties are too light. We can agree that these killers are just sending a message."

"I can't let them murder at will. We have a duty to the law. Right or wrong."

"True enough," Frank said as he rose from his chair and turned to leave. "Adios," he said from the doorway.

Bob picked up his phone and dialed zero. When Louise answered he asked, "Is Sally Sonders still waiting in the lobby?"

"Yes sir."

"Will you please ask her to come in?"

"Your office?"

"Yes, please."

"You got it." Louise clicked off the line.

Bob clicked the receiver and pressed a hotkey.

"County Fire-Rescue," a voice answered.

"Jerry? Bob Schwimer."

"Hi Bob. Don't tell me another boat accident in the bay?"

"No. I need a favor."

"What do you need?" Jerry asked.

"I've got a guy here who's pretty beat up. He refuses to go to the hospital but I'd like you to take a look at him. Still got your paramedic training?"

"Sure do. Comes with the job."

"Emergency?"

"Not overly."

"I can be there in twenty minutes."

"Thanks Jerry." Bob hung up the phone as Louise appeared in the doorway with Sally.

"Welcome. I wanted to talk to you privately."

"Anything detective." She was visibly shaking. Her eyes still nervously flickering and on the edge of tears.

Bob took her hand and led her to a seat, trying to assay her fear, "Russell will be okay. I've got a paramedic coming over to take a look at him. What can you tell me about this morning?"

Chapter 46

Bob's cell phone rang as he sat at his office desk. Donald Rudolph's name appeared.

"Good morning, Don," he answered.

"Bob. There's a problem."

"Sounds like my whole week." Bob smiled.

"It just got worse. You are off the case."

"What do you mean? Which case?" Bob's smile turned down.

"I don't know who he talked to, or what was said, but Frank is in charge of the investigation."

"Which investigation?"

"Rickman and Spears. Anything else you've tied in. The whole task force."

"What's going on? How did this happen?"

"I don't know, Bob. It came from the executive office. Right from the top. The new orders are, 'Frank Wysup is State Coroner and all homicides are the state's jurisdiction. Frank is the head of the task force. You are to assist or step aside'."

"Damn it, Donald. They can't do this."

"Technically they can. You could call Keller. You could call the Staties' Secretary directly. I've already done that myself, and they made it clear, *follow orders or step aside*. The same applies to you."

"If Alan... Sheriff Barton was not on the outs himself I might be able to make a case for keeping this downstairs. Barton's corruption problems haven't helped you or anyone else. I am not making the decisions anymore."

"That son-of-a-bitch."

"You don't have to tell me," Donald mused.

"I can make some phone calls."

"Normally I'd say 'no' to that."

"Not this time?"

"I've been steam rolled. I want to know what's going on just as much as you."

"So I can find out?"

"I'd love to know who was driving the truck that ran us over on this one. I knew he was vying for control, but didn't think he had the power to get it done this quickly, or without any consultation from me or you. I've been blindsided."

"We both were. I promise to keep you informed."

"I'll do the same."

Bob hung up and called Frank immediately after talking to Donald. Frank answered the phone on the fourth ring. "I see you got the message."

"What's this about, Frank?"

"I was the Plymouth M.E. before moving upstairs to State Coroner…"

"Save me from your 'hero speech', Frank. Dammit. I've heard it a dozen times."

"Let's just say I don't like your style."

"And I never gave a damn what you liked." Bob's phone beeped and he saw Terri was calling in. He sent the call to voicemail.

"You better start or you can step out. Better yet. Step out. And you can start your departure by handing over all your files. I've already called for transportation of the bodies."

"You what?"

"Yes," Frank sneered. "Terri is off the case, too. The Rickman and Spears bodies are being moved to Dedham where I can review the autopsies and make any appropriate judgments. I would guess your job is on the line. You and Terri. I've already had the Swanson bones moved. Even the FBI is stepping aside. Have Louise pack up your files. A department courier will be there within an hour."

"Are you still in the building?" Bob asked. Frank hung up on him.

Bob left the headquarters. He saw Frank in the parking lot talking to Peter and Wally. Peter and Wally both raised a hand to wave. Frank only scowled at him as he walked to his car. Bob smiled in return. It appeared to unnerve the man, which made

Bob laugh to himself.

He returned Terri's call as he pointed his car towards Bridgewater in search of Joe Patten Junior.

"I know," she said as she answered the phone. "Frank was just here with a group of State Police. They are bagging up everything. I was trying to get a hold of you."

"Make copies of everything," Bob said.

"I already did. I did it yesterday. I always make copies and save everything to a USB drive. I've got it in my car."

"You are great, Terri."

"He threatened to lock me out of my own lab."

"Don't worry about it. Did you finish the Rickman autopsy?"

"Yes, mostly. But I've still got some samples out at the test labs."

"Does Frank know that?"

"No. He didn't ask me anything."

"Good. Frank doesn't know about the copies you made?"

"No."

"Great."

"What are you going to do?" Terri asked.

"I'm going to take this S.O.B. down."

"Do you think he's involved?"

"There's no doubt. I wondered if he just made some mistakes but not anymore. This is an end-run and no one pulls an end-run unless he's hiding something."

"You think he's involved with the murders?"

"No, but he's covering his ass over something."

"What are we going to do?"

"I'm going to continue the investigation. I've got copies of everything too."

"You'll get fired."

"Only if Frank finds out and only if he's not hiding anything. There is no one who is wrong all the time."

"You're taking a chance on your job."

"I'm out of a job already. Are you in or out?"

"I hate that son of a bitch. He's been riding me for years,"

Terri said with all humor gone from her voice.

"That sounds like you are in." Bob laughed. "Here's what I need you to do. Try to stay on Frank's good side."

"That's going to be tough. I called him every name in the book a couple minutes ago."

Bob laughed, "I'm sure he deserves every one of them. Try to get back in. I need to know what he's doing and what he's saying. Apologize if you have to. I'm going to pursue this investigation but he can't know about it. I need to know what he knows and counter his every move."

"So you want me to play nice?"

"Yes. I need a spy on his side. Call me a few names. I'm sure he'll come around."

"I could think of a few. Cheap for one." Terri laughed.

"That's good. Tell him I never gave you a raise."

"Oh. You want the truth."

"You got a raise last year," Bob said flatly.

"Got ya." She laughed.

"That will work. You might want to wait a day or so. Let him cool down and tell him you realized he was right and I was wrong all along. Throw in some poor police work comments and *'finding evidence that I wanted to find'* stuff."

"It could cost me my job."

"It might anyway. As far as I'm concerned we've been fired. They just still send us a paycheck. The only way we are going to keep our jobs is to take this conspiracy down."

"Whatever Frank is hiding?"

"That's not important. Finding these killers will save our jobs."

"I'll do what I can."

"Thanks Terri. And one more thing. Break out your sidearm."

"I hate carrying that thing. I'm always cleaning up the mess after a shooting and I never need it. It gets in the way."

"This is going to get messy and it could turn violent. We don't know who is out there."

"That bad?"

"Bad enough for four bodies and a near-miss. The Mulligans

are in custody. The Bridgers are supposed to be picked up. Houghton is still loose. Nothing good sticks to him yet. There may be others in this vigilante group. Waldon was grabbed by two guys, one might fit the description of Houghton but we have no one for the other guy. It's not Cody Bridger or Shawn Mulligan. So carry your sidearm until we can catch these guys."

"Okay."

"Tell me about the Rickman autopsy."

"I worked all yesterday and Friday night. Even late last night."

"We didn't get to talk much about it yesterday. You do know it's Sunday?"

"I was bored and I'm glad I worked. If Frank got this body before-hand we'd never know what happened."

"What did you find?"

"I don't think it was an accidental death. I x-rayed and M.R.I.'d the body. Rickman's throat was crushed. Exploration of the body cavity, post embalming, indicates there is no water residue in the lungs. The lung tissue I tested indicates no water borne bacteria or any other match with the pond samples I took last week."

"Could be a dry-drowning. His wind pipe could have sealed up involuntarily?"

"For his throat to have closed he had to breathe some amount of water. Dry drowning would have left a tiny bit of residue. The throat closes and traps out the water and traps in the initial amount. 'Dry' is a misnomer. There was nothing. Not even in the wind pipe, but what caused the crushed throat?" Terri asked.

"He could have slipped and struck his throat against the side of the boat."

"Maybe."

"The Houghton's were never overly cooperative."

"You mean the raped girl and her dad?"

"The father hates me. I don't blame him. There was never enough evidence that Rickman raped the girl. Maybe it's time to talk to them again."

"Good luck, Bob."

"Thank you. One question. Terri? How could Frank have got this wrong?"

"He was doing the job of two people, as he likes to remind me." Terri giggled nervously.

"True. He does like to harp about that." Bob chuckled.

"So what are you working on today, besides being fired and possibly charged with obstruction of justice?" Terri's voice lifted in laughter.

"I'm glad you didn't lose your sense of humor. I'm going over to the Patten house. Joe Patten Junior is Russell's friend from the supermarket."

"That's the second boy in Russell's photo." Terri asked.

"The one you found in Russell's boarding room."

"Any reason he could be involved in the kidnapping?"

"Probably not. I'll find out. There is one thing though," Bob replied. "I received a letter saying that the Spears murder is part of a conspiracy to kill people. No name, no address, but the post mark is from Bridgewater," Bob said.

"And the Pattens are from Bridgewater?" Terri asked.

"I wonder if they're getting cold feet."

"You mean they're involved?"

"Maybe."

"It seems a stretch to me. I mean, the kid shows up in a photograph with the kidnapped pedophile who he works with, but that's it."

"True. But maybe the parents aren't too happy to find out their kid is gay, and they would never hurt their own son."

"So they kidnap Russell as part of the vigilante group?" Terri asked.

"Maybe that or they're getting scared and want out of the group. Too many attacks," Bob said

"You only get hurt by jumping off the roller coaster."

"Or turning in your cohorts in crime."

"That too. Can you prove any of that?" Terri asked.

Bob heard Terri breathing hard into the phone. Her adrenaline was up. He realized his was also.

"Not a thing," he said, "I'm just kicking some ideas around," Bob replied.

"Good. I like ideas. I haven't had this much work in forever. Hating Frank at the moment but I love the work."

"Then you won't be needing a raise anytime soon."

"That's not funny, Bob. We'll be lucky to keep our jobs at this point."

Bob laughed. "I'll stop by tomorrow morning. Take the afternoon off, Terri. Frank isn't going anywhere. Anything he does digs the hole he is in deeper and wider."

"If we are dealing with serial killers…"

"They aren't going anywhere. We'll find them."

"Before they kill again?"

"Hopefully. That's why I need to talk to the Pattens. Joe Patten may be next, especially if they sent that letter."

"Or who else?"

"I've been over the crime statistics and the newspapers and unless you can find a new serial-sociopathic-criminal these guys are targeting…"

"That sounds like a challenge. We've got dozens of drug dealers and lots of petty criminals. They could target any one of them at any time. I'll go over my autopsy report on Rickman when you get back. I'll email it to you."

"Don't use the lab computer and email my personal account."

"Right away. First thing."

"Good enough."

"I have to finish typing up the report anyway. Bye, Bob."

"Play nice with Frank, Terri."

"I'll try."

Bob hung up as he turned into the Patten's driveway. It was foe-cobblestone curving from granite pillars at the gate up to a large piazza with the wings of an orderly, almost stately, McMansion extending out to create a small courtyard. The new house stood out from the older, more mature houses in the upper middle class neighborhood.

Bob rang the bell and waited several minutes. A middle-aged and dark haired but graying man opened the door. Bob noted he was the thirty years older image of his son from the photograph with the same high cheeks and round face.

The door was not locked.

"Good morning. I'm Detective Schwimer. County. Are you Joseph Patten?" The man nodded. "I'd like to ask you about your son."

"Joe? What happened?" Joseph Patten Senior asked.

"It's about a kidnapping in Plymouth."

"And why would my son have anything to do with that?"

"That is why I'm here. Is your wife home?" Bob looked at his notepad, "Susanne?"

"No."

"Is Joe Junior home?"

"That depends."

"Yes. It depends on if you would like your name in the newspaper regarding a grand jury subpoena. You both have the same name. How would you like to explain that at the golf course club house?" Bob hoped his bluff would not be called. It wasn't.

"Come in."

Bob followed Joseph into a large foyer where he pointed to a couch and said, "I'll get Joe. He just got back from work." Joseph left the room.

Bob set his briefcase on the floor. He chose to stand while he waited. He looked around the room for any letters or notepads that might give him a handwriting sample. The letter prowled the back of his mind. He wondered if he should ask them for a handwriting sample.

The room was decorated with the finest furniture and paintings of English fox hunts and cottages hung on the walls. Family photos were arranged on the mantle above the fireplace. Prominently placed where several framed prints of a woman and a boy, individually jumping thoroughbreds over fences, or cross rails, or standing beside a bay thoroughbred horse proudly holding blue ribbons and trophies. Bob wondered how a rich teenager ended up in a provocative homosexual photograph with a male prostitute.

Joseph returned with his son, Joe. The boy plopped onto the couch while Bob and the elder Patten stood facing each other, both looking down, like rams preparing to butt heads. Bob took a copy of the Russell Waldon and Joe Patten photo-strip from his briefcase and handed it to the boy. The kiss photo was cropped out. His father peered over to see the picture. "It's a copy. Do you recognize the other kid in that picture?"

"We were just goofing off," the boy exclaimed.

"That's not what I asked."

"We were just having fun. Russell said he tore that picture up."

"My son is not a homosexual," Joseph said angrily.

"No one said he was," Bob replied as he wondered how the man deduced that from the three photos with the fourth one of the kiss removed. Turning back to the boy he said, "I know you and Russell were friends."

"We still are." Joe stood up, clenching his fists.

"Uh huh. Let's say you *were*, until he died." Bob watched the boy's face. It fell hard at the lie.

Tears came to Joe's eyes. "He isn't dead. He can't be dead."

Bob turned to the father and watched the man's expression at his plotted untruth. "He died in the hospital last night. Whoever tried to kill him succeeded in the end. My question is this; Why do you think someone would want him killed?"

The older Patten answered with a tinge of a smile, "Because he is a pedophile. Convicted."

Bob looked at Joe and saw only genuine horror at the death of a friend. He looked back at Joseph and the man displayed satisfied contempt. The two stared at each other until Bob finally said, "You seem to know a bit about Russell Waldon. What else can you tell me?"

"Nothing. He's a pedophile working at the same supermarket as my son. I always track crime and criminals when my family is concerned. I don't want a pedophile molesting my son."

"He didn't molest me, Dad."

Joseph looked at his son, "What did you do?"

"Nothing. We were goofing off."

"This doesn't look like goofing off to me. It looks gay." Joseph took the photograph from his son.

"Gay is not illegal, Mr. Patten. Kidnapping. Murder. That is illegal. So I would like to know exactly what happened a few days ago. This photograph was found in Waldon's room. I just need to know how Joe is involved."

The man turned and glared at Bob. "I think you better find that subpoena or warrant or anything else you need. You can contact my lawyer."

Bob smiled. "Just don't go anywhere. And…"

"And what?"

"I don't think your son is gay." Bob hoped, for the sake of a young man, that the older man fell for his second lie of the day.

"You bet your ass he isn't gay."

"And I don't want to concern you…"

"Concern me? How?"

"I think your son is next."

"That's not going to happen."

"Are you sure? Are you certain? I'm offering you my help. There's a serial killer out there. Actually a group of serial killers. Four or five of them, working together. They have been killing kids for years. Four years at least. They started with a criminal and moved on to sociopaths. They murdered a rapist, a dog killer, an arsonist, a drug dealer and now a pedophile. Two of them are linked, Waldon and Spears. Waldon has a connection to your son. I have no reason to believe that a he won't be next."

"He's not gay."

"We have arrested four of them. One is still out and another one or two exist, but I don't know who they are."

"My son is not homosexual."

"Does it matter if you think so?"

"We'll be fine," Joseph said flatly.

"Are you certain? They don't seem to discriminate against specific criminals, or crimes, or even questionable mores. I think that any kid is a target if they get spotted in these people's crosshairs. They took out a homosexual prostitute that was a known associate of your son."

"I said we will be fine." Joseph walked to the front door and opened it for Bob.

"This is an open offer of protection." Bob intentionally

didn't ask for a handwriting sample. If the elder Patten wrote the letter he had changed his mind. If the younger had written it, telling the elder would put them both in danger... that is, if either of them had written the letter.

The door slammed closed behind him.

Chapter 47

Morning brought the cool hint of winter in the air. The crisp scent of coming snow hung low to the ground. Morning fog lay like a blanket over the lawn. Mary accompanied Bob to the door. She held it open for him as she carried his heavy coat and insisted he take it. "The weather's turning cold, just in case."

"Goodbye, honey," he said as he kissed her briefly. It was the kind of peck that comes with love and affection even after ten years of marriage; mechanical, but done with intent.

"Lunch today?" Mary asked after she kissed him back.

"Maybe," he said, turning to go to the garage.

"Darling?"

Bob turned back around and Mary threw herself into his arms and pressed her lips to his. They held each other close for a long moment, enjoying each other's presence. The kiss reduced them both to laughter.

"What's that?" Bob smiled as she let him go.

"I love you." Mary's fair skin cheeks brightened with red and her lips curved up.

"I love you, too."

"Go to work," she said.

Mary stood on the front porch, her arms wrapped around herself, as Bob backed the car out of the detached-garage. "I think I'll cut the grass one last time before it snows," Mary said to herself. "The leaves are starting to fall. A little yard work..." As she turned to go inside she saw a package by the porch bench. The box was marked "Express Delivery" and she wondered how long it had been there. She picked it up and carried it inside.

Bob's desk phone rang. The call was direct dialed, not patched through from the dispatcher. He pressed the speaker phone button. "Good morning. Schwimer."

"Hello Detective. This is Sally over at the supermarket."

"Hi Sally."

"You know we talked the other day about Russell Waldon?"

"Have you heard anything?"

"Maybe, but maybe not. You know you asked me to keep my ears open, this being the supermarket with so many people coming through all the time. So. It's kinda strange because he's never missed work before and it doesn't seem like him to not call and just not show up. I know he was pretty upset with the Waldon boy kidnapping and everything so I thought I'd call you. Because they were sort of friends. I know it was in the newspaper about that kid being a pedophile, not that anyone here knew he was one, because I never said anything. The parole officer asked me to keep these things quiet a long time ago when I started offering work for them. So, jobs for ex-convicts, that is. But he was always sweet as key-lime pie when he was here and well, they were friends. Do you know what I mean? They hung out together, not that anything happened, so I don't really know if anything happened, Russell being homosexual or bi or whatever. It didn't seem like it. And Joe didn't either. So anyway Joe didn't show up for work this morning and he's usually twenty minutes early, so he's so much earlier than he needs to be, because he's sometimes here when I get here to open up. Waldon doesn't show up until right on time or even a few minutes late. So I waited until after we opened and I got busy with the cash drawers and getting ready, I'd figure I'd see if he came in late. So it got later and I kinda forgot to call you to let you know, but it's probably nothing. So you see why I am concerned? Do you know what I mean?"

Bob smirked but withheld his laughter at Sally's rambling. "Slow down Sally. Who didn't show up for work?" He already knew it was the Patten boy.

"So I called his house and they haven't seen him. They said he left right on time this morning but they seemed nervous. So they said they weren't worried but I could hear it in Susanne's voice that she was worried but Joseph said, Joseph Senior, not Junior, they were both on the phone, different receivers or something, said he wasn't worried and he kinda paused for a minute and then he said something weird."

Bob stopped smiling, "What did he say?" he asked.

"He said that Joe Junior was at home sick and that he forgot he was sick that morning and that they took him over to the uncle's house by the lake because the uncle is retired and he could watch the boy. But they said he left for work, and then said he was home-sick, and then over at the uncle's house, and how could they have forgotten that and this was only a little after eleven and how could they have gone out to the lake and back in just a couple hours. I guess they could have gone out to the lake and back. It's not that far. But to forget that their son was sick and not call into the supermarket, and forgot where he is, do you see what I mean? And the weird thing is that Joe, Senior, not Junior, Senior works over at the telephone company and he was at home today instead of being at work, it being a weekday." Sally stopped. She breathed hard and fast.

"Sally?"

"And the other thing is I heard Susanne crying in the background, like she put down the telephone but I could still hear her. I know what her voice sounds like. Do you know what I mean?"

"Sally? Please." Bob tried to calm her. Who are you talking about?" he asked. His notes were a scribbled mess as he'd tried to keep up. "You mean the Patten boy?"

"Junior, not senior. Russell is still with you."

"Yes. Protective custody for the moment. Can you come into the office this afternoon? Or tell you what, Sally? Can you write down everything that happened and I'll come over and talk to you."

"You are coming over to the supermarket?"

"Yes. And please write down everything you told me."

"Okay."

Bob hung up and headed out to his car, turning left out of the parking lot, towards the highway and Bridgewater, rather than right towards the supermarket.

Chapter 48

Bob knocked on Joseph Patten's door. He heard someone inside shuffling their feet. The lock turned. The sound surprised Bob as he knew it had not been locked when he offered the boy his protection a day before. Something changed.

"Who is it?" Joseph Patten asked as he opened the door a sliver and put his face in the opening. The man was visibly shaking. His hair seemed to take on more gray, and he stood as if he had shrunk four inches; having aged ten years in one night.

"Mr. Patten? Can I come in?" Bob gently pushed the door open another foot and the man's hand shook as he took the business card that Bob offered him. Bob knew the man already had his card, but the action often functioned as an offering, a gift of greeting to make one feel welcome. Politeness would often be returned by opening the door a little more, or giving answers to questions. At least to appease the person and make them go away.

"I'm not sure," Joseph replied.

"I only need a few minutes. I'd like to talk to your son."

"We don't want your protection."

"That was yesterday, sir." Bob stood tall, firm.

"So what?"

"So today your son didn't report to work and you already know that."

"What happened?"

"We need to talk."

"I don't know…"

"I think you can no longer refuse my help. Can I come in so we can talk." Bob did not ask.

"Um... I don't know," Joseph said nervously.

"It will take just a few minutes." Bob pushed the door open another foot and stepped inside. Joseph stepped back. The man's attitude of accusation of his son's homosexuality was gone. The strength and stature of the wealthy businessman the day before, like a proud leader of a wolf pack, was replaced with the hull of a man hung carelessly from weary bones. From a back room Bob heard a woman's voice.

"Joe? Who is it?"

Joseph turned and answered in a forced calm voice, "It's okay, Susanne. It's the detective from yesterday to talk to about that pervert...um... that boy who was found dead." Joseph turned back to Bob with sharp eyes. Bob saw the wolf return for an instant. "We don't need your help," he said.

"Can Susanne come in here? I'd like to talk to both of you. I get a little nervous with someone in the other room." Bob waited for the woman to appear, or for Joseph to call her into the room. Neither occurred. Finally Bob let the question rest and decided to test the man's capacity for truth.

"Do you know where Joe is? I'd like to talk to him." He suspected the boy was kidnapped but he didn't, couldn't, understand why they would hide it.

"He's in Lakeville with his uncle. He was very sick this morning."

"Yes. That's what they said at the supermarket."

Joseph didn't reply.

"So how is he?"

"Bad," Joseph answered.

"In what way?"

"What?"

"How is he sick? In what way?"

"Sick. Just sick."

"There's different degrees of illness, sir." Bob remained polite.

Joseph didn't answer.

"There's coughing sick."

The man remained stone silent.

"There's vomiting sick. Did he have a fever?"

Joseph nodded his head.

"Could be appendicitis?"

The man nodded again.

"Appendicitis? That's bad. He could die. Should go to the

hospital."

"No. He had his out a couple years ago."

"If he was sick enough to miss work why would you drive him anywhere? Shouldn't he be in bed?"

Joseph straightened up, as if he had arranged his lies, however hastily. Bob knew that badly formed lies led to the truth and hasty lies are always messy. "Let's just say its protection. You said he was in danger."

"So he's not sick?"

"No."

"And he's at your brother's place?"

"No."

"No?"

"Um... Susanne's brother."

"What's his name?"

"Um... Vinny Gagliardo."

"Vinny as in Vincent? Not Tim or Timmy?" Bob took a pen from his pocket.

"Vinny."

Bob wrote the name in his pad. "I'll need the address."

"I... I don't really know the address."

Bob looked at Joe with curiosity. He lowered his notebook.

"You said he should be protected, so we sent him away. He's protected."

"I need to talk to him."

"Why?"

"I'll need the address."

"I guess I could look it up in the address book. Susanne? Can you please get the address book?"

Bob heard shuffling feet from the other room and a moment later a woman Bob assumed was Susanne; tall, overweight, middle-aged blonde; sporting tinges of gray in the roots of her hair, brought a small leather address book to her husband. Her hands shook violently as Joseph took the book and opened it. Joe put his hand on her arm to steady it.

"Are you okay?" Bob asked.

"Yes." Her quivering voice belied her answer.

"Joe's uncle? What did you say his name is?"

"It's my uncle, not Joe's," Susanne said as her husband looked at her and frowned with a hint of a headshake.

"Not your brother?"

"No. My uncle," Susanne said. Bob looked at Joseph and saw the statement was untrue.

"Um…" Joseph said.

Bob turned back to Susanne and asked her again for the name.

"Detective, my wife is very upset," Joseph pleaded.

"I just have a few questions. Your uncle's name is Vinny Gagliardo?"

"Can I ask what this is regarding?" Joe's voice grew stronger.

"I said it's about your son's protection. It is not about his friendship with Russell Waldon, or *the pervert*, as you described him yesterday."

"He was a pervert. Everyone knew he was a pedophile. He raped children. He deserved…" Joe's voice died.

Bob noted the reaction in his book and pressed on. "Waldon was convicted of sex with a minor when he was eighteen and working as a prostitute. He was caught with a john who was sixteen. I will admit he's a prostitute but I would hardly consider that to be pedophilia. The district attorney and the judge apparently think differently than I do, and it was in Boston outside my jurisdiction."

Bob looked to Susanne, "The address?"

Susanne gave him the address. He wrote it down and turned towards the front door. Opening the door slowly he pondered for a moment then turned back to the couple. "We can continue this charade. I can go over to Lakeville and find out this is a wild-goose chase, but we both know that Joseph Junior was kidnapped by the same group that kidnapped Russell Waldon." He stopped and looked at the couple, waiting for his words to take effect. Susanne began to visibly cry and Joseph grew angry.

"You have no business saying that. You are upsetting my wife. Just go." The man pointed to the door.

"Now is the time you need me. Yesterday would have been better, but Russell escaping-alive was an accident… an accident these killers won't make a second time."

"Get out of my house."

Bob ignored the demand. "I think you or your son know something about the killers. Maybe you are part of the group. Maybe on the fringe. Supplying money, or information, or something. I think your son was kidnapped. I don't think he was kidnapped for being homosexual. I think it's a warning to you."

Susanne began to wail in grief. She loudly moaned and tears streamed from her eyes.

"Get out!" Joseph commanded.

Bob knocked on the door of a house at twelve-seventy-five Route 105. The house was set up on a rise above the road, overlooking the cattails around Long Pond to the west and Assawampset pond on the east. A young woman answered the door, opening it just a crack. She wore a house dress of faded plaid and her stringy brown hair was like the tail of an unkempt pony.

"Yes?" she asked.

"Good afternoon. I'm Detective Schwimer with the Plymouth County Sheriff's office." Bob handed her a business card and she took it through the crack. "I am looking for the house at twelve-seventy-five."

The woman casually grinned and said, "There's no twelve-seventy-five. This is twelve-seventy-three." She opened the door a little more.

"I see. Do you know a Vinny Gagliardo? Does he live on this street?"

"There used to be a Gagliardo down the road. Are you sure you have the right address?"

"Yes. Um... I must not..."

"Sorry I can't help you." The woman brushed her hair from her eyes.

"Maybe you can. Do you know a Joseph Patten?" The woman shook her head. "Thanks anyway. Sorry to bother you."

Bob returned to his car. He chided himself for not thinking to check the name and address before driving to Lakeville. He wondered if he should drop in on the Houghton's again while he was in town. He could see their docks across the lake. He instead turned to his laptop computer and clacked away on the keyboard.

A moment later he picked up his cell phone and called B.C.I.

"Louise? It's Bob," he said when she answered the call.

"Go ahead, Detective."

"Louise, please call me Bob."

"Yes sir."

Bob laughed. She always agreed but she never used his first name.

"Can you get me Peter on the horn? He's probably on patrol."

A few moments later, Peter's voice came over the radio.

"Peter? I am following up on the Russell Waldon case and I've got a name we need to check into."

"I thought Dr. Wysup was in charge?"

"What he doesn't know won't hurt me. Can you keep it quiet? I need some help, but don't tell Frank?"

"Of course…"

"See what you can find on a Vinny, or Vincent, last name Gagliardo of Lakeville and while you are at it look up a Joseph Patten Senior and Susanne Patten. See what C.J.I.S. has on them, and Homeland Security too."

Bob's radio clicked and Louise's voice came through, "Bob? Pickup the radio. Bob? Bob?" Louise never used his first name before, even after years of him asking her to. He sensed a strain in her normally relaxed voice. Bob told Peter to hang on as he grabbed the radio.

"Louise? What's going on?"

"Bob. There's a fire, an explosion."

"What's the twenty?"

"eleven-eight-sixteen Merryweather, Duxbury" Louise hesitated. "It's your house."

The radio went silent for a moment, then Bob asked, "Is Mary okay?"

"I don't know. Fire and ambulance is en route. Your neighbor called it in."

"Was she in the house?"

"A woman is reported injured."

"How long ago?"

"Just a few minutes."

"Anyone else hurt?"

"Just one."

"I'll be right there. I'll be on the emergency channel and you have my cell."

"Okay."

"Wait. Louise? Radio the Coast Guard in Barnstable and get the medivac-helicopter."

"I called them first. It's on its way."

Twenty minutes later Bob sped down Merryweather with the lights of the unmarked interceptor flashing. The street ahead was blocked with fire engines and an ambulance. In the pasture behind his house a red and white Coast-Guard helicopter wound up its engines and lifted its struts from the ground. Dust rose in a wild vortex and the long grass whipped back and forth. Hovering barely feet in the air it turned in place and suddenly tilted forward, moving at full throttle across the field and towards Boston, rising quickly as it went. Bob watched it clear the trees at the edge of the field and disappear from view. He knew that Mary was alive. He sighed, as he watched the horses running in a wild panic at the far end of the field. Bob closed swiftly on the vehicles blocking the street. He locked up the brakes and opened the door as the car stopped.

He had a foot on the ground when a knock came from the passenger's side window. He ignored it as he looked at his house. Smoke billowed from several broken windows and the front door. Hoses ran into the house and a team sprayed the roof and eves from the yard.

"Hey!" Duxbury Fire-Chief Le'Bourque called.

Bob got out of the car. "Was that Mary?"

"Female. Mid-thirties. She's alive. You just missed the chopper. You could have gone with her," Le'Bourque answered.

"What happened? Was it the gas? I never trusted gas. I don't care if it is a co-op."

"Not sure. The kitchen took a big hit. Probably. The fire

marshal is inside."

"I'll call the team. I want this place secured. When your men are done, my people are the only ones in or out. I want a full investigation."

"Are you the husband?"

"Yes. Bob Schwimer."

"Local cop?"

"County."

"Why don't you go to Boston?"

"How bad is she?"

"Bad. She was in the kitchen. Your neighbor pulled her out of the fire. He probably saved her life."

Bob looked around with wild eyes to a group of neighbors by the fire-engines. The hero was probably in that group. He recognized all their faces but for the moment his mind was blank on their names. "Yeah," he said.

"Go to Boston." Le'Bourque repeated himself.

"Boston?"

"Yeah."

"Not Brockton, or South Weymouth?"

"She's stable. They have the best burn units in Boston. Do you want someone to drive you?"

"Yeah... ah... No."

"I'll have one of my guys take you."

"No. I'm fine."

"Rose-Francis Memorial."

Bob got back in his car and turned it around in the street. He picked up his phone and thumbed through the contact list and dialed a number he hadn't used in many years.

"Boston Rose-Francis," a woman's voice answered.

"I need the emergency room."

"Hold."

Bob fidgeted as he waited impatiently. It seemed like minutes.

"Emergency desk."

"This is Detective Schwimer. You have a Mary Schwimer that came in by helicopter? How is she?"

"What's the name?"

"Schwimer. A Coast Guard helicopter came in?"

"How do you…"

"S-C-H-W…"

"Coast Guard?"

"Yes."

"They are still en route, detective. Should be here in a few minutes."

"I'll be there. Have the doctor call me when he has information." He gave her his number.

"We won't know anything for a little while. The E.M.T. radioed in that she's on fluids and they're administering burn-care."

"Vitals?"

"Weak but stable."

"Have the doctor call me. You got my number."

"Yes, sir. I will."

"Thank you." Bob hung up the phone and it immediately rang again. "What?" he asked.

"Bob, it's Terri. What happened over there? Is Mary okay?"

"She's on her way to Boston. They took her by helicopter."

"Do you want me to drive you?"

"No. I'm on my way to the hospital now."

"Bob?"

"What?"

"It can wait. Maybe I shouldn't say anything just yet."

"Say it."

"I think we are getting close to someone who doesn't want us around."

"I was thinking the same thing. Terri? Get Peter and Wally and get over to my house. Find out what happened. I don't think this was an accident. I think someone meant this for me."

"What about Frank?"

"Fuck Frank. This is my wife and my house."

"Wally is already there and I'm on the way over now. Frank called in sick this morning."

"Good. Surprised Frank called anyone."

"He didn't. I called his office. Receptionist told me."

"You know, Bob? Frank missed a lot in that Rickman

murder."

"Yeah. That was in your report."

"I met with him. He was very upset about the Rickman autopsy."

"You have my attention."

"He was furious. Yelling and screaming at me and basically saying it was his investigation."

"So much for staying on his good side. What do you think that was about?" Bob asked.

"I don't know. He kept saying something about Rickman drowning, not being strangled... Bob? Rickman was strangled."

"That's what you told me. It was in your reports."

"That's what the M.R.I. showed, but not only that. There was undertakers' makeup covering what looks like finger bruise marks, plus the bruising on his arms, and that's not all. Frank said he ordered a cremation for Rickman and he was surprised that the body was buried instead." She paused and then said, "Maybe it's nothing."

"Terri. I'm on the outside looking in. I need your help. If you have something to say about this investigation you gotta tell me."

"I am just not comfortable with Frank leading this team."

"Me too."

"What can I do?"

"It's his investigation."

"I know that."

"Just talk to him only if he talks to you. Don't offer him anything."

"Isn't that interfering with an investigation?"

"Maybe. Technically, probably no. Look he's yelling at you, right?"

"Yes."

"So he thinks you've got everything wrong?"

"Yes again."

"And we know you don't."

"Uh-huh."

"If he called you to ask your advice, give it."

"He won't do that. Can't imagine at this point."

"No problem."

"So what do we do?"

"Us?"

"Yes. Us."

"I'm off the case. It would be improper for me to continue to investigate the murders while Frank is in charge."

"That's not going to happen." Terri stated factually but Bob stayed silent. Police lines were all recorded, incoming or outgoing. "What's going on? What aren't you telling me?"

"Nothing," Bob replied.

"What have you found?"

"Not much. Got another kidnapping. Not confirmed but I'd put my money on it."

"Joe Patten, Junior," Terri said.

"Ah-huh. That's him. I tried to warn him and his father yesterday."

"What can I do to help?"

"Keep Frank happy."

"That shouldn't be hard." Terri said sarcastically. "What else?"

"See what you can find out about the explosion at my house."

"Will do."

Bob hung up and focused on his drive in to Boston.

Chapter 49

Bob looked at the dashboard clock glowing in the early morning darkness. It was nearly five. What day? Tuesday? Wednesday? He was exhausted, thinking slow, reflexes taxed, and he was psychologically drained, but adrenaline kept him awake on the long drive back to Plymouth from Boston. It was early enough to get to the office and try to discover what, or who, tried to kill him and Mary. He couldn't touch Houghton for the Rickman murder with Frank in charge. The Bridgers were out of his hands too for the Swanson bones. The Mulligans were Jasperse's problem for Joel Richardson. Jasperse was under Frank's direction anyway. There was still no primary suspect on Spears, or Waldon, or Patten.

His thoughts were interrupted by his phone.

"Bob, it's Peter. How's Mary? I called the hospital a couple times last night and they said she was in surgery."

"Mary is bad."

"Is she going…" Peter hesitated.

"She will live. They are keeping her in a medicated coma until she stabilizes. They removed some shrapnel. She lost some fingers on her hands. Maybe paralyzed one of her hands. There was a lot of nerve damage. They just finished surgery a couple hours ago. She has a concussion. The blast must have knocked her out. There were some burns from the fire." Bob stopped. He couldn't continue.

"I'm sorry, Bob. Thank God the neighbor heard the blast. He pulled her out. She didn't deserve this."

"It's okay. She's alive."

"God willing."

'God willing', Bob thought. 'What did God care? He let it happen in the first place. Everyone is ready to thank God for the tragedies that could have been worse. At least she will be okay, maybe.' Bob coughed and said, "She'll live."

"Yeah Bob. Don't worry. Okay? Mary is tough."

"We need to pick up Houghton." Bob changed the subject.

"Frank said no."

"What do you mean?"

"No arrest. Frank said Terri's report was wrong. Frank told the D.A. to hold off until he can review all the findings."

"Dammit."

"It doesn't matter anyway. Houghton goes to Florida in the fall." Peter reminded Bob.

"He has a house there. A house and business here. He's got too much to lose to run and hide. Call Louise and have her check the airlines and see if he's got a flight reservation."

"What if he drives?"

"One disaster at a time. Let's find out what happened to Mary. I'll deal with Frank later. I want to get together with you, and Terri and Wally at B.C.I. I want to know what happened yesterday. Mary's surgeon said it was a military explosive."

"Military?"

"Yeah. He said he's only seen damage like that in war."

"An I.E.D.?"

"No. Sort of. He thinks it was a mine. Maybe a claymore." Bob paused to recall everything the doctor had told him.

"Jesus. Who would have access to a claymore?" Peter asked.

"We are going to find out. The good thing is the bomber messed up."

"How's that?"

"Claymore mines are directional. Whoever did this only got Mary's hands and arms with the blast. She's lucky."

"If you call that luck." Peter paused, then said, "Sorry Detective."

"Luck had nothing to do with it. A package bomb is personal."

"As opposed to a gas-line leak or a broken brake line in a car?"

"The unibomber wanted to send a message. Nine-eleven was a message."

"Like Spears' murderers?" Peter asked.

"Exactly like Spears," Bob said. "Except the message with

Spears was never meant for us; not the police, or the government, or even newspapers. Spears was killed to send a message to drug dealers, pimps, pornographers, arsonists, criminals. 'Quit, or else justice worse than jail.'"

"And you think the bomb was meant for you?"

"Exactly. And up until Russell Waldon, no one survived," Bob said.

"The amateur murder league is going pro?" Peter asked.

"Like the Robert Fish book? 1960s? Probably not for pay."

"I mean taking out a cop. Going after the good guys. The bad guys aren't enough. We get in the way, get too close, ask too many questions, so they come after us too?"

"Nothing is too sacred. I think they do it for a higher cause."

Peter laughed nervously, "Not religion?"

"No. Worse. Because they think it's morally correct. They've been getting away with killing for a few years, at a least a few years if not more, and they begin to believe it's right, approved, and acceptable. But they're slipping up and making mistakes. The conspiracy is falling apart. They know we are close and if one card falls the whole house collapses."

"Who are *they*?"

"Houghton for one. Nothing solid on him but he's involved. Got phone calls over to the Bridgers and Mulligans."

"Who else?"

"Them. Bridgers. Mulligans. Time will tell who else."

"If we have enough time?"

"It's a race."

"How many more people die if we don't win?"

"I don't want to think about that. We'll win, Peter. Eventually. Right now I want to know what happened at my house."

"Frank thought it was a gas line blast. The fire chief agreed with him. Wally thought it was a bomb."

"The doctor agrees with Wally. He's ex-military. He'd know," Bob thought aloud. "How did someone get a bomb into my house?"

"Probably a package bomb or something like that. I think Wally is right. Do you think Houghton did it?"

"I don't know but I'm betting he's part of the problem. What about Terri? What does she think?" Bob asked.

"Terri never came out yesterday," Peter said.

"What do you mean?"

"She never showed up. I tried to call her a couple times. Dispatch said she was on her way over to the house. I thought she was with you at the hospital. There's no answer on the radio. She's not answering the phone at her home or her cell phone."

"Call Wally."

"I did that. No one has seen her."

"I'm still over half-an-hour away. Run over to her place and see if she's okay. Maybe she's sick. I'll see you back in Marshfield by eight."

"Yes, sir. Wait. If you think these guys are targeting police? If your house was bombed..." Peter faltered.

"Then Terri might have been next?" Bob guessed at the question.

"Y-Yeah..." Peter stammered.

"Get over to her place. Call in and be back at eight. Got it?"

"Yeah."

"Good. Stick with that. Peter? Don't over-think this too much."

Bob hung up and dialed Frank's cell phone. He listened to it ring four times and then go to voicemail. "Frank. Let's get together at eight. I want to go over what happened yesterday morning. Call me when you get this. And ah..." Bob hesitated. "Don't worry about the Spears Task Force. That's your investigation." He hung up hoping to regain Frank's trust so he could benefit, or at least stay inside the circle of information, on the investigations. He focused on the drive as he exited the highway and made his way to the headquarters.

Chapter 50

Bob walked into his office as his phone rang. Peter's voice came harried and shaking as soon as he answered.

"She's not at home. Her boyfriend isn't here either."

"Terri?"

"Yes. And James too."

"So they're probably out somewhere."

"She didn't show up at your house yesterday."

"Where's Frank?"

"Don't know."

"Terri said he had called into his office as sick yesterday. Can't think why he wouldn't answer the phone today. Same with Terri, and Frank isn't calling me back. Probably didn't get the message. What about Wally?"

"I don't know. The world is caving in," the young officer continued.

"No. It's not. Slow down." Bob tried to lower his own voice. He found some comfort in calming down his deputy, when he had no sleep the night before and his own wife was in the hospital. It gave him renewed purpose. "You couldn't get a hold of Frank or Wally or Terri?"

"No," Peter said.

"I'll have Louise page them. Get back here A.S.A.P."

"I'm almost back now."

Bob hung up and then dialed zero when yelling erupted in the lobby. The sound of Louise's voice came down the hall.

"Calm down! Just calm down!" Louise pleaded.

A man's voice drowned out Louise's request. "I need to talk to Schwimer! Dammit! I have to talk to the detective!"

Bob sprinted to the lobby, his hand on his side-arm, to find Joseph Patten Senior yelling at the top of his lungs.

When Bob pushed open the glass door Joseph grabbed him

before he could say anything. Bob immediately broke the man's grasp and shoved him against the wall. Louise came through the doors from her bullet-proofed dispatch desk.

"You need to calm down." The wall shook as Joseph's head banged into the drywall. He stopped yelling. He slid down to the floor as his legs gave out. A dazed look came over him. "I need to talk to you." He whispered in a hoarse voice.

"Okay. Talk. Not yell. Talk. Stand up. Are you calm enough to go inside and *talk*?"

Joseph nodded his head and Bob and Louise helped the man get back to his feet. Bob flashed a quick grin at Louise. She returned a frazzled smile. The three of them walked back to the interview room. Bob turned to Louise. "Video room."

Louise nodded and left the room. Bob gave Louise a few moments to get the equipment started by offering to get water or coffee. When he passed by the video room he stuck his head in and Louise gave him a thumbs' up.

"Let's get some coffee," he said. "I'm waiting for Peter to get back. Have you heard from Wally?"

"Prisoner transport today."

"That explains it."

Bob and Louise returned with coffee to the video room. On the monitors they watched Joseph Patten pace the floor of the interview room. He walked the ten feet and turned quickly, over and over again.

Peter arrived within minutes. Louise returned to the dispatch desk.

"Come on in with me. Leave the equipment running," Bob said to Peter.

Peter followed Bob into the interview room. He set the cups on the table. "Is this about your son? Joe Junior?"

"Yes. Of course it is."

"You know what happened to him," Bob stated.

"I don't know. That's the problem."

"You knew when you sent me on that wild goose chase."

"I'm sorry."

"Sorry is for later, or never. I offered you my help, and that offer is still here, but you need to tell me everything you know,"

Bob said.

Joseph began to cry.

Peter sat up and leaned across the table and yelled, "What are you hiding? Who are you protecting?"

Bob put a hand on Peter's shoulder. "That's okay, Peter." Joseph wiped his eyes and breathed heavily. "Mr. Patten is going to help now."

"Yes. Yes," he said. "I'll tell you everything."

"Everything is not just about the Waldon case, is it?"

"The kidnapping? No. Everything."

"Hold on a second." Bob checked his pocket for his notebook. He'd left it in his office. "Peter, run down to Louise and grab a notepad." When Peter was gone he said, "I want to get this down on paper."

"We have to hurry."

"Saturday we had to hurry. Yesterday I needed honesty. Now we just need facts. No more lies."

"My son…" Joseph started to cry again. Bob had never seen a man who appeared so strong and tough, crumble so badly.

"…Is probably dead," Bob said.

"You know? You found him?"

"No, But I doubt a second kidnap victim would be allowed the mistake that left Waldon alive. I'll bet your son was taken to warn you."

Joe nodded.

"And if you didn't behave."

"Yes. Stop. Just shut-up."

Bob shut up and waited.

Peter returned with a blank notebook and pens. Bob took the notebook and wrote 'Patten Interview' on the top of the page along with the date. When he was ready to transcribe he nodded to Joseph.

"Joe was very upset about Waldon being kidnapped and when Waldon escaped. When he showed up at the store Joe was ecstatic, but he said he was going to the police."

"And that was a problem?" Bob suddenly realized new light was about to be shined on his mystery.

"Yes, it was, but not any more. Susanne can't take it. She just can't take it that Joe is gone. Someone must have kidnapped him, just like the other boys. Joe said he would go the police and tell them about Russell and tell them about Swanson..."

"Tell us what?" Peter asked and Bob looked up at the deputy. He turned his wrist just slightly and the deputy stopped. He realized Peter had probably never been this close to a murder investigation, being inside an interview room during questioning. "Let me ask the questions, Peter."

Joseph continued, "That he had a homosexual relationship with that pedophile, Russell Waldon. That he knew Susanne and I were involved in his kidnapping. That the Bridger's had that arsonist kid killed after their feed store burned down. That Henry killed that rapist."

"Okay," Bob scribbled his notes quickly. "Henry? Henry who?"

"Houghton."

"Swanson? Samuel Swanson?"

"Yes. I guess. The arsonist kid."

"The Bridger's had Swanson killed?"

"Yes. Them and someone else. Not sure who."

"Does the name 'Mulligan' mean anything?"

"Maybe. I don't remember."

Bob wrote down the conversation. "Let's back up to Joseph. Your son had a relationship with Waldon?"

"That damned pedophile."

"So you wanted Waldon dead?"

"No... Yes. I'm not sure I wanted him dead. I didn't know about the... *relationship*."

"Someone did."

"Yes."

"We talked about it, but all I knew was the conviction, the parole, Waldon's continued prostitution. That's why he was killed. Almost killed."

"Who made those decisions? Just you and Susanne? The Bridgers? Henry Houghton?"

"We had meetings."

"Who did?"

"I'm not sure. The Bridgers. Houghton. We met once. Years

ago. Since then it was always by phone. I didn't know everyone."

"You discussed murder with people you didn't know?"

"Yes."

"You conspired to kill people based on the words of strangers?"

"Yes. It was a group of us. I knew some of them by name, but not all of them."

"Why?"

"They said it protected the group."

"Who was in charge?"

"I donno."

Bob sat back and looked from Joseph to Peter. He thought the look of wonder on Peter's face could be a mirror of his own.

"How did this group work?"

"I would get a phone call. It was always by phone until last week. Sometimes from Henry, and sometimes from Cody. We never used names after the first meeting. Sometimes I'd get a call from someone I didn't know. Couldn't recognize the voice. At least two others, maybe more." Joseph paused while Bob caught up in his notes.

"And?" Bob asked.

"And they would give me a name. Give me some information about the... the *target*. They would be rapists, or drug dealers, or..."

"Or prostitutes? Or arsonists?"

"Yeah. And I would do some homework."

"What kind?"

"I'd check newspapers. Do some sight-seeing in their neighborhood. I'd verify the accusations... I guess I had to justify something."

"That was your job?"

"No. Maybe."

"You needed to feel good about the target?" Bob intentionally used Joseph's word.

The man nodded. "They would call me back a couple days later. Ask me my opinion. Ask me if I could help with the planning. It was supposed to be one per year. Stay off the police radar. Clean up the area."

"Did you have anything to do with the other kidnappings and murders?" Bob asked.

"No. Not really. We just heard some stuff."

"What did you hear?"

"The Bridger's knew this guy who could take care of problems. We didn't know who he was. We only met him the other night."

Peter's eyes grew large. "Did he ride a motorcycle?"

"Yeah. How did you know?"

Bob asked, "How do you know Henry murdered Rickman?"

"He told me he had it done."

"He *had it done*? Or, *he did it himself*?"

"I am not sure."

"What do you know for sure?"

"The Bridger's and this new guy helped them. Someone else too. Someone high up in the police department. Maybe State Police, or FBI."

"Who?"

"I don't know. They never use names. It's always just 'this guy', or 'he will', or 'they did'."

"So these people found out that your son was going to turn them in and now Joe Junior is a victim?"

"I hope not but I'm afraid…"

"You better be afraid."

"What? Why?"

"Did they leave anyone else alive? Besides Russell?"

"No."

"And we know Russell was a mistake. A fluke."

Joe broke into tears again and hung his head.

"What do you know about a Joel Richardson?" Bob asked when the man's sobs subsided.

"Who?" his voice choked.

"A kid over in Raynham. He was murdered a couple years ago. Richardson? Joel."

"No. Nothing about him. But I'll bet the Bridger's and Houghton and this other guy know something."

"How did you find out about Henry Houghton?"

"Wait. I have friends in Raynham. Betty and Shawn. They

own a horse farm."

Bob looked at Peter and then to Joe, *"Mulligan.* I asked you if you knew the name."

"I forgot their last name."

"Did you ever mention anything about Henry Houghton or the Bridgers or any of this to them?"

"I might have. I met the Mulligans through the Bridger feed and tack store, before it burned down."

"That's the final tie we need to put the Bridger's into the Richardson murder. How do you know Houghton?"

"We've been friends for years. I like to fish. Bought my first boat from him. He was very upset about Amelia. He said it wasn't right that Amelia was raped and that rapist was going to go free. He implied he did something. He told me if I ever needed something done that he had connections. That's how it started."

"We know about Houghton. We have enough circumstantial evidence to put him away. If you testify against Houghton and the Bridgers and this other guy we can bring this whole conspiracy down. What do you know about Spears?"

"Who's that?" Joe's face went blank.

"A pimp and a drug dealer found dead by the railroad tracks. John Spears."

"That was a mistake."

"What do you mean by a mistake?"

"The new guy said at the meeting... he said it was a mistake. Russell Waldon was supposed to show up for an arranged homosexual-sex thing and Spears came instead so they whacked Spears. That's the word he used too, 'whacked'."

"Why would they do that if it was a mistake?"

"I don't know. They could have just left. That's the murder from the newspapers? They said he was a pimp. Maybe..."

"Maybe, *what?"*

"Maybe they decided to change the target. These people don't play games. If Waldon didn't show up maybe they went after his pimp instead?"

"Yeah," Bob agreed. "You said the meetings were always by phone until last week. What happened last week?"

"I got a phone call. Someone... Someone I didn't know his name, but I knew his voice, called and said he wanted a meeting at my house. They wanted to talk about the Waldon kidnapping. They all knew where I lived."

"Who was at this meeting?"

"Susanne, Bridgers, both of them. Houghton. Mulligans. Two or three others. There were no introductions. No name-tags."

"What was said at this meeting?"

"We talked about Waldon. Henry did. He and the other guy, the one I don't know his name, said they got Russell and that Spears was a mistake. Henry talked about you. About the bum he hired to rent boats. How he should have killed him too but he didn't want to pollute the lake like he did with Rickman. I thought it was bravado. Just making himself feel better. They talked about the police getting too close."

"Who did?"

"One of them. A tall guy."

"Your age? Forties? Older? Younger?"

"I don't know. Much older."

"Houghton's age?"

"Older, maybe."

Bob looked at Peter and said, "I need you to leave the room for a minute or two."

Peter looked at Bob. Bob nodded.

Peter started to rise from his chair, then froze and stared at Bob.

Bob turned his thumb slightly, dismissively. "Thank you. Peter. It will be okay."

When Peter had closed the door, Bob leveled his gaze at Joseph, "What about my wife?"

Joseph looked up quizzically.

"The bomb that put my wife in the hospital? What do you know about that?"

"Jesus. A bomb? I promise to God, I don't know anything about that."

"At that meeting... You didn't talk about killing me or sending me a message or a threat, telling the police to back off?"

"No."

"Last week they knew we were getting close. Last week? Last weekend? How do *they* know what we know? Who's on the inside?"

"I don't know. I hardly know these people. I just want my son back."

"Even though he's gay?" Bob asked sarcastically. He was frustrated. He was angry that they went after Mary, that he could have protected the boy if the parents had let him. That they refused and now the boy was most likely dead.

"I don't care. I just want Joe back. Susanne is going crazy."

Bob's demeanor became deadly serious. He stood up and leaned on the table. "This is full-honesty time. I can promise you; If you are lying to me about my wife there won't be any immunity. There won't be any reduced charges. I'll send you up, with all the others, for life without parole. Every one of you. I don't care how big of a lasso I have to rope with."

Joe sat back in his chair, exhausted. He put his hands to his face and wept. "I don't care. I'm telling you everything. What about my son? You've got to help him."

Bob sat down again. He stared at Joseph for a full minute. He felt himself getting hot. Sweat soaked his back. His shirt stuck to his chest. He could smell the odor. He didn't care. He gestured to Peter who was staring in the small window in the door.

After Peter entered and sat down, Bob continued, "Joe Junior disappeared yesterday morning. I tried to talk to you about that and you gave me a false address and a false story."

"I'm sorry. I'm just so scared. These guys are killers. They will kill me and Susanne. You have got to save him."

"If John Spears, Russell Waldon, Tim Rickman and Samuel Swanson are any indication it's probably too late. Waldon was lucky."

"This is destroying Susanne. She hasn't been able to handle this since we found out Joe was missing. He was kidnapped right out of his bedroom window. I know it. We thought he ran away at first but the pajamas he was wearing are gone. Susan says he leaves them on the floor. His coat and sneakers are still there."

Bob looked at Peter, "Let's get over there and search the

room for evidence." He looked back at Joseph. "This would have been easier twenty-four hours ago. Forty-eight hours ago it was preventable."

Peter turned to Bob. "What about Terri? She's still missing."

"She may have stumbled into the middle of this mess. Did you talk about my M.E.?" asked Bob.

"Who?" Joseph said.

"Medical Examiner. Terri Cox."

"I don't know."

"You don't know the name or you don't know if you talked about killing her too?"

Joseph shook his head.

"We've got to find her. I'm going to talk to the D.A. and get those warrants for the Bridgers and Mulligans, and your wife, Susanne. Joe, if we take Susanne in, in handcuffs, we can protect her better. Same for you. It will look like she's under arrest. We can talk about cooperation later. We'll need you both to testify."

Joe sighed, "Yes. Anything. We only want our son back."

"Maybe we can get the Bridger's to confess something. First thing is, Joe, you go into protective custody. We'll take you over to the courthouse lockup. You might recognize someone there. His name is Waldon, but you will be in separate cells. Then we pickup Henry Houghton and see what he has to say. By then, I'm hoping the D.A. will have arrest warrants on the Bridger's."

"Bob. I think Terri is in real trouble. She's never disappeared like this before," Peter said as they escorted Joe Patten down the hallway to the parking lot.

"Do you think Terri is the leak in the police department?" Joe Patten asked over his shoulder. Bob stopped and turned the man to face him.

"How do you know about that?"

"They said they had someone who was a cop. They said it was easier that way."

"Who is it?"

Joe shook his head.

Bob looked at Peter and asked, "Do you think it's Terri?"

"I didn't, until now," Peter frowned.

"Let's figure she's still one of the good guys. Maybe she got kidnapped too. Let's hope not. Work the case. We'll find her."

"I hope it's not too late," said Peter.

"Me too."

Chapter 51

They stopped at the door for Peter to handcuff Joseph's hands behind his back and give the appearance he was arrested, and not an informant. Bob held the door while Peter guided Joseph by the elbow.

Peter could not restrain himself from saying, "These guys have been acting as vigilantes for years and we didn't even notice." Joseph hung his head as they crossed the parking lot to Peter's cruiser.

"That Raynham kid was from Bristol County," Bob said. "We never would have heard about that murder if not for Terrance Silverman. Rickman's death was ruled an accidental drowning. A few of the fires were around Wareham and over to Bournedale but most were in Sandwich and Bourne. That's Barnstable County. Swanson even lived in Bournedale right on the county line so his disappearance, and the police and fire response, what little they need, very well might have fallen out of our jurisdiction."

"And out of our line of sight," Peter added.

They stopped by the patrol car as Peter fumbled with his keys.

Bob continued, "It took until Spears was killed, and that was a mistake. Maybe. There was an argument the night before. Whoever masterminded this made it look like they were after Waldon, but they settled for a murder of opportunity with Spears. It was an intentional mistake. I think one of the conspirators had a falling out with Spears and wanted him dead."

Joe said, "The pedophile. They were supposed to take the prostitute, not the pimp."

"What about the homeless? And people say the homeless are of no value. Joe. You and your friends might have gotten away with this if not for Terrance Silverman."

Suddenly Joe staggered sideways and Peter was slammed to the ground as the crack of rifle-fire echoed across the parking lot. Bob drew his Glock from its holster as he held onto Joe's arm. Blood gushed from a hole in the man's neck. His lifeless body slid down the side of the car. His head fell to the side as the blood pumped from the wound in rivers.

"I'm shot," Peter yelled as he tried to get up off the ground. Bob leapt forward grabbing the deputy and pulling him back down behind the car.

"I'm okay," Peter said. He held his left arm with his right hand. Blood was staining his uniform. "I think the bone is broken."

"There was only one shot. The bullet went through him into you. He took the worst of it." They both looked at Joseph as his eyes glassed over and a last bloody breath escaped his lips.

"Stay here," Bob yelled as he scampered around the car and opened the passenger-side door. He pulled out a medical kit and a pair of binoculars stored in the console. He ripped open a large bandage and handed it to Peter, to press on the wound and slow the bleeding. Taking the binoculars, he looked down the street.

"The bullet hit Joe first, and then you. Passed right through. That means the bullet came from the east, towards the sun. Smart man. Keeping the sun at his back. One shot and change position." Bob scanned the streets and buildings. He swept the rooftops until he saw movement.

"What do you see?" Peter asked as he wrapped his arm in the bandage and tape.

"That's it. The sniper is on top of the hardware store. The red brick building. That's got to be almost half a mile." Bob reached into the car and recovered the AR-15 carbine from the center console.

"Go," Peter said.

"Are you going to be okay?" Bob asked.

"Go. I'm right behind you. I'll call for Wally and we are right behind you. I'll see if I can keep him pinned down with that." Peter pointed to the AR-15.

Bob handed over the rifle. He knew Peter could shoot,

having aced his firearm tests at the academy. At the moment Peter was in no shape to take on a sniper with a broken arm but Bob admired his courage.

"Go," Peter said as he hammered the magazine with the heel of his hand, cycled the rifle's bolt, and pressed the forward assist, all with one hand. He dragged his dead arm as he lay prone under the cruiser. He leaned the rifle against the wheel and aligned the sights on the red brick roof of the hardware store.

As Bob ran down the street, he stayed close to the buildings to shield himself. He heard the loud crack of the sniper's rifle and the pavement beside Bob flew into the air. The shot was followed by several .223 caliber reports and he knew Peter was peppering the rooftop. He hoped the sniper would not stick his head up again. Within three minutes Bob was under the sniper's perch.

The first floor was the hardware store and people were scattering at the gunfire. He held his badge in his other hand, to clear the way. He knew that upstairs were apartments but those levels were abandoned from a long-ago fire. He turned down the alleyway as a tall man dropped from the fire escape with a rifle in-hand. The sniper paused to catch his balance and then started to run.

"Stop," Bob yelled as he raised his pistol. The man turned, twisting sideways and leveling the rifle barrel. Bob squeezed the trigger three times. The forty-caliber Glock leapt in his hands and the man crumbled. The rifle cracked and Bob winced as the round ricocheted off the brick wall, splattering him with fragments. The shards of mortar and lead drew blood.

Wiping his face, Bob walked up to the fallen sniper. "Frank?"

"Bob. You bastard." Frank gasped for breath as bloody bubbles appeared on his chest.

"Why? Why kill those kids?"

"Scum. Psychos. Druggies. Rapists."

"That's it? The court system isn't good enough?" Bob looked at Frank. The older man's eyes became distant. A long breath escaped his lungs as his body sagged into death.

"You got lucky. You should have lived." Bob crouched

down and picked up the hunting rifle. He read the barrel stamping: .375 H&H Magnum. He opened the bolt and an empty cartridge casing dropped out. Bob caught it before it hit the ground. It was still hot and it singed his fingers. The casing was *improved*; fire-formed to a raised neck for increased power factor, a modern day elephant-gun, capable of firing nearly a mile.

Footsteps came from behind him. He turned and looked up expecting Peter or Wally. He saw James Sullivan.

"Hi Bob," James said as he stared down the sights of a Beretta pistol. Before Bob could move, James fired twice. Bob collapsed as the rounds struck him in the chest. He fell backwards, raising his Glock but he was unable to obtain a sight-picture. Three more shots rang out and Bob heard a voice.

"Are you hit?"

Bob looked up through hazed vision at Peter running down the alleyway towards him, his pistol still pointed at the body of James Sullivan. His broken arm hanging lifelessly. "Are you hit?" he asked again.

"Make sure he's dead."

"Are you okay?"

"The vest caught it." Bob tried to sit up. His chest hurt as if he had been hit by a baseball bat. He pulled open his shirt and looked at the copper jacketed bullets embedded in the bulletproof vest. Peter leaned down to help Bob up.

Six more shots rang out. Peter spun, struck in the back, side, and chest. Bob fell backwards again, as he was hit with several more bullets, one grazing his cheek and ear.

A voice said one word, "Faggot."

When Bob looked up again, Peter was laying on the ground. Sullivan was gone. He heard the roar of a motorcycle as sirens grew in the distance. Bob was stunned by the multiple hits to his bulletproof vest, but the wound on his cheek burned. His adrenaline pumped. He realized that Sullivan must be wearing a combat vest under his clothing.

The sirens grew louder as Bob picked himself off the ground. Wally, with his sidearm drawn, came down the alley. The sergeant's face went pale when he saw Peter lying ghostly white and still. He moved to Peter and checked for a pulse and breathing and found none. Only a small amount of blood came from the wound. His eyes went to Frank Wysup's body a few feet away, lying in a pool of blood.

Wally cut open Peter's bloody shirt with a pocketknife. A bullet had entered Peter's chest under his armpit, where the vest offered very little protection.

"They're dead," Wally said as he felt Peter's neck for a pulse.

"E.M.T.s are minutes away. Start CPR." Bob laid Peter's body flat and started chest compressions. The grazing bullet wound in Bob's face dripped blood onto Peter's shirt. It mixed with the growing amount of blood that seeped from the tiny hole under Peter's armpit. Wally put pressure on the wound to try to stop the blood flow.

"What happened?" Wally asked between breaths.

"Frank killed Patten and tried to kill me." Bob pushed on Peter's sternum with a *whump* noise. Air and saliva appeared at Peter's mouth and nose. "I killed Frank when he dropped off the fire escape." *Whump.* "Sullivan shot Peter, Sullivan is hit." *Whump.* "That's his blood over there. He's not breathing. Get on it."

Wally started mouth to mouth resuscitations on Peter and they talked between breaths.

"Jim Sullivan? Terri's boyfriend?"

"Yes. And Terri's missing." Bob saw bloody bubbles coming from the hole in Peter's side and he knew Peter was bleeding into his lungs. Wally's breaths were escaping through the hole. That lung had probably collapsed.

"Missing?" Wally asked.

"Gone. No answer at her house. No calls picked up. Gone."

"Where is she?"

"I'm hoping she got away."

"From James?"

"Yes." Bob nodded.

"Where is he now?"

"He escaped. You missed him by seconds."

"Where to?"

"I don't know but we have two places we can check. If he's dumb enough to go there."

"Frank's is closest," Wally said.

"If James isn't going to Frank's he might be heading to his own place."

"Do you think he's that daft?"

"Sure enough he's heading for Terri, if she's still alive."

"If she is alive, James will want her dead now."

"And if she isn't alive, where does he go?"

"I don't know yet. No witnesses. The Mulligans, and the Bridgers, and Houghton are all on that list too."

"They are all in it? Like a murder club?"

"Uh-huh," Bob said.

"I'll call Abington local. If he's heading for Franks' he has to go through Abington. The ambulance is coming. Louise broadcast the A.P.B. Every cruiser and ambulance in town will be here... They are here now," Wally said as an ambulance crew arrived. He called to them from the alley and they went to Peter first.

Chapter 52

Leaving Peter in the hands of the E.M.T.s, Bob and Wally headed towards Wally's cruiser parked at the end of the alleyway. It was still running with the lights on.

"Do you want to call in some backup?" Wally asked.

"I'll call Brockton and Bristol County S.W.A.T.," Bob said as he poured his bruised body into the driver's seat of Wally's cruiser, "Jasperse can meet us with a few deputies. Get on the radio to the air-unit. If they can pick him up, we'll play follow the leader. Then call the local PDs; Hanover, Rockland, Norwell. Ask them to block off the side streets. Tell them to let him go. Stay with traffic control." We have S.W.A.T. and we don't need extra targets if James turns out to be a sniper also. Get them to monitor the major cross streets on Route 139 and the highways, Route 3, Route 24. If they see James' motorcycle..."

"Radio it in." Wally finished the command.

Bob spun the tires as they whipped around and headed west. "Make him think he's getting away. We want him to lead us to Terri, not get him killed in the process."

Wally's radio crackled with static followed by Louise's voice before he could call outbound. "I got a traffic helicopter reporting a motorcycle heading west on 139 at a high rate of speed. They said they will stay with it and give us info. The police unit just got airborne."

Bob responded. "Ask them to keep some distance. We need to know where he's going. Don't tip him off or we will never find Terri."

The county cruiser screamed down the suburban streets at seventy miles per hour, squealing tires on the turns through Hanover, Rockland, and Abington. They passed local police cars having stopped traffic on every major crossroad. In the rear mirror, Bob saw them pull out and follow. It seemed every one of them joined in, not wanting to miss the excitement. The radio garbled with chatter. Every unit wanted to know what was going on. Bob called Brockton S.W.A.T. on his cell phone. They were already on the road heading east, destination unknown. He told them to monitor the radio. Bob hung up and called Jasperse.

"Howdy, Bob!" The sheriff laughed.

"Sheriff."

"Half the state heard you're having some trouble over there."

"You ain't busy are you?"

"Just polishing the brass on my badge. I think I could spare a minute."

"Great. This involves you and that Richardson kid."

"Good thing I'm already doing eighty heading east. Nothing better than an old-fashioned police chase. *Haw-haw.*"

Bob's jaw tightened. "Where are you?"

"Give me a twenty and we'll be there."

"You can head east on 139, Holbrook or Randolph."

"Almost there now."

Chapter 53

Bob accelerated on the stretch of state Route 139 west of Route 18. In Holbrook, down the long straight road, he and Wally saw the lights from several Bristol County cruisers coming up from the west. Bob turned south towards Ames Norwell State Park at the guidance of the helicopter pilot, via Wally on the cell phone with Louise. Jasperse followed at the turn. Minutes later four cruisers and the Bristol County Special Weapons And Tactics armored truck burst through the gates to Frank Wysup's farm, skidding to a stop on the grass beside the long driveway below the farmhouse. Brockton S.W.A.T. stopped in the road. The men were arming themselves from the back. A dozen local police cruisers filled the road behind them with sirens and lights.

"That's Sullivan's motorcycle." Bob pointed at the Harley Davidson lying on its side in the barn door.

Sheriff Jasperse, crouching beside Wally's cruiser, knocked on Wally's window and Wally opened the door to duck out of the car. Bob slid over and followed him out the passenger's side. They squatted down and sprinted from car to car until they could stand up safely behind the S.W.A.T. assault truck.

The S.W.A.T. team gathered around Bob. "I want snipers to take positions in the woods. Surround the property. Sullivan is here. There's a good chance he's in the barn. Check your targets. We have a missing Medical Examiner."

"Do you think she's still alive?" Wally asked.

"Let's think that she is until we know otherwise. We're going to the barn and see if we can get some communication. You and me. We'll drive up in the S.W.A.T. truck. Try to get him talking. There's still a possibility we can take him alive but don't take any chances. Shoot him if you have to."

The S.W.A.T. team nodded and Wally said, "I spent ten years in the military. Saw two wars."

Bob handed Wally an MP5. Wally shook his head. "I'll use

my Glock." He held the pistol at low-ready.

"How many snipers do we have?"

"Three," Jasperse replied as he took an MP5 sub-machinegun. "They are heading to the woods. Let's give them some time to get situated."

"I don't think we have time."

"Terri?" Wally asked.

"Yes. Let's have S.W.A.T. ride in the truck or follow us up the driveway. There's a good chance he's still in the barn. He wasn't that far ahead of us."

"He's cornered," Jasperse said.

"And that's what bother's me, but right now we will assume Terri is alive and held captive."

"He'll kill her."

"God. I hope not," Bob interrupted Wally as he climbed into the back of the S.W.A.T. van and moved into the driver's seat. He picked up the public address microphone.

"James Sullivan. James Sullivan. Give it up." Bob waited thirty seconds before calling again. "James. Jim. It's Bob. We know you have Terri. I can make you a deal."

"What kind of deal?" James voice yelled from the barn.

"You testify against Frank and I'll make it easy on you."

"Frank is dead."

"No. He's alive," Bob lied. "He's on his way to the hospital."

"Jackson is dead."

"No. You're wrong. Peter is fine. His vest stopped the bullet."

"You're lying."

"I'll make sure the charges are accessory or conspiracy. You'll get five instead of life." Bob waited, though no response came from the barn. "It's five years for your testimony. Out in two or three. Snipers are surrounding the house... Jim. You don't have a lot of choices right now."

Bob waited again. After a moment he put the microphone down. "Wally? Get in. We are going up there," Bob called to the back of the truck.

"Is that a bullet-proof windshield?" Jasperse asked as he jumped in followed by Wally.

"It will take three shots of pistol caliber," Wally said.

"What about rifle calibers?" Jasperse asked and Wally laughed.

Bob pulled on a flack jacket handed to him by Jasperse.

Jasperse handed Wally a flack-jacket and pulled one on himself. Then he handed the men helmets. "Bristol County equipment. Try not to damage it. *Haw-haw.*"

"What about waiting? He can't stay here forever," Wally said.

"This isn't Waco. Terri is still missing and if she's here, then she's in trouble," Bob's voice dropped an octave.

"I was hoping you'd say that." Wally smiled again and Jasperse hee-hawed.

Bob started the engine and drove around the cruisers. He hunched over the wheel as he drove slowly towards the top of the drive.

"What's the plan?" Wally's mirth was gone.

"He's in the barn. I figure we drive right up to the doors. You go out the back and circle around the barn. There should be a door there. I'll wait about thirty seconds and go in the front." Bob flicked on the headlights, police lights and spotlights as he approached the barn. He hoped to blind and confuse James.

"Here," Wally said as he handed Bob and Jasperse bandoliers of flash-bang grenades. "These S.W.A.T. guys have all the nice gear."

"Thinking about a transfer?" Jasperse asked.

"Nah. I like a good pursuit. There's more of them in patrol than S.W.A.T.."

Bob rolled the truck to a stop at the double doors of the barn. The motorcycle blocked the path. They all looked inside for James. Suddenly three bullets impacted the windshield with the high-pitched snap of a nine-millimeter pistol. Radial cracks hazed the windshield.

"He's in the loft," Wally said.

"New plan," Bob yelled. "We've got about a foot of clearance on the doorway. The roof is open to the second floor around the hay loft. I'm going to drive right in, throw flash-bangs while you guys go up the truck's ladder. Don't go up until after you hear the grenades. Then I'll go up the hay lift." Bob looked at the conveyor belt tilted up to the loft near the doorway. "Locate him and take him down. On my mark. Go when I say."

Bob backed up the truck and stopped halfway down the drive. Several more bullets impacted the truck and windshield. Glass flew into Bob's face. He was bleeding again. He squinted through the spider webbed glass and wiped away the blood with his sleeve. When Wally and Jasperse were positioned on the truck's rear ladder Bob stepped on the gas and accelerated towards the barn. The assault truck caught the Harley-Davidson motorcycle on its push-bumper shoving it forward until the truck rolled over it. The truck bucked. Dust flew into the air. Gun shots shook the barn and the windshield shattered into pieces.

Bob threw open the side door and tossed two stun grenades into the loft as hard as he could. He ducked back into the truck as bullets struck all around him. He heard two deafening booms.

"Go, go!" Bob yelled and he felt the truck rock as Wally and Jasperse climbed onto the roof.

He dodged out the door and up the conveyor belt with the MP5 in his hands. His thumb went to the safety and made sure it was off. By training he counted James shots. Three in the windshield, then four driving in, and three more as Wally reach the roof of the truck.

The distinctive boom of a .45ACP rang like a church bell. One, two, three followed by three more. Wally was firing controlled shots. He had located the target. Jasperse fired short bursts from his MP5. At the top of the conveyor belt Bob looked through a cloud of dust. James cowered behind a pile of crates and boxes. He fumbled to reload a Berretta 92FS semiautomatic handgun.

Bob lined up the sights on the MP5 and said, "You're done. Jim. Drop the gun."

James looked up. He turned white as he continued to struggle with the Berretta. The crack of a Glock rang out and James fell forward on the floor.

"He's disarmed now." Jasperse's evil grin shined from across the hay-loft and the man let loose a '*Haw-haw*'.

Bob leapt upon James and pulled his gun away. James

recovered from the hit to his bullet proof vest and threw punches at Bob's face. His knuckles connected to Bob's temple, bringing stars. Farming had built hard muscles around James' short frame.

Bob pushed himself away and drew his right fist back to strike as James clambered over him. Fists landed to his sides and kidneys. Bob struck the man's face, aiming for the eyes. First right, then left, and right again. Kicking his legs up, he pushed James off of him. He scrambled to his feet as James ran on all-fours towards a hay rake. They faced off for a moment.

Jasperse laughed, "Can I take him?"

"No. He's mine," Bob shouted, waving Wally and Jasperse away.

James swung the metal hay fork at Bob. The weapon swung wide as Bob stepped back from the sharp metal tines.

James flipped the fork around and held it in two hands, like a spear. He made several wild stabs but Bob stayed out of range. They circled half one way and half the other. Bob stayed between the man and the ladder and hay-conveyor, blocking any escape. He gave ground and took small steps forward again anytime James swung or thrusted the weapon. Bob kept his eyes moving, watching, looking for an opening. In an instant he saw James' mistake. He turned close to the edge of the loft. Too close. James thrust, Bob pressed forward and James took a step back. He hung in trepidatious balance for a moment, his arms going forward, then back as his foot swung into space. He locked eyes with Bob as he fell, realization of his misjudgment filling his face.

A crash followed as he landed on the floor below. His legs twisted. Bob slid down the ladder and ran to the man as he was surrounded by officers, guns pointed. James didn't move. A gasp escaped his lips.

"Where is she?" Bob commanded.

"She's dead."

"She's not dead. She's here."

James smiled cruelly.

"You had no reason to come here other than to kill Terri and you didn't have enough time." Bob turned to the officers. "Search the barn, the loft, the stalls, the crawlspace. Search the house. The attic, the cellar, everything. She's here."

Wally and Jasperse scrambled down the hay-conveyor.

Bob looked at James again. His legs didn't move. "Probably broke your back, but you deserve worse. Where is she?" he asked again but James remained silent, anger filling the space between them.

"We have something." A voice came from behind Bob. He turned. Several officers were shining flashlights into a trap door in the barn floor.

An officer dropped into the hole. Bob left James and stepped down onto a ladder. He climbed to the bottom. In the flickering of the officer's flashlight Bob saw the walls of an earthen cellar. The ceiling was low and cobwebs filled the space between the rafters. At the far end Terri sat bound to a chair. Her eyes were like fire and she screamed in fear and anger through a gag. She struggled and toppled the chair. The officer quickly went behind her and cut the cords.

"Terri," Bob called as he pulled a knife from his pocket. "You are okay. We found you."

Bob cut the bonds on her legs and Terri wrestled herself to her feet. She tussled with the cords, making the job harder. As soon as he removed the gag in her mouth she screamed, "Get me out of here."

She rushed to the ladder but her legs refused to work, causing her to tumble and fall. The officer dropped his flashlight and grabbed her. She collapsed in faint as the blood rushed to her stiff arms and legs.

"She's claustrophobic," Bob said as they carried her to the ladder. Officers above lifted her through the trap-door and laid her on the ground. Bob scrambled up the ladder as Terri regained consciousness. He knelt beside her as she lay on the ground.

She smiled as she saw his face. "You found me."

"We found you," Bob echoed.

"How's Mary?"

"Mary is okay. You need to take care of yourself right now."

Terri's smile widened. "I'm glad she's okay." She suddenly looked worried. Fear gripped her and she started shaking. Her eyes, squinting in the bright sunlight, jumped from left to right and back. She sat upright.

"James can't hurt you anymore and Frank is dead." Bob anticipated her questions.

"He smoked," Terri said.

"Yes. Frank smoked."

"No. Frank smoked cigarettes."

Bob smiled as he realized what she was saying, "And Spears' clothing smelled of cigarettes."

"I can't believe he was involved in this."

"Me either. I could of guessed at Frank's behavior, but Jim threw me."

"I never saw a thing and I lived with him." Terri began to cry. "We were trying to have a baby."

Bob opened his arms and she leaned into him, hugging him and crying.

"What did they want? Why would they do this?" she asked.

"I don't know. That's something we'll find out from Jim."

"He's not dead?" Terri's eyes widened and her fear returned.

"No. But he's going to pay. He will be in jail for a very long time. Plus, I think he broke his back. He won't be able to hurt you from a wheel chair."

"His back?"

"I think so."

"He won't be able to farm."

Bob nodded in agreement but didn't comment on her concern for the man who would of killed her and buried her in a manure pile without a second thought. Love was a powerful thing.

 He helped her to his car. She smiled widely as paramedics ran past her to treat James. A female paramedic stopped to help Terri but she waved her away.

"I'm okay," she said through dirt-streaked tears on her face. The paramedic handed her a bottle of water and wiped her face with a damp cloth. She took the bottle but turned her face away. "No. No. I need a hot bath."

"Are you sure? Is she okay?" the paramedic asked Bob.

Bob nodded but said to Terri, "I really think you should go to the hospital."

"No. Take me home." Terri struggled to her feet. Bob helped her towards the cars.

"I'll take you to my house. I don't think you will want to go back home for a while."

"Your house has a big hole in it." Terri laughed, wiping away the tears from her eyes.

"I always wanted a bay window and a skylight."

"You picked a hard way to do it. How's Mary?" she asked again, all mirth gone from her voice.

"Okay. She will be okay. After what happened you are concerned more with Mary? You should get checked out. You don't look very good."

"Tomorrow," she said as he helped her into Wally's cruiser. "And you could use a shave yourself. Being fired doesn't suit you very well," Terri said as her lilting voice returned as quickly as it vanished.

"I might be fired too, when the Staties find out about this."

"You are too valuable. No one is going to fire you. You might even make Sheriff."

"Stay here for a little while. I'll be right back."

"Where's Peter?" Terri asked. Bob looked at Terri and said nothing. Terri realized something had happened. She frowned and her eyes fell.

"I'll be right back." Bob closed the door and returned to the barn and house.

Wally was taking photographs of the barn and house while Lieutenant Singer and Abington and Holbrook police officers collected evidence. Bristol S.W.A.T. struggled to free the motorcycle from beneath their truck.

Chapter 54

"Did you see the mountain bike in the barn?" Wally asked as Bob came up to him outside the house.

"I missed it in the gun battle," Bob replied.

"I'll bet it's Swanson's. Come in here, you have to see this." Wally led Bob to the house. "Frank has an entire bomb making workshop. Bomb Disposal is on its way in. I'll bet they burn the house and barn to contain the explosives."

"That would be a fitting end to Frank Wysup's legacy."

Wally led Bob to a back room. Workbenches lining the walls were strewn with wire, electronics, and tools. Wally read aloud the labels on crates and boxes. "M18 Directional Antipersonnel Mine. Explosive. And that one says, M7 Bandolier. There's several more. Didn't the bomb that got Mary have BB's in it?"

"Made from a claymore. Frank was trying to kill me, not Mary. I'm sure after Frank got the Patten kid, and shot Joe Patten Senior, he intended to kill me too."

"He got Peter instead. James being in Marshfield today was no accident. Wasn't Frank in Desert Storm."

"It's on his resume. Medical unit," Bob said. He pointed to the labels on the boxes. "Look. 1960. 1959. I think we are going to find out a lot more interesting things about Frank than we've known over the years."

"I guess an army doctor would know what damage a bomb can do." After a pause Wally added, "Sorry about Mary."

"Me too. Wally, take pictures of everything. We need this done by the book. No mistakes. Whoever Frank's friends are, this is going to hurt them and hurt them hard. First degree murder brings life in prison if we document this correctly. We'll need bullet proof evidence of the conspiracy and the murders and kidnappings, and we still have Susanne Patten. She's lost a husband and a son and isn't going to want to spend the rest of her life behind bars. She'll talk. The phone records and this house does a lot. James and Terri's house is now a potential crime scene. Amelia acts as a character witness for her father. But that will destroy her."

"What about upstairs?"

"You mean State?"

"Heads are going to roll," Wally said.

"Probably not but if they do, let's make sure it isn't one of ours."

"By the book."

"It looks like Frank and James were trying to clean up their mess when they realized they had gone too far. Their first victim was probably Rickman for raping Amelia Houghton. Maybe. We can go further back and look for victims, but Rickman was a clean kill. I'm certain that Wysup, Sullivan, and Houghton strangled and dumped Rickman in the lake and they towed away one of his own boats so it would appear stolen when it was found. Wysup was the Medical Examiner so he falsified the autopsy. Then at some point, Shawn and Betty Mulligan and James Sullivan meet in the Bridgers Feed store and it wouldn't be much of a coincidence for them to start talking about problems with a dog-killing neighbor kid. Phone records help tell us that."

"And Joel was shot-gunned in Bristol County," Wally said.

"And Wysup used to be the Plymouth M.E., before he moved to State, so he didn't have access to the evidence. But with a long list of people who had motives for Joel Richardson, and no evidence, that case went cold," Bob said.

"Because it was in Bristol County we didn't hear anything about it."

"That's where Silverman ties in and made things easier for us with Spears murdered."

"Coincidence."

"I like coincidence."

"Fate, or whatever brought you Silverman and Joel Richardson and that links in the Bridgers. Do you think Silverman was an active part of this?"

"No way," Bob said.

"Then it's the farmers and rural... um... rich people. Patten owns horses, Sullivan is a crop farmer, Houghton runs a fishing boat rentals. Maybe his daughter takes horse riding lessons from the Mulligans? The Mulligans train and raise horses and give riding lessons... to the Patten kid also? Nice little group of friends all gathered at the Bridgers farm-store picking up supplies and picking their next version of justice," Wally said.

Bob continued the line of thought, "Bridger gets his store burned down by Samuel Swanson, an unfortunate choice for a fire, and suddenly a teenage arsonist would make a good target. So kidnap and murder him and they have no place to hide the body. The Mulligans had their problems solved so they offer, or are forced, to hide the body. The best place to hide a body on a horse farm is the manure pile."

"Why?" Wally asked.

"I have horses, but Terri could give you the technical details. Natural enzymes and bacteria create heat during the decomposition process, which spawns more bacteria and more heat and the decomposition accelerates. The organic material is broken down and effectively burned. And that's why potting soils are black. But it takes time," Bob mused. "And that's how they got caught. The Mulligans sell manure to landscape companies that mixes it for garden and potting soils, but I'd think they would be careful which manure pile to use."

"Or they got their piles mixed," Wally added.

"Unlikely, but when they weren't looking someone happened to be digging manure from the wrong pile."

"...And found the bones."

"Which the Mulligans insisted was a dead horse. Someone gets suspicious with the clothing mixed in."

"Does polyester decompose?" Wally asked.

"Not very fast. So the guy calls Sheriff Jasperse and he has a body and two very probable suspects until we talk to the Bridger's. Bridger makes a mistake and accidentally incriminates himself," Bob said.

"Two suspects for the disposal plus two for motive and two more for means and opportunity. Mulligans, Bridgers, Pattens led by Sullivan and Wysup at the top. Frank hunts and fishes. They could have gotten away with it."

"They did, for a while." Bob frowned.

"What about Waldon?" Wally asked.

"Joe Patten Junior is the gay friend of a newly released pedophile and prostitute. They work at the supermarket. The father is also a customer of the Bridgers, with the horses they have. They have photographs of Susanne and Joe Junior jumping fences horseback. He was on the fringe, only knew enough to tie our case together. That explains the 'Conspiracy' letter."

"That Joe Patten wrote?"

"Junior or Senior."

"Which is why Frank killed them."

"Probably not. Joseph Patten Senior was seated in the middle of this group. He has money, power. He didn't need to do anything except provide money or moral support, until his own son was kidnapped. I'll guess the gay friend of a gay prostitute was a bit upset or angry."

"At what?"

"At his friend being kidnapped. At the attempted murder of Russell Waldon. And if Mr. Patten lost his son, he had nothing to lose by coming to us."

"But why the son?"

"Frank wanted him dead to keep him quiet. Joe Junior probably knew about the murders. His father was tough. Pretty conservative. He overhears a few phone calls and puts things together himself. Russell Waldon gets killed and he loses it."

"Waldon isn't dead," said Wally.

"He didn't know that. When I showed them the photo strip I offered them protection. I told them Waldon had died in the hospital. Not too far off a possibility. They beat him and left him *nearly* dead. They believed it. That unleashed Junior's anger at his father. Maybe he threatened to turn them all in."

"And the father goes to the group? Why would he do that?"

"Patten said they had a meeting. A face-to-face as a group. Something they had not done since he joined. Maybe the kid overheard it or confronted them all. Susanne can confirm that for us."

"So Frank, with or without James, takes out the kid."

"What about Spears? He was a drug dealer."

"And he was Russell's pimp. But that isn't why Spears was

killed. It was the porn video. Remember two guys were arguing in Stoney's Mill two days before Spears was found dead? An old tall white man and a black man."

"Frank and Spears," Wally answered.

"I'm betting it was over the porn videos, profits, money, or something like that. Whatever it was, it was enough to push Wysup to murder him. That's why James Sullivan was back in Stoney's mill with Cody Bridger."

"Are you sure it was Sullivan? I heard them talking but I didn't recognize him when he walked by."

"I'm pretty sure it was. The video from the railroad crossing shows a motorcycle and I'll bet it's the same make and model. The video's are hi-def so the license plate may show up. The facial recognition software proved it was not Frank from your cell phone camera. You said they were talking about 'fixing two problems'; Spears and Waldon. They were 'working a second job too soon'. You said the older man had a daughter or a family."

"Yes. It was something like that."

"Not sure Bridger has a family. He hears about the body on the tracks in the news. It sounds like a 'club plan' but maybe he was left out of it. Fewer people on each job helps keep things clean. Bridger gets nervous after he reads about Spears and he goes to meet James at the bar. Find out what the other members are doing. The same bar Silverman hung out at, the one you went to. He wants to know why the heat is on. Maybe he talks to Henry Houghton and Henry wants to know how Silverman is involved in Spears murder? He wants to know what we know. They might even think Silverman was an under cover collecting evidence for the Rickman murder."

"Wait a second. I didn't recognize those two guys in Stoney's Mill. I'd have known if it was James and I went with you to talk to Houghton and Cody Bridger. So maybe it was nothing. Maybe that was unrelated," Wally said.

"But you told me outside of Bridger's Feed and Tack store that you recognized Cody from somewhere." Bob smiled.

"Bingo. He was the redneck. Lumberjack shirt. But he wears western clothing. Is that close enough? But what about the other guy. The business man?" Wally asked.

"There's a few business people in their little club. Maybe it wasn't Sullivan. Maybe it was Patten. You never met Joe Patten."

"But I could pull him out of a photo line up."

"What about an autopsy photo?"

"That too."

"And we know, or I can guess, that Patten was putting up a good front to the police, but silently harboring fears for the safety of his own kid, who he knew was gay, even if he didn't want to admit it. That might make him nervous enough to meet with another club member. Anyway, Terrance finds Spears' body and he's tied back to Joel in Raynham."

"That's another coincidence." Wally admitted.

"Two. A lot of investigation is hard work and asking questions. Sometimes a lot seems like a coincidence or you could call it, 'being in the right place at the right time'," Bob said.

"Or the wrong time."

"There is a lot of chance in this business. Having someone come forward to talk. Cross contamination. A witness who sees something mundane but calls it in anyway."

"Instinct?"

"There's a lot of that too."

"Instinct doesn't convict."

"But it leads to evidence. Look, the guys over in Brockton solve over eighty percent of their murders within days or a week. How long does it take to figure out who someone's friends and enemies are? People love to talk. So we let them talk. Most murders are by associates for the same reasons why Spears was killed."

"Sounds like Frank screwed up."

"Yes. For sure. They went too far. It got personal for Frank. Killing unknown sociopaths is one thing. Getting away with it made him feel like he has power and can do anything. He decides it's his turn to call in some favors and take out a guy who is screwing him over in the porn business. I think Frank was embarrassed, or was owed money, or was caught on camera in a compromising or otherwise *interesting* position, or had his name published in the credits."

"Something completely looked down upon by the rest of the

group and incriminating to his different group of associates."

"But Frank doesn't tell them that when he decided to take Spears out. He works with Sullivan to meet with a gay prostitute, why make it about the porn business, no reason to chance getting caught by his own vigilantes. Frank changes the meeting and Spears shows up and gets whacked. They leave the body on the tracks as a message that drug dealers aren't welcome on the South Shore."

"And Frank tells James it was a mistake and figures they need to go for Waldon anyway."

"Why not. They got cocky. Bold."

"So what happened to Joe Junior? Is he alive?"

"I think he's dead. I'll need to interrogate James. I want you to finish up here and get over to James' place. I'll bet you the body is hidden there. No place else to hide a body on the spur of the moment."

"Next stop."

"I'll meet you there, after I drop off Terri and pickup Susanne Patten. I think we can assume that Frank is off the task-force and we know why he wanted control of the investigations."

"So who kidnapped Russell? Frank and James? I mean he escaped from a house in Plymouth? The trunk of a car, but who's car? James' place is in Middleborough. Frank is from Randolph. The Houghtons are in Lakeville. The Pattens live in Bridgewater. Mulligans in Raynham. The Bridgers are from the Cape. We don't have any conspirators in Plymouth."

"Russell won't talk about it, or he can't remember. The phone records from the half-way house point to various lawyers and parole departments, lots of civilians. It's used by everyone living there. Might be tough to determine all Russell's johns and associates if he doesn't cooperate."

"Why wouldn't he cooperate? He's facing loss of parole for prostitution and associating with a minor."

"He'll come around, but the truth is he may not remember. Three days in a car trunk is pretty rough. I think Russell knew the man, or would know the man, if he saw him. I figure Frank got word of Russell's parole through the newspapers. Even Pearl Hoffman knew. James and Frank were the two that kidnapped

Russell off the road and they put him in the guy's car trunk as another message."

"Alive?" Wally asked.

"A mistake. They wanted him dead and they wanted to send a message. Maybe the car belonged to a customer of Russell's."

"Stop with the gay prostitutes or you're next?"

"We might never know."

"Peter said Frank took something from Spears' apartment. Any ideas?"

"Probably a porn video. Frank's name didn't show up on any of the credits or DVD cases. If he was more active in the business he might have been in one or more of the scenes, or his photo made the back cover. He couldn't have that showing up in our investigation. It would of linked him to the murder. He probably stole the only copy from Spears' closet."

"And then steals the investigation away from us."

"I've been wondering why he didn't squash the investigation. He got control but I assume he took a look at the evidence against him on the Rickman autopsy and how we were putting together the idea of a group of vigilantes and it scared him. He had to take some drastic measures. He took me off the case, and Terri too, for disagreeing with his original Rickman autopsy. Terri found undertakers' makeup on the bruise marks. There were strangulation marks on the man's throat and no water in his lungs, plus a dislocated shoulder. He covered up the murder. He ordered the body cremated but didn't count on the family being wealthy and paying for a crypt. He couldn't call every one of us off the case without raising suspicion from above. He told us he was in charge, but I think he knew I would continue my own investigation. He had to kill Joe Patten Junior to keep him from talking and he had to kill Joe Senior and…"

"Things get pretty messy with all that killing," Wally said.

"It's a bad business." Bob grimaced.

Lieutenant Singer walked into the house. When he saw Bob he said, "Good to see you, detective. I just heard some news over the radio. It looks like Deputy Jackson is going to be okay. He's in E.R. but his vital signs are stable. The E.M.T. said you saved his life."

Chapter 55

Bob sat inside a small health food store and delicatessen across the street from the Ultimate Boxing Sports club in Brockton. A large thick-necked black man, known to the fighting world as Bishop, appeared at the doorway. His jaw dropped when he saw Bob. He turned, as if to run. Wally and Peter, both in uniform, got out of an unmarked cruiser parked by the door.

Bishop's shoulders visibly sank. His head fell forward and he turned back towards Bob. Bob motioned for the man to join him at the table. He reluctantly waddled to the table and sat down. A waitress took their order. Fruit smoothies for each. Then they sat quietly. Bob staring intently at Bishop.

Bishop looked from Bob to Wally and Peter, and back several times. The drinks came and the waitress left them alone. The fruit smoothies were healthy, good for you. The store was clean and pleasant. The air between the two men was toxic.

They both drank, then Bishop asked, "So what?"

"Nothing." Bob pointed towards Wally and Peter.

"I ain't scared."

"I know that."

"So what do you want?"

"I don't really have a preference."

"Between what and what?"

"This and that."

"You're going to kill me." Sweat formed on Bishop's face. His pupils shrank. His eyes flickered towards the door.

Bob said nothing.

"You'd claim it was self-defense."

Bob continued to say nothing.

"What do you want?"

"I want you to testify in court."

"I ain't doing that." Bishop sat upright in the chair. It was a wire-framed scroll-worked chair that might be better situated in a French impressionist painting rather than threatening to collapse under a muscle-bound mixed-martial arts fighter. Bob continued to quietly stare at the man. He wonder how many steroids were required to get muscles that big. He wondered, very briefly, how much the steroids shrank one's penis.

The sweat ran down Bishop's nose. He sniffed at the sweat and wiped it away with his hand.

Bob smiled.

"You're going to call it suicide by cop." Bishop said.

"I don't call it that."

"What do you call it?"

"I don't call it anything. You're a big guy. A professional fighter."

"Semi-pro."

Bob ignored the statement.

Bishop sighed. His brow furrowed. The sweat continued to run down his face and accumulate on his chin. His face flushed. "You don't let anyone know about this but..."

"But?"

"Okay."

"Good. The way I see it, someone hired you to rough me up. He told you to tell me to back off from my investigation."

"Maybe."

"Maybe you stood back and gave the orders. So maybe you were the lead on this little job."

"Maybe."

"And you took the money and hired some of your fight club pals to go along."

"Maybe."

"And maybe the guy who hired you was named Frank Wysup, or James Sullivan."

"I don't have a name."

"Then take a look at these." Bob retrieved and unfolded six photos from his jacket pocket. He hesitated showing the photos to Bishop, placing them faced down on the table. "It's hard-luck time now."

"What do you mean?"

"If you pick the right guy, you testify, you don't go to jail. If you pick the wrong guy, you testify, you plead guilty to felony assault, spend maybe thirty days in County-Lockup and I get you out for good behavior."

"Do I have a choice?"

"Yes... Pick one." Bob turned over the photos. James Sullivan, Frank Wysup, Cody Bridger, Henry Houghton, Joe Patten Sr., and Shawn Mulligan looked up at them.

Bishop stared at the photos for a long time. Confusion appeared his eyes. He wiped the sweat from his face again. He coughed, sipped some more of his drink, then looked at Bob. Sitting back in his chair and smiling, he said. "It was a woman."

Bob quietly thought about who he could have missed. He thought long and deep, not responding to Bishop's unexpected news. *'Who was it? Jan Bridger? Betty Mulligan? Amelia? No. Elizabeth Harding? No. Or...'*

"You don't know." Bishop gave a mirthless laugh.

"Susanne Patten," Bob said.

"I don't have a name." Bishop stopped smiling.

Bob motioned to Wally and Peter. Wally came to the door and opened it.

"Get my laptop, will you?"

Wally nodded and returned with the computer.

Bob turned it on and waited for it to boot. He clicked and punched the keys and finally turned the screen to face Bishop.

"That's her." Bishop said of the mug shot photo on the screen.

"You'll testify."

"What happened?" Bishop's curiosity got to him.

Bob gestured to the photos. "One of them is dead. Another one is going to ride a wheelchair for the rest of his life, in prison. A few more of them are going to be joining him in prison."

"Jesus. It was a lark. Make a few bucks scaring some guy. She said you were harassing a friend of hers. 'Get him to back off.' That's what she said. I swear I didn't know you were a cop."

Bob stood up quickly and punched Bishop square in the face. Bishop grabbed his face. Blood flowed from his nostrils.

"You broke my nose," the man said through bloodied hands.

"It was a just a lark," Bob said.

The following is an excerpt from *Sullyland,* coming soon...

Sullyland

By Richard Howes

"Wake up, dead man."

"What?" I awoke to the muzzle of a gun staring me in the eyes. I focused and saw a large man pointing my own gun at me. I contemplated taking the gun, my gun, away from him. I wondered if he had racked a round into the chamber.

"Get up. Someone wants to talk to you."

"Who?" I asked as I sat up and put my feet on the floor. The man was tall. He wore Bertuli shoes and a high-end dark blue business suit. He backed away, giving me room.

"The guy you been harassing. Let's go."

"Oh."

"You think you're a big man taking a knife away from a kid?" The man backed to the doorway.

I needed him in close if I was going to act. He seemed to suspect that and he gave space with every step I took.

"At least I didn't kill him."

"He's my brother."

"You want to return the favor?"

"And not kill you?"

"If you insist."

"Ha! Get in the car. Today I don't get to kill you. Maybe later."

"Comforting to know."

The man smiled and backed down the left hallway towards the living room. Another man, shorter, fatter, ex-wrestler or rugby player, stood in the doorframe of the bathroom to my right. The man gestured with a handgun and said, "Move it."

He had a thick Italian accent. My guess was Tuscany, but I could be wrong. He wore slacks from a department store and a golf shirt. Black sneakers completed the classy ensemble.

We went out to the car, a white limousine waiting in my driveway. The driver and another muscleman waited. The muscleman hefted a double-barrel shotgun.

"Where we going, Tony?" I figured someone might be a 'Tony'.

"Get in," the driver said.

I climbed in the back and sat facing forward to see where we were going. Tall-Tony waved a gun inside and said, "Over there," pointing to the backward-facing-seat.

I complied. Tall-Tony and Sneakers-Tony got in and kept their guns pointed at me. I rapped on the glass behind me. The window slid down.

"No bumps, okay? We don't want any accidental discharges back here."

The butt of a shotgun knocked the back of my head.

"Wise-ass," Tall-Tony said.

"Dead wise-ass," laughed Sneakers.

I rubbed the knot that swelled up on my head. The glass slid up. The doors closed. The windows were tinted dark. The men pulled shades down over the side and rear windows. I'd have to find Guiseppi's hideout on Google-Maps, later.

"So what would Mr. Medici like to talk to me about?"

"What makes you think we are going to see him?" Tall-Tony asked.

"Because... When Mrs. Medici hired me, she didn't need four gunmen and a limousine ride."

"Veronika is nice eh?"

"Mrs. Medici? She's a looker."

"She's very nice? Very pretty? I'd like to fuck her. He'd like to fuck her. Would you'd like to fuck her?"

"She's very pretty." I smiled. Tried too anyway.

Tall-Tony raised his gun. "You don't laugh. You don't talk like that. Only we get to talk like that!"

The two Tonys laughed. I frowned.

"Good. You frown. That's good!" They laughed some more.

The remainder of the ride went about the same. They told stupid jokes. I kept my mouth shut. They laughed about it.

We got on a highway, probably I-15 through the middle of Las Vegas, but it could be 215.

We cruised at high speed for twenty minutes and then got off an interchange and went to highway speeds again for another ten, followed by surface streets and six or eight turns.

We stopped and the doors opened under a Mediterranean style carport attached to a Mediterranean style house. Good. I could be at almost any house in Las Vegas, or Los Angeles, if the ride had been longer.

Made in the USA
Charleston, SC
13 December 2011